NOKOSEE
& STORMY
Love and Bullets

by

Holatte-Sutv Turwv Osceola

PB
BOOKS
Palmetto Bug Books
Miami, Fl.

Published by Palmetto Bug Books.
FIRST EDITION
ISBN 978-0-9634499-4-8

For
Haalie

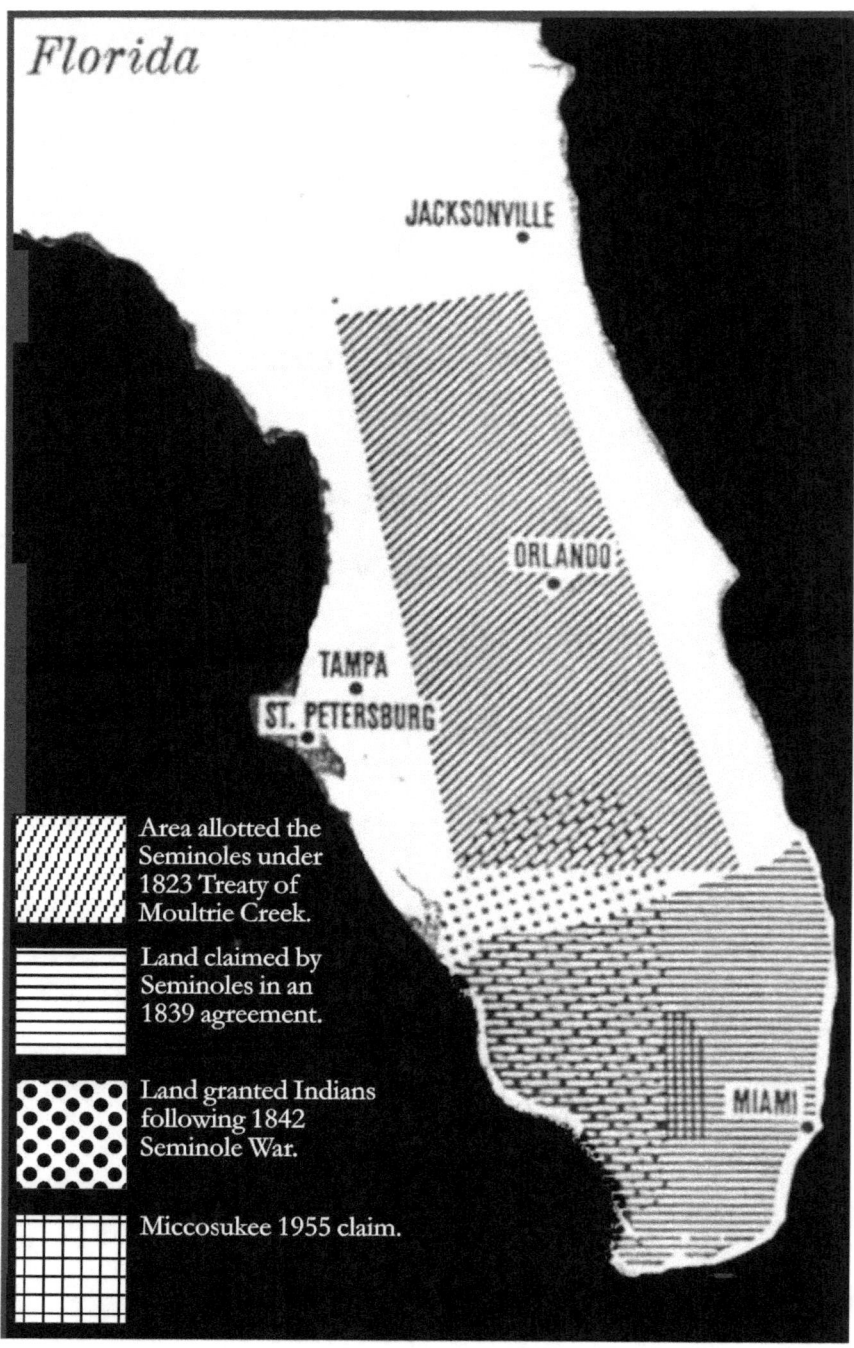

Florida

JACKSONVILLE

ORLANDO

TAMPA
ST. PETERSBURG

Area allotted the
Seminoles under
1823 Treaty of
Moultrie Creek.

Land claimed by
Seminoles in an
1839 agreement.

Land granted Indians
following 1842
Seminole War.

Miccosukee 1955 claim.

MIAMI

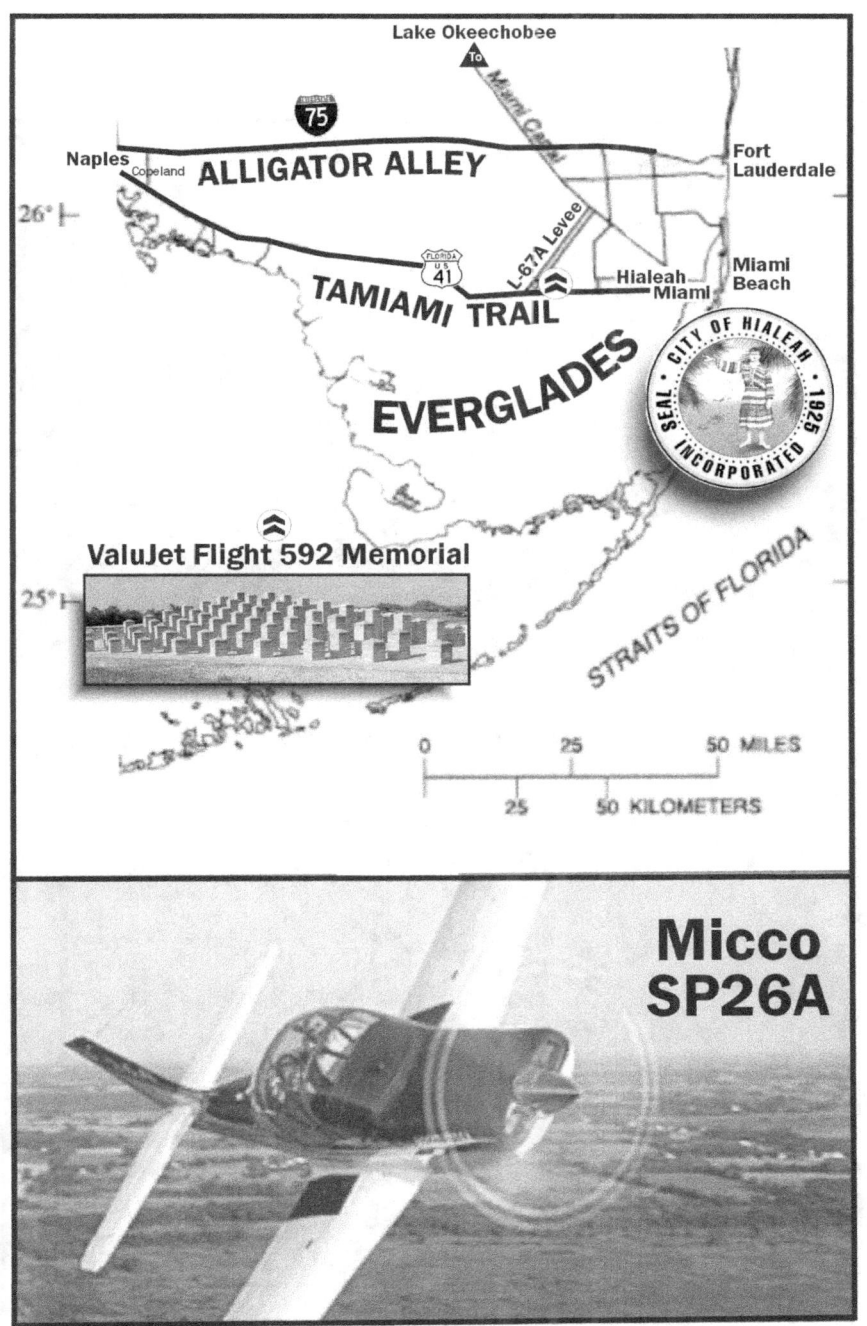

Lake Okeechobee

To Miami Canal

ALLIGATOR ALLEY

Naples
Copeland

26°

FLORIDA
U.S.
41

L-67A Levee

TAMIAMI TRAIL

Fort
Lauderdale

Hialeah
Miami

Miami
Beach

EVERGLADES

SEAL · CITY OF HIALEAH · 1925 · INCORPORATED

ValuJet Flight 592 Memorial

STRAITS OF FLORIDA

25°

| 0 | 25 | 50 MILES |

| 25 | 50 KILOMETERS |

Micco
SP26A

Coopertown Airboat Tour

Swamp Buggy

New Seminole
TM
Brand
BADASS
Spices
Made in the Everglades.
8oz.

Last known picture of 18-year-old Stormy Jones (in her 9th month of pregnancy). Found in the bottom of the airboat destroyed at "Rendezvous Point" as described in the book.

Chapters

Chapter 1
Backpfeifengesicht
Or
Two Weeks Later

It's the ninth month in the tenth decade in the first new century and thanks to my fake I.D, I'm sitting at the bar of my college's Rathskeller nursing a Yuengling, showing off my shiny new gold lamé Doc Martens steel-toed kickers, and trying to forget Nokosee.

And wondering if I'm pregnant.

Yeah, I know, I gave the guy a condom but my body is telling me Trojan owes me a refund. Never been late before until I lost my virginity to Nokosee. Coincidence? I think not. I'd rather have my shiny new Indian mom and dad got me for agreeing to go to college than a baby. Even if it is Nokosee's. Anyway, I'm too damn young to start having kids.

No-go-zee. No go there.

Yes, I know that should have been my mantra then, a play on words with the pronunciation of Nokosee's name but to be honest with you, that's exactly where I wanted him to go so, if I am preggers, I only have myself to blame.

The yahoos around me shake me out of my thoughts with a bar rattling cheer for the team. I look up at one of the TVs mounted over the bar and see our team has scored a touchdown. Whoop-tee-doo. I wish I could get excited about it but after what I've been through (see Micco Mann's rip off of my diary), it's going to take a lot more than a community college touchdown on cable access.

Eddie, my ex-BF, is sitting next to me. He thinks we're back together because I said I'd meet him at the bar for a drink. When I see him I think, what an idiot. He's still the same loud muscle-bound fool I knew in high school. Thinks getting drunk and high is cool. Thinks my showing up means I want to get back together. Doesn't know I needed to get away from mom, her new boyfriend Larry, and another night in the house wondering if I made the right choice in leaving Nokosee. Thinking about him all the time makes me think I made the wrong decision despite knowing his "career path" looks short and deadly. But right now, sitting here in the middle of a testosterone and alcohol fueled convention for those with arrested development, even certain death looks better.

Eddie reaches across the bar, grabs the remote, aims it at the TV in front of us and starts channel surfing. The "Outside" world rushes by with one commercial after the other offering up a better and simpler life if you just buy, buy, buy. Despite getting my new Indian dresser with the classic leather fringe saddlebags, I know that isn't true. I got me a brand new classic V-Twin motorcycle straight out of my *grandfather's* past, but that isn't enough to put a smile on my face. Instead, I feel empty and feel like crying-- even when I'm riding my bike. *Especially* when I'm riding my bike because every time I look at the little Indian head light on the front fender, I can't help but think about Nokosee back in the swamp. Thanks to him, I see the world differently now. It's not all about partying. There's some serious crap going on out there like oil spills and melting ice caps.

Of course, maybe it's all about my hormones. That's what dad, the "Great White Father of the Everglades," thinks. Being the daughter of the head park ranger got me into this predicament anyway. Because of a divorce court ruling, I must spend every summer with my dad, something I've been doing since I was a kid. This summer I met and fell in love with Nokosee. Unfortunately for me, Nokosee wasn't considered eligible boyfriend material. Maybe it had something to do with his penchant for wearing loincloths and the fact that he could kill you with his little finger. You see, Nokosee has been groomed by his nutcase dad to be the first of the "New Seminole" (NS for short) who will "rise from the swamp" and start an eco-war on the "Outside." In retrospect, I can understand why my parents might have a problem with that, but they could have handled it differently instead of trying to break us up the way they did. Trying to get Nokosee packed off to Oklahoma to be studied by a cultural anthropologist "until the day he dies" and me shipped back to New Jersey to live with mom didn't work and only made matters worse, i.e., no one had to die. But I digress. Post-Nokosee, dad now stays in touch more often through daily emails and weekly phone calls from the swamp. He can't understand why I'm not happy. "Hell," he says, "You got an Indian for crisesakes."

"The wrong Indian," I say.

"Don't go there."

I don't. Thinking or talking about Nokosee only pushes my dad and me further apart and it doesn't do me any good either. I make a mental note to stop looking at the Indian head on the front fender. I've already stopped looking at the name painted on both sides of the gas tank. Soon I should be able to throw my leg over the bike without giving it a second thought but somehow that sounds all wrong.

When dad brings up my hormones, I have to laugh. When he cuts my laughing short like only he can, the thought that I've been trying to bury races to the surface: my hormones are out of whack because I'm pregnant and I'm too scared to find out if it's true.

I grab Eddie's arm to stop the channel surfing. Fox News is showing Alligator Alley from the air. The road slicing through the Everglades is backed up for miles. A burning BP gasoline tanker truck is blocking the west bound lanes. A quick cut to another helicopter camera crew on the Gulf side shows another burning tanker truck blocking the east bound lanes. I immediately sit up when I hear the reporter say "New Seminole."

"Nokosee."

"What?" Eddie asks.

I glance at him. He's looking at me like my dad, as if I have something to hide. And he's right. I don't need him getting in my face about Nokosee whom he and just about everyone I know knows about thanks to the freaking media.

"Nothing," I say turning back to the TV.

He's still giving me the once over when, without looking at the TV, he aims and clicks the remote.

"No!"

I lunge for the remote but he pushes me back. I blow my cover even further when I struggle for it. He rolls around to block me with his back. My arm is caught in the spin and I'm thrown onto the bar. My shoulder knocks my beer bottle off the bar.

"Dammit!" the bartender yells. He's frozen, covered in beer and hunched over and dripping Pottsville, PA's finest from his outstretched arms.

"Give it to me!" I yell. Yeah, I've still got a jones for that crazy Indian in the swamp and can't hide it.

"I'll give it to you, bitch!"

Eddie pushes me back and I fall off the bar stool onto the floor. Instead of someone coming to my aid, my contemporaries step out of the way and laugh. More embarrassed than hurt, I look up and see Eddie looking at his bros with an unsure smile, hoping their reaction to what he just did to me is simpatico in their eyes. I look at them and discover by their grins and guffawing it is. That's all I need to get back on my feet. I grab the bar stool and slowly pull myself up, never taking my hate-filled eyes off of Eddie. I hear a couple a guys go "Whoe" in that long drawn out way when they know someone's in for pile of pain. Eddie loses the smile. He knows I can be a handful. I step up to him and he steps back. I search his eyes.

"What a man," I say as I reach for my motorcycle helmet sitting on the bar. "If Nokosee was here, you'd be dead by now."

His nervous smile returns. "But he ain't," he says with as much bravura as he can muster. "So shut the hell up."

Backpfeifengesicht. The word comes crawling out of my "Word for the Day" memory cache somewhere deep inside my brain where I save my favorite words. It's one of those German words that's also fun to pronounce: BUCK-five-en-ge ("g" pronounced like in "go") -zisht. It means "a face badly in need of a fist" and signals my synapses to swing the fist-clenched helmet as hard as I can at Eddie's head but he blocks it with his forearm. His cry is loud and very girly-mon. I probably broke a bone in his arm. I'm sorry to admit it, but that excites me. Adrenaline starts pumping, I start breathing rapidly and I'm ready to take on the world. I look around for someone to hit but they're all backing up and looking at me as if I'm crazy. I turn to leave but my ex throws himself at me from behind and we both go tumbling onto the floor. He tries to wrestle with me but I'm not as drunk or wounded as he is and manage to slip around his pathetic attempts to hold me down, this time connecting helmet to head. He falls in a heap on top of me. The crowd gasps, shocked I'm sure to see this little white chick kick a big jock's ass. I push him off and look at him lying next to me. His eyes are closed and blood is running down his temple and across his nose, a nose that's still sucking in air, albeit noisily and with some effort. And so help me, as much as I know I shouldn't, I'm relishing the moment. Not caring to score any points with the losers in the bar, I rustle up some spit while lying on my back, turn and let lose a flying loogie on Eddie's face. That elicits an entirely different response from the crowd: revulsion. But it works for me. I know at that moment, lying on my back on that bar room floor that, like the old Doors song, I've crossed on over to the other side, that I don't give a damn what anybody thinks and that I don't belong in that bar, that college, or that town. I'm not really sure where I belong but I know the quicker I get to my feet and onto my bike, the sooner I'll learn. I pick up my helmet and slowly rise. I can feel the crowd looking at me, judging me. I turn to them.

"You all make me sick! Grow the hell up!"

Eddie moans and I whip around to what once was my high school boyfriend only a couple of months ago. I can't understand what I saw in him. Maybe I'm growing up. Dad would be proud. And then I go and blow it by planting my gold lamé high-top kicker on my ex's chest and kicking the stirring mass of broken memories trying to get to its feet back onto its back to measured tones of "shut...the...fuck...up."

I make the crowd nervous. It makes room for me to pass. I feel like Clint Eastwood in one of his westerns-- but with sparkling gold lame boots as I walk out of the saloon in a town with no name. I feel my upper lip quivering like his too. Oh, how I love being a badass. I think I've found something I'm really good at. This is my epiphany and I wonder how many of them have come to others staring up from bar room floors. I pause at the door to fish for my keys in my black leather Harley-Davidson purse/weapon-- the cute and dangerous little one with the real chrome air cleaner cover-- and look back at Eddie. He's staring up through my loogie and trying to focus on a flickering neon Budweiser sign hanging from the ceiling and I wonder if he's having one too. I don't know it at the time but as I turn away and kick the door open, I'm leaving one world for another.

Chapter 2
Bye Bye, Mom!

The little Indian head light on my front fender guides my way home. I turn onto my street, the street I grew up on, and pass under the branches of trees I grew up *in* as a child playing tree tag. I turn into my driveway and park outside of the garage in the back. I turn the engine off, kick out the kickstand and let the bike rest on its side. When I remove my helmet I hear insects chirping and can smell jasmine mixed in with the Indian's exhaust. I shake my hair loose and look around. Moonlight floods the concrete below my boots and reminds me of camping out in the backyard with friends when I was a kid. I instinctively turn to the house, hoping to see a light on inside, knowing my dad is awake and there to protect us in case something wicked this way comes. But dad's long gone. Only mom's home, probably with her new boyfriend Larry. I sigh, lift my leg over the bike and walk toward the house.

Thanks to Smokey, my family's pet Dachshund/Chihuahua, I fail to slip into the dark kitchen unseen and unheard. I can hear him barking for all he's worth as I walk toward the door. I peek through the window. His ears are perked up and he's looking at me with eager anticipation. I put my finger up to my lips but that, of course, has no effect on his barking. Instead, it just gets him more excited to the point that he starts executing perfect three-step turns I can only wish to emulate. I should know this by now. He's been part of my life since I was nine. I unlock the door and scoop him up. He buries my face in kisses. I hug him good and strong.

"Darling, is that you?"

Mom's voice is coming from the living room. She's probably sitting on the couch reading a book, a romance novel, something dad detested. I hope Larry isn't there too. I'm sure if I give him half a chance I'll discover he's not such a bad guy after all but I don't care to try. Larry would make mom's third boyfriend since dad and as far as I'm concerned, none of them will ever measure up to my old man. No matter how hard they try to kiss up to me, none of them stand a chance because I'm a one-dad-girl. Despite sharing what dad likes to remind me is a *Cool Hand Luke* "failure to communicate" with each other, for better or worse he more than my mother made me what I am today. In fact, I aspire to be as independent and as self-reliant as he is-- minus his hard-ass approach to the world.

I put Smokey down and step into the warm and inviting light of the living room.

"Yeah, mom, it's me."

I stop short. Larry's sitting next to mom. Both are reading. For some reason that makes me sick.

"Hello, Symona," he says.

Asshole. He has to call me by my given name, the name I hate. He does it on purpose, as a joke. I can't make myself say hello back. Instead, I turn and run up the stairs, two steps at a time. Smokey, barking as if possessed by some kind of devil-dog-spirit, can't keep up with me.

"Symona," mom shouts, "Can't you say hello to Larry?"

"No!" I shout back and see Smokey struggling to clear the last step. He thinks it's a game. I slam the bathroom door in his face.

It's showtime, folks!

Thanks to mom, I hear Roy Scheider's voice in my head over Smokey's incessant barking. While dad tried to make me into the son he never had, mom was pushing musicals and dance my way. Although I may not have become the dancer mom always wanted, I sure know musicals, especially the story about my favorite choreographer Bob Fosse. That was a phrase he always said before facing an audience-- and his fears. Well, it seems appropriate it should rise out of my subconscious now because I finally found the cajones to see if I'm pregnant. Putting Eddie away literally and figuratively probably had something to do with it. Talk about empowering.

"Be quiet, Smokey!"

Why do I even bother? As he keeps barking outside the door I sit my helmet down on the vanity and dig into the back corner between the wall and faux marble top. Empowered or not, my hands are shaking when I pull the pregnancy test strip out from its secret hiding place. I look at the plastic wonder stick and wonder if its 99.9% claim of accuracy is true. It has a little digital read out and looks very clinical and professional which is exactly what I want.

I drop my pants and panties, sit on the toilet and stick the strip between my legs and, thanks to the beers I drank, pee like there's no tomorrow.

"Stormy?"

Mom has joined Smokey at the door. As I lunge for the door and turn the lock, I drop the stick into the toilet. *Dammit!*

The door knob twists back and forth.

"Mom, do you mind?"

"Sorry, I didn't know it was occupied."

"For crying out loud, what do you think Smokey is barking at?" I spread my legs wider and dig into the toilet bowl.

A moment passes during the barking before I hear her ask, "Are you okay?"

"I'm fine, mom."

"Mind if I come in?"

"Yes!"

She tries the door knob again.

"Mom!" I bring up the key to my future dripping with my Yuengling saturated urine and shake it off in the sink.

"Symona, you locked the door."

"Because I want some privacy!" I yell over the barking.

Instructions I read over and over a week ago, that are now permanently embedded in my brain cells, tell me to set it aside for at least 5 minutes which I do.

"Since when did we start locking our doors?"

"Since dad moved out and Larry, Moe, and Curly moved in."

Another moment passes during the nonstop barking before...

"Have you been drinking?"

"No!"

Drinking and driving is a deal breaker with mom and dad and I won't let them take my Indian away for nothing.

"I smell beer."

"Oh, mom, give me a break, will ya?"

"You know you have to be 21 to drink in this state."

"Mom, are you doing this on purpose?"

"Symona, you better not have been drinking."

"Mom, you and Smokey making me crazy!"

I can't wait five minutes, not with mom and Smokey yammering outside the door. I figure at least 40 seconds have passed which is the bare minimum time needed to get a more or less accurate reading so I grab the stick and look at it. The message blinking in front of me says: Pregnant, bitch.

Of course, that's not how the stick lays the news on me but that's how I interpret the data.

The next thing that happens surprises even me: I start crying. I try to stop but mom has great ears. Even over the barking.

"Are you crying?"

"Please, mom, it's been a long day. Just give me a little room. Okay?"

A moment passes before I hear her say, "Alright, darling. I'll be downstairs if you need me."

"Thanks. And take Smokey with you. He's driving me crazy."

The sound of Smokey's barking slowly diminishes. I wipe away my tears and try to compose myself but I can't stem the flow and start crying louder than I care to. I feel sick to my stomach and collapse in on myself. I hold myself tightly, start to hyperventilate and try to stop. I decide being brave and facing down my fears is not for me and vow to never go there again.

So, am I keeping the baby?

That question comes out of nowhere. I'm not ready to answer it so, with some considerable effort, I force myself to get off the toilet, to get dressed and to--

I look in the mirror and stop. My mascara is running down my face and I look older than seventeen. I don't want to look older. I grab a washcloth, get it wet and start wiping away the running lies but when I look up at the mirror, I still see an older, tireder me.

And a frightened me, someone I don't want to be.

I open a vanity drawer, pull out a pair of scissors and without hesitation-- since I've been thinking about this for some time-- start cutting off my hair. It falls in huge blonde and pink lumps around my Docs. I pull out a razor from the drawer and start running it across my temples sans shaving cream. Within minutes I've got a ragged, angry, bloody Mohawk. And I'm no longer that crybaby in the mirror. I'm someone else, someone to be feared.

I pick up the stick, wash it off, put it in its "moisture proof" pouch and stick it in my Harley purse because I'm pretty sure I'll be taking that test a few more times just to make sure I really am preggers. I pick up my cosmetic bag from under the vanity, grab my helmet and open the door.

I scream and stagger backwards. Mom's on the other side looking at my new dew with crazy, uncomprehending eyes.

"Symona! What have you done?"

My heart is racing as I quickly collect my new riot grrl self and push mom out of the way.

"Symona!"

She follows me down the hall to my bedroom.

"You *have* been drinking. I can smell it."

"Is everything alright?" Larry shouts up from the staircase. I glance that way and see he's got Smokey in his arms and the barking starts all over again.

"She's been drinking, Larry!"

I slam the bedroom door behind me and turn the lock. Mom starts shouting and banging on the door. I go into my closet and pull out my canvas Army and Navy olive duffel bag and start throwing clothes and stuff into it.

"Symona?"

All three are at the door. I grab my cash stash under my mattress and my iPod on my dresser.

"Let your mother in." Even Smokey seems to have turned against me.

I look around one last time for something I might need as they pound on the door and twist the lock back and forth but there isn't anything I need anymore from here. I open my bedroom window, throw the duffel bag out onto the sloping roof and follow after it just as Larry breaks down the door.

"Symona!" mom yells.

They rush for the window but it's too late. I'm already sliding down the roof towards the tree branch that's always been there for me for as long as I can remember. Like an old friend who supported me when I spent my summers wishing on all 300 sextillion stars hoping at least one would bite, I jump into its open arms and slide down its kid worn familiar trunk to the ground. I look back at my bedroom window. Mom is holding Smokey and yelling over his barking for me to come back but Larry isn't anywhere to be found. I figure he's racing down the stairs to stop me. Good luck with that one.

I blow mom and Smokey a kiss and tell them I love them before running over to my bike and throwing the duffel bag across the handlebars, my leg across the seat and the helmet onto my head. I start her up and gun the engine a few times and with each rev, a light comes on in a house in the neighborhood. As I turn the big bike around, I'm thinking they'll be talking about my exit for years to come. Especially how I stuck out my big, in-your-face gold steel-toed DM Shine and used it like a lance to knock Larry into mom's prized begonias when he came running at me from out of the shadows, arms chopping the air and screaming his ass off with a less than manly high-pitched *kei* like some kind of martial arts wannabe.

Chapter 3
Pushing Buttons on the Trail of Tears

Before getting on the "I," I stop at a local gas station to fill up, get a cup of Joe, and to buy a map. My plan, which I'm formulating as I go, is to take as many backroads as possible in case mom and dad got the cops looking for me. Well, as I'm pumping gas into my tank, sipping my coffee, and listening to some music through my earbuds and trying to forget the heartbroken look in Smokey's eyes, a bunch of yahoos pull up behind me at the next gas pump. Because they're making a lot of noise, I turn to look at them. That turns out to be a big mistake. I had taken my helmet off to drink my coffee and as soon as the girls (a blonde and a brunette about my age) see me, well, for some reason they take my glance as a threat and the next thing you know the bitches are in my face strutting ghetto style and threatening to do me in. Maybe it's my smile or the way I sadly shake my head, but just after putting my ex-boyfriend away I am far from impressed and turn away. That's when Blondie pushes me from behind. The hot coffee goes all over my motorcycle jacket and my gas tank. I'm stunned as I look at the mess while their boyfriends cheer them on. This is not the way I wanted to flee mediocrity. I just want to break the bonds and to get out ASAP hassle-free-- and not to feel guilty about leaving Smokey behind. When I sigh and put the pump handle back on its cradle, I get pushed again, this time into the pump. This is really not the time to be pushing my buttons. Again, I pause to take a deep breath, turn back to the tank and screw the gas cap back on. I'm trying my best not to lose my cool because the last thing I need is undue attention but then the brunette has to prove to her buds she's got balls or something and pushes me hard against my chest. I don't know what her problem is but as it turns out, that was one push too many. Like my dad taught me when I was twelve, never start a fight but never run away from one either. With that kind of parenting, I'm eager to get at it, my mind having been made up five years ago when dad signed me up for summer karate classes and gave me his blessing for unbridled mayhem on the bad boys and girls of the world. Smiling, I methodically raise my index finger to ask for a moment so I can dig into the top pocket of my motorcycle jacket to pull up my iPod. This kind of catches them off guard as I scroll for a good fighting song. Got it: Green Day's *American Idiot*. As soon as it comes on I start thrusting my arms into the air and dancing in place. Again, they don't know what to think.

Thirty seconds into the song when Billie Joe Armstrong rails about "a new kind of tension," I let go of my own kind of tension and two American idiots are left bleeding on the concrete and crying for their boyfriends. When their idiot, mouth-breathing lovers try to do the manly thing, I fall into a fighting stance and urge them to come and get it. They look at me as if I'm crazy and stop short. Maybe the ragged Mohawk has something to do with it or my wild-eyed gaze which I know can be pretty scary having seen it looking back at me from the full-length mirrors on the walls in my karate dojo. They look at each other and then their crybaby girlfriends lying in the blood and oil on the concrete and, I swear, without saying a word, turn, get back into their car and drive away. I can't believe it. The girls can't believe it either. With some effort, they get to their feet and hobble after the retreating car, cursing, screaming, and crying. Talk about an adrenaline rush. When I throw my leg over the Indian and start her up, it's nearly 10 o'clock at night and I feel as if I've just wakened from a long and restful sleep instead of coming off of an 8-hour shift at Hot Topic and kicked three asses in the space of an hour (well, four if you count Larry).

"And I'm pregnant, too, you losers!" I yell at the girls as they're sucked up by the foggy New Jersey night.

Yes!

I punch the air for emphasis, rev the big V-twin a couple of times and smoke the tires as I fishtail out of there.

I take the "I" that night through Philadelphia, Washington, DC, all the way to Richmond, Virginia before getting off and following backroads the rest of the way down through towns and places I never heard of before. I sleep during the day anywhere I can that offers shelter and a place to hide. When I'm hungry, I look for a drive-through because I never want to leave my bike out in the open for too long. I recycle the greasy hamburger wraps as toilet paper because one thing I learned from Nokosee and my short stint in the Everglades is to never go into the woods to pee or take a dump if you don't have a big leaf or something to wipe yourself with when you're finished.

As soon as I reach the Florida border two nights later, I ditch my helmet. It rolls down a grass embankment and disappears into high weeds. Like my dad, I never liked wearing them. They always seemed counter productive to the whole idea of riding a motorcycle and the state's helmet option law makes it all perfectly legal. Going back through the states that aren't as enlightened won't be a problem because I won't be going back-- *ever*.

I have to force my eyelids to stay open until I can grab my Wayfarers from my motorcycle jacket and put them on. This doesn't help at night so I take them off and slow down which is the last thing I want to do. I need to end the constant fear of getting caught. I want to find myself in Nokosee's strong protective arms *now*.

Florida's pretty freaking long and heading south on its backroads is taking forever. Still, if I hadn't taken "the road less traveled," I wouldn't have had the following experience that begins innocently enough at a stoplight, again around 10 o'clock at night. I'm at an intersection stopped behind a panel truck in a small town somewhere near Lake Okeechobee, a place called White City. But it isn't a city by a long shot. If anything, it's what my dad would call a one horse town. Anyway, I'm waiting for the light to change when I hear what sounds like a raucous party approaching from behind. I look around and see a school bus driving towards me. Harsh ceiling lights reveal it's full of high school marching band kids, cheerleaders, football players and, apparently from the sound of their screaming, shouting, and brass heavy music, are returning to their high school victors of that night's football game. The bus stops in the left lane next to me. Now you know I have a problem with football and all the shit that goes with it and I guess when I glance up at the bus and don't get into the rah-rah mentality, I piss some of them off because the next thing I know they're screaming and throwing stuff out the windows at me and calling me a freak. I mean, come on, everywhere I go someone wants to do me harm.

It's gotta be the Mohawk.

Of course, that's it. Once they get to know you, they'll love you like a friend.

Puhlease.

Like I care. Anyway, trying to pretend the big yellow school bus filled with a rabid student body foaming-at-the-mouth isn't there is pretty much impossible-- especially when someone launches a loogie the size of a pancake and it splatters against my shaved skull.

High school students chew tobacco? Where the hell am I anyway?

That's the first thing that goes through my mind. Crazy, I know but when I wipe the slimy glob away and look at it, tobacco is the only thing I can come up with.

How about karma?

What?

What goes around, comes around.

I pause to study the tobacco-laced-loogie oozing over the side of my palm and to listen to the voices in my head.

Idiot! Eddie, for crying out loud!

Aw, geese. I get it. Anyway, the bus explodes in laughter when I make the mistake of bringing my hand up to my nose to smell the foul item just to be sure.

It's chewing tobacco alright, you damn fool.

When the dark brown goo drips onto the only pair of jeans I have, the bus starts rocking from side to side with the loudest laughing I've ever heard. I'm so embarrassed I blush, a first for yours truly. Assuming girls don't chew, I start looking for a boy with tobacco dripping from his lips and instantly find him chewing and grinning high above me from one of the open windows. I narrow my eyes, invert my hands and point them at him, steadily curling my fingers toward me over and over again to get the Neanderthal to climb down out of the bus to take me on. When he stops chewing and gives me the finger, I get off the bike and start towards him. This elicits more screaming and yelling and jumping in the aisle but I'm surprised to hear that most of it is aimed at the mouth-breather with taunts and dares and verbal assaults on his manhood. In fact, I even hear a couple of "you go, girl"s which is encouraging considering I'm standing alone in the street and looking up --

At the biggest, fattest collection of human flesh I've ever seen gathering itself up to tower over everything we hold sacred!

Okay, maybe he isn't that big, but from my point-of-view on the street, the guy looks like he *is* the football team. He's still wearing his dirty uniform-- including shoulder pads-- and from the numbers on it I can tell that by his size he's fulfilling his destiny in that game: he's a lineman. When he walks toward the front of the bus, the bus dips from side to side with each step. With each step the screaming and laughing gets louder. I swallow hard. This is not good. By the time he gets to the front of the bus, my legs are shaking uncontrollably. Again, a first. I never knew fear like this. Adrenaline is pumping so hard through my arteries it's causing me to lose control of my body. Dad tried to explain this to me so that someday I might be able to control it and not be controlled by it.

Gee, thanks, dad, I thought then. *You never know when your daughter is going to need that kind of information.*

Like right now.

Know what's going on and work your way through it. Hit something. Hit the bastard that's trying to hurt you first. You'll get the use of your legs back real quick.

I hit the side of the school bus with my fist. My legs stop shaking but my hand hurts like hell. The kids on board yell, scream, jump, shout, blow their instruments, beat their drums and shake the bus from side to side.

"That bitch is fucking nuts!" a girl screams.

"Ou-u-u, is she going to get it now!" another girl yells.

As I'm shaking my hand and looking at it, the bus doors snap open.

You gotta be kidding me! I can't believe the bus driver let this guy out. Where are the coaches? The adult chaperones?

On the other bus, the one pulling up behind this one.

When the White City Hulk steps down out of the bus, the whole thing springs upward and groans a mechanical sound of relief. The bus grows silent.

"You got something you want to say to me, bitch?" the giant says with a voice all hoarse and harsh, a voice that sounds like it's been chewing tobacco from the time it was given life in the bowels of a mad scientist's laboratory.

Remember, never run from a fight.

Yes, Obe Wan Kenobi-father, I hear you. Now would you please shut the fuck up? I'm trying to concentrate here.

"I was going to ask you if your momma had ever taught you how to treat women but after seeing you outside the bus, I can tell you never had a momma."

The whole student pimply-faced body gasps.

"Say what?"

"I say you look like some kind of Frankenstein monster and probably never had a mommy so I can't go blaming her for not teaching you any manners."

I hear another hopeless communal groan.

The giant looks up at the cowering villagers and silences them but when he looks down at me, I see his eyes betraying his resolve in adding me to his legendary body count. It's like I caught him questioning whether or not he wants to continue in the role of the school bully-- if that's what he is-- to follow the same path mapped out for him since grade school.

Of course, I could be wrong.

That's why I don't wait to find out. Thanks to my Wonder Woman-adrenaline-fueled legs, I'm at his side before he can react and kick him hard in the knee cap with my gold, steel-toed DM. That makes him cry out and brings him to his knees. He yells a second time when the shattered knee meets the pavement. As he tries to support himself with both hands on the street, I lay a well-placed round house kick to his face and break his nose. Blood squirts onto the yellow school bus and runs down the side. The kids-- my contemporaries-- excited by the blood and mayhem outside their windows, are jumping up and down and screaming now as their school bully, someone they probably grew up with and feared all their lives, is blindly clutching at the bus to keep from losing his balance. Even on his knees, he's still as tall as I am but that makes it easier for me to center myself in front of him and throw one short quick punch up at his larynx. His eyes bulge wide and he immediately forgets the pain in his nose and knee and tries to find something to hold onto when he grabs his throat and starts making choking sounds. A girl screams on the bus. Yeah, I don't blame her, it's not pretty. Especially when I deliver the coup de grace: a back kick to the side of his head which throws the giant up against the school bus.

"Oh, my god, you killed him!" a girl cries as the school ogre slides slowly down the side of the bus, leaving a trail of blood behind it.

I'm breathing hard and my heart is racing as I watch the monster fall away from the bus and onto the street. But it's not from exertion because it only took three kicks and a chop to end the fight in less than ten seconds. It's the adrenaline coursing through my body, the same stuff that ran through David's when he cut down Goliath.

Yeah, that's right, I'm comparing myself to David and you would too if you could see how big this guy was-- and "was" is the key word too because right now, he's way smaller than me.

The light turns green and the truck drives away but the bus doesn't move. I hear crying and look up at the kids looking out the windows. That shuts them up real fast. They all-- including the boys-- look scared shitless and for some reason I like that. In fact, I like it a lot. Right now I feel like I can take on the whole fucking world in an octagon cage match and not lose. I turn back to the fallen giant and walk towards him. The sound of a collective sucking in of the night air escapes from the bus because I'm sure these high school kids think I'm going to kill Goliath just like David did but they're wrong. I'm just checking to see if he's alive because what if I did kill him? I couldn't live with myself. Thankfully, he is. I step back even more elated-- relieved actually-- turn and walk back to my bike.

"What have you done?"

I turn to the voice behind me. A high school coach is running towards me from the other bus.

"Taught him some manners."

I face him with the expectation of getting tackled but he runs past me to his fallen player.

"Stop!"

It's another coach coming at me with purpose.

"Fuck you," I say with as much disdain as I can muster. I guess it isn't enough because he keeps coming.

"Watch it, coach!" someone yells out of the school bus. "She's fucking crazy!"

Coach should have listened. His fat, giggling stomach runs right into my fist. Shot from the hip, it's the first punch you learn in karate. It comes with a *Ke-i!* too and passes through his body. Well, at least in my mind it does. It drops him like a sack of wide-eyed bricks onto his knees at my feet.

"Oh, my God!" a girl screams from the first school bus. "She's killed Coach Bogart!"

Coach Bogart, stunned, is holding his stomach, turning red in the face and looking at nothing when I raise my gold lame DM Shine, place it against his chest to get his attention and with just a little effort push him backward. He falls onto his back into an unnatural but impressively flexible position over his bent legs. His eyes are open and fixated on the stars above him. I lean over and stick my head into his view of the Milky Way to see if he's still alive. His eyes blink as he tries to focus on my face.

"Guess you thought I was just a little girl, right? Didn't see that punch coming did you?"

He doesn't say anything. I slap him across his face to get him breathing again and he sucks in the world in one huge gasp which echoes through the school buses. I look up. The student body is stunned, speechless. The other coaches-- and the other half of the football team-- that were following him out of the bus have stopped in their tracks, not sure what to do, wondering what they stumbled upon in the middle of this lonely country road and who the heck this petite blonde with the raggedy Mohawk is crouching over one of their own. I turn and point at them, pausing for effect, daring them to come closer. They don't. I turn and walk toward my bike, ambling now like some kind of shoulder-swiveling tough guy across the road, a thing that requires my full attention since I'm genetically predisposed to swivel my hips. It's just me and a couple of school buses full of silent, shell-shocked high school cheerleaders, marching band members, football players-- and now coaches-- who have had the euphoria of winning ripped from their hearts in the course of 30-seconds. When I throw my leg over the Indian I see the bus driver standing in the open doorway. It's a black woman, hard worn, probably in her fifties. No wonder she let the giant out; she's not getting paid enough to keep him in. Still, by the way she's looking at his fallen body, I'm sure she's wondering if she did the right thing and wondering what to do next, wondering if she's going to get fired.

"Yes!"

I turn to the bus.

"Yes!"

It's a cheerleader. She's leaning outside the window and shaking her pom-poms high in the air.

"Yes!"

She's looking straight at me.

"Yes! Yes! Yes!"

The pom-poms become exclamation points with each shout. Seeing her do that puts a smile on my face. I rev the motor once, twice, three times echoing her cries. Others join her until it seems like the whole damn bus is cheering me on with trombones and trumpets shoved through the open windows, stabbing the air with praise and thanksgiving. Raised fists are thrust into the air each time I rev my deep-throated motor. It's like that final scene in *Billy Jack* when the star get's a hero's raised fist send-off for standing up to the bad guys, but mine comes with pom-poms, trumpets and flutes attached. The celebration ratchets up onto another level when they start screaming and shaking their heads and slamming their bodies indiscriminately up against each other, the seats, and the walls.

My God, they're humping the bus!

What once was a staid school bus has been transformed into a rockin' bacchanalian mosh pit on wheels.

And now the party is spilling onto the street! The bus driver can't stop them from getting off the bus as they push her aside and start dancing joyfully, uninhibitedly in the street!

I don't know if what I'm witnessing is a release of some kind of long festering communal tension because I slew the village ogre, or how I stood up to their coaches and put one down like so many may have wished they could have, or if it's just pure, unbridled teen spirit gone wild sparked by the sight of blood and violence-- something I can identify with because I'm as jacked as they are, probably even more so since I did the violence and made the blood. I keep revving the motor hoping to find out, to see how far I can make them go before they explode into gooey bits and pieces of benzoyl peroxide drenched teenage protoplasm. But it's something I'll never find out as they start to surround me because I hear an approaching police siren. I twist the accelerator one final time for good measure and slowly let out the clutch to ease through them with both boots on the ground. I stop to look at the fallen giant. The coach who ran past me sees me and stops administering aid to the poor dumb punk. He steps back expecting, I suspect, that he's next on my shit list when a cheerleader shouts, "You own them, girl!" But when I look at the football player lying on his back and writhing in pain the only thing I own is regret that I hurt him. I feel terrible and wish I had waited for him to have made the first move instead of me striking before he was ready, wish I had stopped at the first kick. It reminds me of what my high school guidance counselor use to tell me not all that long ago that, among other things, I've got an anger management problem. I learn tonight I also have a problem with authority figures. I'm surprised I have no sympathy for the coach lying on his back and staring at the stars and wish I could care. I find myself unexpectedly wanting to cry but I put the brakes on that emotion, gun the bike and roar away.

I check my rear-views and see my new found champions have been turned into dancing silhouettes by the headlights and flashing light of the police car. They're blocking its path and I want to believe they're doing it for me, their biker-chick-hero. As I rocket down the two-lane blacktop and vanish into the night air, I can't help but think those high school kids will be talking about this for years to come, that they'll pass down the story of this fateful night to their children and grandchildren and it and I will become legend.

Little do I know that my legend-in-the-making is getting a jump start. It appears some of the students had smartphones and were taking videos of me taking out the giant and their coach. By midnight yours truly is on YouTube and by the time I roll into Miami the next morning, my picture is gracing the front page of the Miami Herald above the fold.

Damn technology!

Chapter 4

Makeover

I'm riding an adrenaline high and listening to Wayne Cochran's *Going Back To Miami* when I enter Miami through its back door, US 27, an infamously deadly road straddling the western advance of civilization and the Everglades. I'm happy and singing out loud, changing the lyrics from "girl" to "guy" to make it work for me. I haven't a clue I'm more famous than I ever wanted to be. But that's all about to change when I turn onto S.W. 8th Street, a.k.a Calle Ocho, an official name reflecting the Cuban impact on Miami. I turn into one of the many strip malls lining the street and stop in front of Ocho Tatuajes, a tattoo shop.

Jose, the owner, is expecting me. Since my cell phone is basically worthless because they can trace the calls, I called him last night from a phone booth in front of a gas station near Ocala-- before the close encounter with the White City Giant. I've known him and his staff since I was twelve and started spending my summers with dad in the swamp. I found it a lot easier hanging with them instead of dad and the four walls at Ranger HQ which is 30 miles in a straight line further west along the Trail. When dad thought I was taking in a movie or taking my karate classes in a dojo in the same strip mall, in most instances I was hanging with the Cubans, learning how to curse in Spanish, and dreaming of the day I'd be old enough to get tattooed without mom or dad's consent. Although I'm still not old enough-- Jose and the guys think I'm of legal age-- that time has finally arrived.

Jose sees me through the storefront window and motions for me to drive around the back to park. He knows I'm on the run and has saved a spot for me behind the shop that is hidden from the prying eyes of Miami-Dade's finest. He's waiting for me there when I pull into the spot.

"Ola, Stormy."

"Ola, Jose."

We bump shoulders and man-hug.

"Have you seen this morning's paper?" he asks.

"No."

"Looks like the karate classes paid off."

"What do you mean?"

He hands me the Miami Herald and this is when I discover how much I hate technology. And bad lighting.

"I look like shit," I say.

He laughs and tells me I look much better on TV.

"Oh, God, no," I moan.

He laughs again, puts his arm around my shoulder and leads me past the garbage cans through the shop's back door as I learn from reading the paper that I'm wanted for questioning.

Beautiful.

"Ola! It's One Punch Jones!"

I turn away from the paper and see Jose's crew standing around a barber's chair cheering and applauding my entrance. By that time I'm watching myself bringing the giant to his knees on a monitor suspended on the wall behind the barber's chair and completely miss their heartfelt welcome and congratulations. I'm transfixed by the grainy, shadowy YouTube image of me kicking butt and can barely respond to the backslapping and shoulder bumping solidarity the guys are offering up. The shop has the monitor hooked up to a computer and I see that since my performance went viral last night, out of the half-a-dozen videos uploaded by the kids, the one I'm watching now has close to half a million hits.

Well, so much for being stealthy.

I stop watching myself only after the video plays out and the guys overwhelm me with a barrage of questions about last night. I can't keep up with the questions before Jose thankfully steps in with a drawing.

"Cut her some slack. Is this what you're looking for?"

"Perfecto."

They laugh and escort me to a barber's chair where a tat doc is waiting for me to take my seat. I feel like I'm stepping into an operating room for major surgery as I climb into the chair and they lower the back a little so that I'm reclining comfortably. As each side of my skull is shaved and what's left of my hair shampooed, I try to focus on them, on their wisecracks, their questions about being on the run and, of course, Nokosee. I say try to focus because I'm nervous. Very nervous. I've never had a tattoo before, especially one on each side of my head. I'm afraid it's going to hurt like hell and I wonder if I'm making a mistake.

Whom am I doing this for?

That question has been turning around in my mind during the whole ride down from New Jersey and I'm still not sure whether or not I'm being truthful to myself.

I'm doing it for me.

I'm pretty sure of that since Nokosee doesn't have any tats. Whether he'll be impressed or not remains to be seen. For all I know, he may think it's revolting. Hopefully he won't. Hopefully he'll dig it as much as the tat guys do hovering around me, congratulating me for my very large cajones.

Just before they start applying my tats I ask them to twist the chair toward the monitor and hit "Replay" because big cajones or not, I need to distance myself as much as possible from the little needles. Unfortunately, I can't watch it more than a few times before I start feeling sorry for the giant and angry at myself. I ask them if they have any movies to watch, preferably comedies. They do and I start losing myself in the first of what will be way too many mindless crude movies about men and their eternal quest to get laid.

Despite my efforts to focus on the crap they think is funny, I can't escape the pain of guilt and the needles. I got a guy on each side of my head working at the same time. It's long, bloody and just about as painful as I thought it would be. As it turns out, the skin covering the head is pretty thin so every once in a while the needle actually bounces off my skull. Aspirins don't help. I ask for a joint or a drink but these guys do everything by the book so I grit my teeth and do this thing hallucination and inebriation-free. In the end, I learn to embrace the pain and hope by doing so it will make me feel better about myself.

You are one sick chick.

It goes on for hours with the guys taking turns applying the tats, taking breaks to eat and using the john. I eat in the chair and only have to use the restroom twice-- and not once do I look in the mirror. To be honest, I'm kinda afraid I might not like what I see-- despite the constant positive reviews I'm getting from the tat docs circling my head.

"Yeah," I say to them, "if it's so cool why don't you guys got tats on the head?"

"'Cause we doan got no cajones," Jose says in a mock Cuban accent on the right side of my head.

"But we do got bats in da belfry," John, the token Anglo in the shop, says from the left side.

They laugh and for some reason I unintentionally join them and laugh until it hurts. They see me flinch and stop to refocus.

"No more jokes, Jose. No?" John admonishes while wiping a tear away from my cheek.

"Si."

Six hours and three movies later it's over. But I won't look at it until my hair is done. They bring in a woman who adds hot pink tipped highlights to my Mohawk so that my hair when groomed and sprayed to stand upright looks like feathers in a war bonnet.

Yes, I'm a member of the Baredak tribe.

Baredak, Nokosee told me, is what they call a gay Indian. Says there's a whole tribe of them living on "Injun bad lands" west of Ft. Lauderdale. While most of the Seminoles got out of there about 30-years-ago once the county built a municipal and medical waste incinerator nearby, some stubbornly refused to leave despite warnings that they and their land might become contaminated by mercury poisoning. According to Nokosee, mercury is a "known endocrine gland disruptor" which governs the flow of hormones. He said with the straightest of faces that within a decade the men got queer for each other. I told him he was full of shit. He said University of Florida researchers can back him up with studies that show wading male birds, particularly the white ibis, went all "limp winged" for each other where ever they fished in water with even the lowest levels of mercury. When he told me the gay white ibis inspired Miami Beach's annual White Party, the gay world's yearly bacchanalian bash attended by thousands of men and women wearing white clothes-- well, at least until they get all rowdy and randy and start stripping down to nothing-- I asked him if he had a problem with gays because I certainly don't (just assholes). He laughed and told me the North American tribes were the least homophobic group of people on the face of the earth and that I should be thankful his mom and dad moved out from under the shadow of the incinerator soon after he was born or we might not ever have hooked up the way we did, no matter how much I was attracted to him. I'm pretty sure he made all or part of that up but with Nokosee, it's pretty hard to tell sometimes unless he's trying to keep something from me and then he's easier to read than a 20-foot-tall billboard.

Anyway, by the time I'm done, over seven hours have passed and I've become the center of attention for a growing number of customers and friends of the flesh artists who have been called in to see their latest work of art. Including Sensei Steve, my Jewish karate instructor a few doors down. He can't brag enough about his "star pupil."

Despite all the nice things people are saying about me, I don't like being the center of attention especially when I'm "wanted for questioning." Who knows, maybe there's a reward out for me and one of these people staring at me is itching to make some money and won't think twice about turning me in.

You're paranoid.

Yeah.
You don''t like being the center of attention?
Yeah.
Then why did you get tattooed?
I don't know.
Not good enough.
Because I'm nuts.
That''s a given. Tell us something we don't know.
Because I need to punish myself.
That'll do.
"Ready?"
For what?
"Stormy? Are you ready?"
For what, for crying out loud?
I open my eyes and realize it's Jose talking to me and not myself.
You're only 17 and you're already talking to yourself. This is not good.
Tell me about it.
I close my eyes and nod. They raise the back of the chair so that I can see myself in the mirror.
"Go ahead, Stormy, open your eyes."
I can't but my growing legion of fans encourages me to take a look.
"C'mon, girl, you rock!" a girl with a Mo says. "Girlhawks rule!"
I don't feel like it. Instead I feel like a damn fool. Exactly what I've been trying to avoid. Still, I gotta see what all the hullabaloo is about and I slowly raise one eyelid.
Whoe mama.
The other eyelid jumps open so that the eyeball behind it can confirm what the first eyeball saw. To paraphrase Samuel F.B. Morse when he sent the first telegraph message in 1844, "What has Ocho Tatuajes wrought?"
To say it's "over the top" would be a fitting and truthful play on words because its amazing, beautiful and scary all at the same time. Below my 12-inch blond war party Mohawk, I got spears sporting eagle feathers arcing across each side of my shaved head. My new look is met with applause, whistles and shouts of encouragement from what my dad would consider a freak show. Cell phones are held up to me by tattooed hands and pictures are taken; flashes are popping all around me from digital cameras held high by a mixture of ethnicities with multiple piercings and total body art. I fantasize about the crowd lifting me above their heads and parading me through the streets. Then some guy says "I want one" and he's immediately ridiculed for

not having the cajones which I apparently have an abundance of and I wonder what my Seminole name would be for "She's Got Balls."

She's Got Balls rides her Indian onto the Seminole resort compound after her "makeover" and is an immediate sensation.

Or so the headline goes in my brain, a brain I fear has finally thrown in the towel on making me think twice before making any decisions regarding my life. Which is to say, my head is going to take me some time getting use to. Until then, it's a constant reminder of all the wrong decisions I've made. I can only hope living with the hawk and the tats gets better. And that Nokosee digs them.

I have to wait until the next day to "create a fuss" as my dad would say. My original plan was to stop by the tattoo shop, get my head done and then ride in to Injun Territory. Unfortunately, I had to wait for the swelling of my head to come down to a point where it wouldn't scare small children and dogs. Ice packs over twin burn wound bandages on each side of my head and plenty of prescription strength aspirin helped. Also the kindness of strangers. Jose let me sleep overnight on his couch in his apartment he shares with his girlfriend Mercedes which wasn't easy what with the ice packs, the pain and the questions. Aside from asking me about the fight in White City, they kept asking me what the New Seminole were all about and I did my best to explain it to them. They said it sounded crazy. I agreed. Anyway, in case I actually hook up with the swamp renegades, Jose told me to offer them discount tats, that he'd even meet them in the swamp for a group rate they couldn't say no to. I told him I should get a commission. He reminded me I had already gotten a major discount on my "head makeover" because he's known me since I was a "kid" and shouldn't be greedy. Thanks to his "discount," I'm broke and riding on empty. My Hot Topic stash that I accumulated after lots of long hours and overtime disappeared on the road and in the barber's chair faster than I could ever have imagined. I alluded that there were hundreds of New Seminoles hiding in the swamp who'd love to get the tribe's logo-- a raised red fist holding a tomahawk designed by Nokosee-- emblazoned on their bodies and if I couldn't get a commission, he could pretty much forget about me hitting them up for his services. Well, to make a long story short, not only did I get my commission, I was able to wrangle my favorite Dunkin' Donuts #4 breakfast and gas money out of him too.

Maybe it had something to do with the pain killers but by mid-afternoon I'm feeling great and ready to venture forth. The swelling has disappeared, the bandages removed and the pain replaced with a general but tolerable numbness. My tats and newly shaved head are protected from the harmful effects of the sun with a nicely massaged in good slathering of 50 proof sun block soothingly applied by Mercedes. I say adios to the people at the tat shop, slip on my Wayfarers, and make sure to gun the Indian enough to make a loud impression on them when I peel out. Looking in my rear view mirror tells me it worked. It's nice to have fans.

I find out real quick riding my Indian with my 12" Mohawk takes some getting use to, i.e., keeping it centered and together with just hair spray doesn't work. It needs something more, something with industrial strength properties so I pull off the road, drive behind another strip mall and kill the engine. I unzip my duffel bag, grab my cosmetic bag and rummage around for what I hope is still there. It is. Butch Wax. Dad uses it on his stupid "flat top" to keep the longest part of it standing up in the front of his head. I discovered it years ago as a kid watching dad "lacquer up" each morning before going to work. It's hard to find nowadays so when I had the chance, I swiped me one one summer from our shared bathroom while doing my sojourn in the swamp with the "Great White Father." I pop the lid off the "control stick" and, using one of my rear views, start running it up on both sides of what's left of my Mohawk. By the time I'm done, it's straight as a board and doesn't move no matter how much I shake my head. When I put it back in the cosmetic bag I see my lipstick and wonder if I should apply it too. I take it out, unscrew the top and...I can't do it. It doesn't work with my tats. Too much color. I'm starting to look like some kinda circus freak as it is. I figure it's probably more "politically correct" with the NS if I deep six the make-up anyway so, as I drive past a dumpster, I say adios to that part of my life too. Except for the Butch Wax or, as I like to think of it now, the Bitch Wax.

Back on the road, I look at my one-inch Glamour Nails and know they too will become a thing of the past. Talk about commitment. I wonder if it's only my out-of-whack hormones making me do this. My psych class would blame it on an immature prefrontal cortex which scientists discovered about ten years ago doesn't fully develop until the late twenties. It's supposed to be responsible for forming strategies and controlling impulses. Combine that with the normal number of raging hormones racing through your average teenager's body and throw in a pregnancy cocktail of even crazier glands gone wild for good measure and you get... crazy little ol' me.

Maybe I should be committed.

I know that's what people driving beside me are thinking, judging me by the number of my piercings and, of course, my outrageous Mohawk.

Screw 'em. Bunch of losers hiding behind their air-conditioned rolling cubicles.

With each new mile I put between them and civilization, I find myself caring less and less about what anyone thinks. As Joan Jett would say, "I don't give a damn about my bad reputation" which I sense is only going to get worse.

You can see the Miccosukee casino hotel and convention center resting on the side of the Tamiami Trail from miles away. The Trail, dug out of the mosquito infested swamp of the Everglades in 1926, was the first road to connect southeast Florida with cities on the Gulf and in fact stayed that way until Alligator Alley opened in 1969 about 30 miles north. At one time it was dotted with Miccosukee and Seminole chickee huts offering souvenirs and airboat rides. Only a few remain. Since casino gambling came to the swamp in 1979 when the Seminoles opened the first Native American "gaming" enterprise in the U.S, the tribes discovered very quickly it's much easier, faster and efficient to run casinos than it is to sell their crafts along the roadside to make a living. Today the Las Vegas style resort looms over the flat expanse of the Everglades and is probably the one main symbol of just how much the world has changed in one generation for everyone living down here.

As I near, I see that because dad still hasn't put out the fires, a few skeleton TV crews are still encamped in the parking lots with their telescoping dish antennas pointed eastward toward Miami, some 30 miles away. I circle around the back and turn in to the employees parking lot and spot J.T. Osceola's custom chopper first off. Sitting in the tribal chairman's reserved parking space, it's one expensive radical beast with its fat ass rear tire and a tricked out Seminole patchwork quilt design painted along its black gas tank. This, as it turned out, was "Osceola's Spear," one of the needful things Nokosee's dad had longed for, had hoped his "first of the New Seminole" would bring back to the swamp as a souvenir from his walkabout. Maybe if Nokosee and I had had the time we could have pulled it off but as you may already know, with cops and lunatic parents on our tail and a handful of rednecks trying to kill us, well, you can see why we couldn't work it in to our schedule. Too bad because I fantasize about what it would have been like if we had. I know I'd be driving the bike with my pagan caveman boyfriend on the back, arms wrapped tightly around my waist. Although Nokosee might be one fearless lean, mean fighting machine, he doesn't know how to drive a motorcycle because his nutcase dad hadn't gotten around to teaching him.

Of course, that could never have happened back then because of yours truly. I wasn't ready to make a commitment to such a cockamamie cause that included living in a bug slapping, alligator infested swamp without A/C. That included being willing to die for something bigger than myself, especially if the "something" was totally outrageous and insane. But that was then and this is now, before the Gulf oil spill, a chunk of ice four times the size of Manhattan broke off the coast of Greenland, and the baby growing inside me, now confirmed after a fourth reading on a far less stressful pee at a Georgia truck stop.

I drive up and park next to the *Spear* because I have a plan, a plan formulated over weeks without my Nokosee fix and 1,200 miles of on-the-road cogitation: I'm going to steal it.

Chapter 5
Hello, Nokosee!

Stealing a motorcycle isn't that difficult if you know where to start and what wires to cut and splice. I learned how by Googling it. Suffice to say, using only a blade from the Leatherman knife and multitool thingie dad gave me when I turned thirteen-- in yet another one of his ham-handed attempts at changing me into the son he never had-- I'm able to start the big twin engine. In less than a minute I become a grand theft chopper chick. It's exhilarating and I don't recommend it to the faint of heart because I think I'm going to die when I rev the motor. "Loud" can't do it justice in describing the way it sounds or the way it shakes my body. It's not until I throw my leg over the beast and sit down on the custom leather seat with the hand tooled spears and feathers stamped onto its surface that I start having second thoughts. This is one mean machine with more instant brute power than I'm use to. I freeze. I'm too scared to let out the clutch and give it some gas.

Until I see J.T. Osceola running my way and screaming his head off.

J.T. might not be a lean mean fighting machine like Nokosee but he's big and fat enough to cause me some serious damage if he doesn't die from a heart attack first before he gets to me which is more than enough incentive to twist the throttle.

I do a wheelie and hold on for dear life. J.T.'s eyes suddenly turn into big white and brown circles of fear as I come roaring toward him. He jumps out of the way just in time and falls against the hot asphalt which is scraping the gold lamé off my gold lamé DMs right down to their steel toes. Sparks fly from my boots as I'm dragged across the parking lot. I let off the gas and the front wheel falls back onto the ground but I have to fight to control the machine as it wobbles back and forth to a stop. I look back at J.T.

"Trade yours for mine?" I shout. "The keys are in the ignition!"

I give the *Spear* some gas and fishtail across the parking lot.

A security guard comes running out of the building and gets all Barney Fife with me, pointing his gun and trying to get a bead on my head.

"Don't shoot!" J.T. yells from behind me. "It's Stormy Jones!"

The guy lowers his gun and lets me roar by. I round the main building and see a TV reporter with a microphone in front of his face talking to a camera lens until he *hears* the chopper. He and everyone else around him turn to look at the rolling soundtrack from hell. I get inspired and throttle the beast right up to the guy with the mic.

"Yo," I shout over the fire-breathing cacophony. "Is this on?" I ask nodding my way cool in-your-face Mohawk toward the camera.

"Hey, you're that ranger's kid, aren't you?" he shouts back. "The one that's all over YouTube, right?"

I nod that I am.

"Little darlin'," he says while sticking the mic in front of my face, "You're on live."

I lean over and shout into the mic while eying the camera. "Hi, remember me?" I ask, lifting my shades. "Just thought I'd let you know Stormy Jones is back in town after a short stop in White City and I just stole J.T. Osceola's badass bike."

I rev the motor for affect and turn to see J.T. rounding the building huffing and puffing with half a dozen security guards.

"Tell Nokosee to keep an eye out for me! I'll be waiting for him by the third alligator on the right."

And with that, I leave a nice patch of burnt rubber on the parking lot for my fans and the media to remember me by.

Chapter 6
Renegade on the Run

Wanna get famous fast? Slay a giant and steal a $70,000 chopper from some powerful big-shot during the 6:00 News. On camera. Then do an O.J. by racing up the Interstate during rush hour so that all the news stories of the day are preempted so the three major local broadcast news helicopters can track your every move from the air.

I look over my shoulder and I see a cop helicopter has joined my aerial pursuit northward on the Palmetto Expressway, a.k.a, State Road 836, because they can't get me in the stop-and-go traffic crawl on what the Weather Channel has described as the nation's 10th worst congested road.

I love it.

With my chopper, I can weave between the stopped cars and trucks, ride the shoulders of the road and, more or less, do exactly what I want because cops in cars can't do what I can do.

Twenty minutes later I'm in Ft. Lauderdale and racing west on I-75. Two FHP motorcycle cops have joined the chase now but they can't catch me. There's no speedometer on the bike but I can only guess as I fly by the cars on the road that I must be closing in on 100 miles-per-hour or more. I discover the only problem I have driving at that speed is keeping the Mohawk more or less perpendicular in the wind stream. By the time I near Alligator Alley, I've managed to learn how to use it to help keep my body centered and low on the gas tank in the turns. Pretty cool.

That's right, my head is a big freaking tail fin.

People are waving at me from their cars and shouting encouragement as I roar by because they've heard about me on the radio or seen me on TV or on their smartphones. It appears my fan base is growing by the mile.

Cars are backed up at the exit. I brake hard and fishtail onto the shoulder. Smoke rises from the back tire. Cops are blocking the exit up front. I look back. The two motorcycle cops are closing in. I give it some gas and slowly swerve between the cars.

"Go, Stormy!" some girl about my age yells from her car.

"Go, 'Noles!" some guys yell as I pass by, pointing at my tats and then back to their baseball caps and the Florida State *Seminoles* logo which appears on the team's football helmets.

Is that where I got the idea? From "watching" too many football games with my dad? I was zoning out most of the time. Thinking about anything but football. Damn, I thought I was being freaking original!

The subconscious works in mysterious ways.

Horns start honking and people are getting out of their cars to see me and cheer me on. This puts thinking about the lack of my creativity and the difficulty of changing the tats on the back burner as I redirect my attention to easing the bike between the cars, trucks and people.

"You go, girl!"

"I'm doing my best," I answer as I try to steady the big chopper with both boots on the ground.

I see cops near the exit trying to sneak up on me, guns drawn. I turn off the road and slide down the grass embankment, bouncing up and down like I'm on some cheap carnival ride because of the chopper's extended front end and narrow front wheel. I twist the throttle, fishtail in the grass and just avoid a flying-tackle-by-cop.

"Don't you dare shoot her!" a woman yells behind me. "I've got a camera!"

I look in my rear view and see her recording it all on her smartphone. I love her! And technology-- despite the NS belief it's the cause of all of the world's problems.

But you hate technology!

Not today.

You're nuts.

Tell me something I don't know.

The cops raise their guns. The last thing they need is getting caught on camera shooting an unarmed 17-year-old-girl who's about to be a mother. Well, in nine months for sure.

Unless I'm already a mother because I'm pregnant.

No, you're just pregnant.

I'm confused. It's hard to think straight when it appears some people have a jones for killing you all over again.

I gun the chopper and race past my welcoming committee-- and the spike strip they threw at me that got snagged on the thrower's shoe and fell way short. Dad taught me to respect the police but I gotta tell you, I feel like I'm in the middle of a Keystone Kops comedy. Talk about incompetence.

Anyway, I slip past the roadblock and head toward the Alligator Alley entrance. To my surprise, no army's there to stop me.

Hey, grrl, you're not that big of a deal. Yet.

Although a concrete barrier has been set up blocking access to the toll booths, it's there to stop *everybody* because of what the NS did a few days ago: blowing up the gasoline tanker trucks on both ends of the Alley. From what I saw on TV last night, they're afraid of more "terrorist activity" along the Alley and are keeping it closed until they can be sure its safe.

That's fine with me as I blast by the lone cop on his radio. Guess he got the message too late because he sure wasn't prepared to stop me. I look back and see that I've got a whole slew of cops chasing me from all jurisdictions, some on bikes, most in cars. By now it turns out I've even got cops in the air gaining on the news copters and jockeying for airspace over my desperate run to...

What?

That's the big question right now running through my addled mind as I accelerate westward. Nokosee and I joked about seeing each other again less than a month ago, said he'd be waiting for me on the Alley by the "third gator on the right." I'm hoping he's watching TV somewhere in the swamp, sees me and is mounting a rescue party.

Or something.

Pretty sad, isn't it? Basically, I don't know what the hell I'm doing except running. Running from something to something... better. Hopefully.

I fly by the blackened skeletal wreckage of the fuel tanker now pushed off the side of the road, and nearly lose control of the chopper. The heat was so intense it melted the asphalt, leaving big. jagged holes on the surface. Construction equipment sits on the side ready to make the damage and the very thought of domestic terrorism go away.

"Stop your vehicle!"

I look up and to the side. A Broward Sheriffs Office helicopter is flying next to me, low to the ground, communicating with the renegade-on-the-run through its exterior speakers. Two SWAT guys clad in black, hanging from the open side, got me in their crosshairs with high velocity sniper rifles. I turn away, twist the throttle till it can't twist no more and pull away, hoping the news copters are still trailing me, hoping the cops will be intimidated enough not to shoot me on camera.

How about off camera?

That too.

The sun seems to be setting dead center on top of the Alley. Heat waves shimmer off the hot pavement and I have this weird feeling that I'm heading for that final white light that supposedly is waiting for all of us when we die when the road suddenly starts exploding in front of me.

The cops are shooting up the road to try to stop me!

Sharp edged chunks of asphalt sent flying into the air smash against my sunglasses and rip into my face. Blood rolls across my shades. I lean forward over the tank and hug it tightly, trying to become one with the beast to avoid the crap in the air but it doesn't work. I can hear it hitting the gas tank, see it pitting the custom paint job, feel it tearing into my scalp. I start swerving back and forth from lane to lane to avoid the flying debris and squint my eyes to see through the rolling, tumbling dust cloud kicked up in front of me.

And then I see a solitary figure up ahead, silhouetted against the red-orange sun setting behind him. He's walking toward me out of the dust storm, casually, with something over his shoulder. By the time it registers with me who he is (Nokosee's father Busimanolotome) and what he's got (an RPG-- a rocket propelled grenade-- something I discovered the crazy bastard had hidden along with Stinger missiles in every camouflaged NS chickee in the Everglades), I've already raced pass him at over 100 miles-per-hour. I look back.

Busimanolotome fires the RPG and the cop chopper explodes in the air in a ball of flame as bright as the setting sun.

I slam on the brakes and swerve the bike into a slide off the road and onto the grass. I can't believe what I see as I'm ripped and rolled from the bike and come to an abrupt stop in high grass next to the canal: the disintegrating, burning helicopter's momentum is racing toward me and crashing into the embankment. I bury my head in the grass and cover it with my hands as flaming body parts and metal contraptions hurtle past me, so close I can feel the heat. The ground shakes with their rapid, staccato impacts. The onslaught of bone and metal is over with in an instant but I'm afraid to look up, afraid something with my name on it is still coming at me but the heat of the burning copter is too much so I start backing away, scared and crying, head still buried in the grass when I'm lifted to my feet and my Wayfarers fall off my face.

Busimanolotome's got me by the back of my motorcycle jacket, the smoking Russian RPG slung over his shoulder. He's wearing war paint-- his eyes are blackened out-- and his Purple Heart medal is pinned to the center of his headband clasping eagle feathers. He's holding me up with one arm while looking at my tats and new Mohawk, his face ablaze with the flickering fire of the burning wreckage less than fifty feet away.

"What the hell?" he shouts over the roar of the fire and the final small explosions of the dying copter echoing, I'm sure, what my father will say when he sees them for the first time too. And then he sees *Osceola's Spear,* drops me on the ground and starts off for the bike.

"Dad!"

I look up. It's Nokosee, jumping off the bow of an airboat with other NS running toward me from out of the tall cattails lining the canal bank. My heart races and I come alive again. And then it skips a beat and I have to put the brakes on my jones to see Nokosee as my brain cells OD and synapses are forever irreparably destroyed as they go into turbo mode in trying to process what I'm seeing: jeggings. My big strong pagan caveman is wearing jeggings, camouflage jeggings to be exact. Not that they look all that bad on the guy because he's got muscles on muscles but it's *so* metrosexual. And then my rattled over-worked brain starts trying to accommodate the other data rushing in: the whole damn NS tribe is wearing jeggings. Some look like stone washed jeans, others are sporting earth tones with the odd fall leaf color thrown in which doesn't work at all with the Everglades palette. It's too much to take in all at one time. I close my eyes and tell myself to focus only on Nokosee.

He's wearing my *Chief's* Seminole jacket-- the "gang" jacket I gave him the night we did "it"-- unzipped, the sleeves removed now to accommodate his big muscles. A machine gun hangs from a strap slung around his shoulder. The loincloth, I guess, is a thing of the past, a relic of his walkabout before he officially became the "First of the New Seminole."

Is that his dick?

Focus, idiot, focus!

I hear machine gun fire and turn from Nokosee. NS are firing on the cop cars and motorcycles that were on my ass, scattering them in all directions except forward. The lead motorcycle cops lose control of their bikes and slide across the asphalt and become airborne over the grass embankment before somersaulting into the water. The cop cars rear end each other and start piling up and when the lead car runs sideways across the road, a chain reaction starts behind it, flipping one, two, three cars multiple times through the air as if they were in a major fail at a NASCAR race.

I close my eyes, cover my ears, and bury my head once again in the grass and dirt, sure that one of the cars is going to spin out and roll right on top of me. But that doesn't happen. Instead of dying in the middle of the shootout with bullets flying all around me and cop cars flying overhead, Nokosee grabs me under my arms and helps me to my feet. I open my eyes and look at him. I'm sure I must look frightened, crazed. I put my arms around him and squeeze him tightly. He pushes me back and runs his hand gently across my forehead, moving the blood aside before looking at my Mohawk, a little tilted now and littered with grass, leaves and grains of sand and asphalt thanks to the Bitch Wax.

"Is this the third alligator on the right?" I ask, my voice trembling, betraying my false bravado.

He finally looks at *me*. He's still beautiful; gorgeous, really. I want him so badly I can't help but latch on to his body. I look up at him with my big cry baby blues and he looks down at me and I hope he wants to kiss me.

He hands me my Wayfarers and nods at my tats. "Had a slow day, did ya?"

A bullet kicks up a clump of sand and grass next to us. I jump and scream, he doesn't but holds me even tighter. And then, when the gunfire becomes even more intense, and bullets are ricocheting all around us, he gives me a kiss to die for, a kiss that makes it all worthwhile. It's Scarlett O'Hara and Rhett Butler all over again with the fire burning down Atlanta in the background but amped up a notch with a *Gunfight at the OK Corral* thrown in for good measure. We kiss like there's no tomorrow, feverishly, changing from side-to-side, my Mohawk slapping his forehead with each impassioned kiss, hoping all the while that a bullet doesn't kill us.

I want to live! I want to live!

They're my thoughts but thanks to mom and pop, Susan Hayward is saying them for me, screaming them as they lead her to the gas chamber. I'm the result of a kid torn between divorced parents, one trying to shape her into a movie star in the fall, winter, and spring and one into a Scorsese slash Peckinpah slash Kurosawa loving cinephile of the machismo during the summer.

"Get a grip," Busimanolotome shouts.

Nokosee tries to pull away but I don't want to stop kissing him because I know when I do the movie I've been dreaming will come to an end and I'll hear men screaming as they burn to death, I'll smell their burning flesh and a bullet will strike me and Nokosee dead.

"I could use a hand here," Busimanolotome drawls even louder over the cacophony of the war raging all around us.

Nokosee pushes my head aside and I see Busimanolotome struggling to walk the fallen, smoking and broken chopper through the grass popping with bullets.

My God, his old man is wearing jeggings too! Forest green ones! He looks like Robin Hood!

Nokosee breaks my hold and runs to his father's aid.

"C'mon, Stormy," Nokosee shouts back at me. "Help us push."

Real men don't wear jeggings.

It's my dad's voice pushing through my misfiring synapses but it's the bullet that whizzes by that snaps me out of my misplaced priorities-- for me and them. I can't believe they're even bothering to salvage the bent and busted *Spear* but standing there in the open questioning their fashion sense seems crazier. I slam my Wayfarers back on and with my hands flapping nervously and embarrassingly from limp wrists held out to the sides--

Yes, I truly am a member of the Baredak Tribe--

I scream like a girly-mon's girl and run tip-toeing through the deadly tulips sprouting at my feet and past the burning wreckage of God-knows-what across the sloping grass embankment, praying no bullet finds me but understand if it does.

I fall in behind Nokosee on his side of the bike and help him and his old man push it through the high grass and the whizzing bullets. One strikes the *Spear* and ricochets into the ground with a loud clang.

"Dammit!" Busimanolotome screams in frustration.

I swear, I almost pee my pants over that one, it was way too close for comfort. But no matter, the Osceola boys never lose a beat and continue to push the stupid chopper across the grass.

I see the helicopter burning out of the corner of my eye but I won't look at it. I see a burning, overturned police cruiser out of the corner of my other eye but refuse to look at it too. Reality wants to rub my face in the horror, the horror when the wind shifts and blows a thick acrid black smoke over us and the very real smell of death. The film strip of my movie runs off its sprockets, forcing me to face the fact that I'm responsible for the deaths of innocent people and inexplicably, I start thinking about Ken Kesey, author of *One Flew Over The Cuckoo's Nest*. Thanks to my dad, I learned that Kesey approached life as if it were a movie of your own making, something I failed at immeasurably. Of course, he was consuming large quantities of LSD at the time and was very forgiving and tolerant of the surreal and the inexplicable which helped him see his movie more or less the way he envisioned it. I don't have that luxury. I start coughing and want to hurl as we push the chopper through the blanketing smoke toward the cattails now burning along the canal and wish I had a tab of acid that would put me on a trip out of there.

For the record, I've never done acid but from what I read, if there ever was a time to justify giving it a shot, this is it

Busimanolotome yells something at a fat black guy with long dreadlocks who-- and I never thought I'd say this-- has thankfully forsaken jeggings for hip-hop clown pants, you know, the wide-legged extended shorts that hang off a guy's ass exposing his pride-and-joy boxers and stop somewhere around mid-calf. This dude, standing next to one of the airboats, pushes a button on a ghetto blaster and suddenly I hear "Run away! Run away!" echoing across the battlefield. It's the voice of King Arthur from *Monty Python's The Holy Grail* and I don't know whether to laugh or cry until I hear another recording, this time of a bugle and I half expect the U.S. Calvary to come charging on horseback out of the sawgrass and tall cattails to save us all.

Instead, the NS, a rag tag mixture of NAs and Outsiders, some with warpaint and feathers, some wearing army surplus camo fatigues and combat boots, and way too many of them sporting jeggings, emerge from the smoke and fire walking backwards, shooting their weapons.

We're retreating! Thank, God!

A couple of NS take the *Spear* from us and load it onto the airboat while another records the event on a small video camera. As I climb on board with Nokosee I look up and see a single TV news helicopter with its rotating ball camera mounted in the front zeroing in on us for what I'm sure the cameraman thinks is a sure fire Emmy Award-winning moment. I'm surprised Busimanolotome doesn't care as our NS war party, abandoning the protective cover of the tall sawgrass, reeds, and cattails, scrambles to board its airboats and swamp buggies until he turns to one of the NS guys running by.

"Take this!" Busimanolotome shouts.

He throws the smoking RPG at him and the guy stops to catch it which turns out to be a big mistake: a bullet strikes him dead. I scream as he falls backward and rolls down the embankment into the water, the smoking RPG rolling after him.

Busimanolotome, never missing a beat nor taking his eyes off the helicopter, sticks his hand out to the last of his ragged band of warriors hugging the embankment to keep from getting killed and shouts, "Tracer, please!" One of them heaves a machine gun up across the embankment and Busimanolotome grabs it on the run, turns and fires a long line of bullets which you can actually see flying across the darkening sky toward the helicopter. Later I learn they're called tracer rounds and are used to help the shooter lock onto his target. The TV news copter whips around and flees back to Miami trailing smoke, disappearing behind cypress trees and finally the endless, ever burning, sawgrass horizon, a thing, like my love for Nokosee, my father can't put out.

Chapter 7
Frank Mills Salutes You!

It's night now as Busimanolotome, sitting high up in the seat of our airboat, leads other airboats and swamp buggies deeper into the Everglades. With only the stars to guide him and the red glow of the summer fires to define the horizon, Busimanolotome threads his way through the countless unmarked hammocks, lost only in a Time-Life collection of music from the sixties in his big ear encompassing headphones.

Nokosee and me are sitting in the hull below his daddy's feet, holding each other. He wants to kiss me but I can't kiss back anymore because I can't shake the feeling that people have died because of me. I think he knows how I feel because he gently pulls me closer, puts his big strong arms around me, and starts telling me how part of my movie came true. He whispers into my ear, loud enough to overcome the sound of the airboat engine, but soft enough to keep it from becoming unpleasant. I learn he knew I was coming at least a day ago when he was checking out the latest YouTube uploads off a laptop connected to a portable military grade satellite receiver. Since then he and his family kept a vigilant eye on the TV news and the Miami Herald's online website to catch any updates on my status. He was lying in the family chickee with his family watching TV when they saw me interrupting the live update re the Everglades fire. Nokosee says he jumped straight up, yelling and pointing at the TV; that his mom and his sister got closer to the screen to see me but none of them had expected me to look like the Last of the Mohicans. He said even his dad sat up and took notice-- not as it turned out for me but because he recognized the bike. I asked Nokosee if my new makeover disappointed him and he emphatically said, "Hell no!" that in fact, it excited him. As soon as they heard me mention the bit about the alligator, Nokosee knew where I was going and cajoled his dad to marshal the troops to save my ass which is something I don't think would have happened if my ass hadn't been sitting on top of *Osceola's Spear*. In any event, Busimanolotome rounded up a NS war party, jumped in their airboats and swamp buggies and were heading for Alligator Alley before I even reached the Interstate. Once they got there, they picked a spot and waited for me to make my appearance.

I look up at Nokosee and smile. He leans over and kisses me. And he won't let me go. I open my eyes and look over his shoulder and see airboats and swamp buggies trailing backward from our lead boat, stretching out across the black water of the Everglades, disappearing into the night. For some reason, despite my overwhelming guilt, the combined sound of all of those engines exhilarates me and I feel empowered, a feeling I know I'd never get back home in Milltown, working at Hot Topic, and going to college. Yeah, getting chased down by cops, shot at while racing along at over 100 miles-per-hour on two wheels, seeing people die over you and surviving it all only to fall into the arms of the guy you love has a way of putting the kibosh on ever wanting to finish your homework. I rest my head on Nokosee's he-man chest and know that I've crossed on over to the other side for good, that there's no turning back. I slowly exhale and close my eyes and for the first time in a very long time I feel oddly at peace and wonder if I'm a psychopath. Nokosee puts his hand over my outside ear and my new life grows quieter. Within minutes I fall into adrenaline sapped sleep because my body and my mind have nothing else to give to love, the movie, or The Cause.

Nokosee wakes me with a whisper in my ear. I look up and see the airboat bow gently, and quietly meeting a hammock bank lit by the flickering orange light of glass lanterns and the green light of glow sticks held up by more New Seminoles who have come down to the water's edge to greet us. The hammock, like the other NS encampments, is draped in camo netting which creates the feeling of entering a giant glowing circus tent. Nokosee jumps out first and then turns to offer me his hand. I take it, step out of the airboat, and fall into his arms. He holds me tightly and beaming, turns to the others.

"New Seminoles," he says loudly, "meet Stormy Jones, our newest member of the tribe, the giant slayer you've all heard about, the warrior chick who fetched *Osceola's Spear!*"

Men are rolling the bent and misshapen bike out of another airboat onto the hammock beach when I'm suddenly yanked out of Nokosee's arms and put onto the shoulders of two men and paraded triumphantly toward the bike with cheers and "Stormy!" shouted by the group of wild-eyed, long-haired, face painted, tree hugging, militant vegans, and old and new hippies, all channeling, as I learned later, their "inner wildness," a return-to-nature philosophy advocated by Daniel Vitalis and tweaked for extreme pro-activism by Busimanolotome Osceola. I suddenly feel at home, that I'm finally on the other side-- the *right* side; the Inside-- until they turn me toward Busimanolotome. He's still sitting in the airboat seat and looking down at me with nothing short of contempt. The others see it too and within seconds my righteous dreamed about movie welcome with fits and starts, finishing with a general communal unease.

"Dad," Nokosee says in frustration, "cut her some slack and give it up for her. You know she deserves it."

Aside from the constantly croaking frogs, it's probably not more than six seconds of totally awkward human silence before the old bastard says anything, but in that short amount of time I immediately get a sense of who's boss and why: Busimanolotome scares the living bejesus out of everyone.

Except the frogs.

"Put her down," he finally says.

They set me down and step back and suddenly I feel all alone again. I look around for Nokosee and miss seeing his father getting down from the airboat and hopping on to the hammock beach.

"You look different," he says.

I jump and whip around to his deep, infectionless voice.

Man, the guy is really, really good at sneaking up on you.

"So do you," I reply angrily. Compared to the last time I saw him when I was lying on my back in knee deep swamp water pointing the "most powerful handgun in the world" at him-- and pulling the trigger-- he looks smaller and less frightening. In any event I've never liked bullies and won't be intimidated.

"Not as scary?" he asks.

I take time to scope out his jeggings before turning to him with what I hope is an incredulous look. "Yeah."

"I'll have to work on that."

He slips his thumbs into the top of his jeggings, pulls the elastic edge away from his round, middle-aged paunch and lets it snap back.

A scattering of nervous laughter rises from his not-so-merry-men.

Screw you, you old goat.

Of course, I don't say that to his face but it's not because I'm afraid of him. Hell, I've got Nokosee by my side now, he's grabbing my hand, and I know he wouldn't let anything happen to me. No, for some reason, Nokosee's old man doesn't scare me at all. Maybe it's because I've been around hardass, monosyllabic guys like him all my life, i.e. my dad, and I've gotten use to them. Of course, kicking your ex-boyfriend's butt, a couple of bitches, your mom's boyfriend, a giant and a football coach on the road builds confidence too. And just coming down from an adrenaline rush like no other also has to be factored in. Anyway, it's better to be polite right now instead of a smart ass since I'm on his turf and standing in front of a group of people who I want to give me the benefit of the doubt before passing judgment on me. In any event, I have no desire to piss their "Chief" off by embarrassing him within the first few moments of meeting his loyal following. And besides, I'm just too damn tired.

"Yeah, Kemasabe," a woman's voice breaks the uneasy human silence. "Cut her some slack."

I turn to the voice, soft, sweet and feminine, and see a woman holding a Coleman lantern stepping out of the shadows of the jungle hammock. I figure she's in her 50's as she parts the New Seminoles like Moses through the Nile. There's a teenage girl with her too. Both are wearing cropped Seminole patchwork tops over the traditional patchwork full-length skirt with beaded headbands. Thanks to some Googling I did on the Seminoles after I got back to Milltown following the bloody climatic ending to the first part of my story, the airy tops follow an even older tradition before the Southern Baptist Convention started turning the Seminoles into Christians as far back as the 1840's, before they were taught displaying a bare midriff was immodest.

Practical *and* sexy.

Right. Anyway, the woman looks like Cher might look like if she didn't do plastic surgery: slim with long black curly hair with streaks of gray framing a weathered, tanned face and an amazingly trim tummy for someone her age. The teenager is thin and tanned too, with the same long untamed black curly hair reaching her waist. When I notice how much she looks like Nokosee, I make the connection: it's his Cuban mother and younger sister.

"Where's that famous New Seminole hospitality we've heard so much about?" she asks her husband.

I turn to Busimanolotome. He just sighs and sadly shakes his head.

"Holatte-Sutv Turwv," she says.

I turn back to her. She's greeting me with open arms and that catches me off-guard. I stumble backward, anxious, and open my mouth.

"That's easy for you to say."

I got to learn to stop talking when I get nervous.

It doesn't bother her. She never misses a beat and continues to walk toward me with open arms.

"'Sky Eyes,'" she says as she takes my hands and looks at me. "It's the name Nokosee gave you."

"Right. I told him it sounds like a Starbucks coffee."

I get a few laughs on that one.

"You got balls," Busimanolotome says behind me.

I whip around even quicker than even I thought possible and turn on him. "And you need to see a shrink. How could you kill all those people?"

Silence. Real silence. Even the critters have stopped critting as Nokosee's mom draws me close to her side. The only thing I hear is the sound of the lens retracting on the digital camcorder that guy used to record my rescue, that he's now using to document my appearance in Busimanolotome's movie. I figure I'm a goner now, even if Nokosee throws himself in front of the arrow I'm sure Busimanolotome is going to shoot me with. Instead, after a long nerve wracking interval, I get this:

"It's funny no one asked that question in 1868 when Custer massacred over 150 Cheyenne men, women and children who had gathered peacefully along the Washita river in Oklahoma to surrender."

"Say what?"

"The Cheyenne and nearly 9,000 other Human Beings were told by the government to assemble along the river in the dead of winter for transfer to a reservation in Indian Territory. As it turned out, it was only a ruse to get them in one place so they could be easily attacked. Do you know why?"

I shake my head no.

"So the government could render null and void the Treaty of Fort Laramie of that same year which essentially gave the Human Beings all of the Great Plains."

"Why would they want to do that?"

"If the Human Beings are all dead, there's no treaty and the government can reclaim the land for itself."

"That's crazy," I say.

"And so was what happened today. Only difference is, we weren't fighting back with bows and arrows this time around. And we didn't come to surrender. As you may know, we're not the surrendering type."

Right. The only tribe that never signed a peace treaty with the Feds. It's something the mainstream Seminoles and Miccosukees are quite proud of and never get tired of reminding everybody. I don't know what to say and turn away.

"So, to answer your question, it was instinctual, something the Outside's war machine taught me as a boy right out of high school. Besides, I got the law on my side."

I turn back to Busimanolotome. "What?"

"Florida's Stand Your Ground self-defense law gives me the right to shoot back."

"Hell, Micco," some twitchy little dude cradling an AK-47 adds, "it gives you the right to shoot *first*."

"You're right, Indian Larry," Busimanolotome says. "My kinda law."

Yeah, I know all about that new law. It's controversial as all get out. Makes it open season on anybody threatening you with deadly harm, effectively "eliminating a citizen's duty to retreat from a deadly threat" while bestowing "immunity" on people protecting themselves with lethal force.

"I don't think that exempts shooting at cops," I say.

"That's something for the courts to decide."

I laugh derisively. Like you'll ever show up in a courtroom to stand trial. Unless, of course you harbor a secret desire to be a martyr like the first Osceola. Or Billy Jack.

His eyes narrow on me. "They were trespassing on New Seminole land," he continues in a tight-lipped inflectionless cadence, "and we had the right to shoot back."

"Sounds like you're struggling to come up with a viable reason to justify it all."

He pauses for a moment to look me over, to size me up and concludes I'm not worthy of arguing with before advising with utter contempt: "It was all about self-preservation of the New Seminole nation."

"That sounds real noble and all," I say, "but there are still a lot of dead guys lying around out there because of you."

"And you."

"Me?"

"If you hadn't came back in the way you did, none of this would have happened."

Now I really don't know what to say. I may have been thinking the same thing, but the old bastard had to go and say it out loud-- in front of everybody. Now I'm not only feeling guilty as all get out, I'm embarrassed too. I look away and inadvertently catch the eyes of some NS looking at me. They don't know where to look either. It looks like we're all a little embarrassed by the whole mess. And then, as if to put all of us out of our misery, Busimanolotome changes the subject.

"You musta been going 200 miles-per-hour on my bike," he finally drawls out in a voice that mixes the soft deliberate cadences of NA speech with that of a down home redneck.

"Your bike?"

Nokosee's mom tightens her grip on my hand.

"It is now," Busimanolotome says.

"Thanks to me."

"Consider it tribute."

"'Tribute?' Screw that."

This is where I should have kept my mouth shut. Again. Now *I* got everybody too scared to move or say anything. Except Busimanolotome. After another long drawn out moment, he says:

"What else would you call it?"

He asks it real slowly, coolly with narrow eyes and a fearless smirk. I don't know what to say. He reminds me of Nokosee, when Nokosee laid it out plain and simple for me when we first met and were getting to know each other in the swamp: what are you going to do about it, Stormy? You're just a girl without a clue in the middle of nowhere. I could kill you if I wanted to and there isn't a damn thing you can do about it.

"A gift," I finally say. I extend my hand to shake. Busimanolotome looks at my hand and then turns to me as if I was some kinda fool. And then I look at my hand, sitting out there all alone in the humidity and see it shaking.

"Just like an Outsider," he says. "Flavor-of-the-Month, when you can hold your hand still, then I'll shake it, then you'll be worthy of making a deal with the descendant of Osceola."

"Oh,yeah?" I ask while withdrawing my hand. I turn and start looking around. "Where is he? I'd like to meet him."

"Harde-har-har-har," Busimanolotome says. "You've got yourself a real comedian here, Nokosee, a real Joan Rivers."

"Hey, dad," Nokosee says while grabbing my free hand, "she makes *me* laugh and that's all that matters. And she's more than worthy with me. If you can't see it, that's your problem. C'mon, Stormy." Nokosee tries to drag me away but with his mother holding my other hand, the exit is a bit awkward and clumsy.

"It takes more than tattoos and a Mohawk to be a New Seminole," he shouts after us.

Nokosee shakes lose, whips around to his dad and lets him have an earful in my defense. It's like watching an episode of *American Chopper* when Paul, Jr and his old man are going at it, each jabbing the air with their fingers to make a point and bringing the frogs back to croaking.

"Don't listen to him," Nokosee's mom whispers as she continues to quickly lead me away. "He's got some control issues. Likes having the last word on just about everything. Anyway, darling, you're more than welcome to stay here as long as you want."

I'm caught off guard. Aside from loving a boy, it's hard for me to show any real affection for anyone. I chalk it up to my upbringing and pray it isn't genetic.

"Thanks." I can barely squeak it out.

"Love your doo," she says.

She's looking at what's left of my righteous Mohawk. I search her eyes to see if she really means it but can't tell. I try to straighten it up but its beyond help, resembling, I'm sure, brains bursting through a crack down the center of my bald head-- which would explain all the bad decisions I've made in the last three days. She laughs and turns to her daughter.

"Gerrycurl, hold the lantern."

Nokosee's sister takes the lantern and holds it up toward my head as her mom gently tries to help me straighten it up with both of her hands rising along the sides. She gently pushes my head to the side to check out my tats.

"Nice touch. What do you think, Gerrycurl?"

Nokosee's sister sticks her head in to get a better look and I remember Nokosee telling me when we first met that Gerrycurl is her nickname. Gerryragni is her real name, a name he said was Seminole for "Hair." Later he admitted she was named after Gerome Ragni, one of the guys who wrote *Hair,* his dad's favorite Broadway musical.

What a kidder.

His dad likes Broadway musicals?

She's got big, brown beautiful eyes and eyelashes to die for. Just like Nokosee. She turns to me and smiles.

"Pretty cool," she says. "Did it hurt?"

"On a scale from one to ten I'd give it a nine."

"Ow," mom and daughter reply in unison.

"How 'bout the piercings?" Gerrycurl asks.

"Compared to the tats, a one."

"Really?"

"What, are you thinking of getting some, daughter?"

"I don't know. Maybe. When I'm older."

Nokosee's mom smiles and then turns to me, putting her arm around my shoulder and pulling me tightly against her body. She escorts me through the parting war party up the beach into the dark hammock.

Even my mother didn't hold me like this.

I glance back at Nokosee. He and his dad are done yelling at each other and he's caught up with his sister who's fallen behind. Gerrycurl reaches out and takes his hand. I turn to Busimanolotome. He's still staring at me like only he can do and I wonder if he'll ever accept me and how could he have produced such loving children.

Their mother, that's why.

I turn to Nokosee's mom and try to speak, but my voice trembles and I can barely hide my jangled emotions.

"Love your matching top and headbands," I say.

"Yeah, aren't they a fashion statement. If nothing else, the New Seminoles sure know how to dress."

She has an ironic sense of humor, something I've always admired in a person and I want to smile but can't.

"Nokosee has told us so much about you," she continues, turning to look me in the eyes, "that I feel I've known you forever."

"Are you saying he can't stop talking about me?" I ask, my voice breaking in mid-sentence.

"Stormy," she whispers, "my son's in love with you."

Whoe, I didn't see that one coming.

"He sure has a funny way of showing it," I say.

"What do you mean?"

"Why didn't he come and get me?"

I didn't see that one going. I've been wondering about it the whole way down and the question just kind of slipped out.

She stops and turns to me. "Stormy," she says earnestly, "you dumped *him*. What did you expect him to do?"

"No, no, I hesitated but I ran after him. I called his name."

"Darling, he didn't hear you."

"He didn't hear me?"

She sadly shakes her head no.

"But I shouted his name over and over again."

Maybe you should have yelled a little louder.

"I don't know what to tell you, Stormy."

"It was the helicopter," I hastily add as tears start to well up in my eyes. "He couldn't hear me because of the helicopter."

She shrugs and offers up a sad little smile.

"And he still loves me?" The question spills out of my mouth right along with my tears.

"He's nuts about you."

"I love him, too," I say while wiping my tears away. "A lot in fact. I didn't mean to. It just happened. Is that okay, Mrs. Osceola?"

Is it okay that I'm a lamo heartless psychopath who has to ask you for permission to love your son?

She laughs and pats my hand. "Call me Demaris."

"'Demaris?'"

"Before I met the Micco at Hialeah High I was once known as Demaris Rodriguez."

"'The Micco?'"

"Micco means chief."

"Do you have an Indian name too?"

She laughs again. "Yeah, but it's a mouthful. Trust me, Demaris will get my attention. So will Mrs. O. Or mom."

"'Mom?'" I ask hesitantly.

"Yeah, everyone here calls me mom."

Oh, thank God. I thought you were implying Nokosee and I should get hitched or something.

You mean married, don't you? Why can't you just say it?

Because it scares me. I don't want a marriage like my mom and dad had. But don't think I haven't thought about it. Especially after discovering I'm pregnant. All the way down from New Jersey. Twelve hundred miles of thinking about it. I mean, that's what you're supposed to do, right? I wish I could do a Lorelai Gilmore and just take off and have the baby and start a whole new life without the father but I can't. I can't imagine living without Nokosee. And I can't imagine having an abortion. Especially now thanks to Busimanolotome telling me-- and the whole New Seminole Nation-- what I already knew; that too many people have died because of me. Trust me, there's just no way I'm adding another one to that list. I guess we could live together, but that doesn't seem right to me either. I want a commitment to match the one I took on to get here, one that makes everyone who died on account of me count for something.

Whoe, sounds like you're looking for a "Saving Private Ryan" kind of commitment.

That's right, on that level. Right now, the more I think about it, as far as I'm concerned, marrying me is the *least* Nokosee can do.

Poor Nokosee. Sounds like there's going to be a lot of snapping to attention and saluting for him in this marriage.

Damn right. I earned it.

Listen to yourself.

I know. I'm losing it. It's one subject that makes me crazy. Getting married is one of the things I kept seeing in the movie in my mind all the way down from New Jersey. Unfortunately, it had two versions: one was a romantic comedy, the other a horror film. I worked hard at making the former my vision quest, the thing that kept me going: getting married and living happily ever after with Nokosee. I know, when I see it written down, it looks stupid and silly but that's me. I'm a mixed up kinda girl. I just wish the first act of my movie had ended differently. Maybe it wasn't destined to be a romantic comedy, but I didn't expect it would actually become a horror movie either and wonder if I can still find redemption-- in the real world where the real guilt resides.

"We saw what happened on the Alley," she says, snapping me out of my thoughts.

I don't reply.

"Live. On TV."

I start to cry.

"I'll pray for those men tonight. And their families."

I fall into her arms and she holds me tightly. I try hard not to cry.

Tell her it's not her fault, 'Mom.'

I start crying uncontrollably.

"Stormy?" Nokosee asks.

"Nokosee," his mom says, turning back to look at him. "She's tired. She's been through a lot today. She needs to rest."

Nokosee walks up to us and takes me from his mother.

"She can stay with me."

But 'Mom' hasn't told her it's not her fault.

Or that it's okay for me to love her son.

"Mom" doesn't say anything as he lifts me up and carries me away. That surprises me. My mom would have a real problem with some boy hauling me off like that. My father would be drawing a bead on him right now with his 30-aught-6. I look over Nokosee's shoulder at her and through blurry tears see her standing alone in the path until Gerrycurl walks over and takes her hand. They look anxious as they look at me and I start wondering what makes them tick.

When I turn around, I see the alligator pit.

"What the hell?"

A channel has been dug through the hammock leading to the water and the penned in gators are reaching up and snapping at us.

"They're our Kamikaze back-up," Nokosee informs me. "Each camp has one. If we're attacked, we set them loose."

"Isn't that dangerous?"

"Hell, yeah, that's why it's important to watch your step around here."

"But what's going to keep them from eating us in an attack?"

"Loyalty."

"Frank Mills salutes you," someone says.

I see a man holding his raised fist in the air as we walk past and notice the guy with the camera following and watching us on his camera's viewfinder and wonder if my movie is a documentary.

"Frank Mills!" comes from the opposite side, this time from a woman, her fist held just as high and staring ahead like a soldier at attention. This unleashes a chorus of "Frank Mills!" from more New Seminoles as we walk through them.

"What gives?" I ask Nokosee. "Who's Frank Mills?"

"It's the name of this camp."

"What, did he die for The Cause or something?"

"No. Dad names his camps after characters or songs from *Hair*."

"Hey, Stormy Jones!" someone yells from a chickee. "Take a look! You're on TV with the Governor."

Nokosee walks up to the chickee and we look inside. People are lying on the log floor, watching a small black and white TV, its weak signal sent down wires attached to an old school antenna aimed at Miami from the top of the thatched roof. Mom and dad are on TV, on each side of the Governor, at what must be a press conference. I'm surprised to see mom there. She must have flown down as soon as I left home. Seems to have a real jones for pith helmets and khaki. Dad's public image is forever associated with olive green ranger uniforms, shorts, and a crew cut, this time thankfully covered by his Smokey-the-Bear hat. It's like they're constantly on an expedition searching for their lost daughter. This time, instead of a blow-up of what seems to be the only picture my parents have of me doing my best James Dean while holding my middle-finger up to the world, I see a digitally enhanced still from the YouTube hit of me looking up at the school bus and daring the giant to get off for an ass kicking.

"Oh, lord," I sigh.

"Four dead," the governor is telling the media. "Two cops and a news team. 30 injured with 21 in serious condition. 40 patrol cars and two helicopters destroyed."

I'm shocked. I didn't know the TV news copter was shot down. Idiot fool that I am, I thought-- hoped-- Busimanolotome was only trying to scare it off. My heart sinks further into my body and I deflate in Nokosee's arms.

The governor tells his audience to watch a video clip. It's me as seen from one of the news helicopters. I'm racing down Alligator Alley with a slew of cop cars on my tail. The New Seminole start cheering, pumping their fists in the air. From this angle high above the road, you can actually see Busimanolotome firing the RPG and taking out the cop copter. This sends the people who have gathered around us into a frenzy. I have to turn away.

"Nokosee, get me out of here."

Nokosee turns and carries me away, pushing past the guy documenting everything with the camcorder.

"Give it a rest," he says.

The guy backs off and lowers his camcorder.

"Nokosee," I say, "I can't believe they cheered those deaths."

"Welcome to my world, kid."

"You don't condone what happened, do you?"

"Of course not. No one is supposed to die. Our war is with the infrastructure. When it's missing, we expect the Outside will find someplace else to live."

"But--"

"I know," he interrupts, "Dad's plan needs a little work." He stops and asks, "So what do you think?"

I turn around to look. It's a chickee along the water's edge.

"Nice," I say.

And then I see my salute to James Dean picture torn from the Miami Herald less than a month ago when I got lost in the swamp. It's stapled to one of the posts.

"You gotta be kidding me. Is this your crib?"

He doesn't answer but instead lets me down and grabs me closer.

"Why did you come back?" he asks.

"'Cause you," I pause, my eyes racing across his face, taking in everything I love and missed for too long, "'cause you make me crazy."

I kiss him with extreme prejudice and thankfully, he does the same.

He lifts me up and throws me into the chickee. I scream thinking I'm going to land on the hard raised log floor but instead land on an air-mattress, like the kind you find floating in a swimming pool.

"Are you crazy?" I ask.

What a stupid question to ask.

He jumps up and crouches in front of me.

"Damn right. Just like you."

He grabs a lanyard hanging next to a post and gives it a yank. A plastic bamboo blind all the way from China drops to the floor behind him.

I scoot back. "And just what do you think you're doing?"

He rises and pulls another cord and another plastic bamboo blind drops from the thatched roof.

"Making up for lost time."

When he drops the fourth and final blind, I watch it unroll across the surprised faces of his mother and sister, stopped dead in their tracks by Nokosee's impetuousness. When I turn away, he's on top of me.

"Oh, you *are* a pagan caveman," I say.

Nokosee lets out a Tarzan yell and I have to pull him down to cut it short so as not to alert Frank Mills that we're about to do it. Sweet, unadulterated, psychopathic passion overtakes us and, even though I know that making love just after causing the deaths of innocent people is frowned upon by civilized society, I can't help myself. I really am a bad girl and deserve to be spanked which is what Nokosee does more than once per my request after each round of slamming, bamming, and thank you mamming before I fall exhausted into a deep and welcomed sleep.

Chapter 8
There's A New Day Dawning

I wake up in the morning to the sounds of a rooster crowing and mosquitoes buzzing around my head but I don't want to get up or open my eyes because I know I'm a sinner. I wonder if slapping at them is a good sign, that a really depressed person wouldn't even make the effort. I wonder if not slapping on purpose is just me trying to be depressed, to punish myself because I know I don't deserve anything more than death by mosquito bites. Or maybe I'm so screwed up nothing matters any more.

I hear voices outside the chickee as the New Seminole goes about its crazy business of winning back south Florida for the "Human Beings." I extend my hand to see if Nokosee is still lying beside me. He isn't but it was a nice gesture on his part to hold me in his arms last night and to kiss me gently to sleep. Maybe if he was there I would have opened my eyes just to look at him, the father of my baby, our child. I wonder if and when there will ever be a good time to tell him. Trust me, right now isn't the time.

I hear music. It surrounds me, softly, as if it were the song of the hammocks but when the volume slowly increases I know it's far from a mystical experience I'm having but something else as it reassures me a new day is dawning and that it belongs to you and me.

"Hippie claptrap," I hear my old man saying. One summer I was having another slow day and started going through his antique record collection, real vinyl albums chronicling what he likes to call the "Golden Age" of rock and roll. For the most part, I can't argue with him on that. There was some amazing stuff back then in the late 60's and early 70's, beautiful songs that came out of nowhere from the first wave of baby boomers. Unfortunately for my dad, after returning from Viet Nam, he pretty much couldn't stomach anything as uplifting and positive as this song.

I open my eyes. Sunlight is filtering through the camo netting covering the thatched roof of the chickee hut. It reminds me of my first encounter with Nokosee. I was on crutches and hobbling around one of the NS's secret chickee hideouts scattered across the Everglades when I fell and knocked my head on the log floor. Before passing out, I remember looking up through the thatched roof and seeing a small TV satellite dish. At that time I thought I was being held for ransom by Nokosee and his nutcase dad. As it turned out, Nokosee was saving me and making me fall in love with him. I wonder if this chickee has a satellite dish too. Probably.

The music grows louder and I turn and see the same fat black guy with dreadlocks playing the bugle retreat on his ghetto blaster during yesterday's "skirmish." He's carrying his "bugle" on his shoulder and looking at me through the open chickee.

"You know," I tell him, "You can get arrested in Opa Locka for wearing your pants like that."

It's true. Opa Locka, another Indian word hi-jacked by the Outside to name its towns and cities means "The high land north of the little river on which there is a camping place" which has nothing to do with the town's "theme." Just northwest of Miami, the town was laid out in 1926 with street names like Ali Baba Avenue and Sesame Street and an architecture that looked like something out of the Arabian Nights with minarets and domed roofs, many of which still exist. Somewhere around the 1980's it became south Florida's first black run municipality. Today its elected officials want to put the kibosh on this ghetto-rooted fashion statement by promising its young men fines and arrests if they don't pull their pants up.

"You got balls," he says.

"So I've been told."

"Boom Box, leave her alone."

It's Nokosee, emerging from the hammock with a tin plate of eggs and bacon. "And turn down the volume for crisesakes on the PMD."

"No problemo." Boom Box removes the huge radio/CD player from his shoulder, sits it down on the raised log floor, and twists a knob so that the volume is at a level that even my dad, despite the song, could tolerate. He turns to me and says, "Hope I didn't wake you."

"No problemo." I smile and shake my head he didn't.

He smiles back. "See you later."

He turns to Nokosee, salutes him smartly, twists smoothly on the balls of his combat boots, and marches off, stiff of arm and stiff of boot like some kinda Nazi soldier on parade, albeit with one hand reaching behind his back to hold his pants up just for me. I cover my mouth and laugh.

"Did he wake you up?" Nokosee asks as he crawls up onto the log floor.

"No, I was awake."

"He's in big trouble with dad."

"Why?"

"Dad didn't appreciate the Monty Python retreat."

I smile and turn to look at Boom Box marching away. Nokosee looks at me.

"It's his job, you know, waking people up. Here, have some breakfast."

He hands me the plate and a plastic knife and spork. I look at the food and sigh. I can't make myself eat it.

"Anything wrong?

"Not hungry." I sit the plate down.

"You okay?"

"Yeah. What do you mean 'it's his job'?"

"The NS all have jobs. Boom Box is our bugler with a twist."

"'A twist?'"

"Yeah, we've updated the bugle to a boom box or as we like to call it, a Portable Music Device, or PMD for short."

I roll my eyes and sigh.

"What, you think it's silly?"

"Hey, whatever makes it work for you guys." I look at Nokosee. He's watching me intently, almost like his old man.

"Are you sure you're okay?"

"Couldn't be finer."

"You seem kinda down."

"Just tired." I lower myself onto the air-mattress and stare up at the thatched roof. A moment passes before Nokosee speaks.

"Stormy, don't blame yourself for what happened yesterday. You didn't kill those people. My dad did."

Oh how I want to believe him but I know the law. In Florida, you can be charged with murder even if you weren't directly responsible if the person you're with pulls the trigger, jabs the knife, or explodes the bomb. I wonder if I broke a law regarding engaging in lewd and lascivious activity too soon after being responsible for killing innocent people? If there is such a law, I'd sure like to know how long the waiting period is. Not that it matters because I'm pretty sure I didn't wait long enough, law or no law.

You're not liking yourself much this morning, are you?

I close my eyes and extend my hand towards Nokosee. He takes it. I pull him to me. "Hold me," I say.

He does, coming up from behind and wrapping his big strong arms around me.

And then Boom Box, as if on cue from somewhere in the hammock jungle, starts playing another song, a song from my dad's approved play list, a song by the great Mel Carter, a song that always makes me cry because it's so beautiful. Mel keeps asking the woman he loves over and over again to "hold me...until you've told me what I want to know" so she can make him tell her he's in love with her.

Make me tell you I'm pregnant.

"Kiss me," I say.

He does.

Make me tell you I'm pregnant.

Thanks to Boom Box, the Alan A Dale to these modern day men and women of Sherwood Forrest, it looks like I now got a soundtrack to my movie.

"I love you, Nokosee."

"I love you, too."

And then he kisses me gently on one of my tats.

It's night now and we're moving across the Everglades because that's how the NS travels, under the cover of darkness. We broke camp just after I forced myself to take a shower under another improvised contraption I've become use to since first meeting Nokosee; when I slipped on a bar of soap and pulled the whole thing down on top of me.

But you still don't feel clean, do you?

Nope.

As the sun sets I'm guessing 200 men and women and their roosters and chickens-- but no children, dogs, or cats-- have climbed into their black airboats and swamp buggies and started the trek southward, deeper into the Everglades. Bithlos, the Seminole's dugout canoes, are tied to the sides to accommodate those who can't find a seat in the machines of the Outside. Nearly every airboat and swamp buggy is mounted with a large machine gun and they all travel side-by-side, dodging mangroves as they go because the prop blast makes it impossible to travel comfortably in a single file.

We leave *Osceola's Spear* behind. I'm surprised but Nokosee says if his dad is meant to have it, it will be there when we return. Anyway, it's not much good to anybody broken and out here in the middle of nowhere.

I'm sitting up next to Nokosee as he slowly maneuvers his way through the night and the uncharted obstacles in front of us. He's given me noise blocking headphones to cover my ears and I imagine I can finally hear the engine that propels the world, humming low, turning the planet and spinning out the wind. I look across the inky-black shallow water at the airboat at the head of our broad delta wing formation, a glow stick hanging from the back of the driver's seat. Busimanolotome, wearing lime green plastic Crocs stolen from a truck he hijacked on Alligator Alley is, of course, leading us toward our next campsite where we'll stay all day, hidden beneath camo netting and the spreading hammock branches of gumbo limbo, cypress, mahogany, and sable palm. Mrs. O is sitting next to him and Gerrycurl below them. Mrs. O waves to me. I wave back just before the setting sun's afterglow disappears and all things, including the woman who wants me to call her "Mom," become indecipherable shadows in the dark.

I look at her son, my love, as he puts on his night vision goggles. Despite the fact he's also wearing a pair of those stupid Crocs-- hell, the whole damn NS nation is traipsing around the swamp-- and tripping-- you can't walk in the colorful plastic clown shoes-- he looks older now and more mature but it's only about a month since we parted ways in the swamp where more men died and the scalpings took place. I wonder if I'll ever be able to shake those images out of my subconscious, to keep them from revisiting me in my dreams. Although I may wake with a start every now and then, it isn't out of guilt because I know I was shooting a man who was trying to kill Nokosee and me, a man who deserved to die. No, my nightmares are totally image based and have nothing to do with guilt. Yet. Maybe tomorrow the bad dreams will come for the dead guys on Alligator Alley.

Busimanolotome killed that guy, the guy who was trying to kill Nokosee. You just blew his hand off.

Yeah, I know. He stabbed Bart Rader through the back, the knife popped through the front and he ran it up his stomach, see-sawing it all the way to his breast bone. And then he scalped him.

I wonder how Busimanolotome sleeps, a man who keeps the black mummified ears of Viet Cong soldiers he's killed on a necklace around his neck, who jokes about hanging shrunken heads and scalps outside his chickee. Surely Mrs. O must have a problem with that.

Busimanolotome's a psychopath and probably sleeps like a baby.

But what about Mrs. O?

She's probably a lot like you.

What do you mean?

She's in it for love and love can be very forgiving.

Unless she's crackers too.

Like I said, she' a lot like you.

I turn away to look at the burning glow of the Everglades fire on the horizon and start thinking about my dad and suddenly, in comparison to Nokosee's, he starts looking pretty good. But I don't miss him or mom. Yet.

You will. Trust me.

What, you know something I don't know?

You'd have to be a damn fool not to see where this is going.

I know. It doesn't look good. I try not to think about it and turn away.

I do miss Smokey.

Well, that's something. There's hope for you yet.

I hope that last memory I have of him whimpering and looking down at me from my bedroom window with his sad little anxious eyes will soon fade away. As much as I try, I can't shake the feeling that was the last time I'll ever see him.

Of course, it was the last time you'll ever see him. Unless you're planning on visiting your mom in Milltown with Nokosee, how will you ever see that innocent little dog again?

When I'm dead and in Heaven.

Listen to yourself. It's embarrassing.

I know.

With your record, what makes you think you'll get into Heaven?

At night the stars and the greenish-yellow light of glow sticks surf the shallow black Everglades water, appearing and disappearing in the machinery of the the Outside's spreading, undulating wakes. It's magical.

Busimanolotome cuts his engine and signals us to stop. He rips the glow stick off the back of his seat and hides it under his Seminole jacket and the swamp suddenly loses its phosphorescent pin-points of light, one airboat and swamp buggy at a time. I take my headphones off. A moment passes in total darkness and silence before we hear a helicopter. I think back to the first time I heard one at night in the Everglades. Nokosee had just found me wandering aimlessly in an Everglades fire and was trying to keep me from running into a clearing so the pilot could see me. I screamed and fought like hell back then because I thought I was being kidnapped but I couldn't overpower my macho man. Now I want to hide with the NS, to slide into shadow and disappear in the hammocks with my lover's arms wrapped around me.

The helicopter flies over us and is swallowed by the night. Busimanolotome's glow stick comes back out and the swamp slowly comes back to life, a world spotted with chemical fireflies. I can see his face and Mrs. O's too glowing in the eerie light as she stands and ties it onto the back of his seat.

Something explodes in the distant darkness. Everyone turns to see what it is but all we can see is a faint, pulsating glow as if something is burning. I wonder if the helicopter crashed or if it was shot down but I don't remember seeing any sentries left behind. I turn back to Busimanolotome. Mrs. O is looking up at him with angry eyes. He ignores her, starts the airboat engine and the NS are moving again like stars on the water. I turn to Nokosee for answers. He just says, "Frank Mills is dead," before starting the engine.

"What?" I shout over the engine's roar.

"We can't go back there ever again," he yells "The Outside has found our camp."

As we join the exodus across the river of grass, neither of us knows someone else has died too, someone once real and alive, someone we both knew. That revelation is still to come and will test my love for Nokosee.

Chapter 9
It's My Movie & I'll Cry if I Want To

When "Mom" tells me to ignore the shrunken head and the scalps outside their chickee at Camp Claude, I know *my* movie has taken an unexpected and alarming twist and that something isn't quite right with Mrs. O. I half expect Boom Box to supply pounding, unsettling music to emphasize the moment but to be honest, scary music isn't necessary to put a shiver down my spine or to make me feel faint. For the first time, I feel like I'm trapped in an asylum in the middle of nowhere.

I look at Nokosee and he rolls his eyes like it's no big deal, that it's only dad after all. A month ago I would have found his reaction "cute" and a positive sign of worthiness. Now it's lost its luster as he leads me past the chickee house-of-horrors.

"Are you kidding me?" I ask.

"We're working on him," he says.

"What do you mean by that?"

"Family counseling."

"'Family counseling'?"

"Yeah, deep woods style."

I shake loose and stop short. "Explain, please."

"It's a weekly thing. Mom, sis, and me take dad out to a hammock away from everybody else so that we can talk about his problem."

I look at him with the best piercing eyes I can come up with.

"His need to act out, you know, by following in the footsteps of all the badass chiefs that came before him. He's studied up on them and unfortunately, they really were blood thirsty savages."

I can't believe I'm hearing this.

"He takes pride in combining modern day technology with their old school take on torture and blood lust."

"Nokosee, tell me you're trying to be funny."

"I wish I was. Dad's one loose screw. Anyway, it's not much different than what you guys did to Osceola."

"'You guys'? What are you talking about?"

"I'm sorry, Stormy. Despite your new look, I still have a hard time forgetting your roots. Maybe it has something to do with your eyes.

"What about *your* roots? You've got a Cuban mother for crisesakes."

"I know but I've only known her one way: Seminole. Anyway, getting back to Osceola, the Outside chopped his head off and sent it to New York for exhibition."

"Are you kidding me?"

"No. As dad explained it to mom, it's tit for tat."

"Because she had a problem with it, right?"

"Right."

Thank, God. At least there's hope. I turn away to massage my tats.

"You okay?"

"I've got a headache. Listen," I say, "do me a favor, will ya?"

"What's that?"

"Please, please lose the shrunken head and the scalps as soon as you can."

A moment passes. I don't hear anything. I look up. Nokosee appears to be thinking it over. He looks at me and his eyebrows rise, his eyes widen and a stupid smile grows across his face before saying this to me: "No can do."

"Why not?" I shout.

"That stuff keeps him centered. Take it away and daddy goes gaga."

"Are you kidding me?" I ask loudly. "Are you freaking kidding me?"

"Stormy," Nokosee says, as he moves quickly toward me, "just try to ignore them for awhile. Let me see what I can do."

I push him away. "Nokosee, I knew those guys. I grew up with them. Do you think I need to be reminded about what happened to them every time I walk past your parents' goddamn chickee?"

"Of course not. Let me see what I can do. I promise I'll come up with something fast."

"You better or else..." I don't know where to go with that thought.

"Or else what?"

"Or else I'll leave you all over again." I can't believe I said that. Especially after just getting there and going through everything I had to to do it.

Nokosee doesn't say anything but looks at me with uncomprehending, blinking, vacant eyes.

"Understand?" I unexpectedly add for emphasis. It's as if I'm on a roll and can't keep my mouth shut. I'm, as Regis Philbin would say, *out of control!* I push him aside and walk a few more steps before I realize I haven't a clue where I'm going. I stop short and turn on Nokosee like a banshee. "So where are you taking me?" I shout.

I got my big strong macho man hobbling like a scared pussy cat as he hops to it and scuttles past me to lead the way. "This way," he adds nervously and I have to confess I'm relishing the moment, discovering I'm much more powerful than I ever imagined. But like all power, I remind myself, it comes with responsibility and I must learn to control it, to use it wisely and only when necessary.

"This is it."

He stops in front of a chickee on the edge of the hammock near the water's edge. I can see the sun rising over the sawgrass and know it's time for the vampires to dig in beneath the protective canopy of the hammock and its camo netting to escape the prying eyes of search aircraft and, of course, satellite imagery, something Busimanolotome has ingrained into the NS to be constantly vigilant of. In the short time I've been with the NS, I've come to the conclusion that the best way to spot one of them out of a crowd of vegans, tree huggers and back-to-earth types is to look for people spending an inordinate amount of the time searching the sky. Which is to say, the NS is one paranoid group of...

Terrorists.

I don't want to think that, but basically, from what I've already seen, there is no other way to describe them.

Man, can you pick them or what?

Up until yesterday, they had only destroyed property. Now the murder of two cops, a TV news cameraman and his pilot changes everything. And I'm right in the middle of it. I'm sure Micco Mann has already moved me up the ladder "with a bullet" on the FBI's Ten Most Wanted List. I want to check their website and wonder if Nokosee's chickee has Wi-Fi?

"Does this come with Wi-Fi?" I ask.

"No, just me."

He offers me his hand to help me up onto the log floor. I take it and without looking at him, climb inside.

"You're welcome," he adds.

I stop and let out a breath.

"Nokosee, I don't want to fight with you. I'm sorry I got all crazy on you."

"Crazy?" He looks around before turning back to me. "I thought that was normal for you."

"And he still loves me, my oh my," I say like some kind of southern belle. "How lucky can a girl get? Anyway," I say, switching back to my New Joisey in-your-face roots, "just accept my apology and let it be. So much has happened in the last few days I'm kinda overwhelmed by it all."

"I understand. Get some rest. I'm gonna rustle up some grub."

"Okay, pardner."

"Are you trying to be funny?"

"Are we going to be talking like cowboys?

"I hope not. I'm an Indian for crying out loud. If anything, we'll be talking like Indians."

"Does that include sign language too?"

"Sign language is optional."

"Good. While you're at it, see if you can *fetch* me some aspirin."

He smiles, shakes his head and walks away. I turn and fall onto another air mattress only this time it's lost most of its air and my elbow pays the price for not looking first as it strikes the log floor. After rubbing it enough to start a fire, I find the mattress valve and start blowing air into it and within minutes I'm pooped and the mattress has less air in it than before I began. I sigh, lie down, and decide to let Nokosee do it. Within minutes I'm asleep.

I wake in a puddle of perspiration. I look at my watch. I've been asleep for six hours. I sit up and look around. Aside from two sentries I can see walking-- and stumbling-- the camp's perimeter in their ridiculous neon colored Crocs, everyone seems to be asleep. I turn to find Nokosee. He's lying beside me, asleep, his massive he-man back turned toward me on the now inflated air mattress. I snuggle up behind him and try to wrap myself around his body.

"Nokosee?" I whisper.

He moves a little and mumbles something.

"I'm pregnant," I whisper softly.

Just trying it out, seeing if I can actually say it out loud. In any event, I get nothing. I don't know if he heard me or not. Maybe I stunned him with the news and he can't speak. I peek over his body to see if he's awake. He's dead to the world. I ease back and slowly scoot away. I don't have the courage to tell him again. Not yet.

I'm starving. I remember Nokosee was going to fetch me some food and start looking for it, to see if he left it somewhere in the chickee. He did, an MRE of beef Stroganoff and a slice of apple pie. It's cold and the gravy has congealed but it's still bug free and I attack it without care. While eating, I look around. This is a pretty good sized camp with at least a dozen chickees scattered about under the hammock canopy and camo netting. But the scene is far from idyllic because a closer inspection reveals combat boots sitting on the ground outside of the chickees (along with a rainbow coalition of Crocs), assault weapons leaning against the chickee posts, and Stinger missiles and bazookas on the log floors. Some of the airboats were driven up into the hammock and parked next to the swamp buggies to conceal them from the ever vigilant prying eyes of the government's spy satellites. The remaining airboats in the shallow water surrounding the hammock are draped in camo netting. It's so quiet, eerily quiet. It's as if all the insects have ceased to exist because they have nothing to say that hasn't already been said in the last few hundred million years or so.

As mom-- my mom-- instilled in me, in polite society I have to "use the facilities," i.e., take a dump. I look for one of those camper toilets Nokosee had in a hammock chickee when we first met but can't find one. I wonder if the camp has a central latrine or something like that and decide to find out. I slip my legs over the side of the raised log floor, lower myself to the ground, and start to look around, keeping in mind that one careless step could mean death by guard-gator feeding frenzy.

Except for the weapons, I feel like I'm walking through some kind of hippie commune. Lots of untamed hair and beards, old and ripped jeans-- and now jeggings-- a kaleidoscopic array of Crocs lined up in neat little rows on the chickee floors, chickens wandering everywhere, and the smell of pot.

Heavily armed pot heads taking on the U.S. government. Gee, I wonder who's going to win that one? Talk about a recipe for disaster.

I can't find a toilet anywhere but I do find a cache of TP under the floor of one of the chickees. I grab a roll and head for the bushes. Thanks to an earlier lesson I learned the hard way from Nokosee, I now know never to assume the TP or a broad *soft* and poison-free leaf is nearby when nature calls. When I'm done, I emerge from the underbrush and step into the path connecting the chickees. Busimanolotome is waiting for me. I scream and stumble backward. Besides wearing his ever present Seminole jacket, he's also got on a pair of way-too-tight burgundy jeggings and his stupid looking neon lime-green plastic Crocs. I wonder if it's the ugly shoes or his innate Indianness that makes him such a great sneaker-upper.

"You scared the shit out of me," I say as I grab my chest.

"Really? Maybe I should rent myself out as a laxative."

Papa Big Chief's Miracle Salve.

That's the first thing I think of, Nokosee's Bactine laced healing potion. On its "label," I pictured Nokosee's gorgeous face.

"No, just your face," I reply.

Busimanolotome doesn't think it's funny.

"We need to talk," he says.

"About what?"

"Why did you come back?"

"Why do you think?"

"I ask the questions," he says grimly. "You answer them."

I look up at him and with as much defiance as I can muster say "Nokosee."

"Then you wasted your time and caused the deaths of innocent people for nothing."

"Hey, stop trying to lay that on me. You're the one who shot down that helicopter and ordered your troops to shoot the cops."

"If you had stayed where you belong, it never would have happened."

"Give it a rest," I say. "If--"

I stop short when he pulls one of the longest knives I've ever seen out of the sleeve of his Seminole jacket. It has a serrated edge on the top. I later learn it's a bayonet. He keeps it close to his stomach, as if he's trying to hide it. I step back, unsure of his intentions but fear the worst.

"Nokosee isn't yours to keep. He's mine."

He points the knife at me and starts toward me.

"I'm pregnant!" I shout.

Now it's his turn to stop short.

"I'm carrying Nokosee's baby."

I could have blindsided him with my crash helmet if I had it with me. He never would have seen it coming he was so discombobulated with the news.

"Hey!"

It's Nokosee coming up the path in a pair of camo jeggings and hot pink Crocs and I don't know whether to laugh or cry. Busimanolotome slides the bayonet back up his sleeve.

"You guys having a pow-wow?"

Nokosee puts his arm around me and holds me tight.

"Your dad," I say, looking the old bastard hard in the eyes, "was just thanking me for delivering him *Osceola's Spear*." I stick out my hand for the Chief to shake it.

"Yeah, ain't that something, dad?" Nokosee asks anxiously. "Talk about counting coup."

Busimanolotome doesn't say anything but just keeps staring ahead at nothing.

"Go on, dad, shake Stormy's hand."

Busimanolotome's eyes blink. He turns from his thoughts and looks down at me and then my hand hanging-- but not shaking-- in the oppressing heated air.

"Notice," I say, "no shakes."

He looks at me with that same baleful stare he's reserved especially for me and, without saying a word, turns and walks away.

"Dad!"

I shout after the old man. "Sure beats that shrunken head and scalps thing you got going outside your chickee!"

Nokosee gives me a look that says "cool it" with Great Chief Run-a-Muck. But I'm on a roll and thanks to my nervous energy, can't keep my mouth shut.

"That stuff is so yesterday. You might want to lose them for something more subtle."

Nokosee grabs me hard and pushes me down the path.

"I mean," I shout back over my shoulder, "it screams someone's over-compensating for his 'shortcomings.'"

Nokosee shoves me away and I stumble backwards. "Are you crazy?" he asks in a harsh whisper.

Yes.

I look over Nokosee's shoulder at Busimanolotome. Chief Looney Tunes is walking slowly through the clearing in his lime green clown Crocs, probably trying to decide on whether or not to kill me. Or how to kill me without arousing the suspicion of the First of the New Seminole. I figure this is a pretty good time to tell Nokosee he's going to be a father. I turn to him and grab his hand.

"Nokosee, we gotta talk."

Chapter 10
We Gotta Talk

"So what do you want to talk about?" he asks after another round of love making.

Somehow I couldn't find the right moment when we got back to his chickee, especially after we started kissing. I tell you, once you get me kissing, I'm a lost cause to propriety. At least with Nokosee.

I look at my watch. It's four o'clock-- in the afternoon. On the way back to the chickee after the close encounter with Chief Crazy Loon, a NS sentry in baby blue Crocs told us the old man called off the nightly trek across the Everglades so it looks like we're going to be holding up at Camp Claude for awhile and it's expected that we adjust our sleep patterns accordingly. As it now stands, I couldn't move even if my life depended upon it because Nokosee's stolen my mojo. But how can you say no to a guy like this when you're both stark naked and he's lying on you and kissing you all over. At the beginning of our "afternoon delight," I kept looking through the plastic bamboo blinds expecting to see people queuing up and buying tickets to the show but that never happened and, after awhile to be quite frank, I got caught up in the moment-- scratch that, *moments*-- and completely forgot about doing it in the open air with only some cheap Chinese imitation bamboo blinds separating us from everyone else in Camp Claude. Even though we're dripping wet from perspiration and slipping off of each other, lying in our own pool of sweat on the hot vinyl air-mattress, with used condoms scattered everywhere-- hell, they're even sticking to us-- we can't stop-- and I can't tell Nokosee we don't need a condom.

"Stop it, Nokosee," I finally cry, "I can't take it anymore." I try to push him away and he grabs my hands and starts kissing them.

"So I guess you're happy to see me?" I ask breathless.

He looks up at me. "What gave it away?"

"You're killing me."

I try to get up but he holds me down and lies across my body. We're eye-to-eye when he says, "So, baby, what do you wanna talk about?"

She's Got Balls can't find them right now.

"What's with the jeggings?" I ask.

"Like 'em? They're fresh off a Macy's truck."

"I hate 'em. They make you all look like a bunch of mincing fools."

"'Hate 'em?' They're freaking fashion statements. Do you realize how much the Outside is willing to pay for these things?"

"Screw the Outside. When did you start caring what it thought?"

"When I met you. I can't believe you don't like 'em. You're a Hot Topic girl for crying out loud."

"Was. Do me a favor and ditch 'em. I can't believe your father is wearing the stupid things."

"Robin Hood. It makes him feel like Robin Hood."

"You gotta be kidding me."

"No kid. He may not admit it, but according to mom, the old TV series really made an impression on him. Besides, they were free. The NS rarely says no to free."

I can't tell if Nokosee is kidding or not. I can only hope he is because I know if I ask him, he'll just deny it. I sadly shake my head and look away. After an uncomfortable moment knowing Nokosee is looking at me, won't take his eyes off of me, I take a deep breath and turn back to him as my words come spilling out, tripping over each other to get to the point.

"Nokosee, remember the night we did it for the first time?"

Nokosee leans on me and smiles. "Yeah, I remember. It was wonderful. It'll probably be my last thought when I die with a smile on my face."

I look at him and I think he actually means it. I mean, where did this guy come from anyway, right? He completely freaks me out.

"Correct answer," I say. "You win 10 points." I kiss him on the lips which, it turns out, is a mistake because it only starts him up again. I push him away.

"This is the best birthday present a guy could ever want," he says. "Don't stop now."

He tries to kiss me again but I hold him off. "It's your birthday?"

"Was. A few weeks ago."

"That's what I thought."

"We *really* like celebrating our birthdays."

"So you're...18 summers now?"

"That's right."

"July 27th, right?"

"Aw, she remembered."

"A Leo."

"According to the Outside."

"What about the Inside?"

"That's not really our thing, looking at a bunch of stars to explain it all. We're more land based."

"That explains a lot. Like your name."

"That's right. When I popped out of mom, dad looked right and saw a bear looking back at him."

"So he named you 'bear,' right?"

"Correcto-mundo."

"You know, maybe your parents should stop having their kids at ZooMiami. God forbid you end up with a brother or sister called warthog."

"Funny, but I think they're long past having kids."

"Have you ever thought about having kids?"

Nokosee pauses for a moment. "Not until I met you."

Whoe. I didn't expect that.

"Really?"

"Really."

He kisses my forehead for emphasis and then starts working on my tats. I have to push him away.

"Nokosee, stop. There's something I have to tell you," I say as I try to hold him off.

He stops short.

"Yeah?"

"You know, Mary was only 14 when she had Jesus."

"Okay."

"In the olden days, everything happened earlier."

"Damn right considering everyone was dead by 40."

He head fakes one way and goes another and manages to sneak in beneath my guard to put another hickey on my neck.

"Too bad," I try to say, "teenage sex is frowned upon today."

"Heck, Stormy," he manages to mumble between sucking my neck like a man truly possessed, "it's not so bad so long as you don't get pregnant."

I don't say anything, don't kiss back, and don't move. Gradually Nokosee stops and looks at me.

"Well," I say with a big silly grin, "besides being a lean mean fighting machine, it appears I should be adding 'fertile' to that description too."

Nokosee sits up.

"Are you kidding me? Are you trying to tell me you're... you're pregnant?"

I just smile, shrug and throw my arms open wide. "Happy birthday, baby!"

"But I wore a condom."

"What can I tell you, Tarzan. Me pregnant. You big pagan caveman stud. Condoms don't stand a chance against you. T'ank you veddy much." I say it like Andy Kaufman, a dead comedian my dad introduced me to one summer. Jim Carrey played him in a movie. I want to be funny, to downplay the seriousness of the moment. I pull him closer so that I can put my head against his chest, hoping that he'll squeeze me tightly against his body. It doesn't happen but I hear his heart racing and his voice with an inflection I never heard before: scared.

"Are you sure it's my kid?"

"*Our* kid, numb nuts." I push him away to look him in the eyes. "Whose kid do you think it is?"

"That idiot's back in New Jersey."

"I left him in a pool of blood a few days ago." I slide out from under Nokosee and shift my weight onto one elbow. "So you're telling me you think I screw around? You don't believe I was a virgin when we did it?"

"No, I...Jeeze Louise."

He's looking at nothing, looking lost with a touch of panic thrown in for good measure. Boy, telling the Osceola men you're pregnant is like a well-placed kick to their balls. I make a mental note for future reference in case I ever need a second or two to extricate myself from a sticky situation of the crazy Osceola kind.

"What's wrong, Nokosee? Don't you want to have a baby with me?"

He doesn't answer and starts looking like his old man with each passing second. It seems both have a tendency of staring at nothing when confronted with the unexpected. This is not a good thing especially when you're on the run from people who might be sneaking up on you.

"Say something," I implore.

"Baby."

The word rolls slowly out of his mouth while his eyes blink uncomprehendingly.

"Baby?" He says it again.

"Yeah, 'baby.' You know, the cute little bundles of joy."

"Wow." He says it softly, like it's still registering.

"Yeah," I say to help him along, "like wow."

He takes a deep breath and exhales. "Wow."

"You said that already. Let's move on.. to...the," I reply, rolling my arm impatiently to speed him up, hoping that he'll live up to my expectations, that he isn't as slow as he appears to be right now, that he's just a little surprised to say the least. Finally, a smile starts growing on his face and his head starts bobbing in agreement with these words that took way too long, in my opinion, to come stumbling out of his mouth:

"That's a good thing."

He turns to me.

"Yeah, that's a *very* good thing," he says.

He reaches over and pulls me to him. He kisses me softly on the lips and then takes my head in his hands and kisses my tats on both sides before holding me close to his body. He rocks me slowly back and forth and we just sit there in the sweat and the used condoms on the sticky air-mattress, holding each other in silence until he says:

"Did I tell you I love your spears?"

Tears are welling up in his eyes and spilling over the sides of his chiseled cheek bones. Even though he's been bred by his father to be a lean-mean-killing-machine, it appears the old bastard wasn't able to beat all of the humanity out of him.

"Yeah," I say as I unpeel a used condom stuck to his rock hard bicep, "with each thrust."

He stops short. "Stormy, if you're pregnant, why'd you make me wear a condom-- con*doms*?"

I sigh. "Well, I meant to tell you once we got back to your love shack but, uh, one thing led to another and--"

"You should have told me when I asked for a condom."

"Yeah, I should have."

"Why didn't you?"

I pause but refuse to pull an Osceola and look away. Instead, I turn to Nokosee and force myself to look him in the eyes. "I didn't know how you'd take it. I didn't want to find out you didn't want the baby. I was scared and too horny to tell you."

"Where's your purse?"

"Why?"

He pushes me aside and starts looking around. He finds it, the black leather and chrome Harley Davidson purse-slash-weapon, and starts rifling through it.

"Hey!" I protest.

He pulls out my last box of Trojans and throws it against the plastic bamboo blind.

"You won't be needing these anymore," he says. "C'mere."

He grabs me and we start kissing all over again until he pops up and asks:

"So, it's okay to keep doing it?"

"As far as I kn--"

I don't get to finish the sentence before he throws me down onto the air-mattress and starts kissing me again but this time with a scary animal-like passion. I try to say a little prayer of thanks because, well, a girl never knows how a guy is going to react to that kind of news but I cut myself off in mid-prayer, abandoning all hope for forgiveness and redemption from God to wallow in the sweat, the used condoms, and precious bodily fluids of our love making.

Chapter 11
I'm Not Worthy

"She's what?" Mrs. O asks.

"Pregnant," Nokosee says again.

"'Pregnant?'"

"Pregnant."

I shrug, roll my eyes and try to smile. It's not easy what with Chief Crazy Loon standing there in his maroon jeggings and neon lime Crocs staring me down as only he can. Even Gerrycurl is giving me the evil eye.

*Like, what's **her** problem?*

Nokosee sees me and starts laughing. I guess he's as nervous as I am. He has to look away to try to stop and when he does I start laughing too.

I swear, this baby doesn't stand a chance with parents like us.

Next thing I know, Mrs. O, a.k.a "Mom," gets all spooky on us when she "floats" across the dirt-- her traipsing little feet are hidden by her full-length Seminole skirt-- and glides right up to Nokosee and slaps his face. That knocks the smile off of it real fast. Mine too. But when she tries to slap me, I don't know, I guess I saw it coming-- knew instinctively it was coming-- I reach out and grab her wrist just before she can lay one across my face.

"Whoe, now, Mrs. O or 'Mom.' You don't wanna go hitting me. I'm *pregnant*."

I say it with defiance and draw it out real long like some kind of toothless country hick out of frustration and anger.

I can't believe you talked to her like that!

She takes another swing at me with her free hand. I catch it too.

"Really, *Mom*, this is no way to treat your *pregnant* teenage daughter-in-law."

"'Daughter-in-law?'" she screams just before switching to Spanish to curse me good.

Nokosee steps between us and struggles to pull us apart.

"Mom," Nokosee says, "we're getting married."

Mrs. O suddenly stops cold.

"'Married?'"

"I love her-- let her go, ma!"

She reaches around Nokosee and grabs my Mohawk. I scream like hell.

"Let go of me, you crazy old bitch!"

We start turning in a circle, me screaming and she cursing me in Spanish before Nokosee can pry her hands away from my hair. When I look up through the tears in my eyes I see clumps of my hair in her hands. I scream again as my hands shoot upward to feel the damage to my Mohawk.

"Are you insane?" I shout.

Nokosee steers her backward into the waiting arms of her cockamamie husband. "Stop it, ma! I love her!"

"'Love her!' She's the *only* girl you ever met, you idiot!" Mrs. O screams. "You just can't go marrying the first girl you ever saw!"

"I'm bleeding for crying out loud!" I'm looking at the blood and hair on my fingertips.

Nokosee lets go of his mom and backtracks to me. Busimanolotome struggles to hold her back as Nokosee pulls me close to his side, pushes my hands away from what feels like a Mohawk on fire and gently examines my scalp.

"Don't need to look further, ma. Holatte-Sutv Turwv is my soul mate."

He kisses my wounds and then holds me tight.

Holatte-Sutv Turwv still sounds like a Starbucks coffee. Why couldn't Sky Eyes sound like Sacajawea or Pocahontas or something? I mean, you can't even pronounce your own stupid Indian name for crying out loud.

Yes, that's what was going through my mind. Instead of thinking, "Oh, what a nice thing to say" and how gentle and caring he is with me, I focus on my Indian name. Talk about a disconnect. Maybe it had something to do with the horrible pain that comes with having the hair on your scalp ripped out by the roots, a pain so excruciating it automatically kicked in an escape mechanism in the brain to dull the pain and make me forget.

"Oh, lord." Busimanolotome doesn't try to disguise his great disappointment as he attempts to drag "Mom" away.

"Busi," Mrs. O implores, "do something."

'Busi?'

"What do you want me to do?" Busi asks. "What can I possibly do? Tell me. Do you want me to make her go away? Forever?"

"Maybe this might be a good time to switch to Seminole," I say. I'm a little put off by the threat and anxious which always has a way of making me open my mouth when I should be keeping it shut.

Busimanolotome turns to address Nokosee since I apparently don't exist. "Nokosee, she isn't New Seminole material. She's not even a Human Being."

"Screw this 'Human Being' crap, man," I shout. "Your wife is a freaking Cuban for crying out loud!"

Busimanolotome turns on me with a fierce rage burning in his eyes, tosses "mom" aside and starts for me-- but instead of hiding behind Nokosee, I surprise myself-- and I think everyone else too-- by pushing away and falling into a defensive martial arts stance.

Am I *INSANE?*

Yes. You and "mom" have a lot in common.

"Kill her, Busi!"

You taking on "Busi," this I gotta see. Where's Digital Camcorder Guy?

Shut up! Did "mom" just tell Busi to kill me? Was that her voice?

Maybe. Or maybe it was just another voice in your head.

"Shut up!"

Busi stops short. "I haven't said anything, you crazy little twit."

Fortunately for me Nokosee intercepts Big Chief Raging Bull, wraps his arms around his body and turns him away. In the struggle to free himself, Busimanolotome yells over Nokosee's shoulders at me.

"You've bewitched my son for now but the world of the New Seminole will inevitably break you!"

'Inevitably?' Is that a word an out-of-control mad man would use? 'Bewitched' seems more appropriate but--

"Don't hurt him!" Mrs. O screams, interrupting my chain of thoughts. "He's just a boy!"

"Not anymore," Nokosee replies as he throws his father back. The old man hunches over and tries to catch his breath while Nokosee, also breathing hard, continues. "I'm the first of the New Seminole and Holatte-Sutv Turwv is going to be my wife."

Maybe I can get a different name. Hopefully it's not like carved in stone or something.

"Don't be so goddamn naive, son," the old bastard says. "Flavor-of-the-Month won't last long. Once she starts missing her A/C, she'll be history."

"Stop calling her that, dad!"

"Yeah, screw you, you old goat," I yell as I find my own voice in the many floating through my head. "You don't know anything about me!"

Busimanolotome hocks up a giant loogie and spits it at my feet. I jump back and shout:

"Hey, dickhead!"

"Fuck you!" Chief Run-a-Muck replies before turning, catching "mom" under the arm, and walking away in a huff.

"Yeah, fuck *you!*" Gerrycurl echoes with equal rancor and an added bad finger punctuating the air for good measure.

Maybe she's the one that wants you offed.

I must admit the hostility shown by the old man wasn't a surprise but "Mom" and little sister's catches me off guard. I realize at that moment as all three stomp off together through the jungle hammock that not only is Gerrycurl a daddy's girl, the Osceolas are one really screwed-up family. Not that I should talk. I mean, mine is the poster family for dysfunctional BS.

I look up at Nokosee for reassurance that, for some unknown reason, the insanity gene skipped him. He's watching them and sadly shaking his head. He turns to me with a supercilious half-assed smile and, with a not so reassuring shrug toward the spit at my feet, says:

"This is a good thing."

"'This is a good thing?'" I ask.

"Relatively speaking." Nokosee replies as he puts his arm around me and studies the loogie. "Spitting on the ground at someone's feet is your traditional marriage blessing?"

"Oh, really?"

"Yes. What we do is gather up the spit and the dirt and mold it into a 'love ball' and put it under our chickee to insure fertility. Let's make one now."

Nokosee tries to get me to kneel with him beside the disgusting, chewing tobacco laced loogie. I shake loose.

"Screw you, Nokosee. I'm not touching your old man's spit."

Like you did with the White City Giant's?

"Shut up!"

He looks up at me.

"I didn't say anything," he says.

Aw geese, not again.

And what's with all these men spitting tobacco juice at you?

I struggle to keep from shouting either inwardly or outwardly that it's "Karma, dammit, karma!" when I glance at Nokosee. He's looking at me as if I'm nuts. I sigh and shake my throbbing, bleeding head in frustration knowing my days of spitting on men are a thing of the past.

"Stormy," he continues with a smile from his position next to the dirt covered loogie, "don't you want to insure the future of the New Seminole?"

"I don't think the New Seminoles have anything to worry about with you around."

Nokosee shrugs and rises. Taking me into his arms, he kisses one of my tats. "Don't worry, Stormy, he'll come around. Underneath all those Viet Cong ears and war paint, he's a pretty fun guy once you get to know him."

"Yeah, but what about your mom? I thought she liked me."

"Me too. Maybe she knows something I don't. She's usually right about these kind of things."

I punch Nokosee on the arm. "You better be kidding me."

"Ow. Hey, we may be a matriarchal society, but that doesn't give you the right to abuse me. If that's what you think this marriage is going to be all about, you can forget it."

"Nokosee, it's not funny. You better shut the fuck up right now."

"Or what? Are you going to *abuse* me?"

Right now I'd like to knock his block off. Instead, I turn and walk away in a huff.

"Stormy, I'm kidding," he yells

Without looking back, I shoot him a bird and tell him to sit on it.

"Oh," he exclaims, "you are *so* mean!"

I hear him running up behind me. He grabs my hand and turns me around.

"I'm sorry, Stormy. I can't believe I said all that shit. I'm just nervous."

"You're nervous? What do you gotta be nervous about? You're the toughest motherfucker in the swamp for crying out loud." And then it hits me. "Oh, I get it, marrying *me* makes you nervous."

He doesn't say anything as he looks away.

"Well, screw that!"

Tears suddenly make an unexpected appearance and I shake loose and walk away. Thankfully Nokosee runs after me and stops me from following a path to God-knows-where. He grabs me around the waist, pulls me close.

"Stormy, you're not going anywhere if we're not going together. You know I love you and want to marry you. I'd be a damn fool to let you slip away."

"What about your parents?"

"I think they think they're losing me. I can promise you one thing, if they don't come around, they sure as hell will."

"What does that mean?"

"I don't know. Maybe it means living together in the Outside."

"That works for me."

I can't believe he actually said that but it gives me hope that not only do I have a future with Nokosee, it may come with A/C. As we walk back to our love shack I sigh and rest my head on his chest.

Ow! When my bloody scalp meets Nokosee's sweaty chest, the stinging pain is instantaneous.

"Looks like a job for *Papa Big Chief's Miracle Salve,*" Nokosee says.

I want to laugh but can't.

Although I'm pregnant, by definition you can't call it a "shotgun wedding" because there aren't any parents or future in-laws holding a shotgun to anybody's head to force them to get married. If anything, I'd call what is happening to me a "bow-and-arrow wedding." Ma and Pa O, minus the neon Crocs and jeggings and dressed in their finest traditional Seminole technicolor garb, come back the next day to Nokosee's love shack demanding we get married immediately if we truly love each other. No apologies are offered for the way they treated me the day before. It's just a quick, unsentimental, in-your-face demand, as cold as a business proposition sans any fancy ribbons or lace. Nokosee looks at me. I look at him. He shrugs, why not? I turn to the Os.

"This is too easy. What's the catch?" I suspect it's some kind of test to see if I really want to make a commitment to their son and the cockamamie Cause he's been groomed to inherit.

"No catch," Mrs. O says. "Marry him or not."

Whether or not Nokosee laid down the law re our marriage, that if they didn't give it their blessing, he'd be arrivederci, baby, I couldn't tell you. Maybe the crazy Os came to this conclusion on their own. I look at The Micco. He's showing an inordinate amount of interest in his footwear, this time a pair of new Tevas stolen from God-knows-where; probably hoping I'll pass on the test.

"I have no problem marrying Nokosee. I just find this all very strange considering how you both treated me yesterday."

Busimanolotome wants to say something but Mrs. O reaches back, touches his arm, and cuts him short.

"To marry my son you must first prove your worthiness as per New Seminole tradition."

"'New Seminole Tradition?' What the hell is that?" Nokosee asks.

"It's so new," the old man interjects, "even *you* don't know about it."

Mrs. O grabs his arm to shut him up.

"To prove her worthiness," Mrs. O says imperiously, "as the wife of the First New Seminole she must do three things."

Sounds like a Monty Python sketch they've watched way too many times on Movie Night. They truly are Loony Tunes.

Nokosee grabs my hand.

"Mom, Holatte-Sutv Turwv doesn't need to prove anything."

"She does if she wants to marry you," Busimanolotome says.

"Bullshit," Nokosee exclaims.

I look at Busimanolotome. He's turned away from his prized ceremonial Tevas and is looking at me. I can't read his face but his toes are giving him away: they're doing "the wave." I'm sure he's thinking it's only a matter of time before I cop out and run for the nearest A/C unit I can find. Screw that.

"Hey, no problemo," I say. "Bring it on, *Busi.*"

Next thing you know, yours truly is sitting in a sweat lodge in the middle of the freaking Everglades coughing up her insides. The crazy Os had already got one heated up and smoking just in case I was foolish enough to agree to their cockamamie plan. They blindfolded me and walked me through what I'm sure was every prickling, sticking, saw-toothed, sharp-edged manifestation of natural evil they could find on a seemingly never-ending path to the smoke lodge. Once we got there, they ripped off my blindfold, threw me in and told me to stay there until further notice. I'm pretty sure that little dipshit of a sister of Nokosee's threw the door flap down behind me because I heard someone laugh in a way that sounded a lot like that evil little twit. I'm also pretty sure they threw some shit-- literally-- in the fire in the center of the improvised ramshackle collection of bent branches and blue vinyl tarps because the smell is atrocious and more annoying than the sweating.

They are some kinda sick kooks for sure. You gotta be crazy to want to get married into this family. Wait a minute. You are crazy. It all makes perfect sense now.

I strip down to my bra and panties. Both are soaking wet from my sweat.

At least I'm losing weight. Some people would pay big bucks for this.

Looking on the bright side doesn't help. The sweat reminds me of my near scalping at the hands of Nokosee's mother. i.e., the pain is nearly unbearable. I throw up into the fire. It sizzles and more smoke rises. That vomit smell mixed in with the burning shit knocks me flat on my back. I roll onto my side-- sand is sticking to me!-- and try to get as close to the dirt floor as I can so that I can breath but the air there is just as smoky. I make an effort to moan loudly in case Nokosee is nearby and wants to put an end to this insanity.

"You can do it, Holatte-Sutv Turwv!" Nokosee reassures me from somewhere outside.

"This is crazy!" I shout.

"Not crazy," Mrs. O shouts back. "Must do to marry son!"

Holy crap, is the whole goddamn family outside?

"Have you seen your vision yet?" my fiancee asks.

"Vision this motherfucker!"

I hear laughter all around me and realize I've become the entertainment for the entire New Seminole Nation.

I wonder if 'Busi' is laughing?

"Fuck you! Fuck you all!" I scream before the coughing starts back up.

"Are you okay?" my love asks.

I kick at the blue tarp in frustration. That gets some laughs.

"Fucking Nazis!"

The coughing cuts me short. My lungs are on fire.

"Sky Eyes," Nokosee says, "look to the sky for your vision."

"Go to hell!" I yell. I roll over onto my back and look up through blurry eyes into the thick gray cloud of smoke above me and there, poking in and out of the swirling vapor is... my vision. It comes with instructions. Nokosee was kind enough to spell it out for me in big fat Magic Marker letters on the blue tarp:

> Wait as long as you can before seeing your vision--
> an hour is good. BE CREATIVE!
> Love, Nokosee

'Be creative?' Is it all a sham? Is nothing sacred anymore?

I look at my watch. I figure I've been in here about 5-minutes tops. There is no way I can do another 55. I start coughing again, roll over and vomit.

More laughter.

"You sick fucks, I'm pregnant for crisesakes!" I shout. "Doesn't anyone care?"

Apparently not because I'm greeted with more laughter.

How could Nokosee let this happen to me? I swear to God when I get out I'm going to kill him!

I look at my watch. A minute has passed.

Screw this! I'm having my vision now!

Not knowing what having a vision entails, I start moaning. As I get louder I add what I figure talking in tongues sounds like. Finally I throw into the mix my own personal vision.

"Oh My God! I see something... In the smoke... It's... It's an alligator. A big one... A big fucking alligator!... Oh My God! It's King Roar!"

Calling up Nokosee's old pet monster gator wasn't much of a stretch for me because it's something I can't forget. Especially when its skinned carcass is floating in the moonlit water, killed and butchered in front of Nokosee's eyes by the Rader boys. Thanks to Busimanolotome, they're all dead now, been dead and rotting for over a month while their heads and scalps are weathering nicely on poles outside the Osceola chickee.

"He's all white," I continue. "His blind eye is healed and... and he's smiling at me. Is that possible? Yes, he's smiling at me! Like that *Peter Pan* Disney gator! Oh My God! He's coming to me! Swimming through the cloud. He's touching my stomach! With his paw!"

I pause to moan for effect and then start coughing for real. When I catch my breath, I continue to lay it on.

"Oh My God! He's talking to me! How is that possible? He... He wants me to name the baby... Haalpatee. Haalpatee? But that's your name...You know it is, but it also means 'Alligator'... You want me to name my kid *Alligator?*"

I pause and answer the question as if I'm a medium and some ghost with a deep voice is speaking through me: "No... Haalpatee."

"You want me to name my kid 'Haalpatee'?"

"Yes... Gator for short." I reply to myself in the best spooky voice I can come up with. I hope it's convincing.

"Where did you go?" I ask the cloud. "Where are you King Roar? Don't leave me here with these fruit cakes! Take me with you!"

"All right, that's enough!"

It's Busimanolotome and his hand is reaching through the smoke to grab me. The next thing I know, the head nutjob has me standing outside the smoking hut covered in sand in my soaking wet bra and panties and coughing my lungs out with tears streaming down my face.

"You think everything's a big joke, don't you?" he says.

"No," I say looking up through my tears, "just you."

Thanks to my sweat I'm able to shake loose from his grip and stumble into Nokosee's arms.

"Dad!"

I didn't see it coming but I figure the old man was about to take a swing at me.

God, how I love pushing his buttons.

Yeah, as long as Nokosee is nearby, it's fun. Safe. Otherwise, fagidabouit.

I look around. I got an audience of clowns in Crocs. It must have been a slow day for the NS because it looks like they're all here.

"Cut her some slack," Nokosee says. "She's pregnant for crying out loud."

"Yeah, and I'm only seventeen-years-old, you big bully!"

I turn away from Nokosee and let fly an unintentional Linda Blair style projectile vomit onto Busimanolotome's ceremonial Tevas. I hear an "Oh, oh" rise up from the NS surrounding me. I slowly look up at Busimanolotome, sure that he will finally kill me and put me out of my misery. But he's staring at his Tevas, stunned I guess that the best the Outside has to offer in sandals has been basically ruined by yours truly.

"I'm...I'm truly sorry, Busi."

I have to squash a giggle which betrays how truly sorry I am. Anyway, the old bastard doesn't say a thing. He just keeps staring at his prized possessions long enough to make everyone nervous and decidedly muted. The NS start quietly peeling away so as not to disturb the old man in his time of loss. When he finally looks up, it's just me, Nokosee and his crazy mom and sister. I reach back for Nokosee for reassurance and safety. Thankfully, he's there to take my hand.

"Dad," he says.

"I really am sorry," I say, this time almost meaning it.

"You...You..." Busi tries to say, "You're going to pay for this."

"'Pay for this?' What are you going to do, beat me up?"

Cut to me filleting that night's fish dinner for the tribe. I've got my clothes back on, dirty and still full of sweat now covered in fish scales and blood, as I chop heads and slit bellies on a rock near the water's edge.

"This is bullshit," I grumble as I gut a fish in my hand and throw away its entrails, something by the 50th fish and two hours later I'm getting pretty damn good at.

"I agree," my love says as he helps me by dropping the dripping carcasses into a badass mixture of New Seminole spices and herbs guaranteed to make you fart before dinner's over and shit bricks made of fire in the morning.

He only just arrived. I guess he was feeling guilty. Or hungry.

"Hell, it's not like your dad paid for them. They're stolen for crisesakes just like those goddamn Crocs you all are wearing."

"Got a problem with the Crocs?"

"They look stupid, you can't walk in them and it makes the NS look like a bunch of Dutch circus clowns."

"Dutch"?

"Wooden shoes. They look like wooden shoes."

Nokosee lifts a foot to admire his pink neon Crocs. "I dunno, they look pretty cool to me."

I have to stop to look at him. I can't believe he said that. "Tell me you're kidding."

"Holatte-Sutv Turwv, all the NS are--"

I interrupt him. "Listen, about my Indian name, can I change it?"

"Why?"

"It's not working for me. It doesn't feel right."

"'It doesn't feel right?'"

"Right. For one thing, it's unpronounceable. I mean, it's not too late is it?"

"Well, I guess we could call you something other than 'Sky Eyes' but to me, it wouldn't be the same."

"Super. Let's work on that then over the next few days, you know, when we're not gutting fish and making love."

"Okay, if that's what--"

"You know, Nokosee, for someone who says he loves me as much as you do, you sure have a strange way of showing it."

"What do you mean?"

"How could you let them throw me in that smoke shack? I mean, c'mon, I'm pregnant for crying out loud."

"Darling, sometimes you just have to go with the flow."

"'Go with the flow?' Are you nuts? *You* go with the flow."

"Stormy, trust me, I *was* watching out for you. I was ready to jump in there the moment I thought you were in danger."

"How much do I have to cough and wheeze to convince you I might be dying?"

"Maybe if you hadn't had your 'vision' I would have jumped in sooner. As far as I could tell, you were having a good time at the expense of Indian tradition."

"'Indian tradition'? Is it anything like wearing Crocs?"

"There you go again with the Crocs. FYI, Crocs help the NS connect with the NA tradition of anointing ourselves-- especially the males-- with colorful objects like turquoise, fire coral, butterfly wings, and sea glass. Even our warpaint looks better in color which is why we make an effort to secure the best lipsticks and eye-shadows made on our foraging runs in the Outside."

"Tell me you're kidding."

"Coordinating warpaint with our Crocs is going to make the NS famous."

He delivers that line while focusing coating a fish with the evil NS spice mixture. He won't look at me and appears to be serious and I can only hope he's kidding.

"Nokosee," I finally say, "I can't take you seriously when you've got hot pink neon shoes on your feet. You, your dad, I don't care who you are, NS or Outsider, wearing Crocs make you all look stupid. Combine that with this stupid jeggings thing you got going on well, you either lose them or lose me."

"You know, Stormy," Nokosee says while tossing the fish into the growing pile, "some people might think your tats make you look stupid. Maybe even nuts."

"Yeah, well screw 'em."

"Yeah, well screw you."

This time he's looking at me. He looks hurt, disappointed that I dared to question his style. I had no idea he was this sensitive about things like that. Well, live and learn. It appears I will have to learn to live with the Crocs and the jeggings.

"Touché," I say. "Score one for Nokosee."

"Put a feather in my war bonnet."

"You earned it."

"Yeah, it's right up there for wrastlin' bears."

"With one hand tied behind your back?"

"With one hand tied behind my back."

A moment passes before he says, "Flip-flops?"

"What about them?"

"You got a problem with them, too?"

"Yeah. They make people look slovenly."

He sighs and shakes his head slowly. "Wow, you're tough."

"Hey," I say while extending my arms with a fish in one hand and its guts in the other, "what you see is what you get."

And with that, Nokosee reaches across to pick a fish scale off of my nose.

At least I didn't have to fry the fish too. I guess they thought that might be pushing their luck. And it would have. I don't cook. Without any effort I could have easily killed the whole NS nation in one fell-swoop which in retrospect probably wouldn't have been such a bad idea considering what they put me through. But, like that Monty Python scene with the Bridgekeeper where the Knights of the Roundtable have to answer "these questions three" before proceeding on their quest, it turns out the crazy Os still have one more thing up their patchwork quilt sleeves-- besides Busi's bayonet with my name on it-- for me to do. After dinner and washing the dishes by myself, they call me out in front of everybody to let me know they want me to do a "walkabout."

Now it all makes sense. They were just fattening you up for part three in their sick little game.

I don't say anything. I'm hoping the way I look at them says it all.

"Here's your loincloth," Mrs. O says over her very audible and lengthy fart.

I'm taken aback by the fart and its creeping aftereffects and have to roll my eyes and turn away but then, as if the NS were following protocol, i.e., waiting for the Micco and the Miccotess to cut the first after-dinner fart, I'm greeted with a Hallelujah chorus of farts-- the participants, as if following NS tradition to show solidarity with The Cause in a "secret handshake," stand, turn their backs to me, bend over and let loose a series of ground thumping anal anthems both thunderous and squealing all around me. I'm thinking if anyone strikes a match, we're all dead but then the stench is so overwhelming I quickly stop thinking about dying in an NS gas blaster and focus on keeping my balance.

Don't faint. Don't faint. Don't let those sick fucks' farts win.

I try to focus on the spinning loincloth "Mom" is holding in her hand. It looks like a *used* deerskin loincloth.

"You gotta be kidding," I struggle to say, tears running down my face.

"No kid. You wear."

She sounds like Mrs. Kim in *Gilmore Girls* as she throws it at my feet, another show it appears they've been watching way too long. I look for Nokosee. He's walking toward me through the methane cloud and looking like he's as surprised as I am.

"Mom," he says, "you can't really expect Stormy to do what I did."

I can't believe the communal stink doesn't buckle him at his knees.

Hey, he was raised to roast the Jockeys. Or jeggings.

"We don't," Busimanolotome chimes in. "You're always telling us we should cut her some slack like, because you and her got a thing going on or something, that she's entitled to special consideration, a different set of rules than those that are applied to everyone else here."

"No, dad, I don't think that at all. In fact, I wish you'd use those same set of rules for everyone else because I don't remember anyone being asked to do a walkabout. That was reserved just for me."

"And now your girlfriend."

"Why? Why does Stormy have to take more crap than any of the other NS? What did she do to deserve this?"

"Because she wants to marry you and the future leader of the New Seminole will need the strongest, bravest of women by his side."

"So what I've already done doesn't count?" I manage to gasp.

Busi looks up at the darkening sky as if he's actually contemplating the question and then whips back to me with an emphatic: "No!"

"C'mon, dad--"

"'Cut her some slack'?" the old bastard asks.

Nokosee starts for his dad but I grab his arm and step between them.

"No problemo, Mr. O," I say, struggling to find my equilibrium. Before I'm aware I'm channeling some crotch grabbing, shoulder dipping, in-your-face homeboy, I'm all up in front of Chief Crazy Loon's grill. "Dawg, I be chill to yo walkabout." I reach down, grab the loincloth up off the ground and start feeling myself up like I got a pair of big ones. "Bring it on! I can take whatever you throw down and dish it right back cuz I'm a playa and not some lame ol' hammock homicita wearin' wussy lime green Crocs in the middle of bumfuck nowhere. Do you see what I'm sayin'?"

When I'm done, my body still keeps moving back and forth like it belongs to some angry black kid in a signifying rant. No one says anything, they're stunned by what they've just witnessed-- some caught bent over in mid-tradition-fart and, looking back, I can't blame them. It's a sight to behold and hear for sure. I've gotta stop watching BET. Nokosee mercifully stops me by taking my hand away from my crotch and pulling me to his side where I turn back into an angry little white girl with a bad grasp of Ebonics and minus any swagger.

"Are you done?" Busimanolotome asks.

"Almost." I shake loose of Nokosee, turn around, bend over, grab my cheeks and try to let one fly his way. Only nothing comes out. I close my eyes and try to squeeze one out. Nothing. I open my eyes and see the NS looking at me in disgust, some sadly shaking their heads, judging me as being unworthy. I feel like a damn fool. I straighten up and look away. "Yeah, I'm done."

"Holatte-Sutv Turwv, come with us," Mrs. O says in a no-nonsense, overbearing voice.

I look at Nokosee. I feel like I'm going off to war, to certain death, but I don't want anyone to know so I blow him a kiss and say: "Don't wait for me, Nooksy."

The next thing I know, Mrs. O, her little brat and a couple of NS chicks have walked me into the hammock, ripped my clothes off except for my bra and panties and watched me pull up the loincloth. It's a little long. It reaches my knees. I turn to Mrs. O.

"Got anything shorter?" I ask.

"What, are short loincloths in this season?"

"Hey, you tell me, 'mom.' You're the fashion guru here."

"If it was good enough for Nokosee, it'll be good enough for you."

Ugh! Oh, I'm sorry. I mean lucky me!

Mrs. O grabs the leather strap that runs through it and yanks it so tightly I almost cry out-- but I don't because I won't give her that pleasure.

"Why didn't you tell me you were pregnant?" she whispers harshly while holding onto the leather belt.

I pretend I can hardly talk because of the squeezing. "I.. wanted.. to.. tell.. Nokosee.. first."

She yanks the belt tighter. "How could you let this happen?"

"Trust me," I really manage to gasp, "I didn't do it on purpose."

She throws me aside and walks away. Thankfully the bitches allow me to keep my gold lamé DMs which should come in handy against snake bites. (I know, a lot of you are probably thinking that bitch has a lot of nerve complaining about Crocs, jeggings and flip flops when she's running around in gold lamé Doc Martens in the middle of the freaking Everglades but these shit-kickin' boots have a built-in cool factor that the other stuff will never touch.)

As they lead me into an airboat, I'm thinking I look pretty cool, like some kind of Wonder Woman-hippie-Tarzan-chick. Even my bra helps create the feeling: it's a leopard print Victoria's Secret push-and-squeeze model, a little stinky and dirty but still pretty cool.

By the time we pull away the sun is setting behind the hammock. Standing with one hand holding onto the metal frame supporting the driver's seat above me, I look back at the NS sphincter singers gathered along the shoreline for Nokosee. He's there waving and yelling something to me which I can't understand because of the roar of the airboat's engine. I figure he's wishing me good luck and offering me words of encouragement. I put on a brave front and prop a gold lamé DM onto the airboat's aluminum sideboard and start voguing suggestively, hoping the last rays of sunlight are bouncing off my boots in such a way that should I die, at least people will be talking about me for years to come, like they're doing right now in White City.

As it turns out, Nokosee was only trying to tell me to sit down before I fell down which is what I did unceremoniously, nearly out of the airboat. So it goes for my big exit, now memorable for all the wrong reasons.

Chapter 12
My Walkabout

After removing my Wayfarers and blindfolding me in the airboat shortly after leaving the asylum, "Mom" leaves me on a hammock in the middle of nowhere in the middle of the night with only a compass, my watch, a pocket knife, the Wayfarers-- the "official" eyewear of the NS-- and nothing more. Not even a bithlo, a good-bye or a good luck. She didn't even bother to remove my blindfold. I basically don't know what's going on until I hear the airboat start up. When I yank my blindfold off, I'm greeted with a hurricane force wind in my face that knocks me off of my feet and onto my butt in knee-deep alligator infested water which unleashes my first New Seminole butt blast that bubbles up to the surface and makes me want to gag.

What? This couldn't happen when you were bent over and had Busi in your crosshairs? When you had an audience? What a waste of rectal revenge.

What a douche bag.

I know, what a terrible thing to say about my future mother-in-law but, come on, this woman's got a couple of screws loose too. Right? I mean, what's going on here? This isn't normal behavior. This is the kind of crazy red neck, urban *nigga* code people live by in the hollers and inner city streets of America where no one backs down and no one shows any mercy.

And I want to be a part of this?

Hell no. I just want Nokosee. Right now I haven't worked out all of the details on how or *if* I'm going to live this crazy new lifestyle but I figure I'll have a lot of free time on my hands to think about it while I try to find my way back to that bumfuck loony bin. Mr. and Mrs. O were kind enough to "cut me some slack" by giving me a day instead of a week to find my way back before sending out a search party. Still, it would have been a little easier if they had given me a bithlo. Even Nokosee got one of those. I'm guessing-- hoping-- that I don't really need one because I'm not really that far away. I'm also hoping Nokosee's got my back like Busimanolotome had his.

Yeah, God forbid you die and the baby dies with you.

If that happens the crazy Os can pretty much forget about Nokosee taking on The Cause and I'm guessing they know it too.

So, I figure at least they're not going to let me die. Especially Nokosee. I figure I can just wait here until he comes to pick me up.

It's dark now when I look around. This hammock is dense. I can hardly see into it. And it's quiet too. That might be comforting until you hear something move in the water. That's when you get off your ass and your gold lamé Doc Martens high stepping deeper into the hammock, crashing through branches you don't see and slapping away spider webs clinging to your face and remembering how big those giant orb spiders can get. In short, Wonder Woman of the Jungle screams like a *leetle* girl.

A root trips me and I go tumbling into hard edged shadows, bounce off what I'm sure is the state tree, and land in a clump of saw palmetto which lives up to its name by sawing my skin away so that by the time I fall onto the dry ground, I'm bleeding a little here and a little there until when it's all added up I'm bleeding all over the fucking place. But I'm not given the opportunity to savor the moment because something is biting me. In fact, a lot of little somethings are biting me all over. I scream again and get up slapping myself silly because I'm pretty sure I've got fire ants in my pants, so to speak. Within seconds, I'm ripping off the loincloth, throwing it away, and hopping and skipping and falling and getting up again and running back into the water. If there's a gator out there waiting for me, I hope he finishes me off quickly so I don't have to feel any more pain that's how bad it is. I dive beneath the surface to drown the little bastards that might be clinging to my Mohawk and my bush, rip off my panties and try to stay under as long as possible-- which isn't long what with off-the-charts pain receptors hitting me from both ends from the "scalping" and the pissed-off fire ants clinging to my bush and tush. When I come up with the pocket knife in one hand and the compass in the other, I meet the star scattered sky with a loud gasp which scares a giant blue heron sleeping in a tree, its silhouette against the burning horizon abandoning me for a quieter spot in the middle of nowhere. I start jumping up and down in the shallow water to dislodge those little bastards while slapping my ass, farting, and grabbing at myself. I'm sure I must look mental.

Hey, this could be your Pow-Wow dance!

I don't think so. Those events are family-friendly.

When I'm pretty sure a snake is swimming past me, I'm up and goose stepping Nazi style across the Everglades headed God-knows-where with my panties held high in a *sieg heil* salute to my Führer. I stop and look at my compass while jumping up and down and alternately squeezing my buns together at the same time. It's so dark out I can't even read the damn thing. I look around and can't figure out where north south east and west is but because the swamp seems to be alive with all kinds of creepy things, I just start marching again across the Everglades in my gold lamé high-top kickers.

"Nokosee!" I yell, "If you're out there say something!"

Nothing, of course. I remember when Nokosee was on his walkabout, Big Chief Raging Bull was shadowing his every move because God forbid something should happen to the First of the New Seminole. I guess his son's wife-to-be is on her own.

"Nokosee, I swear if you're out there you better make sure nothing happens to me because I'm *carrying your kid for crisesakes!*"

I must have scared a bird flying overhead because it answers me with a shrill cry of its own. From its point of view I must look awfully strange jumping up and down, squeezing out silent killers, and marching bare ass across the Everglades in my gold lame high-top boots. I just hope its not some kinda half-starved hawk or eagle who thinks the shiny sparkly thing down below looks tasty.

Within minutes I'm reminded of my last trek across the Everglades. That one hurt too. Sawgrass has a way of doing that to you. Only this time around, I have even less clothes on. Aside from my boots and my bra I might as well be walking across the Everglades stark naked.

Mosquitoes have found me and I wonder if my farts both loud and quiet have attracted them to my lush but now deadly hindquarters. My butt has become one of those big stinking "carrion flowers" found in Borneo. I start slapping my ass and try to keep from farting in my march across the Everglades in my beautiful way cool high-top gold lamé boots.

"Pumpernickel," my ass teasingly whispers as a fart slips out behind me. Aside from *backpfeifengesicht*, it's my second favorite German word and has kept me from eating the bread once I discovered its meaning: "devil's fart." I reach back across my body and use my fingers to form a cross as if to ward off Satan's smell.

Well, at least you haven't lost your sense of humor.

Humor this, motherfucker.

Is that anyway to talk to yourself?

Bats are onto me next. Following the mosquitoes, these big creepy furry fuckers are swooping around my head with wingspans close to two-feet. Up against the afterglow of this crazy day, I can tell by their silhouettes that they're endangered bonneted bats, something I learned from my dad. Their official names are *Eumops floridanus* but they're called bonneted bats because their big broad ears slant forward over their eyes. I start screaming like a leetle girl again and wish dad hadn't taught me so much because I can't shake the picture out of my head from a book on Florida fauna he showed me one night. We were in his airboat sitting in the middle of the Everglades and he was pointing his flashlight at a picture of one of those little bastards as they flew around us. He was trying to tell me I had nothing to fear from Florida's biggest bat-- unless I was an insect-- and that they were cute but all I could see was one of them latching onto my neck, biting me and giving me rabies before turning me into a stumbling, foot-dragging, foaming-at-the-mouth zombie chick who had never gotten a chance to dance at her prom or lose her virginity. Right now as I slap at the noisy nightmarish creatures-- it's like listening to a flock of mockingbirds on speed-- despite knowing it's really politically incorrect to say so, I wish they were all dead. Especially the one who snatched my undies from my hand.

"No! Come back here you little bastard!"

The last time I see my undies, they're silhouetted against the flickering reddish glow of an Everglades consuming itself with fires that never go out, hanging from the creepy little face of a Eumop as he shakes them back and forth, rising and falling in a mosquito filled sky. I start crying, turn and begin marching across this freakish hell-on-earth.

What if I end up stark naked by the end of my walkabout? What would the NS think? I can't return like that. It'd be too embarrassing.

"Embarrassing?" Are you nuts? Showing up in your birthday suit should be the least of your worries. It sure as hell beats showing up dead!

I slap my bare ass. Mosquito bite. Probably missed. Another bite. Another slap. Another miss. This goes on all night. After a while I actually like slapping my butt because it's like giving myself a much deserved spanking for being such an idiot-slash-fool. I expect by the time the sun rises, my once cute, righteous firm little tush will look like bloody ground chuck thanks to the mosquitoes, the fire ants and my own self-loathing. But long before that, I truly wish those big ugly Eumops would come back to feast on my tormenters and gladly, shamelessly retract any death wish I had toward them.

My boots fill with water and mud clings to each step making it more and more difficult to lift each foot. I slow down. The mosquitoes speed up. Slapping and trying to lift mud encrusted, water filled boots soon becomes excruciating. The mosquitoes are winning. I slap at a bite just above my boot and discover leeches have joined the feast. Blood trails away and runs down what was once my beautiful to die for way cool gold lamé high-top DMs. I catch myself. I *don't* want to die for them any more. I just want to cry.

And despite my efforts not to, I do.

When the sun comes up, I've walked all night, slapping, farting, and crying across the Everglades and forcing myself to put one fashion conscious foot in front of the other.

And planning on how to kill the crazy Os.

From what I can see of my once beautiful hiney, it's covered in red and white bumps and looks inflamed. I want to cry again. I turn away to wipe tears from my eyes and see a hammock up ahead and decide to rest there, hoping to find a place where I can sit down on something that doesn't want to bite me.

I find a large branch lying over the water and decide to make that my bed for the day because it sways like a hammock in the breeze, a breeze that should keep the mosquitoes at bay. I take off my boots. My toes are all shriveled up from soaking in swamp water and mud the whole night. I hang them on some branches to dry out and ease myself back onto the branch but, as it turns out, not slow enough. When my swollen little hiney meets the branch, it's as if the tree-- Mother Nature-- is slapping my ass one more time for good measure. I jump up and try again, lowering my precious brittle bloody buns slowly against the branch. And still, I have to bite my tongue to keep from crying out. I ease backward to settle in the fork so that most of my ass is hanging below the branch which helps make lying on my back bearable. Once settled in the boughs of the tree, I jam the pocket knife in a branch above me, slide the compass into my bra, pull out the Wayfarers and put them on. Sunlight flickers in through the leafy canopy across my body and face and within minutes I fall asleep, exhausted from what Nokosee's crazy family put me through the night before.

I'm dreaming my once beautiful butt now hanging from a tree is dripping a thousand tiny drops of blood from all the bug bites into the water below where piranha are having a feeding frenzy, kicking up the water and jumping into the air to get at yours truly's tush. I struggle to wake up, to remind myself that the Everglades is still piranha-free no thanks to all those selfish dingbats living here who keep them for pets. But I know it's only a matter of time and, not wanting to think about it, force myself to wake up.

I hear an airboat engine. When I turn to look at it, I fall off my branch and into the water. I'm instantly reminded of every cut and bug bite I have. I pop out of the water screaming, my eyes blinking in surprise at a world it sees dripping laconically across its pupils. I see the runny airboat in the distance and start to call out to it, waving my hand to get the driver's attention but I stop short: what if it's someone from the Outside? The cops? Or Feds? I step back into the shadows of the hammock and watch through leaves and branches. I can't tell who they are but I know the NS has an aversion to traveling in the open during the day. I let them pass. Despite my circumstances, I don't need being hauled off to jail. My watch says it's only eight in the morning. I wonder if I'm ever going to get any sleep as I make my way back up the tree and out onto the branch. I'm so weak. I've never felt this tired and I'm back to sleep within minutes.

Pain, shortness of breath and the loudest sustained fart I ever heard wakes me this time around but my sudden start doesn't knock me off the branch and into the water. Instead it only makes the reticulated python wrapped around my body squeeze even tighter until the hideous gasses inside me are squeezed out of me like bullets from a machine gun. One of my greatest fears and biggest nightmares has come true. The monster snake tightening itself around me is the biggest of the snakes and could swallow me whole-- after it's done squeezing the life out of me, an excruciatingly slow death that could take for hours. If Nature had a World Court, this snake would be banned from the Garden because of its cruel and unusual way of killing its prey. If Nature had political parties, this snake would be a member of the Nazi party. I watch in horror as this stormtrooper, brownshirt, diamond-patterned, Frankensnake scuttles across my breasts right in front of my eyes and I think, yeah, this close the pattern does look a lot like its Latin name *reticulatus* which means *net-like*.

Yes, it surprises me too on what goes through my mind in my life and death moments (which I seem to be having an inordinate amount of lately for someone my age) but, aside from a father who made sure his daughter knew all there was to know about the Everglades, I suspect I'm not that much different than any other luckless loser who's got a giant snake wrapped around him squeezing him to death, especially when it's so close you can stick your tongue out and lick its disease ridden scaly skin as it slides by.

The thing is so huge I wonder why its weight and mine hasn't broken the branch until I hear it crack. I can hardly breathe, even trying to scream is an impossibility. I see the pocket knife stuck in the branch above me and wonder if it will be of any use and then remember that outdoorsy guy who fell down a hole and got his arm stuck between a rock and a hard place. His knife was smaller than mine and he was still able to saw off his arm-- not that I need to do anything as drastic as that. If any body parts are going to get deep-sixed, they sure as hell aren't going to be mine I can goddamn guarantee you that. So, with my one free arm I reach for the knife but the branch I'm on cracks again dropping a few inches and the knife escapes my grasp. This time I'm so angry and frustrated I summon what strength I have left and grab the knife just as the snake latches onto my forearm. Its head is enormous, bigger than my hand. Blood runs down along my arm as the snake yanks it back but I grab the knife with my free hand and stab blindly at its body. It loosens its grip immediately and I roll off the branch but not into the water because the snake is wrapped around it. I'm hanging upside-down under the branch, lying and rolling against the slithering snake's thick body, looking at the water. I bring the knife up and draw it hard across its body. It recoils and starts unwrapping itself so quickly that before I know it, I'm spinning and falling into the water head first. I can't turn around and look up fast enough. When I do, all 20 feet or more of reticulated python is falling on top of me. It's like having a 200 pound man dropped on your body. I'm knocked back under the water and can't get up. Pushing against the snake doesn't do anything as it wraps itself around me again and tightens its grip. It's trying to keep me pinned underwater so I start slashing at it and don't stop until I'm breathing air again and the snake is lying lifeless in the water. I fall back against the hammock bank exhausted, short of breath, and frightened. I curse those people who raise them as pets and then set them free in the Everglades when they get too big or they get tired of them.

Motherfuckers!

The snake freaks, not the snakes. It's gotten so bad that the state has begun annual snake hunts to kill them all. It appears they are upsetting the natural balance of the Everglades. I look at the snake lying in the water and see that it was a pregnant female, hundreds of its big cream colored eggs are floating in the water, freed from a gaping knife wound. I sigh deeply. Another mother. I feel terrible.

I decide to continue on because there is no way I can stay here any longer. Remembering how it was trying to walk through the Everglades last night, I cut myself a walking stick, hoping that having a little leverage will make it easier this time around when I struggle to pull my boots away from the muddy bottom. I put on my damp boots and start the trek all over again, this time without my shades because I lost them in the fight with the snake. The stick helps and when I'm some distance away from the hammock and standing in the open Everglades bare ass to the world, I pause to look around. I haven't a clue to where I am. I dig into my bra to pull up the compass and discover I lost it too. I figure if I can keep walking north (wherever that is), one way or the other I will walk onto Alligator Alley. If I live long enough. Hopefully I'll stumble onto Camp Claude before that because, believe it or not, I really,

really want to get back "home" so I can kill all the Osceolas and every last one of the New Seminole.

Hours have passed. Knowing the sun rises in the east I figure if I can keep it on my right as I trudge through the swamp, I ought to be heading north. Because of that, I've got myself a good sunburn now only on the right side of my body. Aside from the sunburn, the bug bites and the hundreds of cuts on my body, I'm constantly in pain and my stomach never stops reminding me how hungry I am. I'm so desperate, I even drink the water I'm walking through.

I can't tell you how many ways I've come up with to kill the "O"s.

More time has passed. It's getting dark. Now I'm also working on a *detailed* list of ways of killing Nokosee.

Chapter 13
Death to Busi

Around dusk I see a hammock silhouetted on the burning horizon. It's glowing. I've been in the Everglades long enough to know that's not normal. I start for it. By the time I get there night has completely fallen and I've convinced myself to be ultra-cautious, not to alert any NS sentries because basically, I plan to sneak up on Busimanolotome and kill him first.

I hear voices as I carefully walk along the water's edge. I see figures through the underbrush. It's the NS camp alright. The jegging-clad fools are tripping and stumbling in their stupid neon colored Crocs. Except the sentry. He's got on a head-to-toe ghillie suit and is wearing no-bullshit combat boots. He looks like a walking pile of leaves, sticks and twigs with an AK-47, the NS's first choice in automatic weapons because it's so easy to get. According to the World Bank, 75 million are out there with the NS tapping sources from gangbangers in Miami's inner city. They're cheap too, reliable, and probably most importantly to their nutjob leader, they're a symbol of the revolutionary spirit that opposes everything American. Thanks to Nokosee and Wikipedia, I discovered the AK-47 is part of the flags of Mozambique, Hezbollah, and is included in the coat of arms of Zimbabwe and the Iranian Islamic Revolutionary Guards, all countries and politically-armed movements that owe everything to the AK-47. I'm surprised some haven't turned it into an object of worship, bowing down to it as if it were a god. Or at least praying to Mikhail Kalashnikov, its Russian inventor. When I asked Nokosee why it wasn't part of the NS logo, he said because his dad didn't want to give any credit to the Outside even if what he "borrowed" from it was instrumental in the war on it.

Makes perfect sense to me.

Shut up!

Busimanolotome made a good choice in making Ghillie Guy a sentry because he's seriously committed to the cause. So, it is with great trepidation that I gingerly step out of the water toward him with the wussy little pocket knife in my hand.

Are you really going to kill him?

I know I should have that question answered in advance because to hesitate could mean I'm the one that gets killed but to be perfectly honest, I can't imagine killing the guy. As he nears, I hold my breath and double-check to make sure my gold high top DMs are below the water line so they don't give me away in the day's last sunlight. I try to become one with the jungle, dark and shadowy. And then a mosquito lands on my ass.

You gotta be kidding me.

Shut up!

You know you want to slap it.

Oh, I can't believe this is happening. Why can't that guy walk faster?

I start squeezing my butt, one cheek at a time hoping it will drive the little bloodsucker off. Nothing. He's just hanging on back there sucking away, getting fatter, and making me want to slap him so badly I want to scream.

C'mon, can't you walk any faster?

Oh, no.

Now what?

I'm going to fart.

You gotta be kidding me. Didn't that goddamn snake squeeze it all out of you?

I guess not!

Oh, you're gonna make a great wife for the First of the New Seminole. Hold it in for crying out loud!

I can't. It's Book One all over again. It slips out like air escaping through the end of a tiny balloon-- slow and steady and... *frapping.* I pray-- *Pray!*-- sentry-boy doesn't hear it.

He stops short and looks around.

Please, please, oh, God, please, please--

He starts walking again, closer, closer, he's getting closer.

Thank you, thank you, God, thank--

"What the..."

He stops right in front of me and starts sniffing.

Oh, my God, he smells it!

He immediately falls into a crouch and aims the AK-47 in my direction. I freeze, pocket knife in air.

"New Seminole?"

Of course. After ingesting those NS "badass" spices we all smell alike.

"New Seminole," I reply in a deep voice.

"What's the password?"

His eyes-- blinking to clear them while his brain tries to digest what he's looking at-- are riveted on my blond bush in the green and woody jungle. It's spotlighted by a shaft of the day's dying light wafting across it thanks to a breeze through the trees. Before the rest of his body can act, I grab the barrel of the machine gun, push it downward, and thrust my puny pocket knife upward towards his throat.

"Password this, motherfucker."

Instinct tells him not to pull the trigger unless, of course, he's willing to shoot himself in the foot in order to worn the NS.

"Stormy?"

"You should be ashamed," I whisper breathlessly while working my cheeks from side to side because, believe it or not, that damn mosquito is still feeding on my hind quarters.

Slap it! Slap it!

Like the mosquito feeding on my once gorgeous glutes, guard-boy doesn't move. I'd like to think it's because I overpowered him with my jungle-fighting skills but from the way he keeps staring at my bush, I'd say it's because, like most men, he's governed by his dick and can't turn away.

"Like what you see?" I ask.

He nods that he does.

"Good, because outside of Nokosee, you're the only one who will ever see it with my permission and live to tell about it. If you cooperate. Are you going to cooperate?"

He nods that he will.

"Good. Now without taking your eyes off my bush, hand me your gun."

He does, very willingly. I take the pocket knife from his throat, throw it in the water and aim the AK-47 at him.

"Now take your stupid hat off."

He does.

"Give it to me."

He does.

"Put your hands in the air and turn around."

As soon as he turns I slap my ass with the leafy, twig filled ghillie hat and cry out.

"Are you okay?" he asks with what appears to be genuine concern.

I have to stop biting my lip to reply. "Shut up and give me your shirt."

He does and I quickly wrap the ghillie suit shirt around my waist, knot the long-sleeves in front of me and slide them to the side so that when I make my grand entrance looking like a pile of leaves, I won't be giving the NS a free show. I jam the AK-47 muzzle into the guy's back and push him firmly ahead.

"Start walking."

Your bush will become legendary.

"Shut up!"

"I didn't say anything," Ghillie Guy whispers.

I push him up to the group I spotted from the water. Busimanolotome is holding court. Mrs. O and Nokosee are there too. Perfect. Sounds like they're debating on whether or not to look for me. I decide to save them the trouble by pushing the world's worst sentry into the group.

"Hey, asshole, remember me?" I say. I got the AK-47 pointed at Busimanolotome's head.

"Stormy!"

It's Nokosee. I turn the weapon on him.

"Don't come near me," I shout, making sure, if they're not already, my eyes are wild and crazy.

He stops short.

"Stormy, we've been looking for you for days."

"Excuse me but, shut the fuck up."

I turn the AK-47 back on Busimanolotome.

"Do you have any idea what I've been through, you motherfucking piece of shit?"

Busimanolotome doesn't say anything and he doesn't try to move either as he looks me steadily in the eyes.

"Do you?"

I fire a few rounds at his Crocs for emphasis. Everyone jumps except him.

"How dare you treat me like that. I'm carrying your grandchild for crying out loud."

I let go another burst of weapon fire, this time closer to his feet. Sand is kicked up onto his stupid Crocs but the old bastard still doesn't move. Probably still believing no bullet has his name on it.

"Stop."

I whip the gun around towards Mrs. O and she can't stop fast enough.

"I can't believe you gave birth to Nokosee," I say through clenched teeth. "He's so loving and you're such a sick fuck."

"Stormy!" Nokosee yells.

I keep the gun on his mom and turn to him.

"How could you let them do this to me? We're supposed to cover each others backs, like your dad covered yours."

"Holatte-Sutv Turwv."

It's Busimanolotome. I whip the weapon around and face him.

"I ought to fucking kill you right now," I shout.

Busimanolotome backs up a little bit, like it finally has registered in his pea-sized brain that I might actually kill him. And then he says this:

"You forgot one thing, little darlin,' there isn't a bullet with my name on it."

*Geese, this guy is **so** damn predictable.*

"That's what you said the last time I pointed a gun at you." I remember the last time he said that to me. I was trying to save Nokosee's life and his old man was coming at me with a knife. I thought he was going to kill me and I pulled the trigger on the Clint Eastwood gun I was holding at the time, a .44 magnum, "the most powerful handgun in the world," but the gun was empty. This time I'm coming at him with a smoking AK-47 pointed at his head. "What if you're wrong this time?" I ask.

"It's one thing to talk about killing a man, little girl, but it's quite another thing to do it. Isn't it?"

"Stormy," Nokosee says softly, "give me the gun."

"I don't know," I say, my eyes still focused on his big bad dad. "I'm feeling kinda trigger happy right now."

"Don't, daughter."

It's Mrs. O coming up from the side. Her voice is soft, much more Lorelai than Mrs. Kim. I look at her.

"Don't go there. It won't make you happy. I want my grandchild to know his mother."

Of course that catches me pretty much off-guard allowing Nokosee enough time to come up on my other side. He puts his hand over the gun and pushes it toward the ground.

"And I want my child to know his mom too," he says.

Tears start welling up in my eyes. It's been a long couple of days and as it turns out, I really don't want to kill anybody, especially the parents of the boy I love. I look at Busimanolotome.

"What about you, fuck face?"

He smiles over that one.

"I'll tell you one thing," he says to me. "You got balls."

"So I've heard."

A moment passes as he looks me up and down.

"Yeah, you're worthy. Probably always were. I'm sorry I put you through this."

"Me, too," Mrs. O says.

"You're right, I need counseling," Busimanolotome says.

"So do I," Mrs. O says.

"Fucking-A," I say in agreement before suddenly and unexpectedly start crying like a real wuss. "You're lucky I'm too damn tired to kill you all."

I take a hand away from the AK-47 to wipe my tears and, weak from fatigue, lack of food and blood loss from thousands of mosquito bites and leaches sucking me dry, let the hand holding the machine gun drop toward the ground. What happens next is sort of a blur-- literally-- as the world spins and I fall dramatically (so Nokosee told me later-- and which is the only way I'd have it!) into his and Mrs. O's arms. From what I can see through eyes rolled to the back of a head flopping uncontrollably from side to side (Nokosee also told me my tongue was hanging out but I think he was just trying to make me laugh-- he didn't but he did get punched in the arm that took my mom's bullet from Book One) is Busimanolotome walking up to me and delicately removing the machine gun from my trigger finger. Now when everyone thinks I'm safely defanged I let slip one last rectal tremor, a real methane bomb I'd been saving up just for this occasion. Although I can't see their reaction, I can hear it.

"Oh, God," Mrs. O cries.

"Holy shit," Busimanolotome coughs.

"I guess," Nokosee pauses to gag, "I guess she's really one of us now, hunh, pa?"

"She sure knew the Gas Word I'll tell you that," Ghillie Guy gasps.

Nokosee lifts me and carries me coughing and wheezing through the jungle to his love shack. Finally, I'm back at home, sweet fucked-up home.

Chapter 14
Prenuptials Explained
or
How Mrs. O Lost Her Quotation Marks

I'm really glad I didn't murder Nokosee when I had the chance. Since my return to the NS, he's taken real good care of me, nursing me back to health with breakfast, lunch, and dinner in bed and the most solicitous medical attention a girl could want-- he can't do enough for my poor hiney and thanks to him, it's beginning to look like the one we have all come to know and love. I think he feels a little guilty about the whole walkabout thing and the way his family treated me and that suits me just fine. Even the crazy Os seem a lot less crazy over the last couple of days, especially mom (that's right, she's quotation marks-free and you'll soon see why). She took me to the side one day and made a point of trying to explain why she was so gung-ho on putting me through all of that over-the-top prenuptial BS: she was hoping, even though I was carrying her grandchild, to drive me away. Why? Because she's got a "bad feeling" about everything that's coming down and doesn't want her kids and grandkids growing up in a world that's trying to kill them. She thought if I took off, Nokosee would follow and she'd make sure he took Gerrycurl with him. I asked her if Mr. O knows about this and she looked at me as if I was mentally challenged. Then she asked me if I was a "true believer" in The Cause and I told her I was here for Nokosee and nothing else. I guess that was the right answer because the next thing I know she's telling me she wants Nokosee and me to jump ship as soon as we can. Right after the wedding if possible. And you know what? I don't have a problem with any of that. Trying to convince the First of the New Seminole to abandon his father and the old man's cockamamie dreams will be the hard part. But it's a project I'm more than up for in pulling off.

Chapter 15
We Gotta Talk II

I'm lying stark naked on my stomach and look back at Nokosee who is kneeling beside me so he can apply his magic fingers and his *Papa Big Chief's Miracle Salve* to my damaged goods. He's staring at my butt, his hands hovering over it as if he was afraid to touch it.

"Go ahead, it won't bite," I say.

"Are you sure?"

"Pretty sure. Of course, you never know. I could still be harboring some badass NS spices in there."

He hesitates. I don't blame him but I can't let him off that easily.

"Nooksy?"

"Yes?"

"Love me, love my farts."

Nooksy winces.

"I saw that."

He pauses, offers up a crooked smile, takes a deep breath and begins to massage my poor swollen hiney.

"So what do you wanna talk about?" he asks in a rush of words before sucking down another lungful of still undefiled air.

"The honeymoon," I say. My eyes are closed and there's a big smile on my face as I relax under Nokosee's expert but tentative kneading.

"What about it?"

"Disney World."

"Yeah?"

"It's so," I struggle to focus on what I'm saying, to come up with the right word what with what's going on with my buttocks. "It's so...lame."

"'Lame'? I thought you wanted to go there."

"Not really. Been there, done it. How about you?"

"Well, I was looking forward to going there with you."

"Really? Well, don't feel you have to do it because of me."

Suddenly the massaging stops followed by silence.

"Nooksy?"

Nothing.

"Don't stop now." I shift to the side to look back at him. Instead of being mesmerized by my great but dangerous ass, he's just staring at nothing.

"What's up, big guy?"

"I've never been to Disney World."

"Are you kidding me?"

"No kid."

I have to laugh and sit up. "But you're the first of the New Seminole, for crying out loud. You're not supposed to want to go there for anything except blowing it up. I thought you were doing Disney World as a favor for me."

A moment passes before he says, "We got reservations."

"Oh my God, I can't believe I'm hearing this." I grab his secret family recipe lotion covered hands. "Nokosee, I'm sorry. If that's what you want, *we're going to Disney World*." I say it like I just won the Super Bowl.

"Really? You're not just saying that?"

"Of course I'm just saying that-- for you. I'm doing this for you. I love you, Nokosee. That's what people do when they love each other. They make sacrifices."

"'Sacrifices?' What do you think I'm doing right now?"

"Massaging my poor ravaged hiney is a sacrifice?" I shake his hands loose.

He grabs them back. "C'mon, Stormy, you know I'm kidding. Anyway, what's the big deal? It's not like you've never been there before."

"Okay, 'concessions.' Is that better?"

Hey, if you have to think twice before opening your mouth with this guy, maybe you shouldn't be marrying him at all?

Shut the fuck up.

"You are so worthy," he says to me.

I sigh and pull my big goomba closer to give him a big hug.

"I can't wait to ride the monorail," he says in my ear.

I whisper back, "That's what I say every time we do it."

He laughs and pushes me away to look at me. "God, how I love you," he says. When he makes a move to take me down to the mat for some "Afternoon Delight" I hold him back because I sense for the first time how naive my big bad lean mean killing-slash-love machine really is and that possibly-- hopefully-- he's not as sold on The Cause as I thought he might be. I decide to use this revelation as an opportunity to run his mom's idea by him, something I've been meaning to do since she first brought it up.

"You got reservations?" I ask.

"Us Injuns all got reservations." He pushes my hand away and moves in on me.

"Funny. No, really?" I slip to the side.

"Under an assumed name." He goes for my neck with a hickey in mind.

"And this is safe?" I fend that move off too.

"As far as I know. Dad's got a mole or two in the mouse hole." He licks one of my scalp tats.

"Okay, if you say so but it sounds kinda risky." I roll my head to the side.

"Risky is what we live for."

He tries to kiss me but I push him away. "I'm just surprised your old man would risk the First of the New Seminole on something that's so, I don't know, so frivolous."

"'Frivolous'? You think our honeymoon is frivolous?"

Wrong word!

"Not the honeymoon, the place. It's probably got more guards than Fort Knox."

"But I've *never... been... there.*"

I shake my head. "Okay, but what if you fall in love with it, the biggest advertisement for The Outside ever, and don't want to come back?"

"That'll never happen."

"Why?"

"It'll just never happen."

"C'mon, you've hardly been in the Outside. Disney World is like a thousand times cooler. It's the "Happiest Place on Earth." You don't stand a chance against it. It's your Kryptonite."

"Well, then I guess you don't really know me then, do you, *Lois*."

I pause. "I guess not." The moment becomes awkward. "Nokosee," I finally say, "what if I don't want to come back?"

That catches him by surprise. "What?"

"Maybe you don't know me either."

"But look at what you went through to get here. I mean, to toss it all aside just to go back to where you started?"

"Well, maybe it wouldn't be so hard to do if you were there with me."

Now he's *really* looking at me.

"Are you suggesting we live in the Outside?"

"Why not? It sure beats wondering if someone is going to sneak up on you and kill you with extreme prejudice."

"Stormy, I can't leave my family."

Ah, geese, I thought that might be one reason so I got a quick response prepared. "We could live nearby, like in Miami or Hialeah or some--"

"I could never abandon The Cause."

Ah, geese again, this is not what I want to hear because I couldn't come up with a response in advance to a reply that implies he's more brain washed than even I thought he was. This is what I feared and realize that if I'm ever going to convince him otherwise, it's going to take some time and won't be happening today. I decide to stop steering the conversation into that direction. "I'm just saying."

He looks at me as if he's trying to read my true intentions.

"Don't worry, Nokosee. Although I may not be as gung ho as you are about The Cause"-- which I sarcastically make sure to add air-quotes to emphasize my point-- "I'm here because of you and I'll goddamn marry you too to prove it."

I lean over and kiss him hard, ramming my tongue into his mouth for emphasis. When I part to see if he bought my explanation I can tell he still has his doubts but he's also willing to give me a chance because, despite his best effort to control the smile growing on his face, he can't.

"¿Comprende?" I ask.

"Comprende," he says.

As he takes me down to the mat and we start doing it, I keep thinking about how I'm making one more in a long line of concessions for love and wonder if I will ever be able to convince Nokosee to make just one for me.

"All aboard the monorail!" he yells.

Chapter 16
Swamp Bride

Since I've given up on trying to convince Nokosee to abandon his family and The Cause for the time being, I've focused my attention on the wedding. Besides, I'm betting the Magic Kingdom will work magic with Nokosee's thing for The Cause without any help from me. If I'm lucky, The Cause will become a thing of the past while we live our new lives in beautiful downtown anywhere-but-heresville. Having Mom's blessing re not coming back, has lifted my spirits which makes preparing for the wedding all that more fun. Case in point: my wedding dress. From what I can tell, it's going to be some kind of communal effort on the part of the NS women that mashes up Seminole with punk rock. Instead of an engagement ring, Nokosee gave me his father's Special Forces knife, the same one I saw up close and personal when I met Nokosee for the first time (see Micco Mann's rip off of my diary). Of course, I don't know what to say. A diamond ring it isn't but for some stupid reason I know it's the most meaningful thing he can give me. I mean, it's symbolic as all get out, right? Talk about re-purposing something; from something that could have been used to kill me to something symbolizing his love for me, well, that's pretty cool. Heck, he even cleaned it up and sharpened it for me.

Yeah, with the big engagement knife in my hand, it looks like Nokosee and me are finally getting hitched. Mr. O has promised with a wink that it will be a wedding no one will soon forget.

I can only hope that's a good thing.

To be honest with you, I never thought this day would come. Especially with Mr. O sitting in for my father and walking me down the aisle, a dirt path between two rows of chickees. I'm really glad the NS have Digital Camcorder Guy recording the moment because I look great in my wedding gown and it's something I want my parents to see-- and my kids too. The NS crew did a helluva job with the dress. It's in the Seminole tradition of the full-length two-piece patchwork design, but they managed to sew in some colorful shiny cloth and stuff to set it apart from the rest of the Technicolor clad NS standing on both sides of me and Mr. O. I really dig how it trails behind me over the dirt and grass and how they left a gap between the top and the skirt so that I could show off my pierced navel, now sporting-- thanks to Nokosee-- a turquoise stud and "diamond" over my belly button with a "dream catcher" dangling from it for the wedding. He "bought" it at a Hot Topic at our "local" Sawgrass Mills, the largest outlet mall in Florida straddling the edge of the Everglades. Said it would only catch happy dreams for our baby. I can only hope so.

With the skirt hanging low on my hips Brazilian style, it has to be one of the sexiest and most colorful wedding dresses ever made. Some NS women made a sheath for my big freaking engagement knife out of colored beads and I'm wearing that tied to a leather strap draped loosely over one hip so that it falls at an angle across my skirt for that warrior princess look which is all the rage here in the swamp.

My Mohawk has been washed and waxed and died in the four colors of the New Seminole flag which is basically like the old Seminole flag except the colors representing the races have been rearranged so that white has been dropped to the bottom and red moved to the top: red, black, yellow and white (my blond hair). The tips are groomed to look like red tipped feathers. Vertically stacked Popsicle orange orchids are woven through my hair and into my bouquet of wild flowers. A single rare ghost orchid, the same flower the movie *Adaptation* was centered around, is pinned to the front of my Mohawk over my forehead. If I look up just a little, I can see its delicate white flower curling in front of me to form the shape of a heart which I think is pretty freaking cool.

Mom rustled up some NS approved lipstick and powder for my face. I applied her mascara to my eyes and extended the color to my ears to make me look like I'm wearing war paint or, as I like to call it, "love paint." Yes, it's all quite symbolic and everything and even though it lacks tradition, it sure isn't lacking in creativity which, I think, makes it even more meaningful. And, of course, all of my piercings are buffed and polished to the max. I will truly be something to behold when I walk down the aisle.

Thanks to Nokosee I won't lack for height either. Although you can't see them under my wedding dress, he was kind enough to "buy" me another pair of gold lamé high top Doc Martens Shines to wear for this special occasion since mine were looking kind of crappy after the walkabout. He lifted them from a store near the Hot Topic. It's only a few miles away from the entrance to Alligator Alley where all the shit went down less than a month ago. With the flowers in my Mohawk and the extra inch from the boots, I almost come to Mr. O's shoulder.

While we wait for Boom Box to turn on the music for the walk down the aisle, I look up at Mr. O. He looks like he stepped out of some old history book, traditional to the max with a turban pinned smack dab in the middle with his Purple Heart holding a couple of eagle feathers. Thankfully, he left his Viet Cong ear necklace back in the chickee. Unfortunately he couldn't shake his thing for jeggings. In fact, he's got a pair on under his traditional coat dress I've never seen before and hope to never see again after today: tie-dyed jeggings. My mind reels and I half expect the Fashion Police to pop through the sawgrass and hammock jungle to arrest all of us at any moment. I force myself to turn away from his hallucination inducing jeggings to the sound of his voice.

"Like surprises?"

"Please, no more surprises."

"What do you mean?"

"The jeggings are quite enough."

"Har-de-har-har--"

"Har!"

I nail the last "har" before he can say it.

"Just like Joan Rivers, right?" I ask.

"Just like her," he says.

He offers me a crooked smile and pats my hand. And to think only a few days ago I had him dead in my sights with my trigger finger itching to blow his brains out.

"Hare Krishna" from *Hair* starts up and that's our cue to start walking down the aisle. This is part of Mr. O's contribution which is pretty amazing considering from the best I can tell the guy's an atheist. In any event, I have no problem with it instead of the traditional wedding march. In fact, over the last few days I've been listening to the old man's CD and have become a devotee of the musical.

As Gerrycurl leads the way, dropping flower petals before us, the NS, clad in their cleanest Technicolored jeggings and Crocs, start singing and swaying to the music. Tears immediately fill my eyes. I can't help it. The next thing I know, I start dancing to the music like those around me. Even Mr. O gets down a little. None of this was planned in the rehearsal. Oh, God, how I love this music. If you aren't familiar with it, you can find it on YouTube. I recommend it for every girl who's not into a traditional wedding.

By the time I get to Nokosee who is standing in front of the main communal chickee, I'm swaying and singing and as happy as I've ever been.

Tears are rolling down my cheeks and I pray my "love paint" isn't flowing with them. I wipe them away and look at Nokosee. He's crying too! Fucking-A! I want to marry this guy so much!

Nokosee is wearing the traditional Seminole patchwork shirt-dress and thankfully has ditched the jeggings. Unfortunately, as it seems to be occurring way too often on my special day, he's added an item of clothing that hadn't shown up in the dress rehearsal: a headdress made from what was left of the top half of King Roar's head. I'm stunned by how hideous it is and its unexpected appearance in my wedding movie. I can't take my eyes off of it. Its skinned back falls across Nokosee's broad shoulders and trails along the ground. Everything about the poor dead gator has been preserved from its ragged teeth framing Nokosee's beautiful, loving eyes to the beast's blind eye which the sun's rays are bouncing off of and making me wish for my lost Wayfarers. I start thinking about the scalps and the shrunken head outside the Osceola lodge and how well-preserved they were too and wonder if this isn't some kind of family tradition they specialize in, some kind of taxidermy wizardry thing that's been passed down from generation to generation. And then I remember how the Osceolas were good enough to take those things down so I wouldn't have to look at them anymore, how they were really making an effort to welcome me in to their loopy family.

Mr. O taps my hand and I shake loose from the spell the gator's evil eye had over me to look at my future father-in-law. By the way he's looking at me, I get the feeling he's judging me one last time before handing me over to his son.

Probably trying to figure out whether or not you got a problem with his son wearing his dead pet on top of his head.

I do but he'll never know.

"Was this the surprise?" I ask. "The dead pet on the head thing?"

He just offers me a cryptic smile before giving my hand to his son.

Nokosee is wiping away a tear and beaming as he turns us toward the Shaman, the oldest Seminole member of the NS. He's gotta be in his eighties and, officially, only speaks Muskogee or Hitichee or Hitachi or some kinda freaking old language only he knows because he's the only one still alive who knows how to speak it. His turn-of-the-century garb includes a Seminole patchwork scarf draped across his skinny shoulders. He digs into a pouch hanging from his waist and throws a mixture of herbs into the air. The stuff makes me cough, and Nokosee too. We both stifle a laugh as Boom Box lowers the music but allows it to play softly in the background. Shaman blesses the four winds and calls on the spirits to watch over us and make us prolific, or so it was explained to me in the rehearsal. The old man digs into his pouch and pulls out a beat-up old metal Altoids tin. He opens it and holds it out for Nokosee. Nokosee rubs his finger in a red powder I was told was made from a crushed and dried orchid with a name as unwieldy and unpronounceable as my own Indian name, a name by the way I have decided to keep for the sake of détente. Nokosee makes the shape of a heart on both of my cheeks. The Shaman holds the Altoids tin out to me. I rub my finger through it and draw hearts on Nokosee's cheeks too.

"You know, Nooksy," I whisper as I work my finger across his face, "this is pretty cool and all but is there any reason why you gotta wear your dead pet on your head?"

"Makes me look taller," he whispers back.

"Kinda creepy."

"So I've been told."

"Do me a favor. After we're hitched, ditch the skins. Okay?"

"No problemo."

The Shaman starts talking again, takes the Seminole patchwork scarf from around his shoulders and wraps it around our hands. As he blesses our union, Nokosee starts moving his hands around under the scarf as if he were playing patty cake. I don't remember this being in the rehearsal and start doing the same because I assume that's part of the ceremony and it's what you're supposed to do until he grabs my hands. I look up at him. He's trying not to laugh. I look at the Shaman. He's pissed off at me. I look at the Os. Eyes are rolling like bowling balls in a bowling alley. I feel like my parents are watching. I turn back to Nokosee and give him a light kick in the shins and he pretends it's worse than it is, even looking at his parents for help and sympathy.

Shaman-boy starts unwrapping the scarf and I swear, its like magic. No one told me about this but smart ass Nokosee was able to squeeze a home made wedding ring onto my finger, one that matches his own that I'm noticing for the first time. Made from colored beads, they reflect the Seminole patchwork designs framing a red heart on a white background. I have to smile. When I look up at Nokosee, he's acting like its just as big a surprise, staring with open-mouthed, eye-blinking wonder.

I want to kiss him right then but its not time yet. Shaman-dude isn't finished throwing more powder into the air and making us cough. He says something to Nokosee and Nokosee turns to me in Muskogee.

"Say what?" I say.

"I promise to cherish you forever," he repeats in English. "Seriously," he adds for good measure.

"That's cool. So do I."

The Shaman says a few more words before looking at both of us, from one to the other. I look at Nokosee for some cues. He pulls me in towards him and kisses me passionately. And so do I.

This sets the NS to a whooping and a cheering and dancing in the aisle and Boom Box to turning up the volume.

Nokosee stops kissing me to say, "Hello, Mrs. Osceola."

"Hello, Mr. Osceola."

Shaman-boy pulls out two Coke cans from his pouch and throws them at our feet. I look at Nokosee.

"What the heck is this?"

"Do what I do."

He stomps one of the cans and it explodes everywhere. I love it and do the same. Nokosee picks up his fizzing brew and squirts me. I pick up the other can and squirt him too-- and then his family, making sure I get my new in-laws *real* good.

Chapter 17
The What

While I was recuperating in Nokosee's love shack in the days before the wedding, Busi and the boys were out rounding up the entertainment for the reception that would follow. Alligator Alley had just reopened and NS intel (they read it on the Miami Herald's website) had it that The What, one of the biggest rock bands of all time, would be finishing their Miami gig and crossing the Alley to get to their next performance in Tampa for a "sunrise celebration" of the official all-clear sign of the clean-up of the Gulf's most recent oil spill, something Busi said was a lie and impossible to pull off in such a short time considering over 200 million gallons of crude oil had leaked out of a burning oil rig-- an amount I learned the U.S. consumes in less than six hours. This "All-Clear Concert" would be on a newly restored beach hosted by the governor and free to the public. Unfortunately for the public, The What never got there. Somewhere on Alligator Alley probably around one o'clock in the morning, their tour bus vanished from the face of the earth. Hijacked by the NS, it was driven off the highway onto one of the many dirt roads leading into the glades and the Seminole Big Cypress Reservation and abandoned. The band was blindfolded and whisked away into the night on an airboat. The blindfolds didn't come off for the most part   until they were due to perform. During that 18-hour period, Busi and the boys made sure they couldn't wait to play at my reception by scaring them shitless with all kinds of threats and bizarre behavior that included brandishing scalps and the shrunken head. I have no idea what is up until Busi takes the "stage" in the communal chickee as a spotlight powered by a gasoline generator comes on. He removes a microphone from its stand and says, sounding a lot like the hippie in the *Woodstock* film my dad and I watched together many times over many summers, "Ladies and gentlemen," insert long pause, "The What."

When Busi rips off the lead singer Billy Joe McAllister's blindfold and exits stage right, it signals NS collaborators to yank the blindfolds off the rest of the band, leaving them stunned and blinded by the spotlight. Billy Joe's covering his eyes with one hand and trying to see past the spotlight. When he realizes he's standing in a hammock jungle village in the middle of the freaking Everglades with close to two hundred hippies, Indians, Rastafarian-looking dudes, young and old green necks, all looking back, cheering, applauding and shaking fake shrunken heads on a stick (Busi's idea), well, it's pretty freaking discombobulating.

"Hello," he says tentatively into the mic.

Distortion. Boom Box in another chickee off to the side with a ton of wires coming out, adjusts a knob on a soundboard.

"Never done a wedding before," he says, the distortion disappearing before he finishes his British accented sentence. "Congratulations."

Nokosee and I, still wearing our wedding threads, are sitting in the center of the group and acknowledge the cheering erupting all around us with limp wrist waves as if we were the King and Queen of England. I reach out to touch Busi's hand as he takes his seat next to Mom and Gerrycurl and whisper a sincere "Thank you." He acts like it's no big deal, that it's nothing more than just another kidnapping of a famous rock band, something he does on a regular basis, and waves me off with a shrug of his shoulders and a "pooh-pooh" smile as if he were a little ol' Jewish man. What a character.

"Never been kidnapped before either."

I turn to see Bobby Gentry, co-founder of the band. Holding a guitar, he's standing next to Billy Joe and speaking into the mic. He looks pissed off.

Indian Larry, that twitchy little dude I met the night the NS extricated me from the fire-fight on Alligator Alley, the one who reminded Busi Florida's "Stand Your Ground" law allows you to shoot first when threatened, unloads a round from his AK-47 into the air. "Shut up and play already!" he shouts.

After jumping back from the mic, Gentry looks at McAllister, McAllister looks at his band and, with just a nod of his head, leads them in the opening chords of one of their hits, *"Love, Give Me A Break."* This is when I discover the NS are a musically inclined terrorists group, probably the only one of its kind. All the instruments belong to the tribe and Boom Box is providing a background soundtrack from The What's CD to play against. McAllister's singing gives me goosebumps. I look at Nokosee, he's swaying to the beat. So are his parents. Even Gerrycurl, the youngest of the tribe, is caught up in the music. When I turn around, McAllister is jumping off the stage and walking towards me singing the refrain like only he can, powerfully, and I figure with a new found purpose, i.e., singing as if his life depends upon it. I quickly look around to see if Digital Camcorder Guy is recording this for posterity. He is.

I got to hand it to McAllister, he is some kind of showman. Despite having a death threat over his head, his song to me is heartrendingly convincing. I immediately become his number one fan when he gets on one knee and sings to me that "Love sweats from our pores when we do it on the shore."

Yeah, baby! Nokosee and you know a lot about sweaty lovers.

He-- Nokosee- squeezes me tight. We kiss. McAllister, with some effort-- the old guy's not in the best shape-- gets to his feet and continues singing right back up onto the chickee stage. While the music is invigorating, timeless, it makes me sad because up close and personal, I see what time can do to somebody-- even Rock gods-- and I'm reminded of how fleeting life is-- especially the time we're given for our teens and twenties, when it's least appreciated. It ain't much, bro. So, I latch onto Nokosee to stay young forever, to stay in this weirdly surreal moment.

The rest of the night passes before my eyes like Kodak moments: special effects smoke rising through the log chickee floor with an accompanying synchronized light show for The What's finale; us posing with the band for pictures in our wedding garb, dropping "gang signs" and voguing like the baddest gangbangers; Busi strapping on a Stratocaster and singing an original song; Busi and Mom dancing like Travolta and Uma in *Pulp Fiction*, and then father with daughter, the unrepentant killer towering over her and gently guiding her in a slow dance across the dusty earth in their neon colored Crocs, shoes suddenly not looking so silly anymore.

And then it's my turn. I've been planning this moment on the sly for a couple of days now to surprise Nokosee. I've corralled The New Seminoles— the NS's baby boomer rock band— to perform back-up for a song I want to sing to Nokosee. After telling him I have to use "the facilities" and he reminds me to check for TP, I disappear behind the stage to find my co-conspirator Gerrycurl waiting for me with my new post-wedding outfit. I quickly lose the wedding getup and start putting on my new clothes: a Seminole patterned vest over my bare breasts tied at the center with a shoestring knot that leaves just enough exposure of my cleavage to get his attention; a metallic miniskirt the NS brought back from one of their raids on the Outside which I repurposed as a loincloth, and bleached deerskin knee-high moccasin boots Gerrycurl uses in Native American Pow-Wow dance competitions among the tribes—well, up until last year before the Feds started zeroing in on them in hopes of capturing Big Bad Busi and the family decided attending them was too dangerous. I also took an assortment of feathered arm bands and silver and turquoise medallions from the Pow-Wow dance competition box and added them to my costume too so that by the time I was done dressing what with my tats, piercings, Mohawk, dream catcher dangling from my navel, and flowers in my hair, I looked pretty cool, in a dangerous, sexy sort of way.

Nokosee is sitting next to his dad and mom on the raised deck on a chickee facing the stage when I walk out onto the stage unannounced and speak into the mic attached to the stand near the front.

"Nokosee, my love, thanks for making me crazy. And pregnant."

That caught him and his parents off guard. When they turn to me he's surprised and smiling. Ma and Pa exchange glances and aren't smiling as Gerrycurl runs up and sits next to them. I look at the NS who are taking their cues from their Chief and Chieftess and they are equally uneasy since it's been less than a week since I threatened to blow Chief Loony Tunes' head off. Anyway, except for Nokosee, I don't care who digs what I'm about to do.

"And happy. Nooksy, this song's for you."

I step away from the mic and switch on the tiny transmitter attached to my metallic loincloth and adjust the small mic hanging from my ear and curving around my face toward my mouth as the band starts playing A Band Called Smith's version of *Baby It's You*, something I've been dreaming about doing at my wedding ever since my dad introduced me to the song when I was a kid.

Hope you can hit those high notes like Gayle McCormick did way back in 1969.

Don't know why I can't. With all the practicing I've done over the years singing to the record in my Milltown bedroom, I *own* that song.

I jump down from the stage and start singing with as much real emotion as Gayle did way back then. Heck, tears are welling up in my eyes as I walk toward Nokosee and when I stop in front of him, I can see he's tearing up too.

I thought you said you could sing. Poor Nokosee.

I can sing, smart ass. He's crying 'cause it's so good and he loves me just as much as I love him.

It's hard not to be moved by this song even if sung off-key. Then I see Mrs. O turn to The Micco with a roll of her eyes and hear her shout over my singing: "Nokosee didn't stand a chance."

Damn right.

Still singing, I take Nokosee by the hand and lead him away from his family toward the stage. Then, as I continue to sing and look at him hard in the eyes, I begin to dance around him, stripping him of his Seminole jacket so that I can see his magnificent to-die-for muscular body. During the song's bridge, I start dancing around him again as if I was a Pow-Wow dancer, hopping up and down and turning in circles. I sing the last stanza in front of him, hitting the last heart-piercing high note like I always dreamed I would and my husband— like I saw in my dreams even as a little girl— grabs me up and kisses me like no man has ever kissed a woman before.

Just like you knew he would.

Damn right.

Returning to the hidden tour bus was never an option because Busi believed it probably had been found and a trap had been set so, following the reception where the band got down and partied with the NS, two camo "Up-Armored"-- more military lingo the NS likes to use-- Humvees crawl out of the Everglades onto the Alley sometime around midnight. These Humvees were hijacked on the Alley over the past year, stripped of their chrome, brush painted in camouflage, and mounted with machine guns resting on a rotating turret cut and welded on their roofs. Parked on the sloping shoulder, the doors open and the band and Busi, with an AK-47 slung around his shoulder, step out while the driver remains inside on guard. Gerrycurl, Digital Camcorder Guy, Nokosee and me-- he's wearing his wedding clothes and I'm in my metallic loincloth!-- climb out of the other Humvee while its driver also remains on guard. Mom, never a big fan of the band, elected to say her good-byes at Camp Claude. By this time we're all great friends.

"Good luck, guys," McAllister says with an extended hand. This starts a round of hand shaking, back clapping, and bro shoulder bumps including performing some fake martial arts moves on me which, it appears, I will have to get use to since my White City YouTube smack down is now numbering close to 10 million hits. When I grab McAllister's hand I give him a DVD copy Boom Box made of the wedding.

"Billy Joe," I say, "would you mind making sure the media get this? It's some pics and video from the wedding and your show. I want mom and dad to know I'm okay."

"No problem, Stormy. Be happy to. And like I said before, look me up if you ever want to sing with us. That was one helluva cover."

"Stormy, even if you don't want to sing with us," Bobby adds, "you've got what it takes. We'd be happy to set up an audition for you at our label."

Whoe, that caught me by surprise. All I can say is "I... I... I..." before Busi interrupts

"So, Bobby," Busi says as he shakes Gentry's hand, "no hard feelings?"

"None. It was a nice diversion. And inspiring."

"Cool. Did you like my song?"

"Very much."

"Hey, maybe you can get it and some others I wrote into the right hands."

Busi slips a CD into Gentry's hand titled *Songs of the New Seminole*. Nokosee did the art on a laptop in his chickee. It shows the clenched red fist and tomahawk NS logo. The rock god doesn't know what to say especially when the wrong words could mean the world finds his famous but lifeless body lying on the side of the road, a feast for vultures.

"I... I'll do my best," he stammers, feigning interest in the tracks listed on the back.

"Pete Seeger always said if you could find the right songs you could change the world. I tried, but I could never find them. So I gave up and took a more pro-active approach. The songs on this CD are from my BV period, Before Viet Nam. Lots of folksy bullshit."

"How 'bout your AV period?" Gentry asks while looking at the CD shaking in his hand.

Busi grabs his AK-47. "I sing through this now."

Gentry looks at the machine gun. "The barrel of a gun? Not very PC."

"Ha, that's a good one, Bobby. Just don't try sticking a flower down my barrel."

Gentry turns to Busi with what appears as genuine concern. "That kind of thinking doesn't bode well for a long life, Chief."

"So I've been told. Anyway, feel free to use the video we gave you for any new music you got coming out," Busi the showman adds.

"Now that's an idea!"

"Yeah, you know, kinda help us get the word out."

"Right-o."

Busi sees headlights approaching. "Anyway, we gotta go. See you later, alligator."

And with that, Busi joins us in our Humvee, gives a signal to the other Humvee to move out, and leaves The What on Alligator Alley, hitchhiking for Tampa.

Chapter 18
The What?

"The What?"

"Yeah, The What!" Busi is enraged. "Those fucking bastards gave us up!"

I can identify with Busi's frustration and sense of betrayal considering we're bouncing across a dirt road at nearly 100 miles-per-hour with our headlights off as our driver, wearing night vision goggles, tries to out maneuver an F-18 Hornet strafing us from behind. The band probably got picked up by whoever was behind those headlights we saw on the Alley less than 15 minutes ago. I'm betting it was military. Phoned it in.

The F-18 roars pass less than a hundred feet in the air. The sound is deafening as its twin afterburners kick in and it arcs into the night sky. Busimanolotome is standing in the Humvee, his upper body sticking through the roof and firing a huge machine gun at the jet, its empty hot shell casings falling all over Nokosee, Gerrycurl and me while Digital Camcorder Guy records from the Humvee's "trunk" behind our seat.

This is *not* the way I expected to spend my honeymoon.

Makes it kinda hard to focus on your life as a rock star too.

Shut up!

The wind blast from the jet rocks the Humvee and the NS driver fights to keep it on the road.

"Dammit!"

The Humvee slides down the embankment and is hurtling toward the water. I'm thrown against Nokosee who's thrown against his dad's legs who's busy shooting at the jet who slams Gerrycurl against the door. It opens. She screams and grabs Busimanolotome's leg to keep from falling out.

"Goddammit!" Busi shouts as his shots go awry and he tries to kick loose of his child's death grip.

Nokosee reaches around his dad.

"Grab my hand!" he yells.

She does and Nokosee struggles to pull her back inside just as the Humvee's rear tires slip dangerously down the the embankment.

"Are you alright?" I scream.

Her chest is heaving, she can't speak but her eyes are screaming.

Busimanolotome, unaware his daughter was hanging on his leg and nearly killed, whips the machine gun around on its turret to face the rear and the second Humvee still on the road and still firing on the jet circling for another pass. It brakes when ours leaps back onto the dirt road and fishtails from side to side, kicking up a flurry of dust and gravel.

"Nokosee!" Busimanolotome is sticking his head down and shouting through the turret. "Tell 'em to get a Stinger ready!"

Nokosee reaches across the back seat, pushes Digital Camcorder Guy aside and with some effort returns with a heavy steel suitcase. He pops it open on his lap, takes out a small satellite dish and has me point it out the window while he makes a phone call.

"We've got an F-18 on our ass! We need a Stinger up its ass!"

Nokosee throws the suitcase onto the floor and climbs up through the turret.

"Dad, they said they see it coming and will shoot it down!" he shouts.

Suddenly the wind is roaring through the Humvee. Digital Camcorder Guy has kicked open the back doors so he can get a better shot at the flashing red lights in the sky and the small explosions racing down the road toward the Humvee behind us.

The second Humvee explodes in a huge ball of fire and smoke, throwing it end over end down the embankment and into the Everglades.

Digital Camcorder Guy is still pointing the camera but he isn't looking through the viewfinder anymore. He's stunned, shocked, just like me.

And then he's dead, just like that. A piece of the second Humvee hurtling through the air stabs him in the heart and punctures the back seat. A sharp piece of smoking metal dripping blood and spinal fluid vibrates just inches from me.

Oh, my God! You're gonna do a Buddy Holly!

No I'm not. I'm not gonna die before I even get discovered. (I know, talk about a disconnect.)

A shell rips through the roof next to Nokosee and Busimanolotome and smashes our driver against the steering wheel, killing him instantly. The Humvee swerves across the road and we're up on two wheels. Gerrycurl screams and I'm pretty sure I do too but that doesn't stop me from throwing myself across the front seat and grabbing what's left of the bloody steering wheel. It slips under my hands as I turn it towards the roll and the big hunk of American ego falls back down onto all four wheels. As I'm fighting the wheel to keep the Humvee on the road, Nokosee is grabbing the dead driver, pulling him out of his seat and throwing him into the passenger's seat. There's smoking, steaming blood and bits and pieces of the driver all over the place and when Nokosee slips in it while scrambling to climb into the dead man's seat, he hits my hands, tearing them from the steering wheel. The Humvee starts rocking from side to side.

"Goddammit!" Busimanolotome yells. He can't get a bead on the F-18, now circling back far out over the Everglades.

I glance at Gerrycurl. She's hyperventilating and staring in horror at something. I turn to see what it is. The bottom half of the broken steering wheel is lying between the front seats, the driver's right hand still holding it tightly.

Nokosee wrestles control of the hurtling iron death trap, leans across the front seat, yanks the night vision goggles off of the dead driver, and puts them on. He looks like some kind of freakish sci-fi monster from a drive-in movie as he tries to see through the black night and the smoke rising up from the engine. He looks in the side-view mirror and I can see it coming too: cannon rounds are tearing up the dirt road behind us and marching toward us in neat orderly tracks. I throw myself onto the floorboard, look up, and see Gerrycurl still transfixed by the dead man's hand. I reach up and grab her and pull her down next to me just as Nokosee whips the steering wheel to the right and then just as quickly corrects himself as the road explodes on both sides of us and hot shell casings from Busimanolotome's machine gun fall down upon us.

"Die you motherfucker!" Busimanolotome screams while firing his big machine gun at the passing jet.

I look up through the smoking, now silent turret and can see the jet banking hard, two tiny glowing furnaces thrown against the night sky. The explosion is hidden by the Humvee's roof but a sudden flash of light fills the truck followed by a shock wave that rocks our six ton vehicle as if it were nothing more than a plastic toy. I sit up a little and peak over the seat through a side window just in time to see the F-18 nose dive into the Everglades. Exploding a second time, I think I can see by the blast-- I want to believe I see this-- the pilot has ejected and is parachuting safely to earth.

"Dammit!"

It's Nokosee. I pull myself up behind him. I can't believe what I see. The exploding jet has lit up the Everglades and hundreds of soldiers are frozen under the light. They had been slogging through the water towards the dirt road. Now they're dying in front of me-- exploding in front of me-- one by one as Busimanolotome machine guns them down as we race by.

"You gotta be fucking kidding me!"

It's Nokosee again. I turn and see more soldiers crawling out of the swamp and climbing onto the dirt road in front of us.

Huge holes are blasted through the windshield.

They're shooting at us!

Nokosee, racing towards them, starts turning the wheel from side-to-side in order to escape a bullet. Busimanolotome has turned the gun on the soldiers on the road and they too are ripped apart as the machine gun's big bullets tear through them.

A soldier's lifeless body is slammed against the windshield as Nokosee plows right through them. I see a "Ranger" shoulder patch with a grinning skull wearing a beret just before the body rolls off the hood, leaving a bloody trail across the windshield to remember it by.

"Get off the road!" Busimanolotome is yelling at Nokosee through the turret. "You've got another Hornet on our tail!"

Nokosee checks his side view mirror and suddenly drives off the road. I look out the bouncing window and see a rocket roaring by. It bounces off the road like a skipping stone and sails into the air. A second later the second F-18 whips past us less than 50 feet above the dirt road. I can actually see the pilot looking at us when Busimanolotome unleashes more machine gun fire. The jet's canopy takes a direct hit followed by a trail of holes ripped across the fuselage and an explosion. This time, there is no mistaking it: the pilot did not survive.

I duck back onto the floor to avoid getting hit by any shrapnel. Gerrycurl is crying uncontrollably. I want to console her but I know I really want to join her no matter how much I know crying won't help a thing.

The Humvee is full of light again as it hurtles through the F-18 wreckage spinning, sliding and tumbling along with us as we race down the road.

And *through* the stream of burning jet fuel lying across the road.

The side windows explode as the air inside the Humvee is sucked out by the fire. Flames are rushing in through the open back doors, sucked in by a natural vacuum. I've never felt heat like this. Busimanolotome's pants start to smoke. He yells and jumps back inside. His headpiece is on fire, his hair and Seminole jacket are smoking and his face is singed; a face that for an instant-- as our eyes lock-- shows fear, something I never thought I'd see. He knows it too and quickly turns to Nokosee.

"Nokosee!"

"I see it!"

The next thing I know, we're back on the dirt road and the head banging, bone breaking bouncing has stopped. I hear the rapid repeating sound of wood planks getting beaten down by the Humvee's tires as we race over a bridge when just as suddenly, we come to a brake-squealing, body-thrown-forward-into-the-back-of-the-driver's-seat-stop.

"Get out!" Nokosee yells.

I look over the front seat. The Humvee is on fire, flames are leaping over the top, smoke is everywhere. Nokosee's trying to open his door. It won't budge. He leans back and kicks it open. I grab my door handle and spring back. It's hot. Nokosee tries to open it from the other side, but flames leaping off of the tires are keeping him from doing it so he removes his Seminole wedding jacket and starts whacking at the fire so he can get to the door handle. When he grabs the handle, he burns his hand too. By this time I'm leaning out of the broken window with my arms held wide screaming his name when a tire explodes. Nokosee is knocked off of his feet and I'm thrown back against the door frame. I catch myself and burn my hands on the hot metal. I look at Nokosee. He's lying on his back, stunned and struggling to gather himself up. I yell his name. He throws his jacket aside, jumps up, grabs my outstretched hands and pulls me through the window. Unfortunately, a piece of jagged window glass sticking up out of the door cuts through my metallic loincloth and leaves a 12 inch gash down my thigh. My scream races across the battlefield.

"Nokosee!"

It's his dad. He's got Gerrycurl in his arms and sliding her kicking and screaming through the window. Nokosee puts me down on the dirt road, takes his sister and sets her next to me. She sees me grabbing my leg and writhing in pain but can't do anything but cry louder.

"Dad, c'mon!"

"Take this!"

He hands Nokosee the sat phone and Digital Camcorder Guy's blood covered Sony.

"Stand back!"

And this is where Busimanolotome makes me a true believer: grabbing the hot door with both hands and with more grace than even a younger man might posses, pulls himself smoothly through the window and *rolls* in a somersault onto the dirt road. We're talking real parkour shit here, man! Too fucking much! When he springs to his feet all smoking and shit, I want to follow him to the depths of hell and have his *son's* baby right now smack dab in the middle of the dirt road with bullets flying all around me.

Busimanolotome grabs the sat phone.

"Where the hell are you?" he barks. "Check your GPS!"

He stops short and lets the phone slip away from his ear to look at something down the road. I turn to look at where we've just been. Dark shadows armed to the teeth are stepping up onto the road, the flaming F-18 wreckage behind them.

A loud explosion behind us shakes the dry dirt up off the road I'm sitting on. I turn to see what it was and guess it's the rocket the F-18 shot at us, finally nose diving into the road disappearing in the darkness ahead of us. The fireball rising in the distance lights up the road and everything on it, including us. High-velocity bullets start tearing up the dirt road all around us and before I know it, Nokosee has grabbed me and is running a zig-zag path toward the side of the road now exploding in puffs of smoke, dust, and gravel. I look over my shoulder, Busimanolotome's got Gerrycurl thrown over his shoulder and the sat phone and running for the side of the road too but without bothering to zig or zag.

Of course, there isn't a bullet with his name on it.

"Into the water!" he orders.

We stumble into the shallow water at the bottom of the embankment. I can hear Nokosee breathing hard but we keep on running deeper into the swamp.

"Nokosee, stop!"

It's his old man. He's out of breath and settling into the water behind a clump of cattails. He puts the small sat dish in Gerrycurl's hands and roughly orders her to point it toward the sky. She tries to stop crying and does her best.

"Where the hell are you?" he shouts into the phone.

The answer comes with the sudden sound of a black NS airboat banking hard out of the night. A wave is kicked up and slams against us. I lose my footing and fall into the water and scream when it hits my wound. Nokosee grabs me, pulls me up, throws me over his shoulder, and runs splashing through the swamp. When he throws me into the airboat, I look around. A NS guy is carrying Gerrycurl and Nokosee is lending his dad a shoulder to hang onto as they slog their way across the swamp toward the airboat.

"Get the sat phone!" Busimanolotome orders, pointing to where it was left behind.

Someone does and before I know it, the airboat turns hard under a hail of bullets and roars into the comforting cover of darkness.

"Give me the sat phone!" Busimanolotome shouts as bullets ricochet every which way across the airboat. He hits the redial button and screams into the phone. "We're under attack! Get everyone out of the camp. Make sure you take our computers. We'll meet up at Starshine."

Chapter 19
Return of the Quotation Marks

Camp Starshine isn't as big as Camp Claude which explains why Nokosee and me are spending our honeymoon night shacked up with the Os. Five people in one small chickee even deeper in the Everglades. Disney World this ain't.

I'm lying barefoot on another inflatable air mattress and Nokosee is holding my hand while Mom and Gerrycurl tend to my "honeymoon souvenir," the 12 inch jagged cut on my thigh. As it turns out, Mom runs the medic division of the NS and she's turning my misfortune into a teaching opportunity for three other people who are hovering behind her, which I learn, is the entire division for approximately 200 people, give or take a few here and there since the last battle. One is holding up a Coleman lantern so everyone can see what Mom is doing. Shadows flow slowly back and forth across us as the lantern sways easily above. My metallic loincloth, long since cut to shreds with pieces embedded under my skin, was so bloody I thought-- maybe hoped-- that I had started my period again.

"There you go, daughter," Mom says when she's finally done, "As good as new."

I look at her handiwork. The 30 neat stitches she sewed are hidden beneath a huge plastic adhesive bandage she slapped down over the wound. I guess you could call it my "White Badge of Courage," although it was won trying to save my own ass.

White Badge of Stupidity would be a better description.

"Keep it clean," she says before I get a chance to thank her. "And be careful with it." And then as an afterthought with a finger pointed at me: "No sex!"

"Hey," I reply defensively, "don't look at me. Tell nature boy here." I nod at Nokosee.

Mom reaches across me and slaps Nokosee across the back of the head.

"Mom!"

That wasn't me. That was Nokosee. Gerrycurl doesn't say anything. I'd be lying if I said none of us were embarrassed or uneasy.

"Keep it in your pants for awhile." she orders. "Do you think you can do that?"

"Of course I can."

"I wonder." Mom turns to me. "If he's anything like his father, you're in for a heap load of slam-bam-thank-you-mam."

"Mom!"

This time it's Nokosee *and* Gerrycurl. He's still rubbing the back of his head and she's giving her mom one of those looks only teenage girls can deliver with devastating simplicity when they've been embarrassed in public by their clueless parents. Unlike the kids, the medics are averting their eyes and I basically can't speak, I'm so taken aback.

"You fall for the first girl you ever met and get her pregnant too." Mom sadly shakes her head. "Unbelievable."

"Believe it, 'Mom.'" That's me, finally finding my voice and my other Indian name: She's Got Balls. And in case you didn't notice, I'm back to referring to her in quotation marks which is better than *bitch,* emphasis intentional. I don't know what her problem is, maybe she's pissed off Operation Disney World fell through, but that's no call for her to go bad mouthing me or my man. "And I'd appreciate it if you'd cut us some slack. I don't need to hear you bitching about the past. Nokosee, me, and Gerrycurl are lucky to be alive for crying out loud."

That shuts her mouth but her angry eyes aren't finished, still shouting volumes in the uneasy silence when suddenly Gerrycurl starts some "deep crying," the kind that racks your body with convulsions. "Mom" turns to her and takes her into her arms.

"It's alright, darling," she says while rocking her daughter slowly from side to side. "Everything is going to be fine."

I really want to believe that but I gave up believing in fairy tales a long time ago. The entire NS medic division uses this moment to excuse itself in a less than smooth but hasty exit.

"Is everything alright?"

It's Busimanolotome. He's standing outside the chickee with the rising sun on his back watching his medical corp quickly retreating and avoiding his eyes. He's just returned from an impromptu pow-wow with the remaining NS and the few wedding guests that opted to escape with us through the swamp. I say "remaining," because some elected not to follow Busimanolotome from Camp Claude to Camp Starshine. Instead, upon hearing about the "skirmish" with the paratroopers and the shooting down of two F-18s, a few dozen elected to throw in their Indian blankets, so to speak, and to take their chances with melting into the jungle and returning to the Outside. When Busimanolotome heard about this upon arriving at our new camp, he basically went ballistic and threatened to kill every last one of them if he ever came across them again.

I have to admit, had I been at Camp Claude and heard what had happened, I probably would have said "adios" too because each time we go deeper into the Everglades to escape pursuit, the more hopeless "The Cause" begins to look.

But I didn't have that opportunity. I was right in the middle of the battle and then running away from it as fast as our airboat could go.

Mrs. O doesn't say anything to him. Her eyes say it all: husband is in deep shit-- not necessarily for putting me and my baby in harm's way (although had my stomach been ripped open instead of my thigh it could have killed the "Second of the New Seminole") but for endangering her kids-- especially 14-year-old Gerrycurl who appears to have been traumatized for life. She scoots back with Gerrycurl under her arm onto another air mattress and they lie down. Busimanolotome looks at me. I shrug "I know nothin'" and ease back onto my air mattress. He motions for Nokosee to come with him. Nokosee, to his credit, checks with me first. I tell him it's okay and my lover boy kisses me on the forehead before sliding out of the chickee. I watch them walk off into the dawn's early light, mumbling to each other in Muskogee and thankfully, for some reason, probably the pill "mom" gave me, fall to sleep not thinking about all the people we are responsible for killing a few hours ago. Or how I'm spending my honeymoon night sleeping with my in-laws. Instead, as I hear Gerrycurl crying softly behind me and my eyelids finally give up and close across my eyes, I'm wondering what the old man has up his sleeve besides that bayonet with my name on it, new daughter-in-law or not. Having seen him shoot down two F-18 Hornets "with extreme prejudice," this is a gnawing mistrust I cannot shake. My gut feeling is if I want to get out of this nightmare alive-- with or without Nokosee-- I need to be constantly on guard whenever I'm around this mercurial, menacing man-- *and* his wife.

And, of course, sleep comes to me with this thought too: how cool it'll be being a recording star.

When Nokosee wakes me up I can tell it's daytime. I look at my watch and see it's around 2pm. I've been asleep for nearly 8 hours.

"What?" I ask sleepily. I see Mrs. O and Gerrycurl are gone.

"I brought you some food and something to drink."

I try to focus on the MRE steaming in front of me: scrambled eggs and sausage with a small plastic tub of hot sauce on the side. He helps me to sit up.

"I want you to take this pill too."

"What is it?"

"An antibiotic."

I make a feeble effort to take the pill out of his hand but he pulls it away.

"First eat something," he says.

He gets behind me and has me rest against his body and then starts feeding me. I look around. Camp Starshine is active with NS rushing here and there preparing for God-knows-what.

"Nokosee, what's up?"

"We can't stay here. We're leaving as soon as we can."

"But it's not dark."

"Can't wait."

"But isn't that asking to get spotted?"

"Maybe, but we'll be traveling under camo."

"What, to Camp Aquarius?"

"Funny."

"I wasn't trying to be."

"No, dad's sure the traitors will give us up so our camps are useless."

"So what are you going to do?"

"Shift to Plan B."

"Plan B?"

"Improvise."

"'Improvise?'"

"Yeah, dad's got back-up sites he hasn't told anyone about especially for these kinds of situations."

I grab Nokosee's wrist and stop another plastic sporkfull of scrambled eggs in mid-air.

"Nokosee, we gotta talk."

Nokosee sighs. "Not again."

"Again."

"About what this time?"

"Everything."

"I don't think we have time for 'everything'."

"Make time."

Nokosee pauses and then settles onto his side.

"Okay."

"I'm having a real problem with all the killing going on. It's not what I signed up for when I joined the NS. I thought we'd be more like Friends of the Earth but just a tad less friendly. You know, maybe blow up a few buildings here and there, hijack a few trucks with a shitload of Crocs, but never anything like shooting down a couple of F-18s or killing soldiers left and right. Do you understand what I'm saying?"

Nokosee doesn't say anything right away as he looks me over. And then he takes my hand and kisses it.

"I love you, Stormy Jones a.k.a Holatte-Sutv Turwv and She's Got Balls."

He licks my fingers, the bastard.

"I don't blame you," he says while licking and looking me in the eyes. "It's bugging the shit out of me too. But what do you want me to do?"

For one thing, you can stop licking my fingers!

But I can't tell him that because it feels so good. With an exertion of what little will power I still have with this guy, I remove my fingers one by one from between his luscious lips and try to concentrate on my concerns with the way the NS is being ran.

"Do we *really* have to kill people?"

"Do they *really* have to shoot at us-- *first?* Did you notice that, Stormy, that they always shoot first?"

I have to think about that. I know it shouldn't matter but for some reason it does.

"I know you think my dad's a major fruit cake, but his first order to the NS is to never shoot first at the Outside-- especially the Outside's army. He might be gaga about saving the environment, but he's not *that* crazy."

I'm not convinced. After a moment I say, "Maybe we should try another way of saving the environment."

"Like through a letter writing campaign?"

"I don't know, Nokosee, but right now that sounds like a pretty damn good idea. At least no one's trying to kill us."

Nothing. I question whether or not to bring up leaving Dodge City but then decide to throw caution to the wind.

"Or we could go away and not come back."

"Are you ready?"

It's Busimanolotome. He's standing outside the chickee with Mrs. O and Gerrycurl. I swear the whole goddamn family has got that sneaking-up-on-you Indian thing down so freaking good it's getting to be annoying, making me paranoid.

I wonder if he heard you.

"Give us five minutes, dad."

"You got two." He turns and leads his wife and daughter away but not before Mrs. O gives me a concerned look of her own.

Nokosee picks up the pill.

"Open up," he says.

I do and in goes the pill. He picks up a bottle of Gatorade and holds it to my mouth so that I can swallow it down. Next thing I know, I'm being carried in his big strong arms through the camp to an airboat at the water's edge. It's completely covered in the bizarre camouflage style called ghillie. Basically, they've strung camo nets over all of the airboats and swamp buggies and ran leafy branches through them to make them harder to discover during daylight. Some NS are wearing Army Surplus store-bought ghillie suits like Ghillie Guy had on when I snuck up on him with my pocket knife. It makes them look like clumps of sawgrass and little hammocks not to mention stupid. Nokosee hands me off to his father who lowers me onto an air mattress in the airboat's hull. While his dad climbs into the driver's seat and starts the engine, Nokosee settles in next to me as we slowly pull away. Every inch of space is crammed with survival crap and weapons. As I look up through the ghillie camo at the passing clouds and sun lit sky, I gotta wonder if this cockamamie idea is really going to work or if we're just asking to get blown out of the water. But again, I don't really have much say in the matter but to accept it and go with the flow. I see Mrs. O and Gerrycurl in a camouflaged airboat next to us. Gerrycurl is crying as her mom holds her. Their airboat, driven by ghillie suited Indian Larry, is parallel to ours and I'm surprised all the Osceolas aren't traveling together. I ask Nokosee why and he says his parents had a fight and aren't speaking to each other. I struggle to keep my eyes open and suspect the pill Nokosee gave me was designed to make me sleep too. Call me paranoid, but I'm pretty sure the captain on this boat doesn't trust me and wants to make sure I remain, dumb, barefoot and pregnant. The last things that go through my mind are that the "fight" was over me, that maybe "Mom" took my side but she lost the argument and that I'm being held for ransom by the old man to secure everyone's future escape from our inevitable entrapment; plus, whether or not Nokosee remembered to bring my gold lamé DMs which I'm going to wear at my Madison Square Garden concert .

Chapter 20
Plan B

When I wake, the world is totally lights out. Even the stars are hiding. It's like waking up blind.

"Nokosee?" I whisper. Nothing. I grope cautiously in the dark, hoping to find him lying next to me instead of touching a spider, snake, or scorpion.

I find him. He's sleeping on his side, turned away from me. I feel his massive back and feel safe. I snuggle up behind him and try to wrap myself around his body but a pain shoots through my leg where the stitches are. I cry out.

"Stormy?" He whips around.

"Sorry. I didn't mean to wake you."

"No problem. Are you alright?"

"I think I might have pulled a stitch."

"Let me see."

I slap his hand away. "No, that's okay. It can wait until morning. Where the hell are we? I can't see a damn thing."

"You're in Plan B."

"*In* Plan B?"

I hear a click and Plan B lights up. Nokosee is propped up next to me with a flashlight in his hand, running the light across the walls of what appears to be a cave. Its roof is propped up with heavy rough-hewn cypress trunks and re-purposed steel beams.

And then I see the airplane wing.

We're lying on an air mattress beneath a black airplane wing.

"What the..."

"It's called a Micco SP26. The Seminoles use to build them. Dad stole one a year ago. Made some changes."

I slowly sit up and touch the wing above me.

"Is this part of the NS air force?" I ask.

"It *is* the NS air force. Take a look at this."

Nokosee helps me slide out from under the wing to show me the little plane's tail. It's wearing the NS logo of the clenched red fist holding a tomahawk. The Seminole tribe's colors are painted in four rows across the tip. This time, instead of the camo job that was hand brushed on the Humvees, this one looks like it was sprayed on with a helluva lot more care.

"Did it myself."

I look at him. He's beaming.

"Not bad," I tell him. I look around. "So, do you mind telling me where the hell I am?"

"Come here."

He takes me by the hand and leads me limping toward the front of the plane.

"Grab this and don't move."

He puts my hand on the propeller, walks a little further away, reaches out and grabs something in the circle of light. He pulls away the cave's canvas twig and branch embedded entrance and I have to shield my eyes as the setting sun, now an undulating bright red disk in an orange sky, fills the space. The whole Everglades seems to have been dropped in front of me, flat and full of water. I step forward a little and see the water is dangerously close to entering the cave.

"Are you trying to tell me the NS dug a cave in--" I stop myself. "Wait a minute, how can you dig a cave in the Everglades? It's nothing but water and more water and a few thousand hammocks only a few feet at best off the ground."

"Come here."

He takes me by the hand and expects me to follow him quickly out of the cave but I can't keep up with him because of my leg.

"Nokosee, slow down."

He turns, sees me holding my leg and without a thought, scoops me up and carries me out of his man cave as if I were as light as a feather. Within a few steps I know what the NS have done. They cut a hole in one of the long levees built to control the flow of water into the Everglades, a hole big enough to hide an airplane.

"So what do you think?" he asks.

"You are some kinda enterprising motherfuckers that's for sure."

He can't hide how pleased he is with himself. He nods toward the plane.

"We added floats to make it amphibious. It wasn't designed for that but it still flies."

"Like I said, you are some kinda enterprising motherfuckers. Mind if I ask how you plan on using it?"

"Why tell you when I can show you?"

Less than thirty minutes later I'm sitting in the cramped quarters behind Nokosee and his dad, freshly arrived with cans of aviation fuel. I'm tied down like a load of cargo with a thick rope wrapped around my waist and bouncing across the Everglades towards a dimly lit horizon. Nokosee is pulling back hard on the wheel to get the little Micco to climb into the sky and I'm praying he can because of the fast approaching hammock at the end of the "runway."

"Dad," Nokosee shouts into the mic on his headset over the engine roar. "I think we're too heavy!"

"I think she lied about her weight." Busimanolotome replies in a steady voice into the mic, his eyes planted firmly on the horizon.

"I did not!"

"How much did you say she weighs again?" Busimanolotome shouts.

Nokosee turns to me. "Stormy, scoot forward a little."

I'm panicking now and struggle to squeeze between the front seats as Nokosee pulls back as hard as he can on the shaking steering wheel. I feel a stitch pop. I want to scream from the pain but I bite my tongue because there is no screaming in front of The Micco.

The plane starts to shake violently. Busimanolotome looks at me struggling to pull myself to the front of the plane and with frustrated disgust, grabs me by the back of my cut-off jeans with one arm and throws me forward. I bang my head on the windshield as the rope holding me down tightens across my stomach and I scream loudly this time, a scream that bounces off the metal interior of the cramped little plane and, I'm sure, across the Everglades as we barely clear the hammock trees.

"Ye-haw!" Nokosee yells.

"Nice job, son! You doan need no stinkin' private pilots license."

With my nose crunched up against the glass as we climb higher into the dying light, all I can see are stunning, gloriously sunset-lit clouds as my stomach drops away to the Everglades below, a place that I always feared but now long to be firmly planted upon.

"Hey, Bal-*ass*," Busimanolotome shouts over the engine's roar.

I look at him. He's looking at me, sees me vice-gripping the dashboard with both hands and breathing hard, sees I'm scared shitless.

"You can let go now," he says. "Stick your bal-*ass* back where it belongs."

"Dad, stop joshing her!" Nokosee shouts across me.

Stop *joshing* me?

Busimanolotome laughs and starts singing "Fly Me To The Moon" as loud as he can. I give him a half-assed smile and let go of the dashboard with one hand long enough to extend my middle finger. That's when he grabs it and sings the following lyrics directly to me as if he were channeling Frank Sinatra:

"In other words, hold my hand; In other words, baby, kiss me."

That thought disgusts me and I shake loose of his grip around my finger and back up into my little space behind the seats. He laughs, turns to Nokosee and keeps singing. Nokosee looks back at me with his "let's do IT" face, the one that comes with a silly smile and eyebrow acrobatics. I try to smile too. I just wish he didn't feel the need to show off to me.

So, besides being able to kick any high school kid's butt in the world, he can also fly a plane. What a guy. Is there anything he can't do?

He can't get a pilot's license because he's wanted by the Feds.

And you can't say 'No.'

I know. As you may have already learned, I'm pretty bad at saying *no* to Nokosee which explains why I'm bal-*ass* 10,000 feet in the air. Of course, the way he presented it, it would only be a short flight and that I'd love it. And then his dad shows up with the gas cans and starts implying I was scared which is all I needed to say "Screw you, let's go!"

It wasn't until we were close to 10,000 feet and I was freezing my bal-*ass* off that it dawned on me that I had been played by the Master and the real reason the old man would even consider taking me along for the ride: he didn't want me captured and spilling the beans about the NS.

So, you can't have these paranoid flavored revelations on the ground? Would that be too much to ask?

My first ever flight in a small private plane comes courtesy of Busimanolotome's paranoid insistence that the Outside knows our every move because we're being watched from above by drones equipped with high-res cameras. This is the only way he can explain how quickly the F-18s and the Army Rangers were all over us following our dropping off The What on Alligator Alley. Despite this new "analysis of the events," The Micco still thinks the band squealed and refuses to ever buy one of their records again. Whether or not any of this is true or just crazy talk by a clinically paranoid man suffering delusions of grandeur is anyone's guess. Although he has secret sites that only he knows about, having this kind of foresight is probably one of the few positive things this fruitcake has going for him.

Besides his loving kids. Thanks to a Google search done by Gerrycurl on a laptop wired through the sat phone, Busimanolotome, who is barely computer literate and tolerates its wonders only to exploit the Outside, learned how high a Predator drone can fly: 25,000 feet according to Wikipedia. He figured if the Micco can reach its maximum altitude of 14,000 feet he might be able to shoot it down with a Stinger missile, something dependent now, as he likes to remind Nokosee with every chance he gets, on whether or not I'm as fat as he thinks I am.

"C'mon, dad, she can't weigh more than a hundred pounds."

"Thanks, Nokosee," I say. I actually weigh a *little* more now because of the baby but it's nice to think he doesn't.

Busimanolotome laughs and starts singing again, this time throwing his arms out to the sides like some kind of sixties tuxedo clad Las Vegas lounge singer as he sings about flying him to the moon and some other planets.

By the time he's done with the song we're closing in on the Micco's maximum altitude and I'm beginning to have second thoughts about our latest mission.

"Ah, Mr. O, sir, if you don't mind me saying, I think what we're trying to do is crazy."

"You want crazy. Look out the window."

Nokosee banks the plane so we can look at the Everglades fast disappearing in the fading light.

"That's the L-6 levee. It's 18-feet high and 100 miles long. It's also our airplane hanger. They built it in the late 60's to drain the Everglades for more Outsiders. Someday I plan to blow it up."

"Now *that's* crazy," I reply. "My dad says we need them to regulate the water or there won't be any Florida panthers or black bears left."

"That's the official party line. The truth is they built levees and dams all over the Everglades to stop the natural flow of water so the sugar barons can grow their sugar cane and people like you can live comfortably in what was once wilderness."

I turn and look at the back of Busimanolotome's head. "I'm not one of them."

Busimanolotome turns to look at me. "So you say. So you say. We'll see."

He turns to check the radar.

"What do you see, dad?"

"Not much. Which is the way it ought to be since we're over," he pauses to turn to look at me, "'the middle of freaking nowhere.'"

"Jesus, will you give it a rest?" I ask. "I love the Everglades. Tell him that, Nokosee."

"She *loves* the Everglades, dad."

Busimanolotome smiles and checks out the radar one more time before looking up through the glass canopy. "Take us as high as it'll go."

Five minutes later Nokosee calls out the altitude: "14,000 feet."

"Circle slowly."

I'm pretty sure I'm suffering the first stages of frost bite. I see my breath vaporizing in front of me, my body is shivering like it's in the worst winter Milltown ever had. Nokosee looks at me. He's freezing too. I think he's checking me out, to see if I'm too cold. I am, but I'm sure as hell not going to let him know-- or especially his father. I won't give him *that* satisfaction.

"Sky Eyes, hand me those binoculars."

Busimanolotome catches me off guard with the way he addresses me. Maybe I'm reading more into it than it deserves, but it seems warmer, friendlier. I look around in the flotsam in the cramped dark compartment they elected to stow me in and come up with the binoculars. I give them to him and he starts canvassing the sky.

"I feel like an eagle," he shouts.

"Yeah, well, Eagle Eyes," Nokosee shouts back, "check the radar. We got company at 25,000 feet."

The radar display shows the "military designated object" with 25,000 printed under it plus its speed of 50 kts.

"I see it," Busimanolotome says, looking through the binoculars.

"Where?" I can't see it, don't know what I'm looking for.

Busimanolotome lowers the binoculars and points to something high above us. "There. It's glinting in the light."

I see it. It's a speck of light moving slowly across the sky and reflecting the final dying light of the setting sun, now below the horizon.

"You're sure about that, Mr. O?" I shout.

"Pretty much. Hold on Sky Eyes."

"Pretty much?"

Before I know what's happening, to really consider the ramifications if he's wrong, Busimanolotome has unlocked the glass canopy and slid it back. The cockpit is suddenly torn apart by hurricane force sub-zero freezing winds.

"Oh, my God!" I shout as I'm bounced around against the walls and the glass canopy. I grip the seats in front of me with all of my strength. My hands immediately turn numb from the cold. As it turns out, while I was looking for the Predator, Busimanolotome was snapping a climbing hook-- a carabiner-- around his belt which was knotted to the same rope that was keeping me from falling out of the airplane. And hoisting the Stinger missile lodged between his legs in the front seat onto his shoulder.

"Are you fucking kidding me?" I try to scream above the unbelievably loud roar of the engine and the eerie cry of the wind.

The old man is scooting up onto the back of his seat so that he can get his head and the missile on his shoulder up above the windshield. The rushing blast of frigid air lifts the Stinger from his shoulder just as he pulls the trigger. The cockpit is suddenly full of smoke and just as suddenly free of it as the missile races upward into the sky, leaving a looping vertical contrail behind it.

Busimanolotome throws the smoking box the missile came in over the side of the plane before falling back into his seat. He reaches up, pulls the canopy shut and tries to follow the Stinger's flight path through the glass canopy. I lose track of it.

"Where'd it go?" I shout.

"Incoming!"

It's Nokosee and he's staring wild-eyed at the radar display. It shows a flashing light closing in on the center of the screen.

"Roll!" Busimanolotome yells.

Nokosee turns the plane hard and suddenly the Everglades is above me and I'm falling against the canopy and all kinds of crap is landing on top of me as I look out and see a missile rush by.

"Goddammit!" Busimanolotome shouts, "they're shooting Hellfire missiles at us!"

Nokosee brings the Micco out of the roll and points the nose skyward.

"Sky Eyes, fetch me another Stinger."

"What?"

"Behind you, give me one of those boxes!"

Oh my God. I swear this is really getting out of hand.

"Nokosee, get us higher!"

"But, dad, we're already at the limit!"

"Do it!"

Nokosee pulls back on the wheel and the little Micco groans as it claws its way upward for more altitude. I pick up a long black box that looks like it might be used to send someone flowers you'd like to see killed and hold it up toward Busimanolotome.

"Is this one?"

I guess it is since he doesn't say anything, just rips it from my hands and assembles it to the firing mechanism.

"Hold on," he says.

He throws open the canopy and once again all hell breaks loose inside the cabin as he scoots up onto his seat and aims the second Stinger. But this time the engine starts to sputter and backfire.

"Dad!"

"Don't rush me!"

A moment later he pulls the trigger and the Stinger explodes from its box and quickly rises heavenward on an arcing trail of fire and smoke. Again Busimanolotome dismantles the box the missile came in and throws it over the side of the plane before falling back into his seat. But this time he doesn't close the canopy as he continues to watch the missile's contrail shrink in size until it can no longer be seen. Moments pass. I don't think I can take the cold and the wind battering me around much longer when suddenly, high above the open canopy and star filled sky, I see a tiny explosion.

"Yes!" Busimanolotome shouts. He reaches up and slides the canopy back and locks it tightly. "I can't believe they mounted Hellfire missiles on it!"

"Dad, what do you expect? They know you got Stingers!"

"Hell, I'm just a simple pagan cave man!"

"Nokosee!" I slap him across the back of the head. The old man is quoting something I only say to Nokosee usually in our most intimate moments.

Busimanolotome laughs and turns to me. "Hell, Sky Eyes, he's told me everything about you."

"Nokosee!" Another slap.

"Not everything," Nokosee shouts while trying to fend off any blows with his hand while flying the airplane.

"I'll admit I had my doubts about you," Busimanolotome says to me, "but after today..."

He extends his hand to me. I've never seen him this happy and as much as I hate to admit it, it's catching. I guess the euphoria of shooting down something you can barely see while escaping death by just inches has a way of doing that to you. I have no reservations about shaking his hand and grab his with as much gusto as any man might. He shakes it hard.

"Welcome to the family," he says. "You're as crazy-brave as any of us. Now high five."

He holds his hand up and I gladly give him a high five. He turns to Nokosee.

"High five!"

Nokosee turns from checking his instruments, looks at his dad and slaps his palm.

"To paraphrase Iron Eyes Cody," Busimanolotome says, "It's a good day to be alive."

"Uh, Mr. O, I think you mean Chief Dan George."

"What?"

"Iron Eyes Cody was the crying Indian."

"And he wasn't even Indian," Nokosee adds.

"Yeah," I say, "he was Italian."

"Hey, you're right," Busimanolotome says. "*Little Big Man,* right?"

"Right. It's one of my dad's favorite movies."

"Yeah, your old man's got some things right."

"Yeah, I guess."

"Say, Sky Eyes, how would you like to be the Chosen One?"

"I thought you already had one."

"Nokosee? Nah, I'm talking about you."

I sigh and pretend it's a real imposition. "What for this time? I mean there are a lot of people who want a piece of me now that I'm famous and--"

"Like me!" Nokosee yells with a raise of his hand.

Busimanolotome and I slap Nokosee, the old man across his hand, me aside his head.

"Seriously, Sky Eyes," Busimanolotome continues, "you could be the face of the Outside for the Inside, for the NS. It would position us as an organization that embraces multiculturalism "

"Position?" "Embraces?" "Multiculturalism?" Who is this guy, Dr. Phil?

That notion and those choice of words catch Nokosee and me by surprise. Dumfounded, neither of us know what to say and are left staring at Busimanolotome with vacant, blinking eyes. He just laughs and starts singing again about flying to the moon and reminds me how much I wanted to send him to the moon one time like Ralph Kramden wanted to send his wife Alice (unless you've been raised by a dad like mine, you won't have a clue about what I'm talking about so just YouTube it). But right now, all I want to do is sing along while picturing myself as "the face of the New Seminole."

Wonder if it comes with a recording contract?

"In other words," I interrupt, singing a little off key because of my chattering teeth, "Hold my hand" and offer him my hand.

Busimanolotome smiles and grabs it. I turn to Nokosee and offer him my other hand.

"In other words," I continue to sing, "Baby, kiss me."

Nokosee grabs my hand, leans back and plants a big wet one on my lips. It's a real kumbaya moment. Any other time it would have made me throw up. But not this time.

By the time it takes to fly back to the hanger dug into the side of the L-6 levee, to the relief of all of us because it's frankly getting kind of awkward, we shake loose of each others hands for solo turns on the song.

Chapter 21
Operation Rory

When we get back that night to a new camp with no name in what I can assume is even deeper in the Everglades, we're given a hero's welcome. All twelve in this little hammock camp thanks to Boom Box are singing along to Queen's "We Are The Champions" as we step off our airboat. Fists are punched high in the air as lighters and matches are lit to show solidarity to The Cause. As we are lifted onto shoulders which cuts our welcoming crowd by half, I try not to think about the lyrics because as much as I want to, I can't help but think we're not "champions of the world." If anything, maybe "for the moment" and hopefully longer, much longer than poor skinny shirtless rock star Freddie Mercury's short-lived life, a man who's voice and music I came to love thanks this time to my mom and the childish thought that because we shared important dates-- he died on my birthday, November 24-- we were in some way linked in spirit. But right now, at the top of the crowd, no matter how small it is, it's good to be the champion of something.

I see Mrs. O and Gerrycurl standing off to the side. They're not singing, just watching. When we're set on the ground I turn to see if I can find them. They're gone, melted into the dark hammock jungle. I don't get it. You'd think they'd be happy to see us again. I mean, we could have been killed. Maybe she's still pissed off at Mr. O and the failure to pull off Operation Disney World. I couldn't tell you because we haven't spoken since she sewed-up my "honeymoon scar."

Which is bleeding again. Probably started when I was lifted into the air. My White Badge of Courage is slowly turning into a Red Badge of Courage.

While we were "on mission," a tent was set up for us away from the others. Mr. O says it's best for the camp since no one can get any sleep what with all of our screaming and moaning. I tell you, this guy is starting to make me self-conscious about doing it. And he's also making me appreciate even more something the Outside offers the Inside doesn't: solid walls.

In any event, Nokosee and I start doing it again as soon as we get inside the tent. Mr. O's rough edged delivery of the truth as he sees it didn't put the kibosh on our natural desire to screw each others brains out. Maybe it had something to do with the fact that we are riding an adrenaline high having just escaped death by Hellfire missile.

The next day, towards dusk as the NS prepare to decamp in order to keep one step ahead of the "enemy," Gerrycurl appears out of nowhere.

"Jesus, Gerrycurl, you nearly gave me a heart attack!"

"Sorry. Is Nokosee here?"

Aside from scaring the living bejesus out of me, this is the first time since Nokosee and I got married that she's even bothered to have anything to do with me so I've got my guard up.

"No. He's having a pow-wow with your father."

"Mind if I help?"

"Thanks, but I'm getting pretty good at this."

She doesn't say anything, just stands there looking at me as I fold the tent. She's cute, skinny, in the middle of turning into a woman and reminding me just by her presence as she stands there in her traditional two-piece Seminole dress that she's less than four years younger than me, something I find hard to believe.

Pregnant at 17 has a way of doing that to you.

I can't remember the last time I saw her smile.

Was it at your wedding?

After an uneasy moment passes I ask if there is anything I can do for her. She kneels beside me.

"I want to go to Miami Beach."

I don't know what to say but she saves me the task of searching for words.

"I don't want to live here anymore."

Tears start filling her big brown eyes.

"Please get Nokosee to take me there."

Her body shakes and she does her best to stop crying but she can't. I surprise myself by reaching out to her to hold her but she pushes me away and wipes the tears away from her face.

Boy, can I relate to that. That's what we do when raised by daddies like ours.

"Gerrycurl, please--"

"I hate my name! It's not even a real name."

I reach out for her again. I can't believe she's a spy anymore, I can't believe she's acting. "C'mere," I say. She won't so I grab her and bring her close to me. "Let me hold you." She won't. "I need to hold you. Please." She gives in, slowly. We hug and all the pent up frustration and anger she has been holding inside erupts in deep convulsive crying.

"Cry all you want to, sister," I say soothingly. "I know the feeling."

"Do you want to leave here too?

"Sometimes. A lot of times."

Maybe she's only feeling you out for her dad?

I push her away to look at her face. They're real tears, alright. Her cheeks are covered with them and those convulsions, if they're faked, this girl deserves an Oscar.

"So why don't you?" she asks.

"Nokosee." It came out of me just like that, so fast, that it surprises even me.

I hope the baby comes out just as fast.

"Aren't you afraid of dying?"

"Yes."

"That's all I think about."

I can't say the same for me. All the love making kind of takes the edge off of it. I'm like an addict, I guess, using *it* to make me high, to make me forget.

"Why Miami Beach?"

"I've never seen the ocean. I want to see it before I die."

"Good-golly, sister, you gotta stop thinking like that. They'll be plenty of time for you to see the ocean."

"No there won't."

I don't know what to say to her probably because I think she might be right. But as I look at her, I kinda think no matter what I say, she won't stop believing she's doomed. So I say this:

"Okay, let me talk to Nokosee."

"I don't want to come back."

Okay, now that could be a problem.

"Geese, I don't know if I can--"

"You can drop me off at my aunt's in Hialeah."

"Hialeah?"

The town's seal shows a traditional Seminole in his coat/dress with one arm extended, pointing to... something. Nokosee told me Mr. O said it had a major influence on his plan of reclaiming the Outside. Seems growing up

more or less on the roadside, i.e., Tamiami Trail, and getting bussed to the
nearest schools at that time meant going to school in Hialeah where every day
for over a decade he had to pass one or more signs featuring the city seal. After
a while, he began to believe his ancestors were using it to communicate their
wishes re The Cause which he initially resisted "listening to" until he entered
his Viet Nam War period where he had an epiphany and finally learned to see
the world as he sees it today. Upon his return to the states, he embraced the
"teachings of the seal" which, according to him, is a warning to the Outside "to
get out of here." Only decades later did he begin to formulate a "rationale" for
The Cause based on the science built on the accidental discovery of a monkey
in a cage in Italy about a decade ago and how it reacted to a human stealing
his peanuts: that we are soft wired to experience another's plight as if we are
experiencing it ourselves, i.e. all of us, because of our genetics, are
predisposed to care about others, to show empathy. Of course, Mr. O, like
most ego maniacal saviors, uses only the stuff that makes his grandiose and
dangerous scheme palatable to the masses. Since it was discovered that we are
NOT soft wired for aggression, violence, and self-interest but rather for
sociability, affection, and companionship, he was astute enough to tap the
latter and package The Cause in "green" wrapping paper tied up with a bow
made of the New Seminole colors as a "return to the earth movement" that
embraces the "re-wilding" ideas espoused by Dan Vitalis and inclusion. Failure
to mention "by any means necessary" is a fine print kind of thing that is never
acknowledged.

"Mom wants me outta here."

"Sounds like Operation Disney World."

"Only if you and Nokosee don't want to come back. Anyway, we need to
get me outta here as soon as possible because I don't think I'm going to be
able to take it anymore. And dad mustn't know."

That goes without saying.

"Gerry--" I stop short. "I don't know what to call you."

"Call me Lorelai. Or Rory."

"Like in *Gilmore Girls*?"

"Exactly. I love that show."

"Me too."

Rory wipes her tears away and finally smiles.

"She's afraid she's going to die?" Nokosee asks.

"Yep. Aren't you?"

He sighs. "A little."

"Me, too. A lot."

Nokosee starts doing that male Osceola thing, staring off into space. After awhile, I grow impatient and interrupt him.

"So? What are we going to do?" I ask.

He sighs again. "I guess sis and I are going to Miami Beach."

"Wrong."

"What?"

"I'm going with you."

"And put the baby in harm's way? I don't think so."

"Trust me, the baby will be safer in Miami Beach than out here in the swamp what with the Feds and the U.S. Army trying to kill us for what we did on our wedding night."

Nokosee doesn't know what to say and I'm pretty sure by now he knows venturing into that male chauvinist world he was reared in to justify ordering me to stay behind is not worth seeing my scary side.

"Okay," he finally says. "If that's what you want."

"That's what I want. If it makes you feel any better, you can protect me."

"Ha, that's a good one. If anything, the Outside is going to need protection from you."

"Trust me, Nokosee. I won't get in the way."

"You'll never get in the way."

He grabs me by the back of my head and brings my mouth to his. We kiss.

"Besides," he says when we part, "you know the Outside better than I do."

"True. So how are we going to get from here to Miami Beach?"

"We're gonna borrow an NS safe car and drive there."

"Oh, now I see. You want *me* to drive the," I pause to add air quotes, "'safe car'."

"*No*, I'll be driving. You'll be looking good in the seat next to me."

"You can drive?"

"Of course I can drive. What do you think I am, some kinda pagan caveman?"

Only in bed.

"You got a driver's license?"

"I doan need no stinkin' driver's license to drive."

"Right, I forgot, The Great Nokosee doesn't need no stinkin' permission from anybody."

"That's not true, Stormy," he says while putting his hand on my shoulder. "I need it from you."

I tell you, this guy has a way of ambushing me with this love crap all the time and like any good ambush if done right, the attackee is caught off guard like I am right now. I basically don't know what to say.

"Was that in the wedding vows," I tentatively ask, "because I think I missed it?"

"You had to be listening closely because the Shaman kinda rushed through that part but it was there."

"Nice. Too bad our vows weren't in English. Are there any other things I might have missed?"

"A few, mostly about being my sex slave and honoring all of my fantasies, but we don't need to go into that right now."

"Why? Is it lengthy?"

"That's what she said."

I wasn't trying to be funny, it just came out that way. I smile and caution him with my raised index finger. "Remember, Nooksy, you need *my* permission."

Nokosee smiles, drops his head, and, with a deep resigned sigh, shakes it sadly.

"Now, regarding the plan, is there anything in it that covers the possibility of us getting stopped by the cops when the Great Nokosee is driving along without a license?"

Nokosee reaches into the back pocket of his jeans, yanks out a wallet and pulls out what looks like his driver's license.

"What's this?" he says.

I take it and look at it. It's his face but somebody else's name and address.

"'Norberto Hernandez?'" I turn to Nokosee. "Don't you think this is the kind of stuff a wife should know *before* her wedding, Norberto?"

He smiles, takes it back and stuffs it into his wallet.

"I didn't say I didn't have a license. I just don't *need* one."

"Why Norberto Hernandez?"

"I speak Spanish so it won't be a problem passing me off as a Cuban which is like more than half the population here. Plus, it's symbolic."

"'Symbolic?'"

"Norberto Hernandez is believed to be 'The Falling Man' in that famous 9/11 photo of a guy falling from the Twin Towers. Dad sees it as a metaphor for the eventual fall of the Outside."

It appears Busimanolotome sees "signs" everywhere and everything is up for grabs for exploiting for The Cause.

"So," I say with a roll of my eyes, "we're gonna check out the ocean and then drop Rory off at her aunt's in Hialeah. Right?"

"'Rory'?" he asks.

"That's her new name."

"Really? I guess I missed the memo on that."

"I'll fill in the bullet points later. Just tell me if that's the plan."

"That's the plan."

"And?"

He pauses, looks at me. "I don't know. Return to the swamp?"

Now it's my turn to sigh. I cock my head and squint before saying, "I don't know."

"Don't know what?"

"Don't know if it's such a good idea to come back here."

"Because of all the shit going down?"

"Like, *yeah*."

He turns away and starts to slip back into that Osceola thing again but I stop it fast.

"Well? What's it going to be? I mean, you've been thinking about it, right?" I ask pointedly.

"I can't imagine living in the Outside."

"I can."

"That's because you're pregnant. You're thinking about the baby."

"Damn right. Plus, I've lived there and it ain't as bad as your dad says it is. At least we don't have to worry about the U.S. Army trying to kill us."

"Yeah, I hear you."

I wonder.

"So?"

"Do I have to make a decision now?"

"No," I say after some consideration. "You can sleep on it."

I know it's a big decision for a guy who's been groomed to be the First of the New Seminole and all so there's no need to pressure him into giving me an answer. The last thing I want to do is to push him so far he shuts the idea down completely. As for me, I've thought about it a lot lately especially after spending my aborted honeymoon night sleeping with my in-laws and wondering if we really could have pulled off Operation Disney World and made our escape to the Outside. Living with Nokosee in the swamp is one thing, living in the swamp with Nokosee while the entire U.S. armed forces and its alphabet soup of government agencies are trying to kill us is quite another. When Tammy Wynette urges women to "stand by your man," I think she would cut us chicks some slack on this one.

Later I decide it's best that Nokosee doesn't get a lot of time to think about making off with his sister to Miami Beach and beyond. With a little cajoling from me, I suggest we do it now, tonight while we're breaking camp and traveling across the Everglades to find more hammocks to hide in instead of putting it off until we're so far out in the middle of nowhere it becomes impossible. And besides, I explain to Nokosee, his dad won't grow suspicious-- if it's possible-- if we're all traveling together as part of the NS's nightly exodus. He agrees and with Rory joining us this time around, it's not all that eyebrow raising.

Except maybe we don't take Nokosee's airboat. If a cop or some governmental dude saw an airboat with a big machine gun mounted on it, that just might raise a few suspicions, don't you think? So we switch airboats with another NS warrior whose airboat is less conspicuous. When the old man asks about that, Rory surprises us by speaking up and saying the machine guns make her nervous. He doesn't say anything as he pauses, sighs and turns away. I mean, what could he say, right? The girl has been traumatized for crying out loud. Who wouldn't believe her? Hell, even I'm a little bit blown away by it all. If I wasn't crazy in love with Nokosee, I'm sure I'd be joining her and who knows, maybe I just might.

Within minutes Rory and me are sitting in the bench seat below Nokosee as he guides us with the NS "fleet" that includes other airboats and swamp buggies from other hammocks deeper into the Everglades night. I'm holding Rory tight as she looks at her mother across the water for one last time. Mrs. O shows no emotion as she turns away. Rory, on the other hand, starts crying as her dad guns his airboat and is swallowed up by the night, save for the little green fluorescent glow stick hanging from the back of his seat.

Nokosee slows down and then drifts behind a hammock to hide. Once stopped, he reaches back and yanks the glow stick off of his airboat and jumps down into the hull where we undress and put on some Outside "reconnaissance" clothes. When we're ready to go, Nokosee climbs back up into the driver's seat, puts on his night vision goggles, and starts the motor. He checks his GPS and slowly emerges from behind the hammock and heads towards Tamiami Trail somewhere south of us. Within minutes we're in the north side canal paralleling the Trail. Since the road is unlit and rarely used now that Alligator Alley is open, trailing the Trail unseen is easy to do. Still, we're so far west and since we can't speed in case there are other watercraft in the canal, it takes us a while to get to our destination point, a little town called Copeland just north of the Trail about 50 miles west of Miami, which is to say, we still have a long way to go. Copeland lies between the western border of the Big Cypress National Preserve and the Fakahatchee Strand to the east. Less than 300 people live there, mostly outdoors men and tomato farmers. And one friend of the New Seminole.

After tying the airboat to an overlying invasive Brazilian pepper bush along the canal next to some airboats, we climb the embankment and follow County Road 837 into beautiful downtown Copeland. Traipsing around at night is easy since there aren't any streetlights but that doesn't stop me from looking up at the sky. Despite shooting down one drone, I can't help but think the Feds already got another one or two up there to take its place.

Nokosee's been here before, so there's no need for a map. We turn into a dead quiet nondescript mobile home park and within minutes, Nokosee is cautioning Rory and me to lay back in the shadows as he walks up to a weather-worn trailer tied to the earth with big steel chains wrapped across its roof and embedded in a thick concrete pad beneath its wheels. It looks like it belongs to someone who's been through a hurricane or two. Nokosee walks up two steps and knocks on the screen door. Somebody opens the inner door.

"What the..."

"Hey, Billy Bob."

"Billy Bob?"

The guy opens the screen door. He's a balding white guy about Mr. O's age, unshaven, wearing a dirty wife-beater over a beer belly. He's got a Budweiser in one hand.

"Nokosee, what the hell are you doing here?"

"Nice to see you too," Nokosee says.

"The FBI has been out here a couple of times. They know I know your father."

"Think you're being watched?"

"Probably."

"Then you don't want me standing out here on your doorstep any longer than I have too. We need to borrow the van."

"No problem."

He reaches behind the door and grabs the van's keys.

"Here you go." He gives Nokosee the keys. "Bring it back with a full tank."

"No problem. If dad calls, you don't know nothing. Okay?"

"I know nothing.'"

Just like Sargent Schultz.

"Thanks. See you later."

And just like that, we have some wheels.

Billy Bob stores the NS van on his property behind the trailer next to his swamp buggy. It's not much to look at and that's a good thing because the last thing we want is drawing the attention of the cops. The tinted windows are a plus. Before driving out onto the Trail and heading due east, Nokosee switches the license plate-- enclosed by a "Life Member" NRA chrome frame-- with another one lying in the van. I also discover the van's hiding an AK-47 under a beach towel.

I feel so much safer now.

Nokosee has stuffed his long hair inside his shirt collar. I'm riding shotgun, my Mohawk now lying flat across my tats. I look at Rory sitting in the middle bench seat and staring at the world as it goes by. She's no longer looking like she stepped out of an old faded and spotted black and white photograph showing her ancestors posing along the Tamiami Trail in their traditional garb. Right now, she could fit in anywhere in the Outside.

Almost an hour has passed when we pass the lonely memorial to ValuJet Flight 592 that crashed into the Everglades in 1996. 110 concrete pillars of differing size for each person aboard the jet point to the actual crash site 8 miles north. It brings back memories of that one unforgettable night my dad drove our airboat to a place in the Everglades I had never been before. We had been gigging for frogs, an act that involves sweating, sliding silently up on the critters in your airboat, sweating, blinding them with a light, sweating, spearing them with a three-pronged trident, sweating, and hauling them in. Trust me, I hated every second of it but it was dad's way of showing he loved me. Go figure, right? Anyway, I thought we were finally on our way home when he stops the airboat, turns off the light, and says "this is hallowed ground" and commences to tell me the horror story. You never would have known such unimaginable violence had happened on that fateful day because the place was indistinguishable from the rest of the swamp. The jet had just taken off from MIA when within minutes it nosedived into the swamp at over 500 miles-per-hour. Dad said it was hard to find anything. It was as if the Everglades had opened up and swallowed it whole. He told me children were on that flight and then he stopped talking. Without the airboat light on and knowing the place's history, it gave me the creeps. I couldn't wait to get out of there. When he fired up the airboat and drove off, I can't tell you how relieved I was because I thought we were finally heading home. Then he drove up to the memorial. At midnight. It was erected alongside the Trail's canal in 1999 and was meant to be seen and visited during the day because it has no lights. During the day, the 110 blocks look like a modernist cemetery with nothing explaining what they are to anyone passing by but in the full moon's light which heightened the disquieting experience, those 110 blocks took on a whole new meaning for me. I was shocked and dismayed to see they had been tagged with graffiti. Dad was livid. While he was cussing and kicking the dirt in frustration, he missed the single most important change in me since I had my first period (which he also missed because of the divorce): the chip I was growing on my shoulder had flowered and taken over my whole body. On that night, I became permanently pissed-off at the world. Busimanolotome says that's a prerequisite to becoming a New Seminole and he's doing his best in "channeling my anger into pulling the trigger," something I don't think will ever happen because I'm in it for Nokosee and the baby, not The Cause.

Later Busimanolotome filled in the missing parts of the horror story. He says greed brought the jet down because a company that serviced the airline was cutting corners on safety to save money. He also said the Outside should get use to these kinds of things as we enter the Age of Aquarius (approximately 2,150 years) where the earth, now out of balance due to man's careless stewardship, tries to correct itself and to cleanse itself. He said the most notable example of this cosmic shift was the Exxon Valdez oil spill in 1989, an environmental catastrophe brought on by a drunken captain. It was the earth's first wake-up call to the Outside, to get it's attention and to clean up its act-- the second one was the fall of the Berlin Wall later that year. When nothing changed, when conspicuous consumption and exploitation were still propelling the Outside, Busimanolotome took it upon himself to step in to make the corrections necessary to enter the Age of Aquarius.

"So," I say with my hand raised under a chickee's thatched roof during one of the brainwashing-- excuse me-- brain*storming* sessions in which all the NS participate in, "we got like over 2,000 years to save the earth, right?"

Busimanolotome sighs. "Theoretically."

"So why are we in such a hurry? I've heard of 'proactive,' but taking on the US Army is kinda crazy."

This makes the NS "warriors" sitting around me uncomfortable and causes The Micco to sadly shake his head.

"Holatte-Sutv Turwv, it may seem like we're in a hurry to you but I've been thinking about this since 1979, ten years after seeing *Hair* on Broadway."

Busi did Broadway?

I look at Nokosee who is sitting next to me. He's surprised too.

"I didn't really start acting on it for another 10-years. So, you can't say I'm rushing into anything. Trust me, little girl, I've given this lots of thought."

"I'm sure you did but so did Hitler."

"Ay-yi-yi," Nokosee says in frustration. He turns away and looks at nothing. I ignore him. I've got a point to prove to the old man.

"1979? That's the same year 'Forest Man' started planting trees."

Now Nokosee is sighing. I punch him in the arm without looking at him.
"Ow!"

Nokosee's heard my rant on this before but his dad hasn't and this seems like the perfect moment so, as Nokosee rubs his arm, I continue pressing my point.

"You've heard of the guy, right?"

"'Forest Man'?" Busimanolotome asks with one arched eyebrow. "Can't say that I have."

"He's an Indian-- you know, the kind that live in India-- who started single-handedly planting trees on a barren sandbar in the middle of a lake. He still goes out there every day and plants a tree or some kinda plant. His forest is now about twice as big as Central Park. Just think of what you could have accomplished if you had chosen that path instead of this one. Unlike you, he's a frigging hero over there, gets all kinds of medals and stuff for what he's doing."

Silence. Except for the uncomfortable rustling of NS butts on the log floor.

Busimanolotome points to the Purple Heart in the center of his bandana holding two eagle feathers. "Does he got one of these?" he asks with a wide crazed look in his eyes, like Jack Nicholson's "Here's Johnny!" from *The Shining*. But I ain't no Shelley Duvall.

"Ay-yi-yi." That's all he's going to get from me. I give up. There is no reasoning with him.

Forty-five minutes and about a thousand paranoid glances in our rear view mirrors later we're crossing Biscayne Bay on the MacArthur Causeway heading toward Miami Beach. The City of Miami at night looks stunning sitting on the water with towering new condo towers crowding Biscayne Boulevard. Too bad Nokosee has been taught that they look better as a large pile of rubble. PortMiami, home to the largest cruise ship port in the world, is to our right, bereft of vessels at the moment since it's the weekend and they're all out to sea. To our left, private islands with multimillion dollar mansions dotting the bay between mainland Miami and Miami Beach. Traffic slows to a crawl. Club-goers from the mainland are driving in to party down at the clubs in SoBe, an acronym for South Beach. It's around 10pm, an ominous time for me based on past experiences but nothing gets started earlier in this town until midnight. It's crazy.

Rory sits up as we get closer to the clubs along Washington Ave. The street is swarming with young people dressed in all the latest fashions. Although most of the young men look like losers wearing their ghetto inspired t-shirts and clown pants, the women are chic, high of heel and skirt. We have to laugh when some of the girls try to cross the street in their stilettos and agree that they should have spent more time practicing in front of a mirror before taking it public.

Nokosee turns north onto Ocean Drive. On our right, the Atlantic Ocean, barely visible beyond the hundred yards of freshly pumped up beach sand. To our left, row after row of re-born neon-lit Art Deco hotels and their accompanying nightclubs, restaurants and sidewalk cafes. The sidewalk is swollen with all kinds of pedestrians, some dressed for the clubs, others dressed for the beach. Loud Latin music competes with thumping hip hop beats. A few drunks are staggering between cars parked on both sides of the street and crossing dangerously between the stop-and-go traffic. I look at Rory. It seems she's becoming more alive, as if she's absorbing the energy of the street. I smile.

"It never fails," Nokosee says.

"What?'

"I always find a parking spot," he says as a car pulls out in front of him.

"How many times have you been here?" I ask.

"Never," he says as he flips on his turn signal.

"So you're one for one. Trust me, it's a lot more difficult when you live here."

"Can't you be happy for me?" Nokosee asks as he drives ahead of the spot to back in.

I look at him. He's smiling. I have to laugh.

A horn honks. He hits the brakes and we lunge forward. We check our mirrors. Some Jap sports car is trying to inch into the space. I look at Nokosee. He's got a tight smile on his face and continues to inch slowly backward. The driver behind us leans on the horn.

"Nokosee, it's not worth it."

"Yes it is."

"You'll blow our cover."

Bumper meets bumper, the van shakes, but continues to move slowly backward into the parking space. The driver behind us stops honking his horn so he can shift quickly into reverse and backs into bumper to bumper traffic creating a mad symphony of irate horn honking. When we're parked, the guy in the Jap sports car pulls up alongside us yelling and cursing at us in Spanish. Three other guys are with him, adding a chorus of curses of their own. Nokosee starts to lower the side window and I grab his hand.

"Nokosee, don't."

Nokosee does. But he doesn't say anything to them. He just stares balefully, something it appears he's picked up from his crazy old man. This does not go down well with the hot heads. They take it as a dissing of their manhood and proves to me that less isn't always more. But none of them is ready to step out and go mano y mano either with Nokosee. Thankfully cars are backing up behind them and their angry and frustrated drivers, leaning hard on their horns, encourage the hotheads to make the right decision which is to move along because, let's face it, Nokosee would have made mince meat of them. As they smoke their tires, we're given the four bird salute, one from each side window.

"You know, Nokosee, if we're going to pull off 'Operation Rory,' we gotta be as inconspicuous as possible. Getting into a fight with some yahoos on Ocean Drive isn't the way to do it."

"I know," he says while rolling up the window and watching the car drive off, "but I have a real problem with assholes."

"So do I, but this isn't the time to address those issues."

He looks at me.

"'Address those issues?'"

"Lots of high school counseling. Sorry."

A thin smile grows across his face as he grabs some change to feed the parking meter.

"C'mon. Let's go see the freaking ocean."

Chapter 22
The Freaking Ocean, Drug Dealers & More

It's big. The neon lights along Ocean Drive give the waves breaking softly on the beach a luminous, other-worldly vibe as we walk barefoot through the water, our Crocs and Doc Martens held in our hands. Nokosee and I have our free arms wrapped around each other as Rory walks ahead of us, hands dug deep into the pockets of her jeans. She stops to examine a blue Man-O-War that has washed up on the beach. When she starts to reach for it I tell her to stop, don't touch it unless, of course, she doesn't mind getting stung. By the way Nokosee looks at me, I get the feeling brother and sister were never taught about anything beyond the Inside. For their safety I suggest we sit on the beach to watch the waves. Rory settles between us. Nokosee and I exchange glances. I smile, he rolls his eyes and all three of us start watching the waves curl lazily, hypnotically in front of us. Because of the overpowering sound of the sea at our feet and the width of the reconstructed beach, we're far enough away from Ocean Drive so that we can hardly hear any music, horns honking, or drunks yelling. It's like we've been transported to a far away tropical paradise, a place much more tropical and much more paradisier than Miami Beach. After about twenty minutes of watching the waves and the occasional strollers walking barefoot through the foam cast shore, Nokosee says to nobody in particular, "My dad says in less than 50 years there won't be any beach."

I sigh and shake my head. Anytime Nokosee begins a sentence with "My dad says," I know it has something to do with 'the science behind The Cause.'"

"Global warming, right?"

"Yep. Besides the rising oceans, he says more ships are sinking every year because global warming is making monster waves everywhere."

"Nokosee?" Rory whispers.

"Yeah?"

"Could you please *shut the fuck up?*"

"Excuse me?"

"You're ruining my moment. Just once I'd like to appreciate the world the way it is and not the way it's supposed to be or will be."

"Sorry."

He looks at me and rolls his eyes until he sees I'm on Rory's side. He turns away with a sigh and looks at the black ocean-- now lying in wait in all of our minds-- ready to pounce without warning to drown us all. Rory gets to appreciate the world the way it is for about 15 more minutes before Nokosee asks, "So, what's next?"

"What do you mean?" I ask.

"How much longer are we gonna sit here watching waves?"

"As long as Rory wants to," I say. "What, are you *bored?*"

Nokosee sighs and looks away. I look at Rory. She's staring at the ocean, tears welling up in her eyes and doing her best not to cry. I put my arm around her and pull her closely. She rests her head on my shoulder and cries louder. Nokosee hears her and turns to look. I catch his eye and give him my own version of the Osceola baleful stare. He looks embarrassed and turns away. A moment passes before he shifts in closer to his sister, puts his arm around her and gives her a squeeze.

So what's next?

That's a good question. I wish I had an answer. Dropping Rory off at her aunt's won't solve the bigger problems for her. Living without her parents and brother around her won't be easy, especially since that's all the people she's known for most of her life. Knowing that mom and dad might die a horrible death at any minute isn't something easy to come to grips with either.

This is how the Apaches led by Geronimo must have felt.

Another epiphany. I never know when they're coming, never thought of what it must have been like for his small tribe of renegades-on-the-run. The pictures of him and his group always make me sad. They look so poor and desperate, so out-numbered and out-gunned and not a chance in the world.

Yeah, that's us alright. It's déjà vu all over again.

After he calms down and stops breaking heads and kicking trees, maybe something can be worked out with Micco Meshugana where all of us can visit Rory once in awhile. I don't really know. I can only hope that Mr. O learns to accept that this is the best thing for his daughter. I'm also hoping Mrs. O is doing what she agreed to do by telling him now so he gets all the yelling, kicking, and stomping over with before Nokosee and I return.

If we return.

The more I think about it, the more I feel sorry for the kid. I give her a hug and kiss the top of her head.

"You know, Rory," I say, "I think things will turn out alright for everybody."

"You wish," she says softly.

"We could visit you on weekends."

She stops crying, pauses, and then looks at me as if I was crazy. So does her brother.

"Pinche pendejo, voy a matarte!"

A coconut hits Nokosee's shoulder and before I know it, he's up and facing the four hotheads descending on us from Ocean Drive. It appears they still haven't gotten over losing their parking space.

"No esa ojete," Nokosee replies in a steady, calm voice as he frees his hair from the bondage of the shirt collar.

Rory and I jump to our feet and stand behind Nokosee.

"¡Que te follen!" the driver yells.

He's running through the sand toward Nokosee with a raised fist. When he swings, Nokosee catches it nicely and diverts the guy into the sand. But he doesn't let go, instead he twists the man's arm while blindly kicking out his leg at the second guy on him, catching him squarely in the face. Second Guy drops to his knees in the sand crying and grabbing his bleeding mouth, trying to keep his busted teeth from falling out of his hands and getting lost in the sand. Third Guy grabs Nokosee's outstretched leg and throws him backward but Nokosee still doesn't let go of First guy's arm. When First Guy's arm breaks at the wrist, a loud girly-mon scream races across the sand as Nokosee rolls with the attacker and lands on his back. Third guy tries to land some punches on Nokosee but my man won't keep his head in one place so he can do it. Nokosee knees him in the balls which brings him to his knees and close enough for my lean-mean-killing-machine to put him out of his misery with a head butt that knocks him unconscious. Unfortunately, before Nokosee can push him off, Fourth Guy is standing over them and pulling his unconscious buddy out of the way so he can shoot him.

"Nokosee, he's got a gun!" I shout.

As Nokosee tries to keep unconscious guy Number Three between him and gun wielding guy Number Four, that's when I step in with a nicely placed kick with my gold lamé DMs to the side of gun guy's knee. He screams, shoots his unconscious buddy in the back, grabs his knee, and falls beside Nokosee. Nokosee doesn't give him a chance to get off another shot when he grabs the guy's gun and turns it outward and upward. Although it fires again, this time into the sky, the shooter's trigger finger has been broken which unleashes another round of Spanish cursing and crying like a leetle baby. And, if you want to know, I feel exhilarated. In less time than it took me to slay the White

City Giant, Team Osceola has put four attackers away and given them permanent injuries-- one possibly fatal as a by-product of screwing with us-- that will remind them for the rest of their pathetic mercurial and possibly short lives to think twice before losing it on people they don't know.

"Are you alright?" I ask as I help Nokosee roll the guy with the bullet in his back onto the sand.

"My God, Stormy," Nokosee says as I help him to his feet, "the guy was trying to kill me for crying out loud!" He slips the gun into his waistband because no good NS lets a weapon go to waste. "Is that normal?" he asks while brushing sand off of his clothes. "Does everyone carry a gun around here?"

"No, only one in four. Now let's get out of here before it's too late."

I start to run up the beach when Nokosee grabs my hand and stops me.

"You were pretty fucking-A impressive, Mrs. Osceola!" Nokosee says.

"Thanks. We make a good team. Now let's go."

"Shut up!"

It's Rory, yelling at the guys lying, moaning and crying loudly in the sand. They try their best to obey her, settling into whimpering and blubbering. Apparently, that isn't good enough and she kicks sand in their faces which gets them adding coughing and spitting to their miserable repertoire.

"Whoe, little sister," Nokosee says.

"I'm mad! They messed up my quiet time!"

"Okay, okay," I say, "Calm down, Rory. Let's just get the hell out of here."

When we get back to our van, we see the four assholes had gotten there first. All four tires are flat. Nokosee is fit to be tied.

"Nokosee, what are we going to do?" I ask. "How are we going to get back?"

My answer comes in multilingual cursing and fist pounding on the van's door. I can see he's trying to come up with a plan so I opt to keep quiet. After a moment, he unlocks the door and slides it open, grabs the license tag and wraps it and the AK-47 in the beach towel lying in the back of the van.

"What are you doing?" I ask.

"Covering our tracks." He slams the door shut. "C'mon!"

Rory and I race after him back down the beach.

"Nokosee," I implore, "please don't kill them."

"Don't worry. I've got something else in mind."

The four assholes started crying louder once we left and drew a crowd. Nokosee pushes his way through them and throws a good Samaritan off of the driver who, when he sees Nokosee, screams louder than ever.

"¡Ghiata puto!" Nokosee shouts.

The guy does his best to obey while Nokosee digs into his pockets.

"¿Donde se hizo el parque, hijo de puta?"

"Hey," someone says to me, "aren't you that--"

Before one of the bystanders can finish the question, there's a flash. Someone has snapped a picture of us just as Nokosee rips the car keys and the place he parked from the wincing guy below him. He jumps up and starts out after the guy that took our picture but I hold him back.

"Forget it. We gotta get out of here."

Forty-five minutes later thanks to the car keys and the information Nokosee extricated from the driver where the Jap sports car was parked, we're in Rory's aunt's Hialeah living room looking at ourselves on TV. We're the lead story on the eleven o'clock news. I tell you, it's getting more and more difficult each day trying to be renegades-on-the-run what with smartphones and TV stations making it easier to upload pictures. The only good thing that came out of this is that the four assholes we left broken and bleeding and almost dying on the beach were Colombian drug traffickers on holiday. You'd think seeing them led away in handcuffs and on gurneys might count for something in the bigger scheme of things, right? That we might catch a break from the universe what with all the crap that's been coming down all around us lately? Not a chance. We're the real story on all three local network stations plus Spanish language Telemundo and Univsion with warnings to all viewers that we're possibly armed and surely dangerous.

"Next time we venture forth into the Outside, let's *NOT CALL EACH OTHER BY OUR REAL NAMES!*" I shout.

"Like that matters when they've got our pictures on TV?" Nokosee replies.

"Shut up!"

It's Rory again and she's very frustrated. She walks up to us and starts pushing us out the door.

"Please go! Before the cops get here!"

Nokosee turns to his aunt.

"Remember, tía Maria, when they get here, you had no idea Rory was going to be dropped off."

"Rory?" aunt Maria asks.

"That's my new name!" Rory shouts as she slams the door behind us.

I can't tell you for sure whether or not Mrs. O called her sister in advance about the plan because there's a good chance she thought the phone line was tapped and wouldn't risk it. And/or tía Maria is one hell of an actor. If that's so, tía Maria won't have a problem passing any polygraph tests. One thing she'll be able to truthfully tell the cops is that she didn't know Nokosee had swiped her car keys and had stolen her beat-up Honda Civic because Nokosee didn't tell her. Or me for that matter. I found out outside the small Hialeah home when he pulled me toward her car when I was going toward the stolen drug cartel's car. Of course, it makes sense when the cops are looking for that car and not tía Maria's car. Assuming they're a little slow in making the connection to the aunt, there's a good chance we might just escape.

Plus, how do we know aunt Maria's phone line is tapped anyway? Or that they even know Mrs. O has a sister? Maybe we're just being overly paranoid.

In any case, it's probably better to be safe than sorry.

"Nokosee, I feel like we're abandoning her," I say as we drive along the Palmetto Expressway south to the Tamiami Trail exit.

"I do too."

I look at him. It looks like he's about to cry.

"So what do you think will happen to her?" I ask.

"Well, assuming they find her, the worst thing that could happen is they interrogate her a bit and then let her live with her closest living relative which is tía Maria."

"You don't think they'll want to lock her up? Put her in reform school or something?"

"For what? She never hurt a soul."

"Yeah, but she's the daughter of the guy responsible for all this megadeath crap going down over the last month. I mean, come on, wouldn't you use her to get to him?"

"You mean like a hostage? I don't see that happening. I think it's against the rules or something."

"Let me get this straight. You still expect them to play by the rules after all the laws we broke? I mean, come on, Nokosee, get real."

He doesn't say anything but I can tell he's thinking about it as we exit onto Tamiami Trail, a.k.a Calle Ocho. As we head west, passing one ugly nondescript strip store after another, all lit up with garish neon and fluorescent lighting so you can't miss the litter in their parking lots and signs mostly in Spanish, I wonder as we pass my tattoo shop if it's not too late to re-up our membership in the Outside. I know, it sounds crazy wanting to become part of this landscape, but at least the United States of America isn't trying to kill me or my baby.

"Maybe we shouldn't go back," I say rather tentatively.

"What?"

"We're already here, in the Outside. Maybe we should stay here. You know, melt into the population."

"And do what?"

"Live lives of quiet desperation?"

He looks at me as if I'm crazy.

"It's safer," I offer.

"It sounds boring."

"Boring has its merits. At least people aren't trying to kill you."

After about 5 minutes, I broach the subject once more as the ugly strip stores start looking better and better after we pass a sign notifying us that we have entered the town of Sweetwater, a small burg founded by a troupe of Russian midgets in 1941 and the Outside's last major western outpost before crossing over into the official boundary of the Everglades.

"So, do you wanna pull off the road and start a new life in Sweetwater?"

"For better or worse," Nokosee mumbles. "For better or worse."

"Oh, was that in our wedding vows? I don't remember hearing them. It all sounded like some kinda mystical mumbo jumbo gibberish to me. Anyway, I think getting shot at by Army jets preempts me from putting up with anymore 'worse!'"

Nokosee doesn't say anything, just grips the steering wheel tighter, clenches his jaw, and stares ahead.

A half-hour passes without us speaking to each other. I know we're both trying to figure out what to do and I know it's got to be a lot harder for him than me to see that although the neon light of the Outside world reveals it at its tackiest worst, at least its safer. I keep thinking I'm ready to jump ship at the next stoplight. Unfortunately, there isn't a stoplight for the next five miles as we venture further into the Everglades. When I finally see one, it marks the intersection leading to the Miccosukee gaming resort looming over the Everglades, now long since drained so the Outside could live and prosper. It looks as if Las Vegas has been transplanted in the middle of the swamp, complete with neon lights and the promise of riches. And sex. I look at the top of the hotel for the Presidential Penthouse Suite as we pull up to the light.

"Remember the last time we were here?" I ask, hoping a fond memory will lighten the moment.

"Yeah. Your mom shot me."

"Not that, silly," I reply with a playful tap on the shoulder that took the bullet. "The other thing."

"Hey," Nokosee replies, feigning pain. "It still hurts."

I sadly shake my head and start to roll my eyes as we come to a full stop until I see the following message spelled out in big black plastic letters on a sign below a larger one announcing a weekly car giveaway: *R.I.P J.T. Osceola*. I grab Nokosee's arm and point to the sign.

"Nokosee, what's that supposed to mean?"

Nokosee pauses for a moment and then sighs with a shake of his head.

"J.T.'s dead. Dad killed him."

"What?"

"He blew up with *Osceola's Spear*."

"What are you talking about?"

"The night we left Frank Mills, do you remember the helicopter flying over us?"

"Yes."

"It belonged to the casino. J.T. was in it along with your father."

"My dad?"

"Yeah, but your dad didn't jump down to retrieve the bike. When J.T. touched it, it blew up."

"Your dad booby-trapped it?"

"Unfortunately."

"Why would he do that?"

"Because he's crazy."

I sit back in the seat, stunned with this new revelation. That motorcycle was the only thing Busimanolotome wanted from the Outside. To blow it up makes no sense. To rig it to explode to kill anyone who touched it is sick, beyond anything I can comprehend.

So that explosion was the sound J.T. Osceola made when he blew up. It was loud and fitting for such a man larger than life.

I can't imagine seeing J.T. dead. I can't say we were friends but I knew him for a long time. He and dad would take turns having each other over for dinner. I got to meet his wife and kids. I know they're going to miss him. He didn't deserve to die like that. Had I known then what I know now, this story would have a different ending. Especially if my dad had died with J.T. But of course, I didn't know that muffled, distant explosion was the sound J.T. made when he left this world.

But Nokosee did.

"How long have you known?" I ask, still looking through the windshield at nothing.

"I figured it out the next day when I heard mom and dad going at it."

"When were you planning on telling me?"

"Never. But I promised myself I'd never lie to you either. I don't want you judging me by what my father does."

A moment passes as I try to remember that night and then it hits me.

"You knew it was booby-trapped, didn't you?"

"No, I didn't. I knew the camp was booby trapped, just like all of them are. I didn't find out until the next day that dad had also wired the bike to explode if someone tried to move it."

As much as I want to believe him, I'm finding it hard if not outright impossible. I figure he's had enough time to get his story just right and that no matter what question I have, he'll have a reasonable answer for it. I don't know about you, but murder is a turn off for me. Even if Nokosee didn't set the trap, he was complicit in letting it happen. So was "Mom." By the way she eye-balled her husband that night, you could tell she knew something. I feel sick to my stomach because I know I also have to include myself in this murdering madness: I knew the camps were booby-trapped, not thinking they would kill anybody is no excuse. When the light turns green, I can't make myself throw open the door to make a mad dash to freedom and away from insanity.

Nokosee doesn't say anything and we continue to drive westward in silence until we have to stop because of some kind of road construction.

"Dammit," he says, "this wasn't here when we drove by a couple of hours ago." He starts to roll down the driver's side window.

"Nokosee, what are you doing?"

"I wanna ask this guy what's up?"

He's talking about a county cop brown-shirt wearing a reflective vest and directing traffic with a red-tipped flashlight.

"Do you think that's a good idea?" I don't. I like flying under the radar.

"Just act normal."

"Oh, you mean like I'm scared shitless?"

Nokosee stops the stolen car in front of the cop and without a second thought, starts talking to him in Spanish. The guy leans on the door and looks in the car and at me as if he was the coolest guy around instead of someone standing in the street in the middle of the night with a flashlight in his hand directing traffic. The conversation ends with him and Nokosee tapping fists and calling each other "bro." As we're waved on. I see a huge hole in the east bound lanes thanks to bright industrial strength work lights that have been erected on telescoping poles around the hole's perimeter. A gasoline tanker truck is sticking out of the hole and a torrent of brown muddy water is shooting over it and onto the street. The flashing red, white, blue, and yellow lights of the the fire engines, police cars and county maintenance trucks add more light and excitement to this stretch of wilderness-slicing road than it's seen in decades. Eastbound traffic has been diverted onto our westbound lanes reducing what was once four lanes to two. As we slowly drive by cops sitting in their air-conditioned patrol cars and looking at the glowing words and pictures on their computer screens, I pray no one looks up as we pass. And then one of them looks up as we pass and sees me.

"Oh, man," I whisper as I sink below the window.

"Dad predicted this shit was gonna happen," Nokosee casually remarks as if he hadn't a care in the world while driving slowly by the guys who would be more than happy to arrest us and, if need be, shoot us-- with one hand on the steering wheel and his arm resting on the open window frame. "The Outside would self-destruct because of its crumbling infrastructure. Our job is to hurry it along." He laughs and turns to me. "You know, if that water main had broken a couple of hours earlier, Operation Rory would have been a no-go. Isn't it funny how things turn out?"

"Yeah, real funny." I peek at the side-view mirror. The cop's speaking into the transceiver hanging from the epaulet on his uniform.

"I guess it was meant to be."

"'Meant to be'?" The cop is looking at us, talking.

"Yeah. Like you and me."

The cop hits his lights and a quick piercing siren blast gets Nokosee jumping up and looking in the rear-view mirror.

"You gotta be kidding me!" he yells.

Nokosee guns the car, steers it onto the grassy shoulder, and drives around the cars in front of us, kicking up a cloud of dirt, rocks, and grass. I look back over the seat and see the flashing red, white, and blue police lights hurtling through the dust and smoke toward us. I turn to Nokosee. He's switching back and forth from the rear-view mirror to the sloping "road" in front of us. Me? I'm bouncing around all over the place. When I turn and look through the windshield, Nokosee yanks the steering wheel hard to the left and we're back on the road with a bounce and a trailing cloud of dust. And a cop car. Nokosee floors it and tía Maria's little brown primer spotted Honda Civic pulls away in a high-pitched whine. What the little car lacks in speed is made up for by Nokosee's balls-to-the-wall driving in and out of the cars ahead of us, something the cop with his larger and heavier Ford Crown Victoria won't dare match unless, of course, he doesn't mind taking out innocent citizenry in an effort to catch us. Still, no matter how hard Nokosee pushes the little Honda, we can't shake the cop on our tail.

"Stormy, hold on!"

Nokosee turns the wheel so quickly to the left I don't even get time to say, "What?"

Or grab something to hold onto.

I slam into Nokosee as we turn, cross the strip of land dividing the the east and west bound lanes, bounce across the road, narrowly avoid getting sideswiped by a air-horn-screaming semi, brake, bounce again for good measure, and slide across a gravel parking lot leading to the "world famous" Coopertown Airboat Tour.

"Get out!"

Nokosee throws his door open before the car has stopped and jumps out, taking the AK-47 with him and disappearing beneath the car and the dust storm it kicked up. I throw my door open, look out, see stones and dust getting kicked up by the front wheel, hear the stones slamming against the door and think, *What, am I nuts?*

As it turns out, I am. I jump out and roll across the sharp-edged gravel like I was taught to do by Sensei Steve. Of course, those falls were on a cushioned mat. And I wasn't pregnant. It hurts like hell. When I stop rolling in the dirt and rocks, I'm bleeding all over the fucking place.

"Are you alright?"

I look up. Nokosee is standing over me, wafting in and out of the dust cloud.

"Do I look alright?"

We hear a loud splash and look. Tía Maria's little Honda Civic has rolled off the parking lot into the water. Steam rises from the hot engine and brakes.

Before I can say "Oh, shit," Nokosee has grabbed me up and is carrying me across the parking lot toward a bunch of airboats floating in the water. He picks a nice big black one, steps in and lowers me onto one of the four rows of bench seats.

"Here," he says while handing me the AK-47, "you might need this."

I look at the gun and think, *I don't think so.*

When I turn around to discuss this with him, he's already climbing up into the driver's seat, ripping the ignition wiring out from beneath the seat and hot-wiring the car engine behind us and the big propeller to life. It's so loud I don't hear the police car siren. But I do see its flashing lights across the air boat and on the water. I turn to look.

The car is slipping and sliding across the gravel, kicking up dust and smoke from its burning tires and heading-- more or less-- toward us.

I'm jerked backward in my seat.

"Stormy, untie the boat!"

I look up at Nokosee.

"Hurry!"

I turn quickly around and see the bow rope stretching taut against a wood piling sticking up out of the black water. I grab the top of the bench seat in front of me and carefully move toward the bow. When I get to the rope I can't lift it over the piling because of the tension exerted upon it by the airboat. That's when Nokosee's knife cartwheels past my head and sticks in the piling. I whip around and look back at him with angry eyes baring teeth that are chewing him out. He just shrugs and smiles weakly. I turn back to the knife still vibrating in the piling, angrily yank it out, slash the rope in two-- and promptly fall on my ass as Nokosee banks the airboat hard to the right out of there.

And then bullets start bouncing off the metal hull, ricocheting here and there, trailing sparks like bottle rockets on the 4th of July. I look back through the prop cage and the cop who caught us in the parking lot is now standing behind the open door of his car and firing his Glock at us, the preferred handgun of law enforcement (according to my dad who carries one on his hip when going to work). Behind the trigger happy cop I see more cop cars racing toward us, their lights now clouded by the dust kicked up from the gravel parking lot but I can barely hear their sirens over the roar of the airboat engine. And then the shooting stops. When I look back at the cop who was firing at us, I see he's flat on his back and soaking wet. The prop wash blew him off his feet.

"Yee-*haw!*"

But somewhere the fat lady is still singing.

Aside from being on the wrong side of the law, it turns out we're also on the wrong side of the Tamiami Trail. We need to get onto the other side, the north side if we ever want to get back to our camp du jour. Why? Because there isn't any opening under the Trail to get from here to there. Conservationists have been raising all kinds of hell about it for decades because it stops the free-flow of water and fauna from the northern part of the Everglades to the southern part. As you read this now, the Army Corps of Engineers is finally getting around to solving this problem by adding bridges to the Trail. Unfortunately, they aren't here when you need them, *really* need them because, as I look across the water and sawgrass racing by, there's a convoy of cop cars with lights flashing and sirens wailing keeping pace with us along the Trail.

And then the ricocheting and the 4th of July fireworks start again. They're shooting at us from their side windows.

"Stormy, grab that A-K and start firing!"

I hesitate.

"Do it!"

A bullet grazes my shoulder and knocks me across a bench seat.

"Stormy!"

Lying on my back, I lift my head to look at my latest wound and notice my baby bump for the first time.

You're starting to show!

Whoe, I guess I really am pregnant. Whomever is beneath that bump and the turquoise dream catcher hanging from my navel needs protecting-- no matter how much I may hate myself. So, not so surprisingly, I forget about the pain and blood rolling down my arm and the fact that I might be killing somebody and pull myself up with a vengeance.

"Where is it?" Maybe I got up too fast; my head is spinning.

Maybe you're pregnant.

"It's on your left in front of the first seat!"

Oh, I know I'm pregnant alright. Morning sickness has a way of reminding you. And for some-- a very small minority, I'm sure-- bullets flying at you to jump start that maternal instinct will do it for you too. I grab the machine gun and start shooting at the cops trailing us on the Trail.

"Hold on!"

I grab the ladder leading up to Nokosee's seat above me but keep firing as we bank hard toward the Trail, skipping and bouncing across the water.

"Nokosee!

I expect he's gone mad like his dad and is steering us into a suicidal collision course when, after a hard bump, we're airborne and sailing effortlessly over the road and the cops and my movie cuts to slow motion as I look down at the kaleidoscopic cop convoy and keep firing my AK-47.

The landing on the other side is less than dreamlike because we *didn't make it all the way across!* Instead, we land hard on the roof of a cruiser, destroying its bank of flashing red, white, and blue lights before sliding off in a trail of sparks onto a third hard landing on the sloping embankment rising out of the canal. The third impact throws me out of the airboat as the right corner of the bow dives below the water. When I emerge spitting and coughing I see the airboat stalled and smoking, its propeller barely spinning and its bow just above the turbulent water. Nokosee is dazed but still hanging on as one cop car after another crashes into each other on the road behind him. One sails over my head and nose dives into the water-- in real time. The slo-mo part of my movie is way over.

"Nokosee!"

He hears me. I start swimming toward him. He falls out of his seat, stumbles across the hull, leans over and offers me his hand. I grab it and he tries to lift me out of the water. He can't. I grab the hull.

"Nokosee, are you alright?"

He feels his rib and winces. Not a good sign.

"Mind if I throw you a rope and drag you back to camp?"

That's a good sign.

"Screw you, Nokosee." I throw my good leg-- the one without the honey-moon wound-- over the transom. "Grab my ass and drag the rest of me in."

He does and I plop onto the bottom of the hull, right on top of the AK-47. The pain is pretty bad but I'll never let him know.

"You're bleeding," he says.

"And you probably got a broken rib."

I manage to get to my feet with a little help from Nokosee. "Let's get the fuck out of here," I say.

I stumble past him and he stops me.

"What? You're going to drive us out of here?"

"What? You're going to climb back up into that seat?" Nothing. "I didn't think so. Sit down and just tell me where the hell to go."

I turn and climb up-- with some effort I'm surprised to discover and more pain than I expected-- into the seat, and give the engine some gas. As we slowly creep away, I look over my bleeding shoulder and see a slew of cop cars on fire, all rear-ending each other, all with their lights still flashing and their sirens still screaming chaotically like a horror movie soundtrack for some of the cops lurching about in and out of the smoke like zombies.

"Not bad, babe."

Nokosee has crawled up to the driver's seat in the airboat and is looking up at me from between my spread legs. About a half hour has passed since I started driving the airboat. We're sitting quietly now in the black water in an offshoot from the canal but my heart is still racing and I'm out of breath. Aside from his pearly whites I can barely see his face but that doesn't stop me from clamping my legs around where I think his head is and squeezing with extreme prejudice.

"Don't... ever... do... anything... like... that... again!"

I squeeze and twist his head as hard as I can but all it does is make him pretend he's Bart Simpson and Homer is strangling him. So I stop and push him away but he holds on to the airboat frame with one hand, swings out with a yell as if he lost his grip but then swings right back smack between my legs again.

"You know, you use to like me down here."

"Is that all you can think about?"

I throw my leg over his head and twist out of the seat. He grabs me around the waist and pulls himself up to my face.

"Sorry, Stormy, but you make me especially crazy when you do big balls stuff like that."

He tries to kiss me but I shove him away.

"Well, then I'm gonna have to stop doing that." I jump down onto the airboat hull-- and feel my insides hit bottom a second later. "Since you're feeling so good," I gasp, "you drive."

"Are you alright?"

"I'm fine. I need a break, that's all."

He looks at me and nods.

"Do you need help getting back up there?" I ask.

"No."

When he starts climbing back into the seat he falters.

"Yeah you do."

I ram my hand up between his thighs, grab his balls and squeeze.

"Ay-yichee-mama!"

Aside from his less than manly war cry, it gets him up into his seat. And gives me a way of releasing some of my pent-up anger and frustration with the way my life is going.

"Do you know how to get us back?"

"Of course I do," he squeaks in a pseudo falsetto.

"Right."

"Excuse me?"

"Of course you do."

I angrily throw myself into the bench seat below him, throw my arms across my chest and wait for the motor to fire up. As we creep away into the darkness, I can't help but think I missed what may have been my last chance to escape with my life from this madness.

Suddenly the airboat is bathed in a white light. I look back. A helicopter is racing toward us.

And you thought the fat lady had stopped singing.

"Stormy, grab the A-K!"

Nokosee hits the gas and has us speeding through the pitch black night without his night-vision goggles on and I wonder how we're not going to run into something as the bow rises and the gun slides along the bottom of the hull into my hands.

I can't believe it's happening again. Not a moment's rest. It's like fate is forcing my hand, that it wants me to show my commitment to this cockamamie cause by shooting at people. I don't want to do it. But when our airboat is raked with machine gun fire I immediately, automatically like a well-trained soldier, take aim over the prop cage at the copter on our tail and fire.

I shoot out its searchlight! Suddenly everything is dark again. They back off. I guess they're not use to getting shot at. Seconds ago I was pissed off at Nokosee and the world but now I'm euphoric. I still haven't killed anybody this time around! Then I turn my head and see the ValuJet Flight 592 memorial falling away from me as we bounce across the water in our mad dash through the Everglades.

Oh... My... God. I've come full circle again. First it was the tobacco-laced loogies being spat at me everywhere I went. Now it's this spooky intersection in the middle of nowhere where I learned to hate with extreme prejudice and now where I first pulled the trigger.

I look behind us. I can't see the memorial anymore. Nothing is following us-- but I *can't see the memorial*. I make no bets on whether or not we're providing entertainment to some young soldier following our every move on a monitor linked to a drone 25,000 feet above our heads because nothing matters more to me right now than trying to see the memorial. I'm obsessed with trying to see it, the singular unexplainable metaphor for my life made real, the touchstone to my past and my future but I *can't see it anymore*. That open window to my life's grand design is gone in a flash, just like that. I fall back onto the bench seat and wonder what just happened. Suddenly, God and angels and the spirit world come rushing into that rational part of my brain that couldn't be bothered with such notions, manifesting itself in an adrenaline rush of hope and fear.

Getting back to the new NS camp proves to be more difficult than fighting off Miami-Dade's finest. First off, pregnant and on a mission aren't a great combination. I have to throw up every now and then which means Nokosee has to stop so I can heave over the side of the airboat. Secondly, it appears Mr. O is becoming even more paranoid-- if that's possible-- because only he knew where he was leading his flock of eco-terrorist wannabes. Nokosee *thinks* he knows where the old man was taking them but after about two hours in the pitch black glades I've learned he doesn't have a clue. When he stops the airboat dead in the water to consult a map he has stuffed his his wallet, I know my lean-mean-fighting-machine is getting desperate. I speak up from the bottom of the airboat hull, lying broken and weakened from everything I've done and learned over the last few hours.

"So?"

"I know it's around here someplace."

I let slip a well-aimed laugh and sigh.

"It's not funny," he says.

"You're telling me. This is a joke. How hard can it be to find 200 crazy loons in the middle of the Everglades?"

"Well, I guess it's pretty hard since no one's found us yet."

"Nooksy, you are *not* instilling confidence in me with your path finding skills."

"Well, it's not like he's infallible or something."

Nokosee and I both jump at the sound of Busimanolotome's voice. The son-of-a-bitch has snuck up on us once again, this time in a bithlo.

"Dad! You scared the living bejesus out of us!"

Busimanolotome is holding onto the hull and looking at the side of the airboat. "'Coopertown Airboat Tours'? I don't remember ever having one of their airboats in our fleet."

"It's a long story," I say.

"So, where's Gerryragni?" he asks while still looking at the airboat.

"Dad, she's scared shitless. She thinks she's going to die any minute what with everyone trying to kill us."

"She's with her aunt," I say pointedly.

"Maria?" he asks.

"Yes."

"Never liked that woman," he says. "Never thought I was good enough for her sister. She still living in that little house in Hialeah?"

"Yes," I say.

"Stormy."

I look up at Nokosee. He's giving me a look that says I should keep my mouth shut.

"Don't worry," Busimanolotome says, "I'm not launching a war party to get Gerryragni back. As long as she's happy, I'm happy."

"You're not mad?" Nokosee asks.

"Was. Hopping mad when I found out what you guys had done. Not so much about the plan, but because you couldn't trust me with it, that you had to hide it from me. You don't think I want the best for my daughter? What kind of father would I be if I forced her to stay in a place where she thought she could get killed?"

"I'm sorry, dad. I just didn't think you'd want to live without her."

"I *don't* like not seeing her every day, watching her grow up but that's no longer an option for me, is it?"

Nokosee doesn't say anything. But I do.

"Not really, Mr. O."

He looks at me.

"Maybe you ought to go live with tía María too."

"Don't think that hasn't crossed my mind."

"Stormy," Nokosee warns me.

"I'd be crazy not to consider it. Especially when I learned tonight you killed J.T. Osceola."

"J.T. killed himself," Busimanolotome says.

"Thanks to you."

"That's what happens when a Human Being sells out to the Outside."

"You wanted the *Spear*, too!" I shout.

"Not the way he did. It was my way of counting coup and that's all it was. Believe it or not Sky Eyes, I'm sorry he died, but that kind of death was waiting for him once he chose the Outside."

"You try to make it sound all noble and mystical as if that makes it okay, but J.T. is still dead and his kids don't have a father thanks to you."

"That's true and there's nothing I can do about it. Sorry."

"I should have bailed at the last stoplight," I say.

"Stormy!" Nokosee says.

"So why didn't you?" Busimanolotome asks.

"I couldn't love myself enough."

"Sorry to hear it. Of course, if you did, the Outside would have thrown you in jail and taken your baby."

"That's the other reason I'm here."

An awkward moment passes before Busimanolotome sighs and says, "Well, if it ever crosses your mind to abandon The Cause again, I won't try to stop you. Both of you are free to go."

"Dad, I'd never leave you," Nokosee says with sincere earnestness.

Busimanolotome looks at me.

"I'd rather keep you guessing," I reply.

He likes that one and smiles.

"I can always count on you for a laugh," he says.

I offer him a tired, sad grin and turn away.

"You know, Sky Eyes," he says, "with better planning, hiding in Hialeah could work. I have some NS sympathizers there who would be more than happy to--"

"Don't think I haven't consider it but I just couldn't live in Hialeah."

"Why not?"

"I don't speak Spanish."

Busimanolotome laughs.

"Well you could learn, you know."

"Naah, it's more than that. The city just doesn't appeal to me."

"'Doesn't appeal to you?' It's a helluva step up from living out here with us."

"Not by much. Anyway, Hialeah doesn't have Nokosee."

I look up at him in his perch in the airboat seat and smile. He smiles back and says:

"*Be-e-e-p!* Ten points for you."

"So," Busimanolotome says, "you're going to stay with *Nooksy* no matter what?"

"Well, despite the everyday threat of a bloody death, it does have its perks."

"'Perks?'" Mr. O laughs, "What pray tell might they be?"

"First off, Nokosee of course. Secondly, I'm never bored. I guess the threat of imminent death has a way of doing that to you. In fact, it's weird, but I've never felt more alive. I can't imagine feeling like this in the Outside. Third, it's probably a death wish: I deserve to die for my sins. Fourth, the al fresco lovemaking. It--"

"Stop!" Busimanolotome orders, his hand held high like a school crossing guard. "Jesus, girl, I get the picture. You know, Sky Eyes, you're one crazy kid."

"Tell me something I don't know. I mean, all you have to do is look at me to know a screw is loose somewhere."

"I think you look beautiful," Nokosee says from the top of the airboat.

"Me too," Busimanolotome says.

Now I'm the one who gets a chance to be surprised. I can't say "thank you," instead, I just roll my eyes and sigh as if they're nuts which, if you think about it, is true about all three of us standing out there in the middle of the Everglades in the middle of the night with spent AK-47 shells rolling around in the bottom of the airboat. My eyes start to fill with tears and with the moment rapidly becoming awkward, I change the subject.

"So, Mr. O, can you show us the way," I pause, thinking I can't believe I'm going to say this, "home?"

"No problemo," he replies.

By the way he's looking at me, I guess he's trying to figure out if I really mean everything I just said and to tell you the truth, I'm not really sure myself. All I know is that I'm tired and want to crawl into something that resembles a bed. He smiles kindly at me, as if he understands, and then reaches into his Seminole shirt and pulls out a gun. That would be an instant adrenaline rush for anybody on the wrong side of something that could kill you, but for me, knowing what kind of a guy he is, it's enough to give me a heart attack. I slide back along the bench seat expecting to get killed.

Instead, he points the gun skyward and pulls the trigger. A red flare carves a crooked trail into the sky until it reaches its zenith and a parachute pops out to let it float slowly back to earth to illuminate everything below it.

"See that hammock?"

He's pointing at a hammock about fifty yards away.

"Yeah," I say. I think I hear cheering, maybe even applause.

"That's Camp Aquarius, our new home for the time being."

"You gotta be kidding me. 'Aquarius'?" I look at Nokosee.

"Yeah," Busimanolotome says, "Nokosee mentioned you were guessing it might be Aquarius. Even though I had been saving that name for something special, I thought, why not?"

"Nokosee, you know you don't have to tell your dad *everything* I say."

"Yes he does," Busimanolotome replies. "That's part of his prime directive."

"Tell me he's kidding, Nokosee."

"He no kid," Nokosee replies.

I pause to look at both of them. They're not smiling.

Boy, they are good.

"Well, screw that," I say while shifting my body uncomfortably into the airboat seat. "And good luck getting laid, Nokosee."

"He's kidding!" Nokosee shouts. "We're just joshing with you."

"Yeah?" I say as I look out over the water, "well, josh this." I thrust my arm into the air with my middle finger pointed over my shoulder at Nokosee.

Busimanolotome can't laugh hard enough.

"Aw, come on, Stormy," Nokosee says, "can't you take a joke?" He can't spit the words out fast enough.

"Not when it has anything to do with our marriage."

"I'm sorry, darling. Pa, tell her you're sorry too."

I turn slowly toward Busimanolotome with my best incredulous look. He tries his best to stop laughing.

"Man, you really are something else," he manages to say. "Only seventeen and you got one of the most fearless personalities I've ever seen. No wonder Nokosee fell for you."

I'm not good with compliments. They make me uncomfortable, especially now when I'm wallowing in so much self-hate. I don't know what to say so I say this:

"So, is this your way of saying you're sorry for all the stuff you did to me?"

Busimanolotome laughs. "Yeah, Holatte-Sutv Turwv Osceola, this is my way of saying I'm sorry."

I accept the apology with a slight nod of my head and turn toward the small patch of the Everglades glowing red under the descending flare and see my new home. Camp Aquarius sounds like a summer camp for hippie kids. If only it were.

"We were that close?" I ask.

"Yeah," Busimanolotome says. "You were providing us with tonight's entertainment. I'm surprised you didn't hear us laughing across the water. I wanted to let you guys keep going but Demaris and the tribe started feeling sorry for you and were getting a little bored too, I think, and finally said enough was enough. Demaris thought it would be good if I was the emissary with the news that we're just around the bend and there's a new day dawning. Damn, I'm beginning to sound like Mama Cass.

I turn to him and reply offhandedly, "Yeah, and you're beginning to look like her too."

"Now, now, missy, be nice," Busimanolotome admonishes. "Save that attitude for the enemy."

This time I keep my mouth shut and just look away thinking, for the first time, maybe Busimanolotome isn't the enemy

"Anyway, there's no hard feelings for snatching up my little girl without telling me about it in advance. In fact, I'm glad you did, only next time, please tell me first. So how'd it go? Did you have any problems with the insertion?"

"Are you talking about dropping off Rory with her aunt?" I ask while looking at Camp Aquarius.

"'Rory?'"

"That's her new name. Picked it herself."

"From *Gilmore Girls*?"

"Yeah." I turn to look at Busimanolotome. "Don't tell me you watch that too."

"I love *Gilmore Girls*. Lorelai is my kind of woman."

"Does Mrs. O know this?"

Mr. O laughs. And then he says this:

"You know, *Gilmore Girls* has one of the few things in the world that you can count on, that will never let you down or disappoint you."

He pauses, shaking his head in agreement with whatever he believes is true, expecting me to take the bait for this revelation which I do.

"Yeah?" I ask cautiously, not knowing what to expect.

"Kirk's film. No matter how many times I see it, it never stops being funny."

Whoe. Who knew, right? He's a riddle wrapped in a mystery inside an enigma. And judging by his ever-increasing girth, a Twinkie® too. (Yes, *Seinfeld* is always on his, Nokosee, and my watch list. We have *so* much in common! *Not.*)

"What's that?" Busi asks.

I look at what he's pointing at. A tiny green light is slowly flashing beneath Nokosee's seat. Nokosee gasps as he tries to lean over to look at it.

"Something wrong, big guy?" Busi asks.

"I think he broke a rib," I say.

"Don't tell me you got into a fight. The last thing we need is the Outside--"

"Too late, Mr. O. They caught us on the Trail and were shooting at us."

"'They'?"

"Cops."

"Damn it. How far did they follow you?"

"Not far. But when we thought it was over and we were sitting in the middle of nowhere, they jumped us again."

"Sky Eyes, mind seeing if you can fetch me that blinking thingie?"

I look up at Nokosee and roll my eyes. He shrugs. I get up out of the bench seat and stumble.

"Be careful, Stormy" Nokosee says.

"You alright, little girl?"

"She took a bullet to the shoulder."

"Damn it!"

"It only grazed me."

"Stop," Busimanolotome says. "Let me get it."

"Too late," I say. "I got it."

I shake it back and forth and discover I can pull it out of a metal sleeve screwed under the seat. Whatever it is it comes with a wire running from the back. I pull it out and hand the "blinking thingie" to Mr. O. He looks it over under the dying light of the flare and then curses.

"Sky Eyes, grab my hand and pull me into the airboat."

"Dad, she's got a bullet wound in her arm for crying out loud."

"Use the other one."

I extend my good hand and he grabs it and pulls himself up out of the bithlo and into the airboat but the guy is heavier than he thinks. I grab the airboat ladder with my other hand to keep me from being pulled out of the airboat and thrown into the water. I strain to keep from crying out because of the pain-- and because the last thing I want to do in front of The Micco is to show any sign of weakness.

"Nokosee, get down from there. I'm gonna drop you and Stormy off at the hammock."

"Dad, is everything okay?"

"This is a GPS device. Coopertown uses them on their airboats just in case one breaks down out here. I'm pretty sure the cops used it to find you. I'm gonna drop the thing on a hammock somewhere far, far away from here. When I get back you can tell me what happened to our airboat."

And now the fat lady stops singing.

Chapter 23
Birthday

It's November 24th and I turn 18 today. A few months have passed since I had my "mystic, crystal revelation" and we sent Rory to Hialeah which, at that time, appeared to have been some form of punishment outlawed by the United Nations. Truth be told, she seems to be doing well considering she and her aunt are now under 24-hour surveillance. Reports are that she has made friends and is often caught laughing and smiling.

Re my revelation along U.S. Highway 41: I don't know if I'll ever be able to shake it; it was so spooky with its implication that my life has a plan. But then, it was too neatly wrapped up to be just a coincidence. Right?

These are the kinds of things I've been thinking about since Operation Rory. But wait, it gets worse. Today on my birthday I'm lying on my air mattress, looking up at the new thatched chickee roof and counting the number of people I may be responsible for killing.

Morbid, yes I know but I just can't shake the guilt.

I stop at twenty. I think I have way too much time on my hands.

Rory was interrogated by a host of alphabet government agencies, was never charged with anything, and released into the protective custody of her closest living relative, aunt Maria just as Nokosee predicted. Seeing her without risking life, limb, and imprisonment is problematic. The best we've come up with is Skyping her from purloined laptops at Wi-Fi spots never visited more than once. Of course it only works if she's at home and online but the payoff makes it well worth the effort.

Sometimes I envy Rory in Hialeah.

Re that new thatched roof: Busi has us building chickees again, a sure sign things are looking up for the NS, that we can finally settle down to living our lives in secret in one place instead breaking camp every other day or week in order to keep from getting snuck up on and killed. Why he kept calling the last half dozen camps Aquarius is anyone's guess. Maybe it's because he's running out of names from *Hair*. Or maybe the name only gets retired after a camp gets evacuated because of a fire fight.

"Fire fight?"

Yes, I'm beginning to sound more and more like a soldier every day thanks to Busimanolotome's NS training program which is wrapped up in a lot of military speak. "Up Armor," anybody? Anyway, maybe I'll ask him some day about the camp names when I have nothing better to do.

Not.

The Coopertown airboat has been added to our fleet. Mr. O wasn't too happy about losing the NS "Operation Rory" airboat to the Feds but our new airboat has been reimangined as our battleship since it's about twice as big as our regular airboats. Twin machine gun turrets have been added behind the driver's seat. It's also been fitted for RPGs and Stinger missiles. The four bench seats now make it easier to accommodate more NS when we abandon hammocks. Billy Bob's van was also confiscated by the Feds. Billy Bob would have been "confiscated" too but the government couldn't prove beyond a doubt that Billy Bob knew Nokosee had taken his van or that the NS "sympathizer" had tossed Nokosee the keys. Since then Billy Bob has "dropped off the face of the Earth." Hmm, wonder where he could be?

Nokosee spent much of the time since "Operation Rory" recuperating from a broken rib. Aside from what I suspect may be a permanent scar from the close encounter of a bullet that grazed my shoulder, I escaped with only bumps, scrapes, and bruises, most of which have healed and disappeared. Still, if I keep going like this, I don't want to think about how I might look a few years down the road. If I live that long.

Following "Operation Rory," Busi, in his infinite wisdom, dropped the GPS device off in a hammock far, far away and made us move that night to another secret hammock hideout.

In any event the last few months have been great for Nokosee and me because it's given us time to get to know each other better, especially since we built our chickee on its own little hammock just across the water from the others at Camp Aquarius the Fifth. That's right, yours truly, pregnant as all get out now, helped Nokosee build our chickee. I had a tool belt strapped across my hips hanging below my big pregnant belly and the cutest little loincloth you ever saw. The result was our chickee came out like my attempts at sewing Seminole patchwork, something Mom-- yes, she's off my shit list again thanks to her major shift in attitude toward me because of my part in "Operation Rory"-- and the real Seminole women are trying to teach me: less than perfect. Actually, it's Seminole tradition to make sure there is at least one bad stitch in the work because only God can make a perfect thing and the women don't want to look presumptuous. I think this is a Japanese thing to, but no matter, for me, imperfection comes naturally so it's not something I have to work at. And thankfully, it's something Nokosee and I can live with. Sure, the chickee's four posts might not be perpendicular with each other and all Frank Gehr*ish* and the roof might leak, but it's truly ours, made by our own two hands.

Building it together was fun but now that it's done, it's even more fun because we're so isolated from the rest of the tribe we can do just about anything and not have to worry about disturbing the peace. Now we hardly ever see Nokosee's mom or dad or anyone else for that matter. One reason is because Mr. O has deemed it necessary that the NS divide themselves up among the surrounding hammocks. In case of future attacks he reasons the NS will have a better chance of survival.

Because of our isolation and because it was still warm out when we started building our new home, we became full-time nudists.

And that suited me just fine. With Nokosee taking on the roll of hunter/gatherer, I basically just laid around all day stark naked on a gumbo limbo branch hanging out over the water soaking up sunshine. Also known as the "Tourist Tree" because of its red and peeling bark-- like the skin of tourists-- Nokosee makes sure each morning before he goes "off to work" to rub suntan lotion all over my body so I don't end up looking like one of them. Of course, by the time he's through, we're so hot we got to do it. And, because there's no one around to hear me, I can let loose some loud, swamp thumping Meg Ryans that clear the hammock of every bird fit to fly and critter fit to run. Yeah, it's not a bad way to start the day.

Up in the gumbo limbo I watch my belly grow bigger and bigger. It's so quiet and peaceful up there. Birds who come there to feast on the tree's fruit have come to know me, and I them. When I hold out a fruit for them, they come and eat it right out of my hand. Their non-judgmental acceptance of me is good for my soul. I have to force myself sometimes to come down to the real world of work and chores and hating myself and the possibility of a bad ending to this story.

It's cooler now and I've given up nudity but still climb up into the tree at least once a day to get away from it all and to find my true self.

On my birthday I feel my stomach and pull back a Seminole blouse that once belonged to Rory to look at it. It looks like I'm sprouting a giant tumor.

On my birthday, Nokosee joins me up in the gumbo limbo and kisses my stomach over and over again. I love him so much.

In comparison to most Americans, we're on the bottom rung of the totem pole. We're poorer than the poorest ghetto denizen or any of the millions of people now out of work thanks to the recession, worrying how they will keep their families fed and a roof over their heads. But I never want.

On my birthday up in the gumbo limbo, Nokosee adds dignity to our way of life by giving me a homemade birthday present: a necklace made from spent AK-47 shell casings. He's polished the brass until they shine like gold and stuck turquoise "salvaged" from the few Seminole and Miccosukee tourists stands still left along the Trail into the openings, carving each one to look like the tip of a bullet. They flare out from a center freaking big .50 caliber BMG (Browning Machine Gun) casing which he stuck a piece of carved isinglass in to look like a gemstone. That centerpiece pendant is nearly as long as a dollar bill. Finding and carving the isinglass was probably the hardest thing he had to do since the NS never seems to run out of shell casings which they dutifully re-pack with gun powder and bullets. Although it's scattered all over southern Florida's limestone pad, the cloudy, whitish-yellow mica crystal Nokosee calls isinglass is harder to find in the Everglades unless you go to one of the mining sites where giant dredges are shoveling up tons of the white oolite for the road building and concrete industries. When they can't dig no more, they abandon these "rock pits" in search of new places to dig. Since the water table is so high out here, the rock pits are full of water and, because they drop off from their placid, inviting shores twenty or thirty feet without warning, they act like black holes, sucking in anything and anyone foolish enough to venture into the water if they can't swim. As it turns out, this big piece of nearly worthless crystal was found by Nokosee when he was a little boy beside one of those rock pits and he kept it as a prized possession ever since. Now he tells me I'm his most prized possession. Who needs diamonds?

I try not to think that my center pendant held one of the bullets that shot down the two F-18 Hornets.

Thanks to our need to keep one step ahead of the Army, Navy, Air Force, Coast Guard, Marines, Border Patrol, ICE, FBI, CIA, NSA, Homeland Security, and everyone else trying to catch us, we were constantly on the run and because of that I've managed to keep the weight off. Now that we seem to be "permanently" based at Camp Aquarius the Fifth, my current regimen of morning group calisthenics followed by intense hand-to-hand combat training Nokosee and I teach together (something he and the NS insisted on since I'm this famous martial arts chick now) and timed marches through the Everglades, has continued to keep me looking pretty good. In fact, aside from my 12" honeymoon scar running down my thigh, my legs and, for that matter my once mangled tush, have never looked better. That's probably because Nokosee, aside from rubbing suntan lotion all over my body every morning, has also been habitually rubbing a special concoction on my butt and the 12-incher for the last couple of months. It's something I hope he'll never grow tired of doing because, although the honeymoon scar will probably never go away-- even though I keep telling him "I think it's working" to encourage him to keep doing it-- it usually leads to making wild, passionate love.

But not every day which is a bummer. That scares me and makes me want to climb back up into my tree where everything is perfect. I guess we're turning into an old married couple. I just thought that happened much later down the road, like maybe after the kids have gone to college or something.

I can't imagine our child going to college. In fact, I have a hard time imagining any kind of future for our baby at all.

You need counseling.

One present I got for my birthday: I didn't once during the whole day think about the poor friendless giant I sent crashing to the street a few months ago. I truly hope he's alright.

I also hope all the killing and running and fear of dying is a thing of the past but in my heart of hearts, I don't think so. I can't imagine the Outside forgetting or forgiving what we did to it. I suspect it's just biding its time for one final assault. Maybe if we keep a low enough profile, nothing will happen to us. I can only hope so.

But then I think about Ishi, the last of the Yahi, and how that approach proved to be not worth a damn. Mr. O makes his story part of the indoctrination all new NS recruits get in "basic training." In the DVD documentary I saw in a chickee deep in the Everglades, Ishi showed up on a California ranch one day in 1911 half naked and starving to death. Because no one could speak his language, it took one of the world's first anthropologists and a team of scientists a long time to discover Ishi had been hiding with his people for over 40 years in the wilderness to avoid being murdered by the Outside. During the 1850's and 60's in California, thanks to the broader interpretation of "Manifest Destiny," it was legal to murder Human Beings to free up the land for commerce. Back then you could get fifty cents for every scalp you brought in; five dollars for every head. In 1854 alone, the Feds reimbursed California Indian hunters one million dollars. When the second to last Yahi died, Ishi, starving and in desperation for human companionship, stumbled into a world that was to him filled with magic and mystery but one we take for granted. The Outside quickly portrayed him as a savage and a caveman and put him on exhibition. He became world famous. When he died four years later from tuberculosis, his handlers were quick to agree that despite the systematic murder of his people by the Outside, the loss of his way of life, and the 40 years in hiding the Yahi imposed upon themselves in order to live free, Ishi never showed any resentment and, in fact, was one of the kindest people they ever met. Aside from choosing the nobler path of never surrendering like the Yahi, Mr. O promises we won't be like that lost tribe in every other way; that we will fight back and flourish and never get caught.

From your meshugana mouth to God's ears.

The GPS reading for our location is a coordinate of numbers that when translated into plain English says "smack dab in the middle of bumfuck nowhere." So, I've finally arrived at that place I always bitched about. Fitting. Actually, as long as we're never found and we can continue living like we are now, i.e., "borrowing" what we need from the Outside, 40 years in the middle of freaking nowhere this time around sounds doable.

As long as Nokosee is doing it with me.

Thinking about Ishi reminds me to stop calling Nokosee a pagan caveman. Even if I'm kidding, both guys deserve better.

One more thing to feel guilty about, right?

Right. I'll just add it to my list.

The NS throw a party for me later in the day. Nokosee risked getting caught by the Feds or some other law enforcement agency when he ordered up a birthday cake from the closest Publix, Florida's biggest supermarket chain. I say closest instead of local because where we are, there is nothing local except loneliness, isolation and pondering the "big questions" up in my tree. He had them decorate the cake with my Indian name, spelling it out for the person behind the counter and didn't leave the bakery department until it was done just in case he was recognized and someone felt like being a hero. Before he left, he bought all the other cakes that were sitting there too so everyone in the tribe could participate in the celebration. I don't know where he got the money to pay for them but I'm pretty sure he used a stolen credit card.

There are hardly any jeggings at my party. Thankfully time has taken its toll on them. After months of wear and tear in the sawgrass infested Everglades, the jeggings have slowly repurposed themselves into fitted briefs worn under jeans, camo pants and shorts. Unfortunately, the Crocs are made of sterner stuff and appear destined to out stay their welcome beyond that of even the lowly and just a tad more gross palmetto bug, i.e. Florida's big freaking flying cockroach.

Still there is hope. A couple of days before my birthday, the NS hijacked a truck load of Prada handbags and shoes that were on their way to Sawgrass Mills, the outlet mall straddling the Everglades where Nokosee got me my wedding day gold DMs. It's the first in-Florida Prada outlet and it was just something the NS couldn't pass up. Today I got enough Prada stuff on my birthday to last me two lifetimes. So did the rest of the tribe who waited until my birthday before splitting the loot. I can only hope they will take a liking to the shoes enough to ditch the Crocs.

On my birthday Nooksy also surprises me with a Nook. He knows I miss reading for pleasure. Books aren't high on Mr. O's priority list unless they're weapons or tactical manuals and books that present the NA side of history like *Bury My Heart At Wounded Knee* (which I highly recommend). Hauling books around the swamp-- even paperbacks-- is a problem not to mention the climate has a way of turning them into paper mache in no time. So, when I get the Nook-- thanks to someone's stolen credit card I'm sure-- I couldn't be happier. It comes with a shitload of preloaded public domain books like *The Adventures of Huckleberry Finn,* and *Moby Dick,* books I'd probably never read if it weren't so damn convenient not to. BTW, Huck Finn is very worthy in its original form, i.e., the one Mark Twain wrote that includes the words "nigger" and "Injun." You can skip the PC version which I'm sure has Mr. Twain spinning in his grave. What a joke. As for Moby Dick, it was a tough one, especially from the top of a tree and I hate to admit it, I couldn't get through it. BUT, I discovered some pretty cool stuff too like an over-the-top essay by Thoreau on "Walking" and anything by that wild man Oscar Wilde. These are the kinds of guys that would make any party worthy and I'm happy they could make mine.

As an aside, when you spend as much time as I do in a tree reading, making love, and what have you, it's natural to want to read up on them. I discovered through my Nook that a large oak tree annually releases 1,000 bathtubs worth of water from its leaves into the air. Pretty cool.

And the gumbo limbo-- don't you just love that word?-- is the traditional wood used for carving carousel horses. So, maybe you rode up and down on a "branch" just like me. Even cooler.

Unfortunately, I also discovered something Busi has been bitching about forever is true. I found a book on the Nook that backed him up about a deadly tree-killing fungus spreading through the Everglades. It got here by an invasive beetle no bigger than Lincoln's nose on a penny. It's called the Redbay Ambrosia Beetle and was probably imported in a wooden shipping container. The fungus it leaves behind is called laurel wilt and has killed trees in over 330,000 acres in the Everglades in just a few years. If killing all those native trees isn't enough, it allows other invasive species to take root where the natives once lived like weeds do in a garden. Right now hammocks-- like the ones the NS use to hide in-- and I use their trees to climb up in-- are losing half of their trees. Once that happens and invasive species take root, the Everglades' natural free-flowin' self starts to back-up and what was once a fragile, unique world in balance for millions of years, tips toward flooding and more loss of species and habitat. So far no one has been able to come up with a remedy for this problem. To me, that's as scary as any speculative sci-fi doomsday story. It's got me checking my sitting-trees every time I climb up in one and I can only pray I never see it here so deep and far in the Everglades.

But I don't want to think about that now on my birthday because in my gumbo limbo I also discovered peace, well, at least something resembling what I think peace might be-- I hate myself less up in my tree than when I'm on the ground. Although I might have found this salve for the soul in a self-help book through the hard-wired memory banks of the Nook, it came to me through the sublimely transformative powers of living in my tree's gently swaying boughs. In my tree I'm a healthy happy fruit, full of wholesome goodness. On the ground it's the total opposite. If you feel like I do sometimes or all the time, go find a tree, climb it and make it your own. Get lost in its branches, close your eyes, and, as the Good Book says as interpreted by Chuck Girard, a "rock 'n roll preacher" my mom and dad turned me on to when we were still a happy family-- and who I listened to riding down from Milltown on my Indian and still do in my tree thanks to my Nook and a pair of earbuds: "Slow....... down....../Be still and wait on the Spirit of the Lord..." Who knows, maybe you'll get lucky and discover you're loved unconditionally no matter how much you've sinned. A couple of times I got that feeling sitting up in my tree but it never came down with me.

One thing that did come down from the gumbo limbo with me: I've become an unabashed, unapologetic tree hugger.

I suspect Busi is up to no good which means he hasn't learned a damn thing and the shit could probably hit the fan at any given moment. Every time I stumble upon him with a group of what appears to be his most trusted associates, he clams up until I pass by. One of these members of the inner circle is Indian Larry. He's the nuttiest nut in the bunch and never fails to whistle loudly like nothing is going on until I pass. What a jerk. As far as I can tell, he's a psychotic Italian out of the Bronx and is about as Indian as I am. One time I caught them rolling up what looked like large blueprints. That's not good, right? Nokosee, for some reason, seems to have been cut off from these pow-wows too.

Which probably explains why I still don't feel totally accepted by the old man despite all of the adventures we've shared together and the nice things he says about me. Still, I've developed a stronger relationship with Chief Nutjob over the past few months than with Mama O. I attribute that to our kumbaya moment following the downing of the drone, my reluctance to leave Nokosee even when faced with death and dismemberment, and the fact that I wasn't a wuss with just about everything that's been thrown at me. I've also developed a genuine fondness for Sinatra which further adds to my worthiness in The Micco's eyes.

Although Mom has become friendlier to the point I can drop the quotation marks when referring to her, I think it's out of a sense of obligation rather than from genuine affection. I guess it will take more than risking my life to get her kid safely out of harm's way for her to warm up to me.

She's disappointed you didn't jump ship and take Nokosee with you when you had the chance during Operation Rory. Can't you see? She's still worrying about her son.

She can stop worrying. I'm taking care of Nokosee now.

Good luck with that.

Screw you. On my birthday she gave me a hug and a tight smile. The smile was tighter than the hug.

Not that I care. I'm here for Nokosee and really nothing else. Yes, I know there's a bigger reason Nokosee and the NS are here, but I guess I'm really not a granola eating "empathic" at heart. I'm more in it for the sex.

Just kidding. A little. I do like other things about my new life. I don't think you can get much freer. Take away the constant buried anxiety that at any moment hundreds of Army Rangers might swoop down on us with wicked revenge in their hearts, living out here in the middle of nowhere has proven not to be as bad as I thought it would be. And it's not like I gave up all creature comforts. Thanks to photovoltaic panels, mini wind generators, and hundreds of stolen car batteries, I can still watch movies and TV, listen to music, and occasionally surf the net on the sat phone when Mr. O lets us. On the rarest of occasions, we even get some KFC when an NS warrior returns from the Outside on God-knows-what kind of cockamamie mission.

It's just the buried communal thought that we're all going to die without a moment's notice that puts the kibosh on this back-to-the-earth lifestyle. That's why I make a major effort not to think about it and to live every day to the fullest.

Unless, of course, it's my birthday. Birthdays kind of have a way of making you think about your life and where it's going. And to be truthful with you, I'm not all that sure I like where it's going-- especially after the "revelation." Because, try as hard as I may, I can't see me living out here in the middle of nowhere forever. Or fighting The Man.

Love is all you need, so sayeth the Beatles in four part harmony.

I don't think so. At least not for me.

Does that make you bad? Less than worthy of Nokosee's love?

Probably. Too many people have died because of me.

But you didn't set out to kill them.

That's true but maybe I could have saved a few if I had ran from the NS right after the "Attack on the Alley" instead of letting myself get sucked deeper and deeper into the Everglades and Mr. O's mad plan.

You should have told Nokosee you were pregnant as soon as you had the chance.

Shoulda, coulda, didn't. I was too scared he'd have a problem with me getting knocked-up; too afraid if I asked him to leave the NS so we could raise our baby where it was safe he'd refuse. Then what? What would I do then? Would I really hitch a ride back to the Outside and try to raise my baby alone? What if I got caught? How could I raise my baby in jail? I couldn't because the Outside doesn't allow that. They take your kid and put it up for adoption. No, although living out here in the middle of bumfuck nowhere is far from perfect, it's better than the alternative.

Yeah, keep telling yourself that long enough and you just might believe it one day. Are you crazy?

Yes. That's something the voices in my head and I *do* agree on.

*You **do** need counseling.*

See, we *do* agree on some things.

*And that's a **good** thing?*

I think so. I hope so. Isn't synching up your thoughts with your actions a good thing?

Only if it has positive results for living a long and happy life.

Can't it be a long and happy *crazy* life?

Not if it means hurting yourself or others. That's sowing bad karma and bad karma always has a way of coming back to bite you on the ass.

Geese.

Anyway, you've got a long way to go before you ever get to Smiley Face land.

Why?

Well, first off, you gotta stop talking to the voices in your head.

Chapter 24
Preggers Forever

"It won't come out. It's lodged inside."

I can relate. *Really* relate. That was Sookie St. James talking to Lorelai Gilmore about the giant baby inside her that won't come out, that's been keeping her from having a normal life for what seems to Sookie like an eternity. Back then when I first saw that episode with my mom, before I was knocked-up, I was just a kid and we laughed together but I really didn't have a clue as to what it must be like closing in on the home stretch nearly nine months later. Now I do and brother, all I can say, quoting another line is, "Get it out! Now!"

It's spring, May I think, and I'm big and round now and really tanned. Aside from the "honeymoon scar" running down my thigh which won't go away no matter how many times Nokosee rubs it with his magic elixir, I look pretty good for being pregnant if I do say so myself.

But I still want "it" out. *Now!*

I'm also a celebrity. Busimanolotome got Nokosee to make a video compiled from clips Digital Camcorder Guy (now replaced by Digital Camcorder Guy the Second or, as we like to call him, DC-G2)) had kept on his laptop and uploaded it to YouTube with a few key search words like "empathic." It's one of the most watched, closing in on 100 million viewers-- far surpassing my measly 20 million views of the White City Smackdown. It has been described by Time as a "meme for the mangled masses." It's basically a recruitment video for The Cause and shouldn't get near the numbers its pulling in and probably wouldn't if it weren't for the "action sequences," the last images Digital Camcorder Guy shot before catching shrapnel during the "skirmish" between us and the F-18s and the swamp army. Because of it, our ranks have swollen right along with my stomach. It appears a lot of people don't take a liking to seeing our little band of crackpots with a jones for saving the environment getting picked on by the greatest badass army on the earth. It helps too that the video has a certain cool cachet going for it too. Picture if you will, Busimanolotome sitting in front of the NS flag with Nokosee and me on each side, arms folded across our bodies in a no nonsense, in your face hip hop stance. At that time my baby bump was just that so I was able to pull off a pretty convincing aggressive and threatening performance. Of course it helps that I got on a big old traditional Seminole patchwork jacket to hide my "condition." Aside from the Seminole jackets, all of us are wearing Wayfarers, "the preferred sunglasses of the NS nation." You can hear my voice on the opening fade-in copy re species lost. After that, Nokosee and I don't say anything, we let Busimanolotome do all the talking in what he likes to refer to as "Indian Speak," a stilted cadence the world has come to expect thanks to countless Hollywood westerns :

According to Conservation International,
every 20 minutes a species is lost.
A third of all species is lost each year.

Friends of the earth and the four winds,
my name is Micco Busimanolotome Osceola.
My tribe is the New Seminole.
There aren't many of us and we're not all Seminoles.
In fact, if anything, we're the true rainbow coalition
of those who want to live in harmony with the land
and are willing to forsake everything in today's world
to build an empathic civilization,
to separate ourselves from a world that
subordinates the fate of Human Beings
and the planet to the relentless drive for profit.
To do that, we have chosen to live deep in the Everglades
in the traditional way my ancestors did,
in chickees without air-conditioning
or any creature comforts.

(At this point, Nokosee fades in footage from the attack
and Busimanolotome's dialogue becomes a voice over)

A few months ago we were attacked
by the United States of America.
Strafed by F-18 Hornets. Shot at by Army Rangers. Why?
What does the most powerful country in the world fear from us?
We only want to live in peace and to be left alone.

It began with the "Attack on the Alley," as the media called it
back then, when the cops were trying to kill
Holatte-Sutv Turwv Osceola--once known as Stormy Jones--
as she raced across Alligator Alley.

(Nokosee dissolves my infamous "finger" picture into
TV news footage we lifted from a local station's website)

Despite what the media has told you, we did not shoot first.
But we did shoot back.
Something else the media failed to mention was the reason Holatte-Sutv
Turwv Osceola risked her life.
She did it for love.

(Nokosee shamelessly added "What I Did For Love"
from *Chorus Line* as background music)

She was racing to get back to my son Nokosee so they could get married.
Maybe it's because they're still teenagers with raging hormones and all that,
but they're crazy in love.
Trust me, you can't keep them apart. I know, I tried.

(Busimanolotome conveniently leaves out the part of us shooting down the two
choppers and our fearless leader's cockamamie plan of reclaiming the Outside through eco-
terrorism. At this point Nokosee dissolves to our wedding picture of us
posing with The What and flashing pseudo gang signs)

But I won't anymore. Holatte-Sutv Turwv
and Nokosee are married now and she is
carrying my grandchild.

(Nokosee finishes the video with some way powerful Digital Camcorder Guy footage
which climaxes with DCG getting killed and the camera falling into the back of the Humvee)

Later when the Great Black Father in Washington
sent his eagles to kill us from the sky
and his best warriors to kill us from the ground,
we were forced to fight back.

Despite what your government is telling you,
we did not shoot first.
That attack was an act of premeditated genocide
by the United States of America.
And we regret the loss of life-- on both sides.

(A close-up of Busimanolotome fades in)

So, let's call it a truce. No more war.
We lost people. You lost people.
Now please, leave us be.
An old Seminole prophecy tells us
the white man will blow himself off the face of the earth.
But it doesn't have to be that way.
Let us be. Let it be.

(Nokosee brings up the Beatles "Let It Be" as
Busimanolotome lowers his Wayfarers to look at Camera)

Comprende?

(As the video fades to black and the music dies out,
Nokosee inserts the following copy)

This video is dedicated to Digital Camcorder Guy
for his tireless work and his ultimate sacrifice for The Cause.
For more information about the New Seminole including
becoming a member of the tribe, please visit us at:
www.newseminole.com.

That website was basically shut down by the Feds within hours after its posting on YouTube. Media companies soon killed the YouTube video for copyright infringement. Nokosee then made a second video sans any copyrighted material and uploaded it to let the world know what had happened but it too got blocked within an hour by Uncle Sam. Still, we keep uploading it every chance we get and although it gets banned within hours, it's worth the effort because that action by the Feds is responsible for a surge of favorable comments on YouTube and spin-off supporting videos from people around the world. In the beginning, there were more negative reactions to the NS, i.e., we deserve to get killed for our cockamamie ideas. But the second YouTube video brought us so much attention we were able to secure the *pro bono* services of a Miami lawyer to leverage it into some spin-off NS products using roving overseas websites and off-shore banking accounts to sell tees and mugs and stuff like the tribe's most successful product I'm proud to have inspired: *New Seminole Brand Badass Spices* with me posing coyly on the label with my whispering finger on my lips and my loincloth draped hiney pointing toward the consumer. It's an "inside joke" for those who have read this book and "our" little secret. Now, when Busi asks the NS what they've done for The Cause, I happily shout with fist held high proudly in the air, "I gave my ass!" (But not my heart. That's reserved only for Nokosee).

Anyway, in order to protect our lawyer's identity we call him "Morton Silver" in honor of the legendary Outside lawyer who represented a band of "wild" Miccosukees-- as they were called fifty years ago in a *Saturday Evening Post* story Nokosee made sure I read-- who were-- and I'm not making this up-- threatening to sell over half of Florida to the Soviet Union, Red China or Cuba. The tribe believed old treaties said the land belonged to them and if America didn't stop insisting they take money-- over $350 million at that time-- in exchange for it instead of recognizing their rightful claim, they damn well were going to sell it to the bad guys. If you look at the map in front of the book you'll see that's a whole lotta land.

Unfortunately for the "wild" Miccosukees and Seminoles, the U.S. had a law that made it illegal to give land back to the Indians, i.e. financial compensation was their only option. So what do the "wild" Indians do when they won't sell their land for all the money in the world because they see the land as part of their own body? They get Morton Silver working on borrowing $100 million from the World Bank for legal aid so they can go to the World Court to state their case. That got nowhere fast when the tribe was told the U.S. will never consent to being tried in that court for domestic matters.

As it turns out, in addition to the "Great Seal" of the City of Hialeah, Busimanolotome was very much influenced by these failed legal attempts to reclaim land "rightfully" belonging to his people. Realizing legal action would be a waste of time, he elected to follow what he likes to call a more "pro-active" approach which, unfortunately has turned us into renegades-on-the-run.

Still, thanks to "Morton Silver," the NS has been making so much money it's now able to buy the stuff it needs during its forays into the Outside. This has brought truck hijackings to a near standstill along the Trail and the Alley-- unless, of course, NS intel reveals a shipment of Crocs is on its way (I'm kidding, although I am making an effort to "lose them" every chance I find the offensive shoes left unattended in the various NS camps). That has taken the heat off of us for the last few months and allowed us to live in relative peace which has segued into a chickee building spree.

The general consensus among the NS is that because of all the negative publicity the Feds got from the YouTube postings, the Great Black Father and all his minions are going to leave us alone unless, of course, we start getting all eco-terrorism on them again. And so far, months later, that seems to be exactly what has happened.

Although I've never met him, "Morton Silver" is one amazing lawyer. If Busimanolotome ever steps foot in a courtroom, "Morton Silver" will probably be standing by his side representing him. And winning the case. And saving us all from prison and the death penalty.

If only that could be true.

Nokosee and I are lying stark naked in the shallow water of the lagoon near our hammock soaking up some rays after he finished shaving the sides of my head and Bitch Waxed my Mohawk-- something he loves to do for me-- when for the first time in nearly a year I hear my dad's voice. He's calling out to me through an electronic megaphone.

"Stormy! Give yourself up and come home with me!"

Startled, we swim carefully toward the edge of the lagoon, making sure our heads-- and my 'hawk-- are hidden by the cattails and sawgrass. Dad's piloting an airboat, driving it real slowly through the swamp with the megaphone held close to his mouth with his free hand.

"Have the baby where it's safe."

"You got to hand it to him, Stormy." Nokosee whispers. "He won't give up."

"Yeah, you gotta hand it to him," I reply.

Thanks to the NS, I know he's been trying to find me for the last couple of months in the airboat but I never thought we'd ever see each other again, especially when I'm so, to use some military speak, "in country."

"In Country?" This is Dug-In-So-Deep-The-Sun-Don't-Shine-Country.

There's a standing order from Mr. O that if my dad spots any NS they're not to shoot him but are to take him prisoner. Supposedly Mr. O will have a little pow-wow with him and let him go after dad and I have a family reunion with him promising to forget everything he's seen and to forget about me. Knowing my dad, that might be asking for a little too much so I'm hoping he never finds us. I mean, who needs another confrontation like the one he had with Nokosee nine months ago (see Micco Mann's rip off of my diary).

"He's always been one stubborn son of a bitch," I say upon reflection.

"Like father like daughter."

I hear Nokosee but I can't take my eyes away from my dad. He looks older, desperate, beaten down. I know I should want to go to him, but I can't make myself do it. I can't forget it was him who wanted to break Nokosee and me up, to ship him off to Oklahoma to get studied by a cultural anthropologist until the day he died.

"You really are preggers," Nokosee says.

I don't say anything to Nokosee. I'm still watching my dad, thinking about how much I've changed, how further we've drifted apart. When he disappears behind some tall cattails, I don't try to keep sight of him. I roll onto my back and pat my big round tummy.

"Thanks to you," I say.

Nokosee gently kisses my stomach. He lifts the "dream catcher" hanging from my navel and asks, "Is it working?"

"It's working. Our baby seems happy."

"Aren't you just a little bit afraid of having it way out here 'in the middle of bumfuck nowhere'?"

"Not really."

"Really?"

"Nope. Women have been doing this for 10,000 years without a doctor. Why should it be any different for me? Anyway, your mom said she'd help me out. I mean, she's gone through it a couple of times, it can't be that big of a deal, right?"

"Yeah, but mom had me and my sister in a hospital."

"What?"

"Dad wanted us born in the swamp but mom prevailed."

"Are you kidding me?"

"No kid."

"Why didn't somebody tell me this?

"I don't know. I thought you knew."

"So, what am I like some kind of an experiment?"

"Probably."

I can't believe nobody told me. Not that it makes that much of a difference because I've had enough time to accept having my baby in the swamp. It's just that you'd think *someone* would have mentioned it. I mean, why didn't Mrs. O say something? I tell you, that woman gives me the heebee jeebies. What's her problem anyway?

You stole her son, you big dummy.

Please.

Maybe she thinks having a baby in the middle-of-bumfuck-nowhere will scare the shit out of you so badly you'll hop the first airboat outta here-- and take Nokosee with you.

I'm going to have to have a talk with her.

Yeah, you do that.

Until then, the bitch is *back on quotation marks!*

"Don't worry, darling," Nokosee says. "Since then we've added a midwife to the tribe."

"What?"

"A midwife. She's one of the YouTubers," Nokosee replies, using the word we call our Internet related new recruits. "I know dad really likes the idea our baby will be the first New Seminole actually born in the swamp. You're scoring major points with him there."

"Which is what I live for." Which is kinda the truth. Like it or not, I like it when Chief Crackpot likes me.

"Stormy, come back with me!" Dad's voice echoes across the sawgrass.

"So, you're okay with having the baby out here 'in the middle of bum--'"

"Yes. Hey, if it makes your old man happy."

"Okay, 'cause you know if you're not...'"

"What, you'll whisk me off to the nearest hospital?"

"Damn right."

"Why, are you worried?"

"Not if you're not."

"Oh, my big strong pa--"

I stop short. I was about to call him a pagan caveman. I regroup into my PC mode.

"You're worried about me, aren't you? Isn't that sweet."

I grab Nokosee by the back of the neck and bring his mouth to mine.

"Stormy!" Dad's voice isn't as loud anymore.

Soon, we're laughing, splashing and making love in the water.

Chapter 25
I'm Going Home/I Love You

Recently I've been talking out loud to no one in particular which is, of course, never good. Thankfully, I'm not having a public conversation with the voices in my head and no one has heard me yet. The thing that bugs me though is that I only say two things and I say them over and over in the most unexpected times and places.

"I'm going home" is one of them. It just keeps slipping out of my mouth; especially when my eyes are closed and I'm up in my tree thinking about things. But I don't think I really mean it literally because I really don't miss the BS that came with my old home. What I think it means is that I'm *remembering* the life I once knew as a child, a life of running free without a care in the world and that's the place I'm going to at that moment-- which would make sense considering what's going on in my world now.

Or maybe "home" means Heaven.

Like in a death wish?

Yeah, "like in a death wish."

Could be. I hear they're very forgiving up there.

Where'd you hear that?

Okay, maybe I made that up.

"I love you" is the other thing I keep saying out loud over and over again. Unlike "I'm going home," "I love you" comes out with my eyes wide open. After thinking about it for a while, I'm pretty sure it's not entirely about Nokosee. I think it's my way of thanking God for everything that's good in my life, thanking Him for sparing my life even though I'm not worthy of any such grace.

Of course I could be wrong on all counts.

Chapter 26
Saint vs. Sinner

"You know, Demaris, you didn't have to kidnap me."

The voice and the sound of the plastic bamboo curtain being pushed away startles me. It's around one in the afternoon and I've just come down from the top of my tree where I had spent the morning thinking deep thoughts to get something to drink. Thank God I'm only half naked. I scramble to throw a bikini top on and quickly adjust my loincloth as Nokosee parts the bamboo curtain so "mom" can guide a woman up onto the raised log floor. The woman is blindfolded and dressed in faded jeans and and a t-shirt.

"I would have been more than happy to perform for the Chief," the woman continues. "He and the NS have been on my radar for some time."

While Mrs. O helps her find her footing, I rush to Nokosee's side as he lets the curtain fall behind him. For some reason, he's got an acoustic guitar strapped around his back which is unusual since he doesn't play. I grab his wrist and pull him aside.

"You kidnapped somebody *again?*" I whisper.

"Yeah, mom needed some help."

"Are you fucking kidding me?"

"No kid."

He shakes lose and walks over to his mother who is removing the blindfold from the woman.

"Stormy," Nokosee says with a broad, proud smile, "meet Joanny St. Collins."

Ms. Collins is still blinking her eyes to adjust to the light when she smiles and starts looking for me.

"Stormy Jones is here?" she says all friendly like. "I've heard so much about you." When she sees me, she moves towards me with open arms. "You are so special."

She's deeply tanned and her long black hair is streaked with gray and she could be another Seminole for all I know but the thing I notice most is her smile: it's big, bright and angelic. I don't know what to do or say. It's not every day you get such a loving greeting from someone your husband and mother-in-law just kidnapped. She grabs me up and gives me a big hug. I try to hug back while giving Nokosee a look that could kill since I got no heads-up on another kidnapping which he knows I have a problem with and the fact I look like a wreck and need a bath. When she pushes me away to look at me, I get embarrassed and wish I had done something with my Mo.

"It's a great look, Stormy."

"Thanks," I manage to mumble. Then she puts her hand on my big pregnant stomach hanging out over my loincloth like a beer gut which really catches me by surprise.

"I'm sure the baby is going to be as beautiful as you are."

Okay, I still don't know who she is, but I'm *really* beginning to like her.

"When are you expecting?"

"Late May or early June."

"Boy or girl?"

"I...I don't know."

"Neither did I when I had my babies. As far as I'm concerned, not knowing is the only way to go when it comes to having babies."

"Okay," I stammer. I mean, this woman is like a force of nature. I swear, I'm so discombobulated.

"So," she says as she puts her arm around me and turns to Nokosee and his mom, "when do I perform?"

As it turns out, Joanny St. Collins is a famous folk singer and apparently Mr. O has a jones for her. Because of that, Nokosee and his mom took it upon themselves to kidnap her this morning before she got a chance to perform at some kind of Disney World folk festival or something. Instead, she'll be performing live for the Osceolas-- and surprising Busi-- in celebration of their 20th wedding anniversary. Until then, the co-conspirators are stashing her in our chickee.

Whoe, what Osceola women won't do for love?

Mr. O is, of course, overwhelmed when he discovers a night of karaoke under the big communal chickee has been preempted for a special appearance by (drum roll please)...Ms. Joanny St. Collins!

When Joanny (that's what she insists I call her) walks out onto the log floor with the guitar Nokosee had been carrying a couple of hours earlier and stands in front of the mic, Busi's jaw drops down onto his chest and stays there until he's lifted onto his feet by his wife and son to join the standing O the NS are giving the living legend.

"Happy anniversary, Busi," Mrs. O says, "from Nokosee and me."

"Are you fucking kidding me?" he asks while still looking at Joanny and clapping his hands.

"No kid," she says.

Busi doesn't know who to look at as DC-G2 records it all for posterity.

"Go ahead and kiss her, Micco," Joanny says, her voice amplified by Boom Box's sound system. "She deserves it."

The Micco does as ordered. When he parts to look at his wife, he asks, "How--" but is cut short when her fingers touch his lips. He grabs them, takes them into his mouth and starts sucking and kissing them.

Oh, Lord! Well at least I know where Nokosee gets his mojo.

Mrs. O extricates her fingers from her husband's mouth and turns his head toward Joanny.

"Yeah, Saint!" he yells, jabbing his fist into the air. "Saint! Saint! Saint!"

As others join Busi in the chant, I turn to Nokosee with a puzzled shrug. He doesn't have a clue why they're doing that either but that doesn't stop him from joining the cheer-- until his dad grabs him in a headlock and gives him a noogie and a kiss on the top of his head.

When Busi turns back to "The Saint" to applaud and scream, I'm surprised to report he sounds, dare I say, like a *leetle girl*. I make it a point to yell as loud as I can over the NS cheering, whistling and applause so Nokosee *and* his dad can hear me.

"Why I do believe, Nokosee, your papa's a big giddy fanboy!"

Busi stops screaming long enough to reply, "Fanboy, hell I'm a fucking teenybopper when it comes to The Saint!"

Nokosee and I look at each other and start laughing. Call me crazy but despite what I know about Busimanolotome, that he earned his right to be on the FBI's Ten Most Wanted List-- right up there with me and Nokosee-- I'm happy for him.

When everyone settles down "The Saint" opens with a fitting romantic ballad that makes the old and new Osceolas put their arms around each other and kiss. A few songs later, I get why they call her "The Saint:" her songs-- none of which I have heard of but get the NS to applauding and cheering-- come with a message, usually about standing up for what's right and respecting the land.

When she gets off the stage and walks over to *me* and starts playing a song, I immediately grab Nokosee for support because that kind of attention makes me nervous and I surreptitiously motion for her to sing to the Osceolas sitting next to us, not me. But of course, she doesn't listen being "The Saint" and all and, after playing the opening chords on her guitar, reaches out and puts her hand on my bare stomach and leaves it there when she sings with true passion, never once taking her eyes off of mine, about how babies are sent from heaven to lead us. By the time she takes her hand away from my stomach to sing the chorus to Mr. and Mrs. O, she's turned me into a blubbering, true believer. Oh, yeah, she's the perfect choice for this bunch-- including me.

Especially when you read what she wrote on her guitar.

Yeah, when she was singing to me with her hand on my stomach, it kinda took me by surprise: *This machine kills fascists.* Thankfully she doesn't have a jones for rubbing out losers like me.

She saves her most famous and most moving song for last and sings it directly to the Micco. It's a song about soldiers. Her voice and her words cut me deeply right down to my soul. I glance at Nokosee to see if he's crying like I am. He is. I lean forward to look past him at his parents. They're crying to. Hell, everybody's crying. When she gets to the last lines in the song she looks directly at Busi The Sinner and reminds him that no matter what a soldier does in trying to make the world a better place, war is not the answer.

By now I'm crying like a big baby and have to cover my eyes because I'm so embarrassed.

"Micco, you can't go on like this. You can't win this fight."

I look up. "The Saint" is using her guitar like a rifle, sticking the neck in Busimanolotome's chest and in fact looks like the Marines planting the flag at Iwo Jima. I look around Nokosee at his father. He's looking up at her with an unflinching, steady gaze. His tear-filled eyes are narrowed on her's and there's a slight smile on his face.

"So far we don't seem to be doing too badly."

Mrs. O collapses in on herself and tries to control her body wrenching sobs but she cannot.

"Mom."

Nokosee reaches across his father under the guitar/rifle to touch her hand. She yanks it away, gets up and walks quickly across the open clearing and disappears in the hammock jungle.

"Mom!"

Nokosee goes after her.

Busimanolotome drops his head onto his chest.

"Micco," The Saint says softly, "you--"

He raises a hand and cuts her short.

"I know."

He tries to push "The Saint's" guitar away from his chest but she resists.
"Boss Man!"

It's Indian "The Whistler" Larry. He's suddenly standing next to Busi and aiming his AK-47 at The Saint. Mr. O, without looking at the guy, motions for him to relax as he looks up at the guitar wielding folkie.

"Now, now, Joanny, let's not forget our non-violent roots."

Indian Larry loads a round in the chamber of his machine gun to help remind her.

The Saint isn't intimidated as she struggles to keep the guitar planted in Busi's chest.

"As much as I love your music and what you stand for," Busi continues, "it's no match for the power of my vision."

He sticks his fingers through the strings and into the guitar and starts to close his fist but The Saint won't give up. I look around to see if anyone will help her but they won't look me in the eye.

"Leave her alone!" It's me. I'm standing up and yelling at him and don't know if I'm more angry or surprised I got all in-your-face over his behavior. Of course, he never acknowledges me but instead keeps looking at The Saint.

"Fuck this shit!" Now I'm standing by The Saint and helping her pin The Micco to his chair with her guitar. But it quickly proves to be a fruitless gesture as the old bastard methodically and effortlessly pops the guitar strings one-by-one and, despite our combined struggle to keep it firmly implanted on his chest, rips it from our hands. We stumble into his body and he pushes us back with the guitar.

"And you call yourself a peace activist," he says looking up at her from his chair. "You should be ashamed. Just for that, no guitar for you!"

Busi breaks the guitar across his thigh and throws it on the ground. It looks so sad lying there all crumpled in the dirt. When I turn back to look at him, he's slowly rising from his chair and looking like he's about to bust a valve or something. I step in between him and The Saint.

"Leave her alone," I shout. "She was only trying to talk some sense into your thick skull."

By the time I finish my sentence, he's already towering over me and my perspective on things suddenly becomes more realistic and hopeless.

You really got to learn to keep your mouth shut and to curb your impulses.

How come you're never around to advise me *before* my faux pas?

Focus. The old bastard looks like he wants to slap your head off.

"You touch me," I quickly add, "and you'll lose Nokosee too."

He doesn't move. He just looks at me as if he's seeing me for the first time and what he sees disgusts him.

"I don't take lightly to threats," he finally says.

"Yeah, I know, you're the toughest motherfucker in the jungle but if you keep this up, you'll be the *only* motherfucker in the jungle because you will have driven everybody away if you don't kill them all first."

Busi pauses and then lets out a great sigh before lowering his head toward his chest and his hand to his head.

"You know, little girl," he says while rubbing his temple, "you're starting to give me a headache."

"Good. Think of it as my anniversary present."

He chuckles over that one.

"Okay," he finally says as he turns to us, "I'll take it under consideration. Will that work for you gals?"

The Saint and I are both dumfounded. We were expecting bows and arrows with the occasional Stinger missile thrown in for good measure and got an olive branch instead. Go figure.

"It works for me, Micco," The Saint replies. She grabs my hand and holds it tight.

"Me too," I say. The last thing I want is a riff between Busimanolotome and me. We're basically all living on top of one another out here in the middle of nowhere and it makes life so much easier if you're on speaking terms with the people you bump into on your way to take a dump in the jungle.

"Fine. Joanny, please accept my apologies for the way things turned out." He starts digging into his pant's pocket for something. "How much was the guitar worth to you?"

"Boss Man," Indian Larry interrupts, "what are you doing?"

"What do you mean?"

"Let's hold her for ransom. She's gotta be worth something?"

"Hm-m-m," Busi says slowly, like he's actually considering it, "ransom."

"Mr. O!" I shout.

"I don't know, Indian Larry. She hasn't had a hit in... decades. She probably won't fetch much."

"Mr. O!"

"That's right, Micco," The Saint chimes in, "folk music isn't as big as it use to be."

"Don't worry, Joanny. I'm not going to hold you for ransom. I was just having a little fun with you."

"Damn!" Indian Larry stamps his foot and walks away in a huff.

"Anyway, Joanny, what's that guitar worth to you?"

"It's priceless. It was my talisman against writer's block."

"What, you can't write songs with another guitar?"

"Hey, what can I tell you? I'm superstitious."

"Okay, but priceless I can't do." He pulls out a thick wad of cash. "But I can and want to reimburse you for your troubles."

"Mr. O," I exclaim, "where did you get all that money?"

"I may not be a great host, little darling, but I'm a helluva bank robber. Joanny, give me a number I can work with."

"That's okay, Micco. It's insured."

"What? Isn't my money good enough for you?"

The Saint, being as intuitive as she is, knows it's probably a trick question and pauses before answering.

"Make me a copy of the video and we'll call it even."

"A copy of the video?"

"Yeah. I mean, if it's not too much trouble for you."

"No problem." He turns and nods to DC-G2. "Mind telling me what you plan on doing with it?"

"I liked what The What did with theirs. Maybe I can do the same."

Aw geese. Too late.

"'The What?' Those fucktards. If I ever get my hands on them I'm going to kill them."

The Saint turns to me with a questioning shrug.

"He thinks they squealed on us," I tell her.

"Think? They did! For crying out loud, Stormy, haven't you learned anything about the Outside. It can't be trusted."

"Micco," The Saint says softly, "Demaris needs you."

The Sinner takes a deep breath and nods he understands. "I'll go tell her you're leaving. Nokosee will take you back. Thanks for the great show. It's something I'll never forget."

"Me too," The Saint replies.

"Oh, by the way," The Sinner says as an afterthought, "would you mind listening to my CD? It'd be cool if you dug one of my songs enough to record it."

Chapter 27
"Recalculating."

"Nokosee."

It's Busimanolotome. Like a good Injun, he's unexpectedly outside our chickee. Snuck up on us with our pants down. This is not good.

"We need to talk."

"Right now?"

"Yes."

"It can't wait?"

"No. Pull your pants up and let's go."

"Dad, we weren't doing it."

Aside from his map reading abilities, Nokosee really needs to work on his lying skills. I fear for our lives if he's ever arrested. Lying on his back, he yanks up his jeans and pulls the zipper up, something he's gotten much better at since we first did it in the Presidential Suite.

"Please. I could hear you two crossing the water."

"Is that a euphemism for getting it on?" I shout as I pull up my loincloth.

Nokosee pushes back the Chinese plastic bamboo blind and sticks his head out. "Hey, dad, I have nothing to hide from Holatte-Sutv Turwv."

"That's because you don't have any sense."

"That's not going to get you what you want."

"Okay," Mr. O sighs, "I want you guys out of here."

"Are we moving again?"

"Yeah."

"You gotta be kidding me," I shout as I angrily slip on my white and yellow polka dot bikini top. I'm so pissed-off. Just when I was *really* beginning to like this place.

"No kid" I hear the old bastard say behind the blinds. "Joanny ratted us out."

I shove the monster wedding knife and its beaded sheath through the leather strap holding up my loincloth and stick my head out below Nokosee's, my big bare pregnant belly scraping the log floor.

"You're nuts!" I scream. "She'd never do anything like that."

"Why, because she's '*The Saint*'? She's in it for the money like all the rest."

"This is bullshit! In your mind they're *always* planning an attack on us but it never happens!"

"That's because we've always managed to stay a step or two ahead of them."

I turn and look up at Nokosee. "Nokosee, I can't do it anymore. I can't get up and do it all over again. I can't."

Nokosee turns to his father. "Dad, Stormy's right. You *always* think they're planning an attack. C'mon, already."

"I've never been more sure about this. In fact, I want you both to take a long vacation with your mom and sister ASAP."

"What, are you packing us off to Hialeah too?" I ask.

"Why would they want to attack us now?" Nokosee interrupts. "I mean, it's like they forgot about us."

"Until you and your mom kidnapped 'The Saint.' For crisesakes, what were you two thinking? Anyway, they didn't forget about us. They've been waiting for the Outside to forget about us before they make their move. Word is they've been planning this for months. Kidnapping 'The Saint' just sped things up a bit. They want to take us all down at once."

"But, dad," Nokosee says as he gets up. "I'm not going to leave you at a time like this. I couldn't."

"And neither could I, Mr. O."

I'm surprised I say that but I get up and stand by my man just the same. I never know what's coming out of my mouth anymore. Maybe it's my hormones talking. Or my lack of a fully functional prefrontal cortex. In any event, I think I mean it. I know it caught The Micco by surprise too.

"Sky Eyes, you're carrying my grandchild and I'm not about to let anything happen to you. Anyway, what could you do?"

"Thanks for the vote of confidence but I'm not leaving Nokosee."

Mr. O turns to Nokosee. "Son?"

Nokosee turns to me. "Stormy... maybe it's not such a bad idea. These bastards don't play fair. I--"

"Save your breath and stop being so goddamn chauvinistic. Both of you. You know, Mr. O., I think you really mean the kid. I'm expendable. He's not."

"*'He'?*" Both Os at the same time.

"I'm guessing. Am I right or not?"

Mr. O pauses to look at the "dream catcher" hanging from my big round belly before shaking his head wearily and walking off.

"That's what I thought!" I shout after him. Busi just keeps walking away and without turning back waves me off as if I was some kind of lost cause.

At least he didn't give you the finger. Things are looking up for you and El Nutjob.

Nokosee motions for me to be quiet. Not smart. "Screw you, Nokosee. I'll say what I want."

Nokosee jumps down from the chickee and runs up to his dad, grabs his arm and stops him.

"C'mon, dad, do you really think we're going to be attacked?"

"Yes. Try to convince your crazy wife to get the hell out of here."

"I can still *hear* you," I yell. "Are you sending us to Disney World?"

"Damn right!"

"You know, you're one obnoxious son-of-a-bitch."

He turns on me so quickly I flinch, expecting that bayonet hidden up his sleeve to finally come flying at me but the only thing he hurls my way is this pronouncement with one index finger held high in the air for emphasis: "'Very little of value in the world is done by people who are not obnoxious.' Malcolm Gladwell."

"Who the hell is Malcolm Gladwell?"

"Look it up in your precious Nook."

He turns and continues walking away in a huff.

"Sounds like another obnoxious son-of-a-bitch I know!" I shout.

Busi shoots me a bird without looking back.

Ah, back to normal.

Nokosee gives me a look to "cool it already" before catching up to his dad and disappearing in the hammock jungle. I hear them yelling at each other and arguing the fine points of me staying or leaving with "Mom" and guess who shows up?

"Stormy."

It's the woman-in-quotation-marks stepping out of the shadows and from between the trees. It would be an understatement to say I'm surprised to see her since she's basically kept herself scarce around our little hammock for a good long time; which has always been more than okay by me.

"Mrs. O," I stammer.

"I want you to leave with me," she says as she advances upon me with a furtive glance toward the voices of her son and husband now growing fainter in the hammock jungle. She takes my hand. "From what I can tell, Busi's right this time."

"Sorry, I'm not leaving Nokosee," I say and extricate my hand from her clammy clutches.

"Stormy, don't be stupid! If you stay here you're going to get killed and so will your baby!"

It looks like she really means it, looks like she's scared shitless.

"Don't make me laugh. If you cared about me and the baby, you'd want me to have it in a hospital like you did instead of out here in the swamp."

"I do, darling, but the Micco's afraid it's too dangerous now, that the Outside has figured it's about time you delivered and is staking out the hospitals. That's why he-- and me-- wanted you to have it here with a midwife overseeing it all. But not anymore. It's too dangerous now. You gotta leave with me today ASAP."

Man, she is one good liar. Don't trust her.

I turn away and shake my head.

"You're right, Stormy, I have been treating you badly. You deserve better, especially for what you did for Rory. In the beginning, when I first met you, I really didn't think you'd be good enough for Nokosee. He needs a stabilizing influence and you're too much like his dad."

I turn to her. "Like in *crazy?*"

"Like in angry."

She surprises me with that one. I have to turn away because I know she's right and it's something that bugs me too.

"And then I find out you're pregnant. Talk about a game changer. There is no way we're going to let anything happen to you."

I look at her. "'We're'?"

She pauses and takes my hand again.

"Micco and me. We both adore you and we both fear for your safety. We don't want anything to happen to you or the baby."

"You 'adore' me? You sure have a strange way of showing it."

"Because we've been trying everything we can to make you want to run away, cursing us as you go. It's not because we don't love you, darling. It's for your own safety and the baby's-- and we want you to convince Nokosee to go with you."

Ah-ha! So this is the real reason; to save her only begotten son.

We hear voices. Nokosee is coming back with his father.

"Stormy," Mrs. O says as she backs away, "try to convince him to leave with you. Please."

"Why don't you and The Micco tell him yourself?"

"He's all for getting you out of here, but he won't leave his dad. Stormy, please try to convince him before it's too late."

She turns and is absorbed by the jungle hammock.

I find myself left all alone in the clearing. I don't know what to believe and elect to make myself invisible until I can figure things out, until I can tell who's lying or not.

"Stormy!"

Even with Busi reading the ground for clues, they can't find me. This is not at all reassuring. After all, they're supposed to be these freaking crazy good pathfinders with tracking skills hardwired into their genetic code for crying out loud.

Or maybe you're getting better at hiding.

Puhleeze.

It's been less than five minutes since Mr. O and then Mrs. O tried to sell me separately on Disney World and certain parts of Hialeah. Now Chief Nutjob and the first-in-line to the throne are standing in the shallow water near the hammock's edge calling my name. I'm, of course, hiding among the tall cattails and sawgrass watching them get more frustrated by the minute-- and me even more doubtful of their super sleuthing abilities. I mean, c'mon, I'm less than 10 feet away and they can't find me. It's pathetic.

"Goddammit, Nokosee, can't you control her?"

"No!"

It's all I can do to keep from laughing out loud.

"Well, good luck with that. C'mon, it's getting late. We got to get your mom off to Hialeah."

Land of the "signs."

They turn all hot and bothered and trudge back through the hammock. It's not until they're long gone and I'm left all alone in the suddenly silent swamp that I begin to have second thoughts.

I must be nuts. I'm in the chickee looking at my reflection in a small compact mirror.

I've got multiple piercings on my face and tattoos on each side of my shaved skull for crying out loud-- what girl in her right mind would do something like that?

Well, according to Mrs. O, an angry mixed-up kind of girl with a spear instead of a chip on her shoulder.

Exactly.

I throw the mirror down and fall *awkwardly* onto the air mattress. Even that, I conclude, is abnormal because most girls my age could easily do that without even a second thought but not me because *I'm eighteen, barefoot and pregnant!* I've given up walking for *waddling!*

Waddling in the middle of freaking nowhere! Alone, barefoot and pregnant!

I'm not a happy camper.

Wanting to stay here to face down the United States of America with its panties all in a bunch I blame on my hormones and that prefrontal cortex thing. That's the only way I can explain it. I was never really much into nature. If I have a natural streak of rebellion running through my body, it became more apparent every summer when mom shipped me down to dad's mosquito infested swamp. I wish I could give a damn about saving the world but, as you know, I don't. I can't even get excited about saving the Inside from the Outside. I'm basically a selfish, self-absorbed, hormonally imbalanced nutjob going through the motions for Nokosee and his tree hugging cockamamie family. I'm really not that committed to The Cause despite my revelation which seems to be pointing me in that direction. Dying for it seems like such a waste of time. And lives-- especially mine, the baby's and Nokosee's.

I'm nothing but a big, fat, pregnant hypocrite.

So why didn't you flee when you had the chance?

I don't feel comfortable in the Outside anymore. I'm a freak in that world but here I'm not. In this world, even though it's as dangerous as all get out, I'm loved. And I get the privilege to love back.

So you did it for love?

Maybe. I make an effort to roll over onto my side and reach out for our little CD player and the CDs lying next to it. I find *Chorus Line,* slip it in and play "What I Did For Love," Track 12. It helps. A little.

I feel the baby kick. I put my hand over my stomach. I wonder if he-- or she-- can hear the music. I want to believe my baby can, that he or she loves it and is rocking slowly with it inside me, that he or she can't wait to get out into my world to love life, this great gift. And then the music stops, the batteries have died.

I hope I live to see my baby.

Then maybe you should have left with "Mom."

"Mom?" quotation marks or no quotation marks? I'm so confused.

Tears start welling up in my eyes. I may be nothing more than a big fat confused baby nutjob hypocrite, but I won't allow myself to cry. I'm here in the middle of nowhere, alone and pregnant and have no one to blame except myself. I should have taken the opportunity to get out of harm's way when it was given to me but *no-o-o-o,* I'm *insane!* I'm as crazy as Mr. O.

I'm nothing but a big fat pregnant ***insane*** hypocrite!

You should be locked up. For child endangerment.

I need counseling; lots of therapy. Thanks to my high school counselor I already know I have "boundary issues" which was her way of saying I don't have any, i.e., I don't know how to say "no" which partially explains why I'm all alone in the swamp right now.

Apparently you don't know how to say "yes" either.

But at least I kept the baby.

That little voice. I haven't heard it in awhile. Didn't need to hear it, didn't need to be reassured that I was making the right decisions. Everything was so...bucolic what with me lying around all day naked in the sun and making love with Nokosee. Not a care in the world. Most of the time.

Keeping the baby makes me proud. It's one of the few good things I've done right in this short lived life of mine.

I hear an airboat coming and struggle to get up and stumble out of the chickee.

I'm back in the swamp in my favorite hiding place, standing knee deep in water behind the cattails and the sawgrass watching Nokosee gather up our meager belongings. He's wearing my *Chiefs* Seminole jacket, unzipped down the front, and jeans with no shoes. The sun is setting. Mosquitoes are biting my ass again and I'm wishing I hadn't worn my sexy little loincloth, wishing I had grabbed my gold lamé kickers when I had the chance, wishing I had gone to Disney World with "Mom" (she's keeping them just in case I'm wrong about her) and Rory. I feel like a damn fool standing here, slapping away at the bugs. I don't want to feel like that and I'm tired of losing the bug battle.

You should have sprayed on some mosquito repellent before playing hide-and-seek.

Yeah, I should have done a lot of things but I didn't.

You should add "big dummy" to your litany of self-flagellation.

I decide to sneak up on Nokosee. For a laugh and to see if I can, like I did with Ghillie Guy. I think I've gotten better at it over the past few months. It's one of the few things I'm good at out here in the middle of nowhere. That and making love. In any event, I'm pretty sure he's stuck with me now since "Mom" is probably long gone to Hialeah, "land of the signs." Besides, I don't relish spending the night alone in the swamp. And I'm hungry.

Nokosee isn't that far away. He's busy throwing some loose ends into his machine gun mounted airboat and I decide to use it to hide my approach as long as possible. I come up on the stern, trying to walk as carefully and as slowly as I can. Trouble is, my feet are sucked into the muddy bottom and every time I bring them up, there's the chance I'll create a giant sucking and splashing sound. Sneaking up on him in the hammock is a lot easier. It shouldn't be since he's the big kahuna of the jungle and all, but it is.

"So what made you throw in the towel?" Nokosee asks without turning around. "Mosquitoes or hunger?"

I stop short. "Damn you, Nokosee Osceola!"

He laughs and turns around. I step back, yank the big freaking Special Forces "love" knife out from the beaded sheath hanging from my loincloth and point it at him.

"I'm not going back!"

Nokosee just stares at me. "You should see yourself."

I know.

You look like a wild-eyed, half-naked, confused, insane barefoot and pregnant teen chic in a loincloth with a shaved skull and a limp Mohawk pointing a giant freaking knife at him.

"God, how I love you."

Okay, so he sees me a little differently. That's why I love him so much. I let my guard down a bit.

"C'mere, baby," he says, "let me give you a big fat kiss."

"Promise not to make me go to Disney World?"

"I promise."

"Or Hialeah?"

"Especially Hialeah."

How can I say no to my big macho man? I stick my love knife back into its pouch and walk over to him. He's got his arms outspread and looking at me like Michael Keaton looked at Geena Davis in *Beetlejuice* before he tried to feel her up.

I liked that movie.

When I step up to him, he grabs me up and kisses the daylights out of me which isn't easy considering there's a giant baby between us. He ends the kiss with kisses all around my face and especially my tats.

"Remember when we did it for the first time?" he asks, still holding me up so it looks like I'm standing on the water.

"How can I forget?"

We're eye-to-eye and he squeezes me tightly.

"Remember later when we were catching our breath in bed before the next round and you asked when I saw you standing beside the bathroom door if you reminded me of a famous painting?"

"Yeah, and you said '*What?*' like I was crazy."

"I'd never heard of Botticelli back then or his *Birth of Venus* but I looked it up after you went back to New Jersey. Yeah, Stormy, you did look like Venus and I thought I'd never forget that pose. Until now."

Eargasm!

I tell you, this guy's got me coming every which way but loose. I start kissing him as he continues trying to talk through his adjectives, sometimes slurring them across conjunctions which is exactly what I want when he's done explaining how much he loves me, a big fat wet conjunction, baby.

"God," he manages to say, "you looked so sexy, and cute, and dangerous, and demure, and vulnerable and loveable."

I wrap my legs around him to let him know how I feel. He responds as I hoped and expected but then pushes me away.

"But, Stormy," he says breathless, "please know that everything I said is true but you're still going to Disney World."

"What?"

"But not Hialeah."

He grabs my knife and the next thing I know, he's walking me across the water to his airboat.

"Are you kidding me?" I yell.

"No kid."

"I don't want to leave our chickee!"

"We can come back."

"We never go back!"

"We can build another one."

"No! No! I can't do this anymore! I don't want to leave you!"

I'm so angry I squeeze him with my legs as hard as I can and I'm happy to report it makes him stumble and gasp for breath. But that's about it. Looking back, clamping on to him like that probably just made it easier for him to walk me across the water and step into the airboat. I should have been kicking and screaming. Then I get the bright idea of head butting him which is to say, I forgot everything I learned from my previous experience trying that on him. If you've read Micco Mann's rip off of my diary, you'll know that we had just met (he had me pinned to the ground and I thought he was going to rape me) and that it didn't go very well, i.e, Nokosee's head won. Just like this time around. Again, it looks like everything that happens in my life comes around full-circle, like it needs an encore or something. In this case, full-circle includes watching Nokosee's handsome face and its hard head spinning in circles in front of me.

Your life needs an encore because you don't learn anything the first time around. Talk about being hard-headed.

Only this time, I don't black out.

"Stormy?"

I try to focus on his face which is circling in front of me.

"Are you alright?"

I let my head collapse on his shoulder to catch my bearings. When he uses the hand holding my love knife to push my head back to see how I'm doing, I try to grab the knife and fail miserably. In frustration, I start pounding his chest with my fists. He immediately throws the knife into the airboat, grabs one of my wrists and turns it down behind my back.

"Nokosee, you're hurting me!" I scream.

"Sorry," he gasps.

He grabs my other wrist and directs it around my back too. I scream loudly because of the pain and the anger I'm feeling about the way he's manhandling me. Before I can register how to fight back effectively-- which is a joke in itself because what can I do against a guy like him?-- he's turned me around and tying my hands behind my back with plastic wire handcuffs.

"You bastard!" I yell over my shoulder. I try to back kick him in the balls but he jumps out of the way and I get him in his thigh.

"Whoe, there, little darlin'," he says with a laugh.

"I'll never trust you again!" I yell, tears now running down my cheeks.

"Darling," he says while he leads me backwards over to the bench seat below his, "there is no way I'm going to let anything happen to you. Whether you like it or not!"

"You chauvinistic bastard!"

He puts one knee on the seat and the other across my chest to pin me down as he runs rope through my arms and ties me to the airboat frame. No matter how much I struggle I can't stop him from tying me up. I try to bite him and get lucky. He screams like a big baby.

"Are you crazy?" he yells while trying to shake me loose.

I can't answer because I'm still latched onto his arm. I can taste his blood which only encourages me to bite harder. When he focuses on extricating himself from my mouth, that's when I kick him between the legs just like my father taught me-- and open my mouth. He falls backward onto the airboat hull like a sack of flour, grabs his balls and starts moaning and rolling from side to side while my teeth marks on his arm ooze multiple streams of blood. I'm so crazed with anger I yank at the ropes holding me back like King Kong on that New York stage. I really, really want to do him harm. I taste his blood and spit it to the side and know it must be running down my chin. I look at my heaving, bloody breasts and know I'm close to hyperventilating. I tell myself to think of the kid to make me calm down but I'm so enraged-- *deranged!*-- even reason can't work with me. The only thing that works to quell my anger is fatigue and the headache that's brewing. Nokosee might not be that great at tracking but he ties great knots and there just isn't any way I can fight through them. After a while, I collapse in on myself like a deflated punching doll and start crying in deep heaving sobs.

"You're nothing but a big fucking ignor*anus!*"

"Excuse me?"

"Ignor*anus!* You're stupid *and* an asshole!

Well, at least you didn't call him a pagan caveman.

"I'm sorry, Stormy," Nokosee says softly from the airboat bottom. "Please stop crying. You're breaking my heart."

I look at him through my deflated Mohawk falling across my eyes. He's flat on his back, holding his balls and leaving a trail of blood on the airboat hull as he rolls slowly back and forth and cries for his mommy. Literally.

"Mommy..."

"Is that supposed to be funny?" I ask.

"Does this look funny?" he manages to gasp.

"From where I'm sitting, *YES!*"

There's a distinct paleness to his dark, handsome features. Suddenly I'm feeling a lot better.

"I hope it hurts!" I spit it out with as much conviction as I can muster.

"Oh, it hurts alright," he confirms in a squeaky, grimacing falsetto.

"Good. You deserve it."

"I know I do. I'm so sorry."

He struggles to get up and I take further pleasure in seeing him stumble before my feet.

Not bad for some pregnant chick who's tied to a chair.

I find myself thinking my dad would be proud.

*Yeah, if he could **only** see you now.*

I'm thinking crazy thoughts as Nokosee climbs into the seat above me and starts the engine.

Once I get to Disney World, I'm leaving him.

Which probably isn't all that crazy when you think about it.

It's night, the motor has just been shut off and we're gliding slowly through a moonless Everglades, its horizon still glowing red from fires that seem to have become a permanent fixture. It's been about a half hour since I last screamed at Nokosee when I hear a woman's voice:

"Recalculating."

I look back. My idiot husband, now wearing a makeshift bloodstained bandage around his arm, is looking at his GPS.

Oh, lord, how are these guys ever going to overthrow the Outside if they can't even find their away around the Inside?

"You gotta be kidding me," I say with as much disappointment in my voice as I can muster.

Nature Boy doesn't say anything. I suspect-- I hope-- he's just a little bit embarrassed. I know I am.

"Did you pack my boots, asshole?" I shout.

I'm still tied up and, although my anger has subsided a little, I'm even more sure I'm leaving Nokosee and shaking loose of his facocta family in Disney World.

"I say, did you pack my fucking boots?"

He looks at me as if hearing me for the first time.

"Yeah. I got the boots."

"How 'bout my Nook, *Nooksy?*"

"Yeah, yeah, I got that too." he replies with a tinge of tension in his voice.

"Lost again?" I ask, twisting the words like a knife into his fabulous but dumb-ass body.

"I know exactly where I am."

"And where's that?"

"Right here."

He shows me the glowing, nearly featureless back-lit GPS screen and puts his finger on a spot that could be anywhere.

"And that's...?" I draw it out, daring him to answer me.

"Right where I'm supposed to be."

I look at him and can tell he's lying.

"You haven't got a clue, do you?"

"Nope."

I wait to make sure he's looking at me before sadly shaking my head, rolling my eyes and turning away in complete and utter disgust.

"That was supposed to be funny," he says.

"It wasn't."

"I know exactly where I am. It just doesn't have a name."

"Right."

"So, I guess you're ready to talk?"

"Not really. I just wanted to know if you got my Nook and my boots."

"What, so you can really kick me good in the balls next time?"

"Yes. And smack you aside of the head with my Nook."

He laughs, starts the engine and guns the airboat, banking towards the burning horizon.

"Do you mind!" I shout. "I'm starting to freeze up here!"

He lets off the gas and the airboat continues to glide through the swamp.

"My nipples are hard as a rock, not that you'll ever see them again."

"C'mon, Stormy, how many times do I have to apologize?"

"I can't count that high."

He sighs, turns the engine off and climbs down from his seat above me. When I see him holding his crotch and limping over to the duffel bags thrown haphazardly into the hull, I have to work hard to keep from laughing. He digs around and comes up with my Seminole jacket and a pair of jeans. He gets up and turns to me.

"So, are you going to let me untie you so you can put your jacket on?"

"Are you going to tie me back up after I put it on?"

"It depends."

"Depends on what?"

"It depends on whether or not you try to kick me in the balls."

I laugh and shrug that suggestion off. "Don't worry, your balls are safe with me."

"That's what she said."

I look up at him. "Still not funny."

He doesn't move, just stares at me like Larry David sizing up a guy to see if he's lying (yes, we watch pirated *Curb Your Enthusiasm* DVDs in the swamp). And I stare him down, just like Larry would.

"Okay, I'll trust you, but you better be pretty, pretty good."

I have to smile a little over that one. Just like Larry.

Nokosee limps up to me with my stuff in his hands in a mock defensive stance.

"Promise not to bite?" he asks.

"Please. Just untie me."

He leaves my clothes next to me and this time steps *behind* the bench seat and unties the ropes. I pull my sore arms up over the back of the seat and start rubbing them.

"You know," I say, "you're really never ever going to see me naked again."

"C'mon, Stormy."

"Never."

I grab my jacket and put it on, zipping up the front.

"'Never ever again?'"

"Never ever again."

"Then how are you going to put your pants on?"

"I'll wait until I'm on the bus to Disney World."

I wish I wasn't in such a big hurry to let him know I have it all figured out. If I would have just paused a second or two I might have thought of telling him to turn around so I could put my pants on. But I didn't so now I'm stuck wearing my loincloth until I can at least get somewhere where I can change so that I can keep my promise that he'll never ever see me naked again.

"Okay," he says with an eye-rolling drawl.

"Don't you roll your eyes at me!" I yell, pointing at him as he limps past me and climbs back up into his seat. "I was *brutalized!*"

I fold my arms in front of my chest and let them rest on my big round belly. Settling into the seat resigned to the inevitable, I sigh loud enough hoping that he can hear me. In any event, I get nothing from him as he starts the airboat back up and sends us sliding across the black water through the night. But I can't let it go so out of frustration and for good measure I let him have it one more time.

"Brutalized!"

Chapter 28
Stars Hammock

Well, I never got to Disney World that night. As it turned out, the First of the New Seminole couldn't find his way out of a paper bag and we "missed the bus." What a joke. By the time dawn arrived and we "stumbled" onto the latest NS camp, Nokosee had been subjected to a relentless tireless onslaught of some of my best ball bustin' put downs for being such a doofus; which helps explain why we aren't speaking to each other right now. Maybe I should have kept my mouth shut but by now you must know that pretty much isn't going to happen. I was so angry with him what with my kidnapping and the handcuffs and the uprooting from a place I loved, that I just basically took out all of my frustrations on the poor guy. Whether or not we were being stalked by the almighty Army of the United States of America I couldn't tell you. Never saw any soldiers or heard any gunfire. All I know is I've traded in my nice chickee for a tent and that I've pretty much had it up to here with all of the moving around and false alarms.

The only good thing that came out of arriving late at the new camp is that "Mom" didn't miss the bus. She's long gone and to tell you the truth, despite what she told me last night, how much she and The Micco "adore" me and all, I don't miss her one bit especially with all the crying she was doing lately. It was starting to bring me down. Plus, it saves me time searching for those damn quotation marks on the keyboard. Now if Busimanolotome would disappear too and take his crazy collection of granola-eating, nincompoop pot heads with him, a.k.a. the NS, and leave Nokosee behind so that we could spend the rest of our lives kissing and making up, that would be great. Unfortunately, I don't see that happening any time soon no matter how much I get down on my knees and pray to God to forgive me for all I've done. Some might suggest that I poke Him re Nokosee to help him see the light his mom wants him to see, the light that *isn't* shining in the swamp while I'm down on my knees and praying. But I could never ask Him for a favor like that because it would be insincere, i.e., I don't have the right to ask for *any* favors. Period. Truth be told, in the final analysis, I think I have a death wish. I need to be punished. Not forgiven. Still, I half hope He'll have pity on me anyway-- by "God's Grace" and not by anything I do-- and grant my unspoken wish to live happily ever after with Nokosee and our child. Maybe if I was more of a global warming denying fundamentalist than a less judgmental Lutheran I'd stand a better chance with the Big Guy but having listened to Busimanolotome's rantings long enough now about how right wing Christians are part of the problem instead of the solution re saving the environment, I've come to the hellfire conclusion for my soul that he's right. According to Mr. O, Nature is the real world and Man exists on islands within it like the NS does in the Everglades. The last thing a fundamentalist wants, The Micco says, is someone preserving the environment because it would delay Armageddon, the end of the world, and the return of Christ.

But Busimanolotome doesn't blame fundamentalists for everything. In fact, he likes to remind anyone who will listen to him that more than half the American people don't believe in global warming, evolution, or (and I'm not making this up) gravity and he'll gleefully site the 2009 Gallup poll to prove it and to further justify why the NS are needed: without us the Inside-slash-Nature is doomed because the Outside can't be counted on to save it since it's degenerated into a mouth-breathing, drug addled collection of consumer cultures that can't save itself.

Aside from the fact that the poll implies half of America was high on drugs when it answered the questions, the thing that makes me the saddest about seeing the world like Busimanolotome does is that it makes Man's removal from the scene insignificant in relation to Nature. Not only will life go on without us, it'll probably flourish like all get out. No matter how pristine such a world might be, it would be a Dystopian one for me and that would be unbelievably sad. The idea that our gift of the arts and all the beauty we created is meaningless doesn't compute with me. Neither does a world without the great human attributes of love, valor, compassion, and laughter which Busimanolotome insists can be found in Nature too. Maybe others can find it there, but it doesn't shine as brightly as when it takes human form. I can't imagine a world without any of that. In fact, I've come to the conclusion after sitting for many hours in trees that *my* Nature can't exist without *my* Nature Boy. Of course, maybe if I had been sitting *under* the tree like Newton, I would have come up with a more rational explanation for it all but I don't think it would be an answer I could live with.

Anyway, one of the neat things that came out of all of this arboreal cogitation over the last few months before my brutalization is that I discovered that despite what his father had been trying to beat into him, Nokosee is *leaning* in the direction of the "light." i.e., he's starting to see things my way. At first when Nokosee joined me up in the tree it was for some arboreal fornication, a thing that, according to Busimanolotome who informed us unannounced (as usual) one day at the bottom of the tree, can be seen and heard for miles: "You ought to stick a sign in the ground," he said while looking up at us, "warning anyone should they venture onto your hammock that if they see the tree a rockin,' don't bother a knockin'." To which I replied with a roll of my 'sky eyes,' "Harde-har-har-har" in the same mocking way he did with me on our first argument following the "Attack on the Alley." Except this time around he cut me short like a middle-school kid with an idea he couldn't wait to share: "No, wait, you should also include screaming and moaning too on that sign." When I heard Nokosee laugh, I whipped around to my co-conspirator in all things horny with a look that cut *him* short. As we soon learned that day, Busimanolotome was an emissary sent over by the tribe to inform us that our love making sessions in the top of the tree were, besides scaring the poultry, making it impossible for anyone to sleep. It appears we were shaking the bejesus out of the only tree on our little hammock island and, thanks to my moaning and screaming, the tree appeared possessed, as if it had been singled out by some kind of supernatural mini-hurricane badass spirit. It so alarmed the old Shaman Dude who married us that he begged Busimanolotome to allow him to perform an exorcism on the tree. Busimanolotome told the old guy not to worry, that he'd take care of it which he did: we no longer do it in the air because it's too damn embarrassing. Instead, we've taken to climbing up into the tree to watch a wide-screen view of the far-flung and humbling Everglades which invariably leads us to asking the big questions usually reserved for philosophers and such like, what's up with my revelation? (which Nokosee likes to remind me was God's way of showing we were meant for each other). As Nokosee puts it, I was the one who convinced him his dad was wrong, that Man matters because of *me*, because of my "powerful balls-to-the-wall life force" that made him fall in love with me. Until I came around, he saw "love" as his hardass dad did, unromantically and scientifically. I convinced him by just being the wonderful person I am that Man gives Nature that special something that balances it all out, that puts a smile on Nature's heartless face. He calls me his "true north" and knows without me he'll lose his way in the world-- which probably isn't saying much considering his pathfinding skills-- and couldn't live without me either. It's that kind of talk that makes it really hard for me to stay mad at him for long.

So you'll be forgiving him soon?

Just a little longer. He must learn brutalization comes with a price.

Plus you still need convincing he means everything he says.

True. I know, I shouldn't but I can't help myself. I figure that will only come with time-- after I've had more time to think about all that has happened to me and been said to me, to sort truth from lie.

Because you can only sit so long stark naked on a branch over the water thinking about these kinds of things-- or reading books on your Nook to *stop* thinking about those kinds of things-- before your ass starts developing a rash and you start craving a change of scenery, I decide to climb down from my newest gumbo limbo one day to continue my thinking and sorting from a bithlo. This has allowed me to put some needed space between Nokosee and me since my brutalization because bumping into each other at the base of my tree was becoming uncomfortable to say the least for both of us. In the beginning my excursions into the unknown always kept my new hammock home in view as I stood barefoot in my loincloth and polka dot bikini top in the bithlo and polled it around the neighborhood so to speak. At first it was surprising to see the number of NS and their tents hidden inside the surrounding hammocks but after a short while and many friendly greetings and hand wavings later, I got the feeling that I was living in a cheap, rundown Venetian trailer park where the roads were always flooded and poverty was the norm and everyone knew your name-- even my unpronounceable Seminole name. I began to think of myself as a barefoot Lorelei Gilmore in a loincloth and that I was living in the tent city version of Stars Hollow, i.e., Stars Hammock, a name I gave to our new camp since Busimanolotome appears to have finally run out of names from *Hair.*

With each new day's exploration, I ventured farther and farther away from Stars Hammock with a Prada handbag hanging from my shoulder filled with snacks-- the NS is awash with yummy Lance *Toast Chee* peanut butter crackers and *Cheez Doodles* thanks to the tribe's latest foray into the Outside-- bottled water and a compass. Within a few days not only was Stars Hammock no longer on my horizon, it was also never a hassle to find again, no matter how many miles I might be away from my tent in the wet wastelands. I grew more self-confident in finding my way around the swamp basically because I discovered I'm good at reading my compass and have a gift at spotting landmarks and marking a trail. Not that these are the kind of skills that might get me a job anywhere, unless maybe with the Marines but being on the FBI's Ten Most Wanted List might put the kibosh on that. Anyway, after a while it became a personal challenge to develop this skill to see how far I could go each day into an unknown part of the Everglades before turning around and finding my way back home. And it will certainly come in handy knowing how to actually read a compass, a map, or the landscape when Nokosee gets lost again, which he probably will, my big loveable and currently monosyllabic doofus-in-the-doghouse.

This daily ritual comes to a crashing and disturbing end when I come across a small cluster of hammocks far away from Stars Hammock. I stop polling the bithlo because I'm sure I hear someone crying. Listening intently confirms I'm not hallucinating. That gives me goosebumps. I drop to a crouch in the bithlo and grab my honeymoon knife. It's the most wretched crying I've ever heard in my life. It might be politically incorrect by saying this but its gotta be coming from a woman, wailing uncontrollably, inconsolably. I don't know who she is and don't care. All I know is that the sound of her crying is like a knife in my heart and I want to help her-- even more than finding out who she is. I wonder if she might be a member of the tribe and needs help. Despite how much I hate walking barefoot through the swamp, I slip out of the bithlo into the water. Each squishing step in the muddy bottom sends shivers of disgust up my body but I tramp through the swamp as carefully and as quietly as I can just in case my first instinct to help is the wrong one.

When I push cattails away the first thing I see is the top of a dead tree. And then another one. Oh, God, it looks like that goddamn fungus made it all the way out here! And then I see a small chickee built over the water under a canopy of dead trees. It can't be more than six feet square, just big enough to shelter one person, in this case a woman as I suspected. Her back is to me and she's sitting on the raised log floor, a small camping toilet behind her. She's fat, bordering on obese and her whole body is shaking with each gut wracking sob. Her pantsuit is dirty and torn, her shoes are missing. I want to see her face and cautiously thread my way through the knee deep water, careful not to disturb the water's surface or to create any splashing sound. I hunker down behind a tall cypress tree and peek around its massive trunk.

I've seen her from someplace before but I don't know where. That creeps me out. Was it on TV? The newspaper? (Yes, I started reading the Miami Herald to kill time when I was sojourning with dad in the swamp every summer and became addicted to getting my daily news fix off the ground every morning, including Milltown, NJ ground when I was sent back home). She's old, maybe sixty and she's dressed professionally, like she works in an office. She doesn't appear to be tied up either.

"Sei-*ho*, shut the fuck up!"

Oh, my God! There's someone else out here in the middle of nowhere. I turn to the voice and see another mini-chickee tucked away deeper in the cypress stand and fall back against the tree. There's a man lying on the raised log floor. His hands are behind his head and he's looking up at the thatched roof. He's barefoot and also looks like he belongs in an office. And he's got a small camp toilet too.

"You're starting to give me a headache!" he shouts.

He has a Cuban accent and although I can't see his face, I recognize the voice.

"What have we done to deserve this?" the woman shouts across the swamp.

She also has a Cuban accent and I swear, I know that voice too. This is way too weird.

"Nancy," a third voice shouts, "I'm with Carlos. Shut the fuck up!"

Another woman is shouting across the water. I turn and see a third mini-chickee even further away but still hidden in the dying cypress stand. She's standing, leaning against one of the chickee posts. She's too far away to recognize but from her voice I can tell she's not Cuban. She has blonde hair and fair skin and is wearing a white blouse and a navy blue skirt. She looks like another office worker. She doesn't have any shoes on either.

"You shut the fuck up!" Nancy shouts back.

"No, bitch, you shut the fuck up!"

Oh my God, another voice. This one belongs to a man. I ease up along the tree trunk to see if I can find him. I see a fat black guy in another mini-chickee built over the water behind me. He's sitting on the edge of the log floor looking into the water, his legs and bare feet dangling over the side.

And then it hits me because I know who this guy is. Who else wears gold satin suits in Miami? I mean, he's got one on right now for crying out loud. His name is Dorrance Robb. He's a Miami-Dade County commissioner with a jones for gold satin suits and backroom deals. And the others? I know them all thanks to dad who use to drag me along to county meetings regarding the Everglades. Carlos is Carlos Alvaro, the Mayor. Nancy, is Nancy Seijo another commissioner and I figure the blonde is Sandy Heyluke, one of the few Anglos on the commission.

What the hell are they doing out here in the middle of bumfucking nowhere, where everything is dying instead of living? Are there any more? There are 13 commissioners. Did Busimanolotome kidnap the whole goddamn bunch?

How do you know it was Busimanolotome?

Please.

I start looking around and damn if Micco Meshugana didn't kidnap the whole lot of them. Thirteen commissioners and I'm guessing a few of their aides, and one mayor in about half-a-dozen mini-chickees scattered around the gray-dead cypress stand.

And no one's guarding them?

No, no one's guarding them. I guess Busimanolotome doesn't have to considering at 1.5 million acres, the Everglades is so freaking big, if anyone tried to escape it would mean certain death by any number of means including alligator, snake, bear, panther, mosquito, exposure, and starvation. Considering the age of these people and the fact that they are woefully out of shape, they wouldn't stand a chance.

I hear the rising sound of an airboat engine and sink deeper into the water. I try to become one with the cypress tree as a black airboat draped in ghillie camo and looking like it won The Crapiest Float Award in the annual Swamp Bowl parade slows down and banks into this mosquito infested gulag. Busimanolotome is at the tiller with Indian Larry sitting below him. This guy is my least favorite of the NS. Besides being a smart-ass, he has a short fuse and is, I'm surprised and anxious to see, brandishing his favorite weapon of choice, an AK-47. Of all the crackpots and crack heads in the NS, I can't understand why Mr. O would bring this dangerous nutjob with him. Busi cuts the engine and by the time they slide into the cypress stand, everyone is rising to their feet in their mini-chickees anxious and afraid.

"Greetings, Mr. Mayor and Commissioners," Busimanolotome shouts affably as he throws the ghillie camo net aside. "I hope Camp I Ain't Got No Home has exceeded your expectations. If not, please let us know by filling out our guest response cards and leaving them with our front desk clerk, Indian Larry here, upon check-out."

Ain't Got No Home is right out of *Hair*. Indian Larry, unsmiling, chambers a round in the AK-47.

"Check-out is, of course, at 3PM. If you check-out after 3 you will be charged for an extra night."

I look around at the "guests." They look scared shitless. Fat Nancy starts to cry.

"Commissioner Seijo, please, there is no need for tears. For any late charges, just put it on your county issued credit card, you know, with all the other shit you charged taxpayers for."

Fat Nancy starts crying even louder. Indian Larry shuts her up with a burst from his AK-47 shot into the water beneath her mini-chickee and all of a sudden it becomes quite clear why Busi brought Indian Larry along for the ride. Although words may be more powerful than swords when written down for posterity, nothing quite beats getting your attention and making an immediate short lived impact like a rapid round of gunfire.

"Now, now, Indian Larry, save your bullets. We may need them later for something much more important."

Indian Larry doesn't turn his crazed, possessed look away from the "guests" or point his machine gun elsewhere when he says, "Like the Final Solution?"

"Well, Indian Larry," Busimanolotome chuckles, his head bobbing as if he were channeling Ronald Reagan, "that's not really for me to say. It depends on how the negotiations go."

"Can't I just kill one of them to show we're serious. Maybe one of their lackies."

"I don't think so."

"How about the bus driver? No one will miss him."

"Hey!" the bus driver shouts in his own defense. "I got kids!"

"Maybe later but right now, let's try to be patient. I mean, it isn't every day nearly two million people get their elected representatives kidnapped while on a fact finding excursion into the Inside and held for ransom. We'll give them another day before we address that issue."

"Sir?"

It's the mayor. He's got his hand up in the air and looking up at Busimanolotome as if he were a school boy.

"Yes, Mr. Mayor," Busimanolotome says jovially. "What can I do for you?"

"Like I said before, the county doesn't have a hundred million dollars for anything much less our ransom. We're basically broke."

"No thanks to you and your guests at Camp Ain't Got No Home. Maybe if you weren't locked in to that quarter of a billion dollar baseball stadium giveaway you guys put together at taxpayers expense, there might be some money left over for these kinds of things, you know like funding eradication of that fucking fungus that's killing all the trees."

"Uh, Chief," Commissioner Heyluke says nervously, her hand raised too as if she was a kid in a classroom, "I voted against the baseball stadium."

"Yes you did, Sandy," Busimanolotome replies pleasantly. "Unfortunately, you voted to move the urban development line deeper into the Everglades. That's a real no-no where I come from."

"But I voted against both!" another "guest" shouts from the back of the swamp. I can't place him but he looks like some kind of well-dressed shoeless hipster lawyer.

"And the NS is proud of you. Unfortunately, Commissioner Hardy, you were on the bus with the rest of the usual suspects when we hijacked it. Sorry about that."

"But that's not fair," he shouts.

"Hey, what's fair in love and war, right? Maybe if you guys hadn't cracked down on my bank robbing ways I wouldn't have had to kidnap you and hold you for ransom. You know, Stinger missiles and RPGs don't come cheaply. Anyway, I'm not hear to argue with you. I just came by to say hello, see how you're doing and to drop off more food and supplies."

Indian Larry starts unloading cardboard boxes onto the log floor of the mayor's mini-chickee.

"You'll be happy to know that we were able to score some KFC for you guys. Extra crispy. Hope you like it. I'll let the mayor divvy it up between you. He seems to be pretty good at that."

"Did you get any mosquito repellent?" Commissioner Heyluke asks.

"Gosh, Sandy, I plumb forgot. Maybe next time. Talley-ho!"

And with that, Busimanolotome pulls the ghillie camo net across him and Indian Larry and starts the engine. He turns the airboat on a dime and with Indian Larry firing his AK-47 into the air and the prop wash blowing the boxes of food, supplies, and Fat Nancy into the water, races through the dying cypress stand, disappearing behind the cattails, sawgrass, and skeleton trees.

I don't know what to say or do. My eyes are blinking from sensory overload, my mouth hangs open stupidly, and my head shakes slowly from side to side because I'm basically one dumfounded, smack-me-aside-the-head, mixed-up kinda clueless chic who thought she'd seen it all and had it all figured out up until now.

Now what? Am I supposed to save them? I'm no hero. I'm just a half-naked barefoot and pregnant teenager in the middle of the freaking Everglades. What can I do? It's not like I can call 9.1.1 or something. Oh, man.

Then I see the beady little eyes of an alligator headed my way.

Idiot! Of course Busimanolotome didn't leave these yahoos unguarded. He's got guard gators watching them!

I push away from the tree and try to make a mad girly-girl dash through the water towards my bithlo but my "dream catcher" pendant hanging from my navel gets snagged on a cattail. I cry out and stop to unhook myself.

"Hey, look over there!," someone shouts. "It's that ranger's kid!"

I look back at the gator closing in on me and try to yank the cattail out of the water.

"Stormy Jones! I'm the mayor of Miami-Dade County! We've been kidnapped!"

The cattail breaks loose from the muddy bottom and two giant steps later I'm throwing myself into the bithlo, dragging the dripping cattail from my "dream catcher." I look back. The gator is yanked backwards and stopped dead in the water by a chain tied around its neck.

"Help us, please!"

I turn from the gator as it thrashes against the chain anchored to a cypress tree and look at the "guests" of Camp Ain't Got No Home. They're all standing in their little chickees and looking at me as if I'm their only hope.

"Don't leave us here!"

Aw, geese, why does this have to happen to me?

This is what happens when you get bored too easily. None of this would have happened if you had stayed in Milltown. Or at least back in your tent or in the top of your tree.

Or had gone to Disney World when I had the chance.

I've got to stop talking to myself because I always feel like a schmuck afterwards. I grab my pole and stand in the bithlo, the wet cattail hanging over my big baby belly, and look at them. For such powerful people, they look so forlorn right now. And I've never felt more powerful even though I may look like a damn fool what with a cattail snagged in my "dream catcher" and dripping between my legs. Their lives are in my hands. I've been given this opportunity to redeem myself.

Yes, I know my focus should be on saving their raggedy fat asses but I'm also quite aware that I need redemption if I want to continue living with myself and the voices inside my head. I wish I could be the perfect heroine but I'll be perfectly happy to settle for one who's flawed and I'm pretty sure the ones I save won't mind either. In fact, I'm betting they might even drop some if not all of the charges against me if I can pull it off.

"I'm going to get help," I shout across the water. "Until I get back, whatever you do, stay out of the water!"

I turn and drive the pole into the water and the bithlo glides gently through the cattails and the sawgrass. I can't pole fast enough to get out of there to escape the implications and to find help.

Maybe this is what my revelation is really all about. Maybe this is my true destiny.

"No! Don't leave us!"

I don't look back. I can't look back or else I'll start crying.

Chapter 29
When the Holy Shit Meets the Fucking Fan

It's night by the time I get back to Stars Hammock. Nokosee, wearing my *Chiefs* jacket, is throwing what little possessions we have into our airboat. It's lit only by the the light of a single Coleman lantern as I approach in the bithlo.

"You gotta be kidding me!" I shout.

He jumps, catches himself and does a long sigh.

"Not again?" I ask.

"Again. Dad's sure they're coming this time."

"This is bullshit!"

"I agree but let's get out of here just the same." He jumps into the airboat. "Throw me your line-- and lose the cattail. You could trip over it."

I had forgotten about the cattail snagged in my "dream catcher." I grab the "dream catcher" and yank the damn cattail through it, breaking a few of the silver wires woven around it. Unfortunately, I also yanked the navel piercing enough to make it bleed.

"Dammit!" It hurts like hell.

"Now what?"

"Nokosee," I reply as I cradle my big belly and limp toward the airboat, "I'm bleeding."

"For crying out loud."

He runs into the water, catches me under an arm and helps me walk toward the airboat.

"C'mon, we gotta get out of here!"

I've never seen him so agitated. Maybe he knows something I don't. Maybe they really are coming this time. Or maybe he's just antsy because he isn't getting any lately as punishment for the way he brutalized me a week ago. He bends down, puts an arm under my legs, lifts me out of the water and puts me in the airboat.

"Nokosee, stop a second." I grab his arm.

"What?" he says sharply. "Can't it wait?"

"Nokosee, your dad kidnapped the whole goddamn county commission and the mayor! He's holding them for ransom in the swamp!"

"What a guy."

He shakes me loose, jumps into the airboat and climbs into the driver's seat.

"Nokosee!"

"What do you want from me? The guy's a fucking maniac. It goes with the territory." He turns the engine on.

"Did you know about this?" I shout. Nothing. "Nokosee, we gotta save them before they all starve to death or get eaten by alligators!"

"Later." He slips night- vision goggles over his eyes.

"'Later?'"

"After we save our own asses."

He whips the airboat around throwing me into the seat below him. I look back at Stars Hammock. He didn't even have time to take down our tent, now ripped from its stakes and thrown against the wind whipped gumbo limbo I had taken to climbing in. I whip around, look up at him and shout:

"Did you pack my boots?"

"Yes!"

"My Nook?"

I can't see anything as Nokosee hurtles us through the black night. If it wasn't for his night-vision goggles we would have crashed into a hammock or two by now. The only good thing about this high speed charge through the thickest jungle night I've ever seen is that the bow has come up enough to shelter me a little from the wind.

And then it comes to a bone crunching halt. Literally. Nokosee kills the engine and slams the rudders hard to the right to stop us as fast as he can. I'm thrown onto the hull bottom and all the crap thrown into it seems to find a way of falling on me. I feel like I've dislodged the baby but I know that can't be true as I try to hold onto the cargo sliding down the raised hull because I should be in excruciating pain. And then Nokosee whips the rudder to the other side and I'm rolling head over heels back across the hull again with the cargo. When we finally come to a stop, I push some stuff off of me to look up at Nokosee. He's staring motionless through his night vision goggles at something in the hidden Everglades. I lift myself up to see if I can see it too but I can't see a damn thing.

"Nokosee," I whisper, "what is it?"

"Stormy," he whispers, "get up *real* slowly, as quietly as you can, and come over here."

When I kick something off of my legs, I feel a pain in my stomach and groan.

"Are you alright?"

He's climbing down from the driver's perch, still wearing his night-vision goggles and looking a lot like that freak in the cellar in *Silence of the Lambs*.

"I'm fine," I lie.

He deftly avoids the crap in the hull and helps me to my feet.

"Here, put these on."

He helps me put the night-vision goggles on.

"I want you to drive us out of here."

"Why? What do you see?"

I start looking around and stop short. Another swamp army is advancing upon us. All of them are wearing night-vision goggles but they haven't spotted us yet because Nokosee put a hammock between us and them.

Oh, crap. I really wanted to believe that all the shooting and killing was a thing of the past, that Mr. O was just paranoid as usual. Guess not.

"Use the GPS in the seat and steer us northwest. Got it?"

"Northwest. Got it. What are you going to do?"

"Shoot 'em if I have to."

Nokosee, holding onto my shoulder, pushes me toward the back of the airboat. I stumble through the flotsam in the hull and climb into the driver's seat while Nokosee steps into the center of the machine gun turret behind me. As Nokosee readies the big machine gun, I check the GPS to find out where northwest is. Because the NS use mufflers on their engines, its pretty quiet when I start it up and can't be heard by the encroaching swamp army as I turn the airboat slowly around. But the moment I gun it and pop out from behind the hammock, the Everglades lights up with flashing yellow lights and milliseconds later the sounds of thousands of bullets ricocheting off the steel in a flurry of screaming sparks. The bullets that miss are racing ahead of the airboat on both sides in neatly spaced marching plumes of water.

I look back at Nokosee. He's standing and firing the machine gun over the prop cage, raking it across the bouncing horizon at the popping yellow lights in the distance. Most of the empty hot shell casings are falling into the back of the airboat but some are hitting the spinning propeller and getting hurled back at Nokosee and me. One hits me hard in the back and it's like I've been hit by a hot fireplace poker. Because Nokosee's not wearing night-vision goggles, his aim is a little off. Unfortunately, theirs isn't.

The airboat is whipped with a long loud lashing of bullets smashing into the hull and bouncing off the metal prop cage. It's as if the bullets are wearing night-vision goggles of their own and can't miss.

I start zigzagging through the swamp and try putting as many hammocks as I can between us and them and within the longest seconds of my life, we've outrun the things that are trying to kill us.

A minute flies by before we stop to catch our breath and to look back.

"Holy shit! What was that?" I shout at Nokosee who's standing behind me, looking at the numerous welts rising across his bare chest left by the errant spent machine gun cartridges.

"That was the holy shit hitting the fucking fan."

"We're under attack!"

It's Nokosee's two-way radio squawking to life with Mr. O's voice yelling over shouts and gunfire in the background.

"Meet up at Rendezvous Point!"

Chapter 30
Rendezvous Point!

We switch places to get to Rendezvous Point, whatever or where ever that is, as fast as we can. To me it sounds like a romantic spot on the water, but I'm pretty sure it isn't. Even with his night-vision goggles, I question whether Nokosee can find it without old school or new school assistance knowing what I know about his pathfinding skills, but as it turns out, he won't need them. I can see Black Hawks in the distance, silhouetted against a red glowing line marking where the burning Everglades ends and the night sky begins. They look like bees hovering over a burning flower, their metal bodies reflecting the flickering light below them. I grip the machine gun harder and pray I don't have to use it.

The burning flower is now a hammock. I can see tracer rounds going back and forth as the NS fire back on the helicopters. One of them, circling with its nose pointed toward the hammock, fires a rocket. The hammock explodes in a giant ball of fire and the Everglades is lit up for a moment, just long enough for us to see Army Rangers in inflatable rubber rafts paddling toward the hammock.

Army Rangers are a scary bunch considering what they have to go through in training. Only one in three who applies makes the cut. Those that survive basic Ranger School training can out run, out slog, out swim, out climb, out starve, out pain, and out kill any soldier on the planet. The last thing you want to do is piss them off. Knowing that we killed a few of their buddies, I'm sure they're coming at us with a vengeance that can only be described as Biblical. I start praying to the Almighty Army Ranger God, which I'm sure is the same as mine, asking for forgiveness and protection for we know not what we do.

When Nokosee lets loose a war-hoop and turns into the soldiers paddling and sloshing through the swamp, I immediately know I'm on the wrong side.

But you're only eighteen, barefoot and pregnant for crying out loud! Doesn't that count for something?

I guess not. I'm doomed. Well, if that's the way it's going to be, I figure I might as well go down fighting instead of crying like a big fat baby; just like my father taught me saying, "the meek might inherit the earth, but God only takes warriors." I think dad would have made a great Army Ranger.

Or a New Seminole.

The first soldiers to die are paddling their rubber raft when they're run over from behind by our airboat. Ten dead just like that. Ten dead before we land back on the water. They never saw it coming. Or heard it coming what with all of the sounds of war echoing around them. Ten more die within seconds as Nokosee broadsides another raft. Good young men, I'm sure. All with families who loved them, wives who will miss them, children who will need them forever.

I don't want to be a part of this. I just wanted to love Nokosee and have his baby and maybe move into a nice little trailer with air-conditioning near the swamp to raise our child in peace without any cockamamie agenda. Maybe a place like Copeland, next to Billy Bob who, unfortunately, is no longer there. What a fool I am, so naive. But, when you shoot at me, no matter how big of a goddamn simpleton I may be, I will shoot back, something that appears to be in my genetic code and reinforced by the way my dad raised me during those long hot summers watching the Everglades burn down all around us.

And let's not forget the revelation.

Of course, how could I ever forget that? For better or worse I'm dead-on the course my life is meant to take.

When I pull the trigger to fulfill my role in this giant, cosmic game, my initial aim is off which is understandable when we're bouncing across the water, but with just a slight adjustment of the machine gun, I start finding my targets and one by one, the world's best fighting force is shred to pieces, dropping off their rafts into the water like exploding rag dolls caught in a hurricane of hurtling lead as we race by.

You don't kill her or her baby! She kills you!

And you kill me. My self-hate grows a little with each one of your deaths and I wonder how much do I have to detest myself before my heart throws in the towel and calls it quits.

Nokosee banks around the back of the hammock at such an angle that we both have to hold onto something to keep from falling out.

"Dad!" he yells.

"Nokosee!"

It's Busimanolotome. He's running from the hammock jungle with a wounded NS warrior under his arm. It's Boom Box and he's still holding onto his ghetto blaster, dragging it through the water. Busimanolotome stumbles into the water, gets up through sheer strength of will and sloshes toward the airboat again as it slides toward him. He throws his shoulder into the hull to stop its forward progress and gets pushed back but he doesn't lose his footing.

He grabs the airboat, throws Boom Box into the hull and then returns to the hammock.

"Dad!"

Busimanolotome disappears behind perimeter trees and undergrowth before returning, running through the water as fast as he can, this time with a Stinger missile over his shoulder.

"Go! Go! Go!"

He rolls into the airboat and Nokosee whips it around and guns it.

"Did you let the gators loose?" Nokosee yells.

"Yes!"

I hear screams as the soldiers closest to the hammock are attacked by the guard gators followed by automatic weapons fire. This buys us a little time but not much as I hear shots and then feel the bullets pushing the air away from my neck. Some are smashing against the hull and ricocheting off the rudders and the propeller cage. I whip the machine gun around and fire back at the popping flashes in the night.

"Fuck you, motherfuckers!" I yell.

I'm more enraged than scared at this point. And very, very frustrated. I mean, come on, this is the last thing I want happening in my life: barefoot and pregnant and taking on the best the United States Army can throw at us. And I'm only eighteen for crying out loud! Did I mention that before? I'm not even legally old enough to drink! Let me tell you, living on the edge isn't all it's cracked up to be.

"Goddammit, Stormy," Busimanolotome yells, "get down from there!"

When he grabs my leg a bullet catches him in the chest below the collar bone and sends him flying backwards into the airboat hull.

"Mr. O!"

There's not a bullet with my name on it.

"Duck behind the cowling!" Nokosee yells.

I scoot down behind the round metal sheets welded to the machine gun turret and watch Busimanolotome grabbing his chest and writhing in pain as Nokosee starts wiggling the airboat's tail back and forth to make us harder to hit. Unfortunately, in a world where night-vision goggles are as plentiful as AK-47s (or in this case, the Ranger's M-4 combat assault rifle), everybody's got one and trying to use it to kill us.

"Stormy!" Mr. O yells, "Come down here!"

I look back and peek over the cowling. There's a Black Hawk on our tail and closing in, all guns blazing. I turn back to Busimanolotome and yell, "I don't think so!"

Then bullets start bouncing off the cowling. Nokosee whips the airboat to the side and starts banking so hard that two things happen. One, the Black Hawk overshoots us and two, I slide out of the machine gun turret and onto the airboat hull. Right next to Busimanolotome.

"Take the Stinger!" he yells.

"No!"

"Do you want to live? Do you want your baby to live?"

The helicopter is spinning around, dipping its nose and heading toward us. I grab the Stinger.

"What do you want me to do with it?"

"Aim it and fire at the son-of-a-bitch trying to kill your baby!"

I look back over Nokosee and the airboat prop cage.

"I can't!"

"You can!" Busimanolotome yells. "Just aim it in the general direction! It'll do the rest!"

I see two rows of bullets marching toward us, kicking up evenly distanced explosions of mud and water. Lying nearly prone in the bottom of the hull, held there under the crushing weight of a guilty conscience, I aim and stoically pull the trigger. The Stinger explodes from the housing, bounces off the prop cage-- nearly hitting Nokosee-- and spirals through the night sky leaving a corkscrew trail of fire and smoke.

I feel my soul and my breath yanked out of me as if tied to the rocket and collapse, spent of body and spirit.

A second later, the Black Hawk is down, head first into the swamp, its four blades cartwheeling across the Everglades like a giant malevolent Ferris Wheel. I want to scream as Nokosee unknowingly turns into its path but I can't make myself do it because I just don't care if I live or die anymore. Busimanolotome throws his body over me to protect me just as one of the blades chops through the prop cage and slices through the rudders. The impact is enough to shake him and me and an unconscious Boom Box and all the crap in the hull up into the air. We land hard and this time I scream because of the pain I feel in my stomach when Busimanolotome falls against the baby. We're shaken again for good measure as we bounce out of control across the Everglades, finally doing a 360 into another hammock.

Aside from Boom Box's moaning, the steaming sound of a busted airboat engine, and the sound a fire makes when it burns a Black Hawk, its quiet and best yet, no one's shooting at us. Yet.

"Is everyone alright?" Busimanolotome asks as he pushes himself away to look at me.

I lie and join the general consensus that we are, considering the circumstances.

"Let's get out of here," he orders.

He struggles to get to his feet and once there, offers me his hand. I brush it aside and roll over to look for my boots which turns out to be a mistake because the pain is excruciating. I gasp.

"Stormy, are you alright?"

"I'm fine," I lie. "Let me get my boots on first."

"We don't have time for that!"

"I'm not going bare foot anymore in the swamp!"

I saw them pop out from underneath our stuff when the airboat crashed. Because the airboat is now tilted half in and half out of the water, I roll down the hull and crash against what's left of everything we own. I push Boom Box aside and dig them out of the rubble and the water.

"Nokosee!" Busimanolotome shouts.

"Hurry, Stormy," Nokosee urges as he drops down from the driver's seat straight into the water. Stiff from the shellacking he took bouncing off the airboat's metal frame, he tries to take his dad under an arm but the old man pushes him away.

"I got 'em, give me a sec."

Busimanolotome starts cussing under his breath in Muskogee.

"Hold your horses," I scold him. "I'm almost done."

I don't have time to lace them all up because the ammunition in the Black Hawk is starting to ignite, shooting heavy machine gun rounds in every direction, but at least when I step into the water, I won't have to tread lightly anymore.

"Okay, Mr. O, let's go."

And then I see my Nook.

"Sorry," I say. "One more sec." I grab it up and stick it in my loincloth.

"Nokosee," Busimanolotome sighs, "see if you can help Boom Box. Stormy, come here and help me."

I take Mr. O under the arm and he leads us into the hammock.

"That's one heck of a getup you got going there, little girl," he shouts through clenched teeth over the sporadic popping sounds of the exploding ammunition. He stumbles and cries out.

"Mr. O, are you okay?"

"Gold lamé boots," he coughs, "and a loincloth."

He looks down at me and tries to smile.

"Coming from a guy who has a jones for Crocs and jeggings, I must be doing something right."

His nascent laugh turns to coughing and I have to struggle to hold him up. A moment passes before he finds his voice again.

"I want to apologize for how I mistreated you," he says. "In case things go from bad to worse, I want you to know you truly are worthy."

"Thanks." I'm taken aback because he actually seems to mean it. "Pardon me, Mr. O, but it sounds like you're less than optimistic about the outcome of this battle."

"Sky Eyes, we're outnumbered, outgunned, and out-trained. We don't have a rat's ass chance of getting out of here alive."

"TMI! TMI!" I shout.

"What?"

"Too Much Information."

"Ha! The truth shall set you free, little girl. I didn't want to take the NS in this direction. My plan was to just blow things up here and there, never to kill anyone."

"Did this plan of yours include kidnapping?"

"Yes."

"Mr. O, what's gonna happen to all those people you're holding hostage in the swamp?"

"Damn, not much gets past you, does it?"

"Mr. O, you can't just leave them there."

"I'll tell you what, if we get out of here alive, you and Nokosee can let them go." He stops and turns to me. "Promise me you won't get yourself killed so you can do that."

"Geesh, Mr. O, I'll do my best. For crying out loud, you're starting to scare me."

"Good. Surrender the second chance you get. Take Nokosee with you. You deserve a long life together."

"'Second chance?'"

"Try escaping first."

He starts coughing again and grimaces. I look at the bullet wound. It's bleeding badly. I can feel his warm thick blood on my face. I look up at him, he's pale, his face is nearly flushed of any color.

"You can't just give up like that, Mr. O. What about your motto?"

"What motto?"

"The one about no bullet with your name on it."

"Oh, that one. In case you haven't noticed, *I got one of 'em in my chest!*"

The effort he makes to shout unleashes another round of coughing which shakes both are bodies. When he's done, I gently, hopefully reply, "Maybe it was misspelled. You know, your name's a mouthful."

He laughs. "Yeah, if it was any shorter, it'd probably been a head shot. It's good our Injun names are long." He starts coughing and we have to stop. "Anyway," he says after a moment, "like I said when you were pointing that gun at me when we first met: it's not like I'm infallible."

"Mr. O, you can't let the bullet win."

He coughs I think because he was starting to laugh again.

"That should be your motto, kid."

"Don't you want to see your grandchild?" I ask, nearly in tears.

"Of course I do. Especially coming from you. That is going to be some kinda kid for sure. But it seems the stars and the planets and the U.S. Army have lined up against me. C'mon, let's keep going."

He leads me stumbling deeper into the hammock jungle. I do all I can to keep from crying.

"Stop. See the trip wire?"

"No."

"Well, you see the chickee, don't you?"

I look up. I can barely make it out hidden beneath camo nets and foliage in the dark jungle.

"The trip wire is in front of it," he says.

I look down again. Without any moonlight and tears flooding my eyes, it's hard to see. Busimanolotome grows impatient.

"C'mon, Stormy, it's right in front of you for crisesakes!"

"Hey, what can I tell you. I left my contacts back in the jungle."

"I got them for you," Nokosee says.

I turn around. He's stumbling toward us with a semi-conscious moaning Boom Box under his arm.

"They're in the duffel bag back on the airboat."

"A lot of good that's going to do us," I say testily.

"Can it," Busimanolotome interrupts. "Nokosee, show her where the goddamn trip wire is."

Nokosee sets Boom Box down and inches carefully toward the chickee. He lowers himself slowly onto his knees, and delicately brushes away some leaves and branches.

"God," Busimanolotome says, "I sure hope the kid gets my eyesight. You two are pathetic."

Nokosee and I don't say anything because it's so damn nerve wracking. Thankfully my farsighted lean mean fighting machine finally finds the trip wire, a nearly invisible monofilament fishing line, and uncovers it enough so everyone, including the blind, will see it.

"Thank, God," Busimanolotome says, "I thought the kid would come first. I think I got some RPGs in there. Stormy, give him a hand, but stay on this side of the trip wire unless, of course, you don't mind blowing up."

It appears The Micco is back to being his old cantankerous self as he pushes me away and leans against a gumbo limbo tree to support himself.

Nokosee crawls into the chickee and throws the camo curtain back. Within seconds I'm reaching out over the trip line and grabbing an RPG which I can hardly hold up.

"I don't think this is something I should be doing since I'm *pregnant!*"

"Complain, complain, complain," Busimanolotome complains. He looks at Boom Box. Boom Box sees him looking at him and starts moaning. "Save it, Boom Box. You got *Hair* with you?"

"Always," Boom Box manages to squeak out.

"If it's not too much to ask, see if you can play me some *Manchester, England* since that's where we're at. Let it segue into what ever comes after it."

This hammock is called Manchester, England?

"No problemo, Chief."

Soon we're unloading some very deadly weapons including machine guns while grooving to the music from *Hair* and within minutes we're totally immersed in Busimanolotome's dream world, singing along in four part harmony. When the next song comes up and I take the lead singing how black boys are so tasty, I know I've crossed over finally and completely into the old man's dangerous and deadly make-believe crazy world. When Boom Box takes the lead singing how white boys are so beautiful from his position on the ground in a wheezing, squeaky voice, we all have to laugh. Yeah, this is bonding while living on the edge. I don't know if I'll ever feel more alive.

Or dead. I sing to keep from crying from the hopelessness of the situation. I didn't know it was possible to have these two extremes tearing you apart at the same time but that's exactly what's going on.

The soundtrack to our make-believe movie is interrupted with a whipping wind that shakes the hammock apart and the roar of a Black Hawk helicopter overhead.

"Give me the RPG!" Busimanolotome shouts.

I hand him one without giving it a second thought. I've changed a lot in the last 15 minutes. I'm no longer that girl who had a problem with pulling a trigger. I've become what The Micco hoped I would be.

"Grab a machine gun!"

I do and he puts his arm around me for balance.

"Let's go!"

He turns and leads me deeper into the hammock. I look back. Nokosee is following us with two RPGs slung across his back, a machine gun in his hand and Boom Box under an arm.

My lungs are on fire and I can hardly breath when a sudden pain rips through my side. It hurts so much I nearly black out. I don't know how I'm going to get through this without hurting the baby.

Busimanolotome leads us crashing through the hammock, breaking branches and tripping over things I can't see. I get slapped more than once with branches across my face and my big round belly but I don't scream until we run through a spider's web. That creeps me out so much I stop and let go of Mr. O to slap at it because I know it's got to belong to one of those giant ugly orb spiders.

Busimanolotome of course has little patience for this kind of wussy crap and yanks me toward him.

"Stop it!" he admonishes. "It's just a spider's web. You're a giant slayer for crisesakes. Start acting like one."

Nokosee and Boom Box join us. Both are out of breath.

"Promise me you won't move from this spot!" Busimanolotome yells.

"Why?" Nokosee asks.

"Just do what I say!"

"Dad, I'm your wingman!"

"Not any more. You're hers," he says, throwing me at Nokosee. "I'll see you later."

Busimanolotome disappears, coughing and stumbling into the jungle void.

"Dad!"

A funky beat rises out of the boombox and lifts me up as the jungle starts whirling around us again and we're "walking in space." I look up and see the Black Hawk. Nokosee gives me an RPG.

"Use it if you have to. I'll be watching your back."

He turns and disappears into the jungle, leaving Boom Box with me.

"Nokosee!"

The music scolds those who "dare try to end the beauty."

An explosion shakes the earth and we're illuminated for a brief moment. Another Black Hawk has destroyed the chickee we were just at. Boom Box scoots closer to me as I put a gumbo limbo between us and the Black Hawk overhead as it flips on a search light and starts combing the jungle.

"Boom Box, help me with this RPG!"

Boom Box finally makes himself useful by taking the back of the grenade launcher and lifting it onto my shoulder before falling backward and rolling out of the way. I point it skyward, look through the eyesight and then pop out from behind the tree. The young pilot sees me and yanks the stick back. The helicopter banks over the hammock just as an RPG leaps out of the jungle behind me and hits it in its belly. It explodes and rolls into the hammock. The explosion upon impact knocks me off of my feet.

Our hiding place is uncovered by the bright, flickering light of the flames leaping high into the air. Suddenly bullets start tearing up the jungle around us. We dive and roll through the underbrush trying to make ourselves disappear while the music becomes our soundtrack.

"Ripped open. Metal explosion."

Boom Box is hit. Sitting upright, the impact throws him back across the ground on his ass, with his legs trailing behind. He slams up hard against a tree. His eyes are so wide. He can't believe he's going to die. He looks at the entrance wound just over his heart. Had it been a little lower, it would have hit his boom box and maybe it would have stopped the bullet. Blood begins to run from his mouth. He drops his hand to the volume control and turns it up. The song's gospel rift uses the dreaded "N-word" as it takes him to heaven. I know he's there and, despite everything to the contrary, I know it exists because, although his eyes may be open and sightless, he's smiling.

God save me and the baby I pray.

Another song comes up as Boom Box's poor lifeless body dances with each bullet it takes as if it were on the ends of a mad puppeteer's strings, adding ironic counterpoint to the song's insistence that man is special, noble, angelic and godlike. This is what I believed at the top of my tree but now down here in the dirt as I cower among the bullet riddled trees that are protecting me, I'm not so sure.

"Stormy, are you okay?"

It's my exterminating angel sent by God. He sees Boom Box and closes his eyes but the smile remains as his boom box continues the fight with song.

"C'mon," Nokosee cries.

He grabs me up in his strong arms and carries me running through the jungle, bullets shredding branches and leaves all around us.

"Did you shoot down that chopper?" I yell over the music and the gunfire.

"No. It was dad."

A bullet grazes my calve. I cry out.

It's the same leg with your honeymoon scar for crying out loud.

Nokosee lays me down on the ground and sees the blood running down my leg.

"Goddam it!"

"Nokosee, it's alright. It--"

He whips around to those firing at us and, like a man possessed, screams at them, cursing them in equal amounts of spit-thrown "motherfuckers" and gunpowder-hurled lead which mows down the dark hammock jungle in a marching explosion of branches and leaves until he runs out of bullets, until all you can hear is his labored breathing because even I have stopped screaming-- not because the pain is gone, but because I'm just too damned scared. In that brief moment I hear over my own deep hyperventilated struggle to breathe and to keep my heart from pounding through my chest, that persistent rising voice singing, distant now, trying to convince me again that man is special and worthy. And then a soldier wearing night vision goggles, and another, and then another fall out of the jungle one-at-a-time in a nice single row dead, all dead.

"Run!"

It's Busimanolotome, yelling from the jungle. Nokosee picks me up and starts running again toward his dad's voice. I make the mistake of looking at my wound. When I see how ugly it is, how much it's bleeding, I grow faint.

As Busimanolotome fires back at an angry army of popping red machine gun bursts from the black hammock jungle, the music echoing over the sounds of battle is joyfully trying to remind me that it's a good morning and that the earth is saying hello when we plunge through the underbrush and crash to the dusty earth beside him. The music reminds me that stars are twinkling above and that I'm twinkling below. I look for them but can't see a goddamn one.

"Dad, Stormy's been shot in the leg!"

"Dammit!" Busimanolotome looks at my wound and gently touches my shoulder.

"It's alright, Mr. O. It's just a--"

"Stay with me, Sky Eyes. I won't let anything happen to you. Can you shoot?"

Nonsense words fill the air.

"Dad! You gotta be--"

"--If we're going to carry her out of here, we're going to have to turn our backs on the enemy and I want as much fire power pointed in their direction as possible."

The hammock jungle jingles with a chorus of silly sounding words.

"It's okay, Nokosee," I struggle to say. "Give me something to shoot."

I want to throw up and can't imagine shooting anything but I also want to live.

"That's my girl," Busimanolotome says.

Nokosee, shaking his head in frustration, throws the empty clip away and snaps in another one before giving me his hot steaming machine gun and throwing me over his shoulder. And it's déjà vu time all over again: I throw up all over his back like I did when we first met after we fought off the alligator attack. Except this time, he doesn't pause and do a slow burn and, of course, I'm pregnant. Before I know it, we're off and running, crashing through the hammock jungle with bullets flying in all directions as we join Busimanolotome and I fire back over Nokosee's shoulder.

"Oh, no!" I shout.

"What?" Nokosee yells as he continues to run.

"I lost my Nook."

"Screw it!"

I see it tumbling in the underbrush, falling away from my outstretched hand and finally vanishing completely in the hammock's shadows as Nokosee runs crashing through his father's unforgiving world where things like my Nook have no place being.

The song tries to reassure me that it's all right, because love still reigns, that you can see it in your lover's eyes and that it will protect us.

We're splashing through water now when I cry out in pain and squeeze my legs together.

"What's wrong now?" Nokosee asks.

"I think my water broke!" I shout as I spray the jungle with bullets.

"Dammit!"

He runs up to his father hiding behind a cypress tree and lays me gently in one of a handful of escape bithlos tied-up and hidden among the cattails as bullets scream by, ripping the hammock apart and tearing up the placid surface of the water.

"Dad, get her out of here!"

Nokosee turns and runs toward the gunfire. I moan loudly fearing the worse, that the song is a lie.

"Nokosee, don't!"

It's too late, he's been sucked up by the hammock jungle. I can hear him screaming and returning fire. Busimanolotome looks at me. I can tell by his life-sapped ghostly face he's worried about me and his son. Without a word, he struggles to push the bithlo out into the black Everglades night.

I hear the nonsense chorus again; it's like the earth is sticking its tongue out and laying the mother of all raspberries on me. I close my eyes and try not to listen.

Fool! This is the way the world is now open your eyes!

Busimanolotome screams. I open my eyes. A gator breaks the surface of the water with his leg between its teeth. Off balance, he slams the butt of his machine gun at the wild-eyed gator's head but that just makes it angrier. He tries to hold onto the bithlo but the gator's crazed thrashing nearly capsizes the thing. I try to throw my weight away from the rocking tilt and that sends a ripping pain through my stomach. I scream and fall onto my back in the bithlo. Busimanolotome lets go and it plops back down with a hard splash.

I turn to Busimanolotome and see him looking at me, wondering if I'm alright as the gator drags him away.

"Mr. O!"

He smiles and nods at me before turning toward the gator, his long bayonet knife rising out of the water to strike it dead. He stabs it hard in the the head-- and the knife sticks! Enraged, the gator starts shaking its head and rips off Busimanolotome's leg, throwing it across the water.

"Mr. O!"

I want to hurl.

The knife sticking out of the gator's head cuts through the water like a periscope on a submarine zeroing in on Busimanolotome who's starting to go into shock. He catches it but is thrown backward into the water and struggles to hold the gator's snapping mouth away from his head. I frantically start looking for something to shoot the gator but can't find anything. He screams again. Another gator is attacking him. He looks back at me. He's shivering, losing consciousness.

"Mr. O!"

I use my hands to paddle closer to Busimanolotome, my Micco, my Chief. He sees me and extends his hand toward me to stop me but I grab it tightly and try to pull him back and then the gator with the bayonet sticking out of its head-- the one I knew was once meant for me-- turns and latches on to Mr. O's forearm. Before I know what's happening, the gator bites through the arm and disappears below the water. The arm, now severed at the elbow, twitches uncontrollably in my hand. I scream and shake it loose. I look at Mr. O-- the second gator is pulling him away from me, backward through the water.

"Mr. O!"

He's smiling at me and with half-closed eyes whispers, "Ooshtayke..." before disappearing beneath the black, fire-reflecting water.

Daughter.

I can't turn away as I fall limp into the bithlo. Tears well up and pour over my eyelids and down my face. Another sharp pain makes me cry out and throws me onto my back.

"No!" I cry in angry protest for all that's shitty in the world. "No! No! No!"

Three-hundred sextillion stars but I can't see one, not one lousy fucking star to wish upon. And I can't hear the music either. My eyelids fall slowly with my tears like a curtain across the false promise of Busimanolotome's Aquarian sky, now streaked with tracer rounds, the sounds of warfare and the screams of dying men.

I want to die with them for my sins but even at this moment, I'm holding out for what some people might describe as a dramatic death for a drama queen but it isn't like that at all. I want to die in a noble way, one that will give my life meaning: I want to die in childbirth and I want my baby to live.

I can't take it anymore, Lord. Please let me die.

"Stormy! Stormy!"

Nokosee can't find me. My eyes jump open and as the clouds and smoke and ash of the forever burning Everglades part, I see stars, millions of them scattered across the sky.

"Over here." I can barely speak, the pain is so bad. "Over here!"

He comes running, splashing through the water to the bithlo. He looks at me in horror. I extend my hand to him.

"Help me, Nokosee."

He grabs my hand and pushes the bithlo through the water into the the sawgrass. I see him looking for his father. I squeeze his hand. He looks at me. I shake my head and he starts to cry. And so do I.

Our baby girl is born in the Everglades, among the sawgrass, the tall cattails, the sounds of gunfire and the cries of dying men. No sooner does Nokosee tie a tourniquet around my leg to stop the bleeding, our little darling thankfully arrives. It's as if she knows we're kinda in a hurry. Nokosee, kneeling in the water beside the bithlo, holds her above his head against the burning horizon, still attached to her umbilical cord and to her mother. The baby is a miracle, like all life and Nokosee, speaking in Muskogee, quickly takes time in the middle of the war for the Inside to offer thanks to the spirit of the Great Breath Giver and the protective spirits all around us. Our baby cries loudly against the sounds of men shooting the NS guard gators and screaming as they're ripped to shreds. Nokosee gives me our baby to hold. Seeing her look at me, I feel no pain until she starts to cry.

"Nokosee, she's shivering."

Nokosee rips his Seminole *Chiefs* jacket off and helps me wrap her in it. The little girl struggles to free herself as Nokosee pushes us deeper and farther away from the Outside into a future none of us can imagine.

BTW

We call her Haalie. It's short for Haalpatee, the name that came to me in my "vision." She has my eyes and Nokosee's hair. She's gorgeous and we love her to death.

FBI

What Ms. Symona "Stormy" Jones, a.k.a. Holatte-Sutv Turwv Osceola, conveniently forgot to add is that while the NS were battling Army Rangers in the swamp that fateful night, Busimanolotome, through NS agents, was carrying out his last desperate attack on the "Outside." Thousands of people were killed when his men simultaneously blew up the Lake Okeechobee dike and portions of the L-6 levee. A tidal wave was unleashed on a sleeping, defenseless population with property damage estimated to be a hundred billion dollars.

Reading her book, it is possible the Osceolas didn't know of Busimanolotome's final act of domestic terrorism. If they did, then they will have to live with the knowledge that they are responsible for the single highest loss of life ever perpetrated against U.S. citizens. If they didn't, it is imperative that they surrender immediately in order to escape a "shoot on sight" FBI directive. Because of their age and extenuating circumstances (including the fact they informed the FBI as to the whereabouts of the kidnapped mayor and commissioners which saved their lives), it is possible they will be spared the death penalty. Their child in all likelihood will be given over to Holatte-Sutv Turwv's mother. Nokosee's mother and sister cannot be found as of this date.

Please note we doubt the veracity of Holatte-Sutv Turwv Osceola's story and find it more self-serving than truthful as should anyone reading her account of her life as an outlaw. We also suspect she is no longer wearing her hair in a Mohawk, has changed her hair color, allowed it to grow out to hide the tattoos on each side of her head and Nokosee has cut his hair. From what we can tell, they have melted into the population and may be standing next to you right now as you read this book while waiting in the *Pirates of the Caribbean* line at Disney World.

If you see them, please report their whereabouts to the authorities ASAP. Do not try to apprehend. They are considered armed and extremely dangerous.

Re the New Seminole, although a few of its ringleaders have not been accounted for, notably Indian Larry, it no longer exists except in memory, YouTube, and the two Nokosee books.

Finally, the author's share of profits from the sale of her book are being placed in a trust fund for Haalie Osceola administered by the FBI.

Micco Mann

www.ingramcontent.com/pod-product-compliance
Lightning Source LLC
Chambersburg PA
CBHW072215170626
46813CB00003B/955